D0938419

The
Last
Green
Tree

The
Last
Green
Tree

JIM GRIMSLEY

A TOM DOHERTY ASSOCIATES BOOK
NEW YORK

THE LAST GREEN TREE

Copyright © 2006 by Jim Grimsley

A Tor Book
Published by Tom Doherty Associates, LLC
175 Fifth Avenue
New York, NY 10010

www.tor.com

Tor® is a registered trademark of Tom Doherty Associates, LLC.

Library of Congress Cataloging-in-Publication Data

Grimsley, Jim, 1955–
    The last green tree / Jim Grimsley.—1st ed.
      p. cm.
    "A Tom Doherty Associates Book."
    ISBN-13: 978-0-765-30530-5
    ISBN-10: 0-765-30530-5 (acid-free paper)
  1. Life on other planets—Fiction. I. Title.
    PS3557.R4949L37 2006
    813'.54—dc22

                        2006007390

First Edition: December 2006

Printed in the United States of America

0 9 8 7 6 5 4 3 2 1

For Kathie de Nobriga

Contents

In the beginning was the Word . . . and the Word was God.

JOHN 1:1

The
Last
Green
Tree

The Poorhouse

1.

From his bedroom at the top of the world, Keely could look one way to the endless spires and towers of the city and the other to the middle of the ocean. Both the city and the ocean had names and people had told him the names but he never really wanted to remember them. There was only one city, only one ocean, only one of everything; it was much simpler to think of things like that. When he sat at his bedroom window, he felt as if he were floating along the bottoms of the clouds; the building where he lived reached so high that clouds sometimes wrapped the summit in fleecy white, and Uncle Figg lived at the very top. This was because he was rich and owned practically everything in the world. That is, Uncle Figg was very rich until suddenly one day he wasn't anymore; Keely heard him talking to some of his grown-up friends, and later at breakfast with Nerva, Uncle Figg was complaining about being poor.

"What does the Mage think she's doing?" Uncle Figg asked.

Keely was watching a line of aircraft in the distance; the breakfast room was surrounded on three sides by glass, so he could see nearly the whole sky from his seat at the end of the table. When Uncle Figg said "the Mage," Keely started to pay attention. Keely had a Mage doll, a half dozen Mage games for playing in his head-space, graphic novels about the Mage, a fully illustrated head-world called Iraen, after the country from which the Mage had come; he had a Mage costume, Mage sheets on his bed, a poster of the Mage and her consort, Jedda Jump-up, on his wall. "She's doing magic, Uncle Figg," Keely said, touching the back of Uncle Figg's hand.

"Yes, I know, Keely. She's made all my money disappear."

The moment caused a knot of upset to form in Keely's stomach. Nerva was watching, but she was using her good face and her good voice, which was always the case when Uncle Figg was around. This meant that Keely could feel fairly safe; only when he was alone with Nerva did she make him afraid. The upset at the moment did not come from Nerva, but from something in what Uncle Figg was saying. "All of your money is gone?"

"Ridiculously large amounts of it, yes."

"Excuse me, sir, but the child looks a bit frightened."

"He should be. We'll end up on the street, no better than paupers."

"Really, sir—"

"You think I'm exaggerating? Why, I won't even be allowed to keep the Marmigon."

Nerva was trying hard to look interested in what Uncle Figg was saying, but, behind the pretense, she wanted to figure something else out altogether. Keely was used to seeing through Nerva to what she was really doing; he had to be good at this, because Nerva ruled so much of his life. So he could tell she really felt no sympathy for Uncle Figg whatsoever. "You'll have to sell the place?"

He snorted. "No. I don't sell it. The Mage says I already have too much money, my whole clan and I. So we have to give up the Marmigon, and, in fact, if I want to go on living here I have to buy my apartment. Buy it! When my mother-clan has owned this building since it was built, Ama only knows how long ago."

Whenever Uncle Figg mentioned the name of a Hormling god or goddess, as he sometimes did when swearing, Nerva touched her thumbnail to her brow. She said it was out of respect to her own goddess, who was the only real goddess anybody knew about. Unlike the Hormling, the people of Iraen insisted on seeing their deity every now and again, to make sure she was still paying attention. Whereas, according to Nerva, the Hormling were perfectly willing to worship a god for however long a time without the slightest proof that he or she existed. Nerva came from Iraen and liked to remind people of the fact. This morning, after touching her thumbnail to her forehead when Uncle Figg mentioned Ama, she sipped her morning tea, which to Keely smelled like the flowers on the patio.

"I realize I'll get no sympathy from the likes of you."

"I beg your pardon. What are the likes of me?"

"These new laws don't affect you or your family, do they?"

She gave a decided sniff and looked studiously out the window at a distant helicopter riding close under the shield of clouds. "Nothing is being taken from me personally, no. I haven't checked with the rest of the paupers in my clan."

"I hear your tone. I know I'm being overbearing. But I can't help myself."

"We agree on that much, at least."

Uncle Figg's brown skin got hints of red in it when he was embarrassed or mad. Which was he now? He was staring at the helicopter in the distant sky, fixedly, as if it were very important. Keely's stomach was turning over now that he understood what Uncle Figg was talking about. He knew "Marmigon" was the name for the building he lived in; and so, when he heard that Uncle Figg would lose it, too, he began to picture himself losing all the nice toys in his room, and his room, with the window on the city and the window on the ocean. "Will we have to go back to the Reeks?" he asked, his voice very small, watching the plastic Mage action figure he brought with him to the table, feeling suddenly as if he ought to hide it, if the Mage really were taking away everything from Uncle Figg.

"What?" Uncle Figg snorted. "No!" He gave Keely a serious look. When his expression softened and he leaned with his big hand on Keely's shoulder, Keely flushed with a feeling of safety. "No, son, I'm exaggerating. The Mage isn't taking all my money, just a lot of it. We'll be able to afford to live very well on what's left, I promise you."

"Why is the Mage taking your money?"

"She's taking everybody's money. Over a certain amount. And she's taking property, and she's making it so that a mother can't leave her money to her children anymore. She has to give it up when she dies."

"But why?" Though Keely was asking the question only because he felt Uncle Figg expected it; Keely had hardly understood much of Uncle Figg's careful explanation.

"Because she thinks we have too much money, people like us. While the people who live in the Reeks don't have any. So she wants to take our money to help them."

Keely sighed. "Then that's okay." He looked at the plastic Mage in his hand, twisted her head.

Uncle Figg and Nerva were looking at each other in that adult way, sending messages to each other, probably. Adults could read each other's minds; children never had a chance. "Having him here does put things in perspective a bit," Uncle Figg said, in an adult tone that meant he was talking to Nerva. "I might not mind losing so much if I were sure it would really help people like Keely's family."

Nerva sniffed. "I wouldn't call that riffraff a family. You can't help people. Even Malin will figure that out sooner or later. All the money on Senal won't get rid of the Reeks. You mark my words."

"Now you sound like my matriarch," Uncle Figg said.

Nerva sniffed again.

"What's a matriarch?" Keely asked.

"She's the female head of my family. She's not very happy right now."

"She's not?" Keely asked, but he could feel that Uncle Figg was paying no attention.

Nerva said, "I can't blame her. This is a blow aimed at all the Orminy Houses, anyone can see that."

"We certainly have the most to lose," Uncle Figg agreed. "I expect most of my people will take whatever they have left and emigrate. Maybe I ought to think about doing the same."

Keely only understood part of what Uncle Figg was saying and tried to look hopeful, usually a good choice when he wasn't sure what else to look like.

"You wouldn't mind leaving Senal, would you, Keely? Maybe it would be a good idea to take you somewhere else. You'd like to live away from the city, wouldn't you?"

This was not a real question, and Keely pretended he was watching the helicopter, closer now, but still the size of a toy, suspended between the gray of the clouds and the gray-blue of the waves far below. He felt a sinking in his stomach. Something was about to happen that would change everything again.

2.

Uncle Figg started to talk about living on a farm, what a nice change it would be, and did Keely think he would want a pet like a dog or a cat? Not the enhanced kind but just plain animals, like in the reading lessons about Mike the Kite who lives on Mr. Mukerjhee's farm. Did Keely know Uncle Figg owned a farm?

"I thought we were poor now," Keely said, the edge of a color stylus in his mouth.

"Get that out of your mouth, Keely," Nerva called from the couch. They were in Keely's playroom, the toys neatly lined against the wall the way Nerva liked them; Nerva spoke to Keely without raising her eyes from her book, as if she could see everything without looking. "You're too old to eat your toys."

"I am not too old."

"Yes, you are. Don't wipe your hands on your pants like that, you just put them on."

"I'm trying to talk about the farm," Uncle Figg said.

"I hear that you are." When Nerva was cross, nobody liked to be around her; Uncle Figg was still sitting with Keely, though, a breakfast tray beside him with a bowl of uneaten fruit and bread. "I don't know why you can't bring yourself simply to tell him."

"You don't?"

"It's a simple message. You own a farm on Aramen and we're going to live there."

"Are we?" Keely asked.

"Yes," she said, looking at him with those sharp eyes, the ones that made his stomach turn. He became very quiet and sank into the couch. It was morning, though, which made it all right for some reason. It was morning and nothing else would happen except that the look in her eyes would change to something else and the bad feeling in Keely would go away.

"You seem to forget that ours is a contractual relationship and not a marriage, madam."

She gave him a hard look, set her jaw, made the muscles on the side of her face move like she was grinding something between her teeth. She spoke in a cool voice. "Yes, master Figg. I apologize. I should let you handle the child in your own way."

"This is the only home he's known."

"When are we moving to the farm?" Keely asked.

Uncle Figg blinked. He had a nice face, smooth, skin the color of morning tea and cream. His hair always looked exactly the same, as if it never moved, short on the sides and longer on the top, even the curls in the same place. Uncle Figg had a spider in his hair, a big one, but it was hard to see when it nestled into the hair. "You sound as if you'd like to live there."

"I would. Because of all the animals."

"I don't know how many animals there really are," Uncle Figg said, after a moment.

Keely lay his hand on Uncle Figg's wrist, looked at him earnestly. If Uncle Figg wasn't sure what a farm was, maybe Keely could explain. "Uncle Figg, if it's a farm, there's a lot of animals, and all of them can talk."

Uncle Figg smiled, sipped his tea, and ate a piece of the yellow fruit that tasted sour to Keely.

"Aramen is a very nice place. There are a lot of my people living in the north there, because of the forest."

"My farm is a few hours south of the preserve," Uncle Figg said.

"What's the preserve?"

"Where the trees live," Uncle Figg explained, looking directly into Keely's eyes, the way he liked to do when he talked. "The talking trees, remember? You saw them in the Surround."

"Can I talk to them?"

"Maybe."

"I don't know how anyone can know that a tree is sentient," Nerva said, irritation creeping back into her voice.

"Ask your Mage. She's the one who said so first."

"She's not my Mage."

"Well. She's from your golden country and all."

20

Nerva sniffed loudly. She was reading some kind of book that made her move her lips. "As if you could look at a tree and figure out what it's thinking."

"We don't have to do that. We have those things we make that talk to them for us."

"What things?" Keely asked.

Sometimes the adults forgot he was part of the conversation and looked at him when he asked a question as if he had just appeared out of nowhere.

"Tree people," Uncle Figg said. "They live with the trees and talk to them."

"Elves, for goodness sake." Nerva shook her head. "Fairy tales."

"They're quite expensive to make, actually. They're called symbionts, not elves. My family used to own a piece of the business."

"Can I be a tree people?"

"No, you may not. In fact, it's time for you to start your learning program." Nerva put down her book and busied herself with a frame that appeared in front of her; a smaller version of the frame soon appeared in front of Keely. Uncle Figg brushed off his jumpsuit and stood, running fingers absently in Keely's hair.

"Do good for Uncle Figg," he said.

"When do we move to the farm?"

"Pretty soon," Uncle Figg said. "We have to travel in a spaceship to get there."

Keely screamed with delight and jumped up from the frame, running to the window as if he could see the ship already. "I want to go now!"

"You've spoiled his learning mindframe for a good twenty minutes, he'll talk about nothing except the spaceship." Nerva threw up her hands and leaned back against the sofa. She looked like someone on a vid, as if a lot of people were watching her. Uncle Figg regarded her calmly from the door.

"Twenty minutes here, twenty minutes there, pretty soon it all adds up to a life," Uncle Figg said, and he disappeared.

For a moment Keely felt a cool hand in his middle, fear, and stood at the window watching Nerva. She had her eyes closed, lips moving, and Keely sat down at the window and tried to become very small. He had no idea what made him afraid at moments like this, any more than he understood why he was so certain that he would be all right, that nothing would happen, that the bad Nerva would stay away, because it was daytime.

3.

Even the thought of the spaceship could not guard him from the fear that closed around his middle when Nerva came to get him ready for bed.

When she closed the door, she turned to him with a look of quiet satisfaction and said, "Mode seven."

He had no idea what the words meant, but when she said the phrase a shudder passed through him and suddenly his head flooded with memories, things that he could never recall unless he was in this room at night alone with her.

Her eyes sharpened. "Are you here?"

"Yes, ma'am."

"You're a very childish boy, Keely. All day I've wanted to bring you in here and punish you for your wicked ways, but I forced myself to wait for night. Forced myself to put off the burden of your punishment until now."

"What did I do?" His heart was pounding.

She approached him slowly with that look of murmuring that caused Keely to feel cool fear through his middle, that caused a sickness of fear to sweep over him, so that he drew back against the wall.

"Look at yourself in the mirror. Look what a big boy you are. You're nearly ten years old."

The door to the privacy room had a mirror setting so Keely stood there, palms wet, looking at himself. He was himself, though there was something odd about him; he was bigger than his picture of himself during the day. His heart was still beating hard and he looked at Nerva's reflection in the mirror. She was slowly walking toward him.

"A boy of ten regressed to the age of five, and why? Because you're weak, that's why. Because you can't remember your sister without crying like a child."

"My sister?" He felt something crumbling in himself. He felt older. Terrible memories flooded him and he began to tremble, thin arms laced around his chest as if he were trying to pull himself upright; he remembered Sherry, his sister, and a place where there were a lot of people, someone who yelled at him and made him crawl into narrow, dark spaces looking for garbage, for something people might have dropped. . . . Remembered being afraid of people's hands, the way the hands flew down at him. . . . He remembered a whole life that had belonged to him before he came to live with Uncle

Figg, and he saw himself for the ten-year-old boy that he actually was.

"If you were getting better I could leave you alone at night, but you're not getting better, you're getting worse. Every time I mention your sister's death, you break down like this."

He was sitting on the floor now, embracing himself. He was seeing Sherry's face, dead, knowing she was gone, and feeling a long tearing begin in his middle, a jagged feeling that raced through him, made him sag onto his arms and breathe in a sob.

"You see?" She was standing over him now, looking down at the top of his head. "You're a mess, Keely. You'll never get better."

"You're not supposed to do this," he said, and his voice sounded older now, sounded like itself. "You're not supposed to make me remember."

"Don't tell me what I'm supposed to do," she whispered, and suddenly he was knotted with pain, his throat closed so that he could hardly make a sound. He felt as if his bones were breaking, as if Nerva's fingers were tearing at his flesh, sharp as hooks. "What does it matter anyway? I can say what I like to you, in here. I'm going to make you forget it all anyway."

He could hear her voice but only in a distant way. She was lifting the math box out of her ample skirt. He tried to shake his head but the pain grew worse; he lost control of his legs, of his bladder, pissed himself and lay prone on the carpet.

"You'll lie in your piss till you're done," Nerva said. "I've turned off the smart carpet; you'll just have to lie there in your own filth."

"Please," he said.

"Such a big boy, acting like such baby all day. And then acting like a different kind of baby every night. If you weren't so good at wearing this box, I'd throw you out the window into the ocean."

"Please," he managed, biting his own tongue, hard enough to hurt but not to break the skin. For some reason a pain he caused himself distracted him from whatever it was Nerva did to wrack his body with that feeling of agony.

"If you weren't so good with this box, you'd never see that spaceship you want to ride on," she said, and fixed the headset over his head.

In the midst of the pain that washed over him began that other tearing that affected only his head, the feeling that the math box was reaching into him, writing something onto the cells of his brain; gradually even the pain subsided and the world of the box engulfed him. He was surrounded in a stream of numbers that swam into each other, relationships that somehow became concrete; he was learning numbers of all kinds, in all relations, and after a while they filled him, and he was aware of nothing else.

How long that lasted he was never certain, but at some point he found himself in bed, the math box taken away from him. He dreamed of a sphere that floated near him, that unwrapped wires from itself and inserted their needle-sharp tips into him, coiled metal arms around his throat.

Sometimes in the dream Father was there, different from the father Sherry had described, the one who was in prison in the Reeks for killing their mother and some other people; this was a father bright and new, kind and good, vague in the face but warm in presence. Keely dreamed of him after using the math box.

Tonight Father was helping Keely play with a new Disturber toy with a complex shape. "You like to play with shapes," said Father. "You're talented."

"That means I do them well," Keely said, feeling the glow of the light around him.

"I choose children who do things well," Father said. "I'm a good judge of character."

Keely was changing the shape of the toy now, seeing new kinds of curves and twists.

"Do you want me to choose you?" Father asked.

The thought made Keely feel warm inside. He tried to keep from saying anything, he even tried to keep from nodding, but the question made him feel so special it showed, even in the dream, even though he knew he was sleeping.

"The music in your head is like the math in the box," said Father. "Do you like it?"

He allowed himself to nod the smallest possible nod. He was afraid he would wake up and find out he could not return to the dream. He liked the Father dream when it came, but it only came sometimes. "I hear the number-shapes all the time in the background," Keely said.

"That's good," said Father. "That means you're adapting."

"Is adapting like this?" Keely asked, and he reshaped the curves in the toy again, to make it into a fortress.

"Sometimes."

"I adapt," said Keely.

"When you're afraid of Nerva, Keely, remember that one day you'll be much, much stronger than she is."

The thought made him very quiet. Father had never said anything like this before.

"When she hurts you, remember that one day you'll be as strong as I am, you'll have me inside you, and you'll be able to hurt her." ·

He put part of the toy in his mouth, started to chew it. He could taste the plastic, feel the texture against his gums.

"Do you think you'll like that?" Father asked.

"Yes," Keely said, and he felt warm all through.

A feeling that he was younger, that he was small again settled over him. By morning it was as if he had always been that way, with no memory of either the math box or the dream.

4.

When the day came to move to the farm on Aramen, Uncle Figg booked passage for them all on the Anilyn Shuttle. They waited out the processing of their emigration papers in Skygard after the long ascent on the pulleypod. Keely watched Senal recede beneath him, the curve of the planet emerging as the car rose over everything he could see. He was glued to the window, quiet with wonder at the vision, feeling small.

By then Keely had turned eleven and sometimes felt very old. Furthermore, he was still shy of Uncle Figg at moments, when he was in certain moods, and this was one.

"Don't press your nose against the glass," Uncle Figg said, "it might not be clean."

"Come and sit with me," said Nerva, a shawl spread over her lap and peel from an orange dropping onto the yarn. She was using the good voice and Keely had only the faintest memory of the other.

"I'm all right." Keely, careful to keep his nose away from the glass, turned sidelong to look at her. She was hired to look after him. She was an old lady with a big bosom and a wide lap, and she came from a long way to work for Uncle Figg.

"I'll give you a piece of orange," she said.

"Is it a good idea to bribe him with food?" Figg asked.

Nerva gave him a warning look. "I'm not bribing him, I'm offering him a piece of orange."

"I'm not hungry." Keely sat on his rump for a moment and looked around the compartment. He was sitting on the side with Figg and Nerva was sitting on the other side, taking up most of the room. She wore a wide, long garment of a fabric that smelled like the park on a sunny day, pale blue, with darker patterns in it that were a kind of plant. Keely forgot the names of things but Nerva would remember. Keely held out his hand for a piece of the orange after a moment.

"I thought you weren't hungry."

"I'm thirsty," he said.

She nodded that this would do and gave him a bit of orange while Uncle Figg handed him a bottle of water. "Drink out of your own straw," he said. "We have to share that."

So he sipped out of the blue straw and chewed the slice of orange slowly afterward. The pod was rising far above the clouds that looked like streaks of fishbone, into a zone of violet blue, and beyond it, the fierce points of light that were called stars and planets and worlds and moons and galaxies and black holes. He had seen them all before on episodes of *Sky Captain of the 35,000th Century* and the other Sky Captain serials.

"Fasten your seatbelt tight," Uncle Figg said. "You're floating off your chair."

On Skygard, after the pulleypod ride, Uncle Figg's spider crawled out of his hair and nestled on his arm, and Keely floated out the arrival commons into the central cylinder of the station. He had never been weightless before, but Nerva had him tethered to her hip, the requirement with children in free fall, and made him keep hold of the guy ropes and pull himself along like a good boy. They were treating him like a kid, as usual, and he didn't feel altogether himself, for some reason. He would have liked to push himself off from the wall to see how it felt to fly to the other side, but he followed hand over hand behind Zhengzhou, the bodyguard.

They were all supposed to be flying on a shuttle from Skygard, and Keely kept looking for it everywhere. When Nerva told him it would be outside, not inside, he started looking through all the windows. They came to the part of the station where Keely had weight again and Nerva helped him take the last step off the transfer point. His stomach did a flip-flop and he looked at Nerva as if he was going to throw up.

"Use the bag I gave you if you're going to lose that piece of orange you ate."

"I think I'm all right now," he said, holding his stomach dramatically.

"That's right, now we're on the part that's spinning. That's how they make gravity."

Keely's knees were wobbly but he looked at her with scorn, since he knew perfectly well that gravity didn't come from spinning, centrifugal force did, and that was what they were feeling. He had a lot of information in his head now that he was learning; Uncle Figg said his head might burst if he learned too much and that would be that for him. This was also not true but made Keely laugh anyway. He liked the thought of someone's head blowing up, like in the cartoons from the Surround.

In the shuttle lobby he finally saw the spaceship, the *Glory Bee*, another name that made Keely giggle. He stood in the window and watched it. There was nothing nice about it, there was no needle shape like Sky Captain of Glindy had in the *Verti Viniga*. The ship had no visible cannons or missiles or fighter bay doors. It looked a great lump of metal with boxy stuff all over it and a billion antennae sprouting from it. He was terribly disappointed and sat down. "It doesn't look like a spaceship," he said, looking down at the toy box ring on his finger.

"Do you want some goo?" Nerva asked. "It's all right for you to play in here."

"I said it doesn't look like a spaceship."

"Well, it is one. Do you want some goo for your ring?"

"Yes, please."

She rummaged in her bag and found the container, scooped him out a good heap, and he touched the ring to it and the toy matrix downloaded and the goo assembled itself into a slinky, which he tossed back and forth in his hand.

"Don't get that tangled in anything like your hair," Uncle Figg said.

"Don't be ridiculous," Keely said, a phrase he had been using whenever he could because it was on Corny Cornberg on the Surround.

Uncle Figg was talking to a priest wearing the whole outfit, hood and all. Keely studied the priest for a while. Uncle Figg was talking about Keely as if he weren't there, the way adults often did. "He's the one," Uncle Figg said. "But we don't talk about what happened to Sherry right now. He doesn't even remember her. We've had him regressed a few years in age, for therapy."

"He did seem a bit big for his speech," the holy man said.

"Are you a holy man?" Keely asked.

"Yes," Nerva said, "he's very holy, so holy you mustn't talk to him. Play with your tinky."

"Slinky," he said, and rolled his eyes. He was beginning to think she mispronounced the word on purpose, which was corny like an adult.

"He'll remember her later, when we get rid of some of his therapy issues. He grew up in the Reeks; he had a rough time."

"I know," said the priest, "I saw the vid special about him."

Uncle Figg frowned. "My attorney tried to prevent that. But that was about the time the new laws kicked in and I lost my money."

An awkward moment passed; Keely could feel it, and it troubled him. He concentrated on the slinky but held it still.

"I know that a lot of your people are upset with the Mage about that."

"It's a bit of an understatement, that, don't you think?"

"Maybe."

"My family lost more money than a lot of factions ever see. Along with the property."

"I understand." The priest made a gesture, and Keely copied it. The gesture said, who knew? "Most of my Hormling friends are furious. I wonder if even the Mage will ride it out."

"That's the bitching problem," Uncle Figg said, and he glanced at Keely and then at Nerva, who was frowning with her wrinkly forehead. "Sorry."

Keely was not understanding much of the talk but he understood the bad word and knew he should not laugh at it, especially in public, where Nerva would be most likely to scold him, since it was for show. A scolding in front of other people was always for show, but sometimes that was only a small help.

"That's the problem," Uncle Figg continued, "the Prin will pull it off. They always do. And the Mage has Hanson in her pocket. Hanson is the whole inside of the machine at this point—if he takes away your money it's gone and if he takes away your stocks they're gone and if he says you don't own your property anymore you don't. So the Mage will take care of the ministries and any rebellion, and Hanson will take care of anything else."

"The same thing happened in Iraen," said the priest, and Keely's ears pricked up, since fairies lived in Iraen, and so did witches, and other monsters.

"And?"

The priest shrugged. He drew down his hood. He was about the same age as Uncle Figg and had a funny long nose and thin dark hair. He was like an old man in a cartoon. His skin was the color of chocolate. "People complained. Rich people complained, I mean. Poor people didn't mind the redistribution."

"All the same laws? The abolition of inheritance?"

"Yes. He wanted to get rid of money altogether but couldn't figure out how to do it without the danger of people reinventing it right away. So he had to compromise."

"He? Great Irion?"

"Yes, the person the Mage takes her orders from. If he is a person." The priest opened the long garment, which hung nearly to the floor. Keely wondered what it would be like to sit inside it between the priest's feet. Would it be like a tent?

"I tried to see him once," Uncle Figg said.

The priest laughed. "You did?"

"My one trip to Iraen. The one where I met you, actually. I applied to go north with some of the missions that were opening up trade there."

"You were going to work?"

"Yes. I'll have you know I'm no stranger to hard work, Dekkar."

"You'll pardon me if I'm skeptical."

"Laugh into your hand, go ahead. Everyone's laughing at me now that I'm poor."

Nerva looked at Uncle Figg as if she would like to scold him in public for show, but it was only a mild kind of want, so she held her tongue.

"Fineas," said the priest, "I know perfectly well you were left enough of your money that you'll have a good deal of trouble spending it all in your lifetime. Which you'll have to do, since you can't leave it to your ward."

"I thought I'd rescued him from all that hardship."

The priest made a spitting, laughing noise.

"What's hardship?" Keely asked.

"Be quiet and play with your ring. I'll give you more goo if you want it."

"Keely will have just as much chance as anybody else does to take care of himself."

There were a lot of voices overhead and around but suddenly the adults were all listening to one of the voices, booming in a tinny way.

"We'll talk more about this on board," the priest said. "I'm traveling with you as far as the port on the other side, anyway."

"Are you Uncle Figg's friend?" Keely asked the priest.

The man had nice eyes but Keely thought his nose was crooked and he ought to get it fixed. Maybe Uncle Figg would get it fixed for him.

"Yes," the priest said. "We're very old friends. I met your uncle when I lived in Iraen and we've known each other ever since."

"I don't know when that was," Keely said.

"My name is Dekkar," said the man. "I know yours. It's Keely."

Keely nodded.

"How long does the regression last?" Dekkar asked Uncle Figg.

Uncle Figg looked at Nerva, who said, "This stage ends in two or three days, by the time we get to Jarutan. He'll seem older then and have some of his old memories back."

"You're his therapist?"

"She's my aunt," Keely said.

"I'm his all-around," Nerva said.

"You're from Iraen, too," Dekkar said.

"Yes."

"I like to have your people around me," Uncle Figg said.

"We're not the same people," Nerva said, politely. "This gentleman is Anin. I'm one of the elder people."

"She's Erejhen," Dekkar said, with an amused smile. "They were there first."

"By quite a considerable number of years," Nerva added, her tone not haughty so much as severe, as if it were a fact that ought already to be known.

"My mistake," Uncle Figg said. "I had no idea."

"It's a complicated world," Nerva said. "Gather up your things, Keely. Melt the toy and give me the goo."

"You're my aunt," Keely told her again, looking her in the eye, as he gave her the toy stuff.

"That's right," Nerva said. "But only because someone has to be." She took his cheek between thumb and forefinger, giving him a grimace like she wanted to eat him. He was supposed to be afraid and pretended he was, as Uncle Figg and Dekkar got to their feet.

"Are you a fairy, Aunt Nerva?" Keely asked.

"No. There's no such thing. Don't drag your feet when you walk. Mind and let me fasten the tether, we're going into free fall again."

So Thin a Thread

1.

Each morning Fineas Figg woke to the news of the world, preread and already queued up for his attention.

Figg's personal head-space was orderly, neat, and compartmentalized, old memories trimmed and compacted to make room for new memories to which he might need more access; his aging consciousness was boosted just a bit by streams of newfangled neurons manufactured by the cell factory nestled into the back of his skull. Because he was wealthy and had always been wealthy, there was no sort of modification or enhancement that was out of his reach. Prereadings of the daily news were expensive, requiring the intervention of a human consciousness to do the initial reading, but even in his reduced circumstances, nearly impoverished by the Mage's war on inherited property, he felt he must maintain a certain level of style in his daily life.

Preread news, if it was encoded properly, required only a moment of realization to be understood; the encapsulated information was presented to Figg's awareness, realized, and then captured into short-term memory by a specialized set of cells implanted in his prefrontal cortex. There was a kind of balance necessary to the process, as taking in too much at once could bring on nausea, even convulsions. He took in a burst, considered it, took another, and so on.

During an idle day, such as today, he could draw on the prereadings and savor them more completely, as he wished, while placidly awaiting the transition through the Anilyn Gate.

Much of the news originated in Grand Wheel, the station toward which he sailed, which was shaped like a wheel with many spokes and rims. At the center of Grand Wheel was the Anilyn Gate, through which ships sailed to Aramen—it was the twin, in many respects, of the Twil Gate on Senal, through which ocean-borne ships sailed to Iraen. Here on Grand Wheel lived the Mage and much of her court, including the central nodes of Hanson, the ghost in the great machine. In this solar system the gate orbited high above Senal, and in the other high above Aramen; the Mage and Hanson, by living near the gate, had the most efficient information access to both worlds.

All the power in the world—in two worlds, rather—and now all the money in two worlds were concentrated here.

°1 The first bubble of news he burst was about the Mage, or at least about the Consort, Lady Jedda, who had recently celebrated her 390th birthday on Grand Wheel. Lady Jedda was now officially the oldest Hormling who had ever lived in a single body; only Hansonian multiples could live longer. The Lady Jedda had been Mage Malin's consort since the days of the Conquest, when Figg, who was now a spry 303, was a mere child.

The Mage's celebration in honor of the Consort was notable for the personal appearance of Pods Poxley, sensation of the moment, a new stipple-ball player for a team favored by the Consort. Pods's name, like Figg's, was a pseudonym; most people used registered proxy names in place of their real ones, especially for the purposes of maintaining a public persona.

○2 Fineas Figg remained infamous on Senal as the heir of the oldest of Orminy Houses, brought low by the Mage's reform of the laws of commerce known as the Common Fund Reforms; his departure from Senal to live in seclusion on Aramen was noted in several tidbits of information gathered by Figg's publicity staff. He spent a moment contemplating each of these. One of the reports was notable in that it claimed he was having the Marmigon reconstructed on the north continent of Aramen to escape from the Mage and her secret service agents. None of the rest had the facts any nearer the mark.

○3 Great Irion closed the Twil Gate due to a storm in the Inokit Ocean the day before; his decision to allow the storm to flourish rather than to quell it was debated by nearly anyone with a commercial interest in keeping the gate open. Trade with Iraen remained at its highest levels in decades as more Hormling colonists were allowed into the country. Figg's interest in this subject was unending; he had heard stories of Great Irion since he was a boy and had dreamed of living in Iraen himself one day, though all his applications to emigrate had been denied and he'd been allowed to visit only once. The Mage came from there; the Prin came from there; magic came from there. Skeptical, decadent as Figg had become at times in his long life, he had never lost his childish glee at the thought of magicians. Odd that he felt such innate, childish affection for Great Irion and such suspicion of the Mage, Irion's niece, who ruled the Hormling in his name.

○4 The Marmigon Tenants Council meeting of the day before erupted into near violence over the scheduling of the Autumn Viewing of the Maples and the rival Night of Dead Souls; now that Figg was no longer available as owner of the complex to adjudicate disputes, more and more such altercations could be expected as factions vied for control of Senal's most exclusive address.

His family had owned the place since it was built; it gave him satisfaction to see how quickly the place was going to hell without him. He would miss mornings in the penthouse looking out over the clouds.

○5 Hanson continued to move forward with construction projects designed to bring better living conditions to those in the Reeks, the lower levels of public cubicles and shelters for the billions of Hormling who lived on the minimum. The Common Fund appears healthy and will finance anything we need, says Hanson. Poor people must have decent housing, no matter how far down they live.

There certainly ought to be enough money in that fund, Figg thought. My money and my family's money, every Orminy family I know, every merchant, every corporation, my god.

By now the shuttle was nearing the check station, a robot craft under propulsion that sniffed all sides of the transport as it accelerated just enough to glide through the dark ring at the center of Grand Wheel. The Common Fund lived here on Grand Wheel, if it lived anywhere; and Hanson owned it all, if anybody did. Had there ever been such wealthy tyrants in the world as these two, Hanson and the Mage?

○6 A minor matter, the claim of Celeb Iniman, underdweller, against Fineas Figg, legal proxy for an unnamed party, in the matter of the allegedly illegal adoption of Keely File, underdweller;

aforementioned Celeb Iniman claimed to be the paternal uncle of Keely and entitled to a claim in his custody as sole living relative following the untimely death of Sherry File, Keely's sister. Case dismissed by reason of incompatible DNA as regards to ancestry; Keely File no relation to the complaining party, who therefore had no standing as regards custody of the minor child.

This was a minor news item hardly reported in any media outlet but easily the most important of all to Figg. He had grown far too fond of Keely to allow anyone to take the child away. In the three years since he adopted Keely, one supposed relative after another had crawled out of the Reeks to contest the adoption, in hope of some large financial settlement from Figg's accountant, no doubt. Not one had ever proven any kinship to the child.

The sister, Sherry, had died as part of Figg's three hundredth birthday party; legally licensed for public suicide, she had killed herself at the culmination of the party. The ensuing confusion and scandal was in large part responsible for the public outrage that led to the Common Fund Reforms and the Mage's wholesale changes in Hormling material culture. The same scale of convulsion in Figg's personal life had led him to retire from the public and adopt Keely, in order to rescue the boy from return to life in the Reeks. Figg had seen something in himself at that party, something he wanted to turn his back on . . . he had no words for it.

○7 Marches for liberty and full independence in planetary government continued in the city of Jarutan on the north continent of Aramen; peaceful and orderly demonstrations bringing hundreds of thousands of Aramenians to the streets in support of the cause of freedom from the Hormling and the Prin. The movement was supported by the Dirijhi, the sentient trees who lived in the north of the continent and who considered themselves to be the owners of the planet Aramen since they were the original inhabitants of it.

Figg had been following this thread for some months as he contemplated emigrating to that very place—not to Jarutan but to the north continent, where the farm was.

It struck Figg as odd, this freedom movement, since the north continent of Aramen, called Ajhevan, was already the freest place in the Hormling universe. Under the terms of the treaty with the Dirijhi, the Prin were allowed no access to Ajhevan, and so, over the years, it had become a haven for people who wanted to do business away from the attention of the priests who served the Mage.

○**8** The Orminy clan Urtuthenel booked passage on Fartha Station en route to Glindy; the entire clan decided to leave Senal with what was left of its fortune in the wake of the disastrous Common Fund Reforms. The Urtuthenel, no longer wealthy, elected to ship out to the Glindy colony via station rather than ship, the cost of fast transport being prohibitive for such a large clan. Bitter statements issued from Skygard as the clan matron held her last press conference. About half the Orminy houses had defected to Aramen and about half to Glindy; those headed for Glindy would take slow-side transport to the station and then ride serenely at half-light speed, a journey of something like twenty-five years. Had the clan possessed the resources for fast-side transport—transport traveling faster than the stations of the Conveyance—they could have made the journey in fourteen.

The richer houses were settling on Aramen, the poorer on Glindy. Exceptions were not so frequent as to distort the picture. This newsburst originated from a private data service to which Figg's family subscribed; Figg made it his business, like any good Orminy son, to keep abreast of clan movements.

This era will be spoken of in shame, said the Urtuthenel matriarch;

we have abandoned Home Star to the domination of a deceiver and a low witch.

◦9 Even harder to access was news from within the Prin, the priesthood who served the Mage, but Figg had sources. Today four high-ranking Prin chorists had been apprehended, along with a group of Hormling and Iraenian scientists; the group had been conducting illegal research into the nature of the Prin chant. The priestly members of the group were willing participants; two of them had been employed to keep the research hidden from their fellows, while the other two aided in research. The names in this case meant nothing to Figg, but the fact of the arrest intrigued him. One rarely heard of any sort of schism in the ranks of the Prin.

This or that member of the Prin inner circles denounced this scandalous breach of the respect due to Great Irion, this violation of the discipline of the Oregal. Figg had heard this word before, *Oregal,* transliterated from the Erejhen language, but he had no idea what it meant. The closest translation he had been able to find was "birdcage," but that could scarcely be correct.

Describing the process of absorbing a newsburst requires a much longer time than undergoing it. Figg considered each of these moments of news, sighed in his seat on the shuttle, waited for transit.

He processed many more moments in those few seconds.

◦192 In Feidreh, the capital of southern Aramen, flowers of further new species had been identified, in some cases kin to nothing else ever found in native foliage. Botanists were at a loss to explain what could only be a severe increase in the level of mutations in certain plant families.

Items like this he passed over with a flickering; he vaguely considered what possible algorithm might have caused it to come to his attention. It was as if some hand were tapping him on the shoulder.

2.

Figg saw Keely properly unbelted from the seat on the lander and passed the boy over to Nerva; the older man was tired from the long transit, most of it spent waiting for the moment at which the shuttle would be given permission to accelerate to the appropriate path for passage through the Anilyn Gate to local space near Aramen.

No one knew exactly how much space the gate collapsed or how far its steady flow of traffic actually traveled during that quick, painless transit. Even the Mage, who helped to cause the transit, had no notion of the distance it crossed; such a consideration was irrelevant, or so it appeared. The particulars of local space around Aramen matched nothing in the sky registers of the Hormling taken from any of their worlds on the other side of the gate; one could presume from this that the gate connected two very distant regions.

On the other side of the gate, in local space around Red Star, the shuttle accelerated out of the path of oncoming traffic, then began decelerating in a long curve toward Sky-gard Aramen.

Now came their processing through local intake, most of which was automated and passive; Figg and his party need merely negotiate the free-fall corridors and hand-over-hand pathways toward the lift platforms, followed by the long descent down the pulleypod into the deep atmosphere of Aramen. Their initial destination was Feidreh-Avatrayn, the twin city that served as colonial capital for what had become, under the rule of the Mage, the second-most important world in the Hormling sphere of influence. He had heard again in his newsbursts that the Prin were not allowed to venture into Ajhevan and, following his recent dealings with them, found the prospect pleasing. There was a strong independence movement in the north; at one point early in his planning he had considered throwing in his lot with theirs. Not that he could be of much financial use to them now that the bulk of his wealth had been stripped away. His family name had a certain level of prestige attached to it—not Figg, of course, but his full krys name, Bemona-Kakenet, the oldest and most senior of the Orminy houses.

He was emigrating to this world for Keely. So far the Mage had not extended the reach of the Common Fund Reforms beyond Senal; here, once Figg became a citizen, he could will his property to Keely. The child had brought immense freshness to Figg's life. He meant for Keely to grow up where there was open land, running water, trees, green growing things, all of which Figg remembered from his own boyhood on his mother's estate.

At the moment Keely was tired, head in Nerva's lap, sleeping as the car slowly descended, their bodies gaining weight again, the car warming for a period during the early descent, then cooling as that system kicked in. He woke soon enough, though, when the car landed and passengers disembarked at the foot of Skygard into the Plaza of Two Worlds.

The first thing he noticed was that he felt heavier. Nerva was muttering about it as well; gravity on Aramen was a good ten percent stronger than on Senal. The difference was enough to notice, and Keely was taking slow giant steps as if his feet were made of lead.

To Figg's surprise, Dekkar was waiting at the point of arrival, coat pressed against his body by the wind. He looked concerned and approached Figg right away. A woman was with him, medium height, indeterminate age; she had that look of being permanently in her thirties that most Hormling carry well into their second century.

"Are you listening to the news at all?" Dekkar drew Figg aside from the rest of his party, near a water fountain in the shape of a twist of stone, basin at the top.

"No, I haven't linked in a while; I figured my stat was still searching through local protocols."

"There's a good bit of trouble here."

"Trouble?" He felt Penelope stir in his scalp, stretching her long, thin legs; he reached to stroke her back. Keely pressed against his side, small head under Figg's hand. "I assume you mean something out of the ordinary."

"You're aware of the freedom demonstrations in the north? Jarutan?"

"Yes. I was going over my news filters and had a newsburst about that."

"The trouble's spread here, too, it appears."

"In Feidreh?"

"Yes. I think it's something quite serious. My guide there," Dekkar gestured to the woman, who was standing in the sun looking a bit out of place, her clothes of no style Figg could recognize, leather leggings and a close-fitting blouse, a utility vest over it—odd fashion, looking more like a work outfit.

"Her name is Kitra Poth. She's from Ajhevan, the northern continent. I believe you said you were headed there?"

"Yes."

"Apparently so am I. She's suggesting strongly that I leave with her immediately to get clear of whatever is coming this way."

"Whatever is coming?"

"The military's gone on alert. There are rumors of some kind of violence in the city."

"You think we'd be safer if we came with you now?"

"I have a surface flitter with plenty of room," said Dekkar. "But we need to leave this minute."

He glanced upward, as if expecting to see something beyond the awful turquoise of the sky, a few clouds distant, purpling along the bottoms.

"All we have is our hand luggage," Figg said.

"Can you leave your retainer here to try to gather the rest?"

"I won't have a bodyguard if I do."

"Except Penelope," Dekkar said, being familiar with Figg's partly mechanical pet, who was far more effective as a bodyguard than even so formidable a young woman as Zhengzhou.

Penelope, hearing her name, stretched and preened, arching her velvety back. Keely was watching, round-eyed; he had a great affection for Penelope, and no fear of her at all, or so it appeared.

"You think it's that urgent?" Figg asked.

"Kitra does. She's impatient that I've made her wait this long."

"All right then," Figg said, feeling his heart pick up a beat, looking around at the busy plaza, dotted with green islands, kiosks selling planet memorabilia to tourists arriving and departing; food stands, most serving various kinds of local sausages; street musicians and performers. "Sounds as if we should risk leaving the luggage if that's necessary. Are you ready now?"

"We have a putter parked over here to take us to the flitter landing."

Figg gathered his family hurriedly and gave instructions to Zhengzhou, who frowned and agreed. "Rent a flitter if you can," Figg said. "You've already got the address of the farm, just take everything there as soon as possible; we'll be there ahead of you."

"That shouldn't be a problem."

"I can't stress to you enough how urgent it is that you get out of the city quickly," Dekkar said to her.

Zhengzhou nodded, bundling her dark weather-coat around her, and hurried off into the crowd toward the baggage terminal.

On the top of Figg's head, legs socketed in his scalp, Penelope stirred and went on a state of alert. She was edgy in big crowds, especially now that Figg could no longer afford his customary entourage of security.

Nerva said, "My goodness, what a rush. I was hoping to see a bit of the city before we left. I've heard there's a grand museum of colonial history here. Keely ought to look at the exhibits."

"We'll be living here, Nerva. There'll be time for that sort of travel later. Right now we want to get to the farm, don't we? So this is a good way to do that. I'm for it. How about you, Keely?"

Sleepy, the boy yawned and nodded. "I'm tired. My legs feel heavy. I want to ride in the flitter."

The woman named Kitra waited beside the putter with her jaw clenched. Dekkar sat in the driver's compartment and everyone else found seats in the passenger booth at the back. During the ride through the city, Figg looked about for signs of whatever trouble might be about to surface; the place looked unfamiliar to him, much larger than it had been a century ago when he last visited, during the first boom of out-migration from Senal. The original Feidreh had been engulfed by new construction, including some of the enclave-style architecture common to corporate mega-complexes in Béyoton, but also including friendlier, more open styles of developments and buildings. The city had a different feeling from anything on Senal, which had dug its cities deep and raised them high to accommodate the billions of Hormling who nested there. Here one had no sense of a latticework of people stretching deep into the bowels of the earth. The sky was clear, there were green spaces open to real, direct sunlight, and one could see plazas and open markets where crowds of native Aramenians congregated to do their business face to face. The day had a calm, placid feeling that belied the urgency with which he was traveling.

The putter, under Kitra's aggressive handling, made good progress and soon ramped into a flitter field on a bluff overlooking the ocean in a clean, bright part of town that looked like a tech complex or some kind of campus for a large business firm.

As they were transferring themselves and their luggage into the flitter, a long, low siren began to moan.

"What's that?" Nerva asked.

"It's a big horn," said Keely, looking up at the sky.

Nerva ignored him and looked at Figg, who gestured toward the interior of the flitter, and she hurried into it as the hatches swung upward, hanging over the sides of the machine like stubby wings.

"Get in," Kitra said, "that's an air raid warning system."

"A what?" Figg asked.

"An attack. There's about to be an attack."

"Good heavens," Nerva said, sliding into the flitter.

Figg took his seat. Dekkar was still standing outside the flitter, looking at the sky. Kitra hit the button for the passenger door; it started to swing closed and Dekkar jumped into the seat. "Sorry," he said. "There's an odd smell in the air, some kind of flower I've never smelled before."

Kitra was powering up the flitter; she sealed the cabins as if the machine were flying at a very high altitude.

"What's going on?" Figg asked.

"The independence movement is declaring war," Kitra said. "I used to be in it; I got word yesterday to get out of the capital as fast as I could."

"War?" Nerva asked.

"Like on the vid," Keely explained, "when people fight."

"They've declared war on the Hormling?" Figg asked; the news, if it was true, was astounding.

"Yes. And on the Mage. And on the Prin. And on the whole trade system."

"Are they out of their minds?" Figg asked.

"Oh, no," Kitra said grimly, raising the flitter off the pad. "You have no idea how serious they are."

"But the Prin—"

"The rebels have allies," Kitra said, "strong ones. The Prin are about to find out just how strong."

"But nobody's beaten the Prin in more than three hundred years," Nerva said.

"There's a first time for everything. I can't answer any more questions right now; use your links if you like. I have to get us out of here."

3.

The Hormling link to the data mass on both sides of the Anilyn Gate could be maintained in something very close to real time for all the billions of people who lived on both worlds. A very palpable and superlatively complex netting of connections bound the populaces of Senal and Aramen, information flowing constantly from Grand Wheel, the entire data mass maintained by Hanson and his cohorts, available to any and all. Figg's link was internal, with some additional hardware stored in Penelope.

One moment the data mass felt proper and right, the link up and running, Figg's neat beads of newsbursts queued for his attention, his orderly head-space making short work of each, and then suddenly there was a feeling of convulsion and the link slowed to a crawl.

○1 Reports of an air battle over the northern stretches of ocean, conflicting locations, satellite feeds erratic; there was a delay as Figg realized each of the newsbursts; the prereading service was undergoing a bit of a lag, maybe in response to traffic. Air defense systems had begun going off all across the southern continent, Jharvan. A major electronic pulse explosion over the port city of Chesna dumped ten million people off the network at once; not a jolt big enough to feel in the Surround, but enough to register.

○2 A collision in orbit between a small naval squadron decelerating into a low orbit as part of the military alert and a line of passenger shuttles queued to pass through the gate. Thousands of casualties. The reports so fresh that most of them lacked verbs, static pictures of the beginnings of chaos.

○3 Appeals from the civilian government in Feidreh-Avatrayn for all citizens to remain calm and await further information. An attack was apparently under way by a northern expeditionary force launched by independence advocates on Ajhevan.

○4 Shocked reaction erupted from Senal as the first images broke into the Surround. Citizens of Béyoton were stunned, so many links active in real time that systems were in danger of overload; people were advised to take breaks from the Surround, especially individuals with permanent indwelling links, some of which might under certain circumstances overheat.

○5 This next was not words but an image: a tree root twisting through a cadaver in a busy street, the root like something serpentine, flexing its strength, driving through the body and into the side of a building. An image so vivid it held Figg's attention for longer than necessary. What had been a large, empty retail space lay in ruins and the tree rose out of it, growing as if by will. The image came from a neighborhood in Feidreh where the tree appeared this morning as a seedling and had now rooted through twelve levels of putter parking under a downtown church, which it had also infiltrated. Was this part of the attack?

○6 Failure in communications systems were reported throughout Jharvan, some caused by a fungus that ate electronics and their attendant organics. Rumors circulated of reports of a similar fungus infestation in military installations and equipment. Loss of some technological function even in the capital; loss of some communications satellites in orbit as well, though there were no reports as to the cause.

○7 A long narrative ensued: a journalist was steering her construct via remote control in a borrowed flitter headed south; she flew low over the ocean tailing a spectacular shower of dogfights high in the air; high resolution cameras caught needle fighters, racers, missiles arcing, drones plummeting into the ocean. Close-ups of the aircraft from Ajhevan matched military profiles from the data mass, all identifiable except for a few pale, almost transparent darts and a number of what looked like flocks of dark birds that cut through aircraft as if they were made of pure carbon, flying blades. So many images were gathered by the remote-construct that the Surround was continuing to digest them long after the journalist's proxy was destroyed by one of the invading aircraft firing a regular air-to-air missile. What we're seeing is astonishing, said the voice of the journalist, our camgatherer recorded images of nearly three thousand aircraft, the whole force available to Drakkar Air Station plus a much larger enemy force flown to the coast by the rebels of Ajhevan. This is unheard-of audacity to challenge the Mage in her own backyard. The governor is anticipating a response from the Fukate Choir of Ten Thousand. Everyone is reminded that not a single military encounter with the Prin has ended in anything less than complete victory since the earliest days of the Conquest. This desperate quest for freedom on the part of the rebels in the north is doomed from the start. Perhaps it has been long enough since the last challenge to the power of the Mage that it is necessary for her once again to demonstrate the overwhelming power of the Prin chant. But the Hormling air force appears to be having difficulties in these early stages.

○ 8 Troops coming ashore at the port of Chesna, flitters wheeling and landing in well-formed ranks; discharging squads of rebels in brown uniforms, rising and wheeling northward again, efficient and quick. An army was coming ashore uncontested, landing in our city of Chesna apparently uncontested. The city was experiencing widespread power outages and real disruption due to heavy electronic pulse bombardment. Local choirs of the Prin had been ineffective.

○ 9 A young girl lay near the entrance to a building, gray fungus covering her like fur; eyes open, staring upward, she was breathing shallow breaths. Chaos in the background, what looked to be explosions. The image switched to another body, a large man, clothes bulging oddly, the same fur of fungus over his face and hands. Downtown Feidreh, still peaceful until a few moments ago, had suffered an explosion at a local restaurant, and workers arrived to this scene, a kitchen fire raging out of control and a room full of corpses covered with some kind of plant growth. Some appeared to have died of contact with a virulent fungus, others of allergic reactions leading to cardiac arrest.

○ 10 Reports of trees growing faster than they should, growing back even when ripped up or poisoned, discarded portions taking root in nearly any locale, some of them out of hand by the time they were discovered; a tree growing through the abandoned Cathedral of Mur Under Heaven roof. Victims poured into local hospitals complaining of contact with new varieties of flowers that had been reported across Jharvan; some of the patients presented in acute respiratory distress.

○ 11 From Grand Wheel emerged further reports of mishaps aboard naval vessels attempting to position themselves from space to provide cover for the Jharvan government. The Fukate Ten Thousand were assembling in the Prin College in Citadel. Unconfirmed reports continued to appear of near-human construct troops from Ajhevan landing at various points along the coast, their approach apparently undetected.

○ 12 Unofficial word had been received by the governor from leaders of various northern independence movements that this would be the day celebrated by their children as the beginning of freedom.

○ 13 Difficulties in satellite communication were reported on both sides of the Anilyn Gate.

This was followed by a shuddering, a pulse in the link that manifested in Figg's head-space as a dead silence, a complete disconnect from all those voices of the network, the Surround, the link that had been part of him for nearly three centuries.

A great feeling of surprise came over him, an emptiness except for the voice of Hanson, which survived the convulsion of the link; and then new voices, echoes, resounded in his head.

He was the only one in the car on-link; Keely was too young and the rest were preoccupied with the flight. He looked up at the sky. Some of his alarm must have shown in his expression.

Dekkar looked at him.

"The gate," he said.

Kitra turned her head. "What?" She was looking at one of her instruments. "The link's down. The link to the car."

"It'll come back up in a minute," Figg said.

"How do you know?"

"I was on-link when something happened. The whole Surround went dead. Then it came back up."

"What did you mean about the gate?" Dekkar asked, but he was pale and drawn, as if he already knew.

"That's why the link went down. The gate's closed."

"What?" Kitra asked.

"The Anilyn Gate. It's closed. Someone closed it."

She blinked, as stunned as he.

"Rebels?" Figg asked.

"Hardly," Kitra said. "No one even knows how it operates, how would anyone sabotage it?"

"Great Irion closed it," Dekkar said, speaking with quiet assurance.

"How do you know?" Figg asked, watching the persistant hint of trouble in Dekkar's face; the priest could not quite be rid of it.

"He's the only one who can," Dekkar said. He folded his hands, looking out the window. "I suppose we're on our own then."

Sisterhood

1.

Kitra had spent the last few days piecing together bits of a puzzle that, while still not fully assembled, pointed to the need to get off the southern continent and head north.

She worked for the Citadel, the Prin College in Avatrayn, as a specialist in matters relating to northern politics. For the first decades of her life she had worked for Aramenian independence, agitating against the rule of the Prin as the foundation of the whole Hormling trade system. Over time she became one of the senior leaders in People for a Free Aramen, one of many colonial independence movements that had sprung up in the cluster colonies. But a decade ago she had turned her back on independence and come to the Prin for help. Following a trip into Greenwood to visit her brother Binam, she had changed her attitude.

Her brother had been sold to the Dirijhi at a young age, a voluntary candidate to become a tree symbiont, a human adapted for life as part of its tree host. Symbionts were the means by which the Hormling had established contact with the sentient trees and the inducement they had used to convince the trees to allow Hormling colonists onto the planet. At the time she had seen the trip only as an opportunity to make contact with the Dirijhi, to convince them to support independence. She had been successful in opening a dialog with the trees, but in the process she had seen the conditions under which the human symbionts lived, as slaves to their hosts more often than as partners. She had dedicated her life to getting her brother out of Greenwood, no small challenge since he could no longer feed except from food prepared for him by his tree; in search of allies, she had turned to the Prin. In the past decade she had made three more trips into Greenwood, though she had not seen her brother again.

A ten-day ago she read an article in the morning newsframe about a curious appearance in Feidreh-Avatrayn of a number of new botanical species, new cultivars, or new variants of older flowering plants. Botanists and biologists attached to one of the universities were attempting to investigate the cause of the sudden emergence of so many new variants at once; this must be sign of some ecological shift of which humans remained unaware.

At the same time, in an Enforcement enclave near the Citadel, some armored vehicles and a couple of military aircraft developed a problem with a kind of fungus that had an appetite for electronics, also digesting most of the organic components of the machinery, including a couple of cloned-consciousness supervisory boxes that had been eaten alive.

The Fukate Choir of the Prin, whose chief cantor, Vekant Anevarin, was one of Kitra's close contacts in her work, developed a difficulty in managing the weather over Ajhevan;

this was a problem that recurred periodically when the weather choir went a bit out of tune. Since the Prin were barred from visiting the north in person, management of weather systems there had always been less than certain. But the combination of these factors made Kitra suspicious, and she said as much to Vekant during a meeting to plan her next foray into Greenwood.

"We're seeing nothing in the chant." Vekant had the polished, almost burnished skin of a Hormling, dark eyes, long lashes, his hair a bit fussy and curly; he was stocky and short, not a very fashionable physiognomy, but he was more fastidious in his manner of dress than most of the Prin. He wore all three layers of his ceremonial vestments even at a meeting; his fingers were heavy with rings and his earlobes crusted with piercings. The Mage herself was said to favor simple dress and few adornments. Vekant also wore a light makeup, though it was nevertheless a bit heavier than Kitra's own.

"This is too much coincidence. Fungus here, these flowers, and now the weather gone weird over Greenwood. I think the rebels and the Dirijhi are nearly ready to launch their attack."

Vekant contemplated her carefully, perhaps even showily, as if gauging once again how far to take her into his confidence. They were on a roof park in the Citadel near his administrative offices; he had walked her here to make a quiet zone around them both, which he did by some means she could never detect but which gave him a bit of a tic, one eyebrow bobbling up and down a bit periodically. For all his heaviness and weight of bangles, he moved quietly as a cat. She was sure he was only partly paying attention to her; not unusual for one of his kind. The anxiety of being so near a Prin still made her skin prickle at times. "Do the Dirijhi have any sense of how we do our work in the chant?"

"I don't have much idea myself," Kitra said.

"We learn languages," Vekant said. "That's the primary tool we use to do the work we do. It's a bit of a simplification, but it's true. We learn to speak words that cause things to happen."

"Look, you might as well call it magic, that's what everybody else does."

"Great Irion doesn't like the word anymore; we don't use it unless we have no choice."

"You don't?"

He had a way of speaking that reminded Kitra of vids of frontier schoolmasters, prim and polished and smug. "Great Irion believes we work through some means that is physical and explainable, even though your scientists haven't made much progress figuring it out."

"You think the Dirijhi have?"

When he failed to answer for a while, she felt a sinking in her stomach. "You do, don't you?"

"I suppose that's what I'm thinking, yes. It's only coming clear to me as we talk. It's the weather, you see. We've always had difficulty managing air currents, moisture, front movements, all that, for Ajhevan continent."

"I've always heard it was the distance, the fact that none of you can actually go there."

"We're the Fukate," Vekant said. "A choir of ten thousand ought to be able to manage most anything on a planetary scale. But we've always had difficulty working on Ajhevan. At first we thought the trees simply had a certain amount of re-sistance to us, that it was innate to their kind. This would make more sense if you knew more about the chant; it's certainly possible. But even the Mage never detected any overt sign of true language at work in Greenwood."

"A true language?"

"A language that can affect the physical world when you know how to use it."

"A language that works magic when you speak it."

He sighed. "That's the vid interpretation, anyway."

"Is it a better explanation to call it a true language and change the rhetoric around a bit?"

He gave her the sort of lofty look that she had come to expect from him; he was a bit of a prig on the subject of his knowledge and his studies. He had in fact explained a good deal of this to her before, including several introductions to the term *true language,* but on each occasion appeared to for-get that he had done so, perhaps because he enjoyed the lec-ture. Most of the Hormling who succeeded in making it through their years as a novice had this kind of superior atti-tude, whereas the Erejhen Prin appeared to be arrogant by nature. "Point taken," he said, a bit grudgingly.

"But the Dirijhi don't speak any oral language."

"They use words. I understand they're made up of chains of proteins, or some such? Very slow language, but language." He sighed. "We already know of at least three different true languages from our own history. Iraenian history, I mean."

She was beginning to see his point, now. "So there may be more."

"It's virtually certain that there are."

She sat quietly for a moment. "You really think the Dirijhi have developed true language?"

He looked at her. His brow arched. "I don't know what I think."

"If you think the trees are resisting your magic—your chant—in some way, what else could it be?"

He gave her a careful study; she was meant to feel flattered. He spoke with a dramatic air. "A visitor."

"I don't understand."

"Not only are there more true languages than the three we know, there are more operators than Great Irion and the Prin."

"Other creatures who can do what you can do?"

"Yes. Or to be more precise, other creatures who can do what Great Irion can do."

The thought was too large. Like everyone her age, she had lived with fairy tales about Great Irion for as long as she could remember. "Is there a creature like that on Aramen? Can you tell?"

He was brooding, staring into a frame filled with the morning news. "Do you think your friends in the independence movement will know more about the timing?"

"I think so. My best contacts aren't happy about the partnership with the Dirijhi. They think the trees mean to use them as cannon fodder."

"Anything you can learn will be helpful." He pulled a tin from his robe and slipped a candy into his mouth. "Meanwhile, we're looking at everything that's going on at the moment. Enforcement is studying some of the flowers, but they don't have the staff to study all of them. We're gathering experts from the universities, and the governer and Commander Rui are calling for more help from Senal. We're collecting specimens of all of the new species we can find. There are dozens of new flowers alone; we're seeing the ones in bloom because they're vivid and they stick out. We need a team to examine other kinds of flora that aren't so easy to spot."

"You think these mutations come from the Dirijhi?"

"You know yourself how dangerous it is to travel in Greenwood, you've told me often enough."

"It sounds as though I'll need to leave for the north earlier than planned."

"I think you should go to Ajhevan right away. I don't know who I can send to meet you when you're ready to head upriver but I'll get word to you." Vekant had provided a Prin escort for two of her trips into Greenwood, in contravention of the treaty with the Dirijhi.

He looked as if he wanted to say something more. The eyebrow ticked up and down a bit, and his chin quivered.

"What?"

"I'm assuming we'll have at least another ten-day before the Dirijhi move. But what if we don't?"

"If they attack right now, are we ready?"

"No. The army's on the alert but we don't know what kind of attack to expect. We haven't even figured out how to kill the fungus that ate the flyers and the heavy armor."

"Can't the Prin get rid of these flowers?"

Reluctantly Vekant shook his head. "We can get rid of some. But some of them aren't even identified. We can find the fungus in its adult stage to get rid of it, but who knows how many spores there are? We can't see them well, they're not identified and named. Until something is named it can't be touched with our words. A Drune can do better, but it helps to have a sample of the thing nearby, or a way to identify it in true language."

"So the trees really can give you a run for your money."

"Yes."

"Then Mage Malin will have to come and take care of the problem herself."

"Which she would do, no doubt, except that if this scenario we're discussing is the right one, she may well have her own problems to deal with. There's already so much commotion on Senal because of the reforms to the Common Fund." He stood and wandered to the edge of the garden, looking over the Citadel, apparently; the wall of his office was all glass. Even in his walk he had a kind of fussy self-consciousness, as if he were being careful to project a performance of concern, as if this were a moment in a vid or a play. "We have a choir of ten thousand; that ought to be enough."

"I suppose we'll have to hope so."

"The first step is to find out what kind of time frame we have before the Dirijhi move. I'm checking through other sources, too, Kitra, but you're our best."

"I'll do whatever you need as long as this doesn't delay my next trip to Greenwood. I need an escort."

"I can't do anything to stop a war. With a war coming, I may not be able to spare anyone to travel with you. I'll need every voice for the choir."

She set her jaw and looked at him. "I'm going, one way or the other."

"Even though we can't do anything for your brother?"

"We can keep him alive," Kitra said.

"How will you travel with him this far from his tree?"

"Your people teamed up with some scientists and have worked out a way to store sap. I'll drain some from his host tree and use it. I have to try it, at least. If there's a war, I won't leave him in Greenwood."

"What if I can't sent you protection?"

"I'll go anyway. I'll have my biosuit."

He frowned, more concerned than she had expected, his face heavy and jowlish, clownish in its way. His dark eyebrows knitted together, again with that look of self-preoccupation, as if he were seeing himself in a film about this moment, as if his reviews were good. "I see I can't convince you, so I won't make things awkward by trying."

A story appeared in the news-frame about a tree growing at the rate of a foot per hour in a downtown Feidreh plaza. Vekant was studying the frame with concern as Kitra excused herself.

2.

She did as he asked, and her contact, Shanes Sharma, an electronics dealer in Jarutan, told her to get off of the southern continent as fast as she could. Shanes had no idea exactly how soon the Dirijhi and the rebels would launch their military force, but she knew it would be within a couple of days.

"You can stay with me," Shanes said, a half smile on her face, checking the secure status of the line.

"That's a little dangerous."

"But fun. Or it was the last time."

"I won't be alone, Shanes. Though it's tempting."

"If you have a girlfriend, you're welcome to bring her."

"Not like that."

Which ended the discussion as far as Shanes was concerned, since, as Kitra knew, Shanes had no use for men at all.

Kitra had to wait a day for the arrival of the man she had agreed to guide into Greenwood. This detail she had kept from Vekant; she made it a policy never to share all her secrets in the same place, and this one was worth keeping: a man from the country Irion, or Iraen, as people were beginning to call it. Someone from that fairy-tale place had contacted her only a day ago with a request to conduct him northward into the Dirijhi preserve. He was an operator of a true language, exactly what she needed, one of the Drune priests who spoke a separate language from the Prin and operated singly rather than in choirs. She had verified the fact directly as a condition of agreeing to escort him.

"Yes," he'd answered, his tone guarded. "Though I'll thank you to keep it to yourself at all times during our journey. That's a condition of my taking you along."

"You're taking me along?"

"Yes. I'm going myself, one way or the other."

The words were familiar enough that she paused. Something in his tone made her cautious; or else she was uncomfortable with an ardor that appeared as great as hers. "Maybe I should reconsider," she said. "Somebody who's never traveled there ought to be less cocksure."

He paused, and his voice changed in tone ever so slightly. "I can help you get your brother out alive."

Her heart pounded, and she stood with the link live, replaying his words in her inner hearing. "You know about Binam."

"It's not hard to find out; I have contacts among your ten thousand choir there."

"Vekant?"

"No. You needn't ask any other names, either. I've told you what I can do for you and your brother. But on condition you keep secret what you know about me."

"You sound as if you don't expect to be traveling alone."

"I don't. You'll have to bear with me on that point as well."

His name was Dekkar up Ortaen, an Anin, a fallen Drune priest, meaning he had been kicked out of the Oregal, the master organization of magicians, which was what everyone called them regardless of what they called themselves. She was to meet him at the Plaza of Two Worlds; she had the schedule for his shuttle and tracked it across the Anilyn Gate.

A day later she was in a flitter waiting for Dekkar and his party to come aboard; she was searching northbound lanes for a low, long route to Ajhevan that took her out of the path of any invasion traffic coming across the water. Her passengers had settled into their seats with grave, serious faces, all except the young boy, Keely, who was amusing himself with a Disturber toy, a huge insect with spiky legs. The toy appeared a bit young for him and his behavior struck her as oddly childish.

The civilian fellow whose name Kitra had not caught, one of Dekkar's guests, had a cyborg spider crawling on top of his head, some kind of bodyguard. She found herself keeping an eye on it as he clambered into his seat.

"I have a silvershield that will help hide us over the water,"

Kitra said, when everyone was strapped into safety belts. The flitter swung in a low curve down from the bluff, dropped close to the water, and started to pick up speed. The mag-lev controls were balky at first, as always. "You'll see a bit of distortion through the window. Don't worry about it, that's the silverfield."

"This is your flitter?" asked the civilian man with the spider on his head, and she remembered his name as Figg and felt again as if she ought to remember his face.

"No. It's mine on assignment from the Citadel."

He looked puzzled.

Dekkar said, "That's the university of the Prin, here. Where the Fukate Ten Thousand sing the chant."

"I work for them," Kitra said. "I'm a factor for supplies the Prin buy from Ajhevan."

"Why are we running?" Keely's nanny asked this, a handsome older woman whom Kitra found to be a bit forbidding; the woman was seated stiff as a bolt with a large woven bag in her lap. She kept her attention on the boy, who looked to be about ten or so, small for his age, playing with the intensity of someone half as old, attention fixed on the toy, oblivious even to the choppy ocean across which the flitter glided some scores of meters up.

Kitra said, "There's an independence movement in the north. They have allies in the forest, Greenwood, where the Dirijhi live."

"The sentient trees," Figg said, nodding his head toward the woman. "Remember, Nerva?"

"I want to see the trees if they really talk," Keely said, looking up.

Nerva said, "But they don't really talk, Keely. You'd never understand if one of them said anything to you."

"But it would still be talking," Keely said.

"And you think they're launching their rebellion now?" Figg asked.

As an answer she pointed east, where, high up, lines of aircraft swept overhead, covering the sky as far as the eye could see, some of them hidden at moments behind the clouds. The party in the flitter was long since out of sight of Jharvan continent, but those the aircraft were headed that way.

"Was this just a good guess?" Figg asked. "Or did you have warning?"

She was looking at him in the mirror and had the feeling again that she had seen his face. She answered a different question than the one he had asked, watching him coolly. "We're taking a long route to Ajhevan that will put us ashore well north of Jarutan. The main routes are clogged with military traffic."

Figg touched his temple, where the spider stirred. The thing had been watching Keely's toy in a predatory stance, as if she wished she could eat it. For some reason, Kitra naturally thought of the spider as a "she." That was when Figg announced that the Anilyn Gate had closed.

Kitra had no stat or any permanent link; hers had been removed as part of her work with the Prin, who limited use of the Surround in order to maintain privacy in their own operations. She had some electronics hidden in her scalp that she could make use of for data storage and enhanced analysis, and she had a chip library in the back of her neck with a large store of information hardwired into her, updated periodically in a minor surgical procedure. As the system grew she was having data storage added along her spine, none of it detectable to the naked eye.

After the first impact had soaked in, when it was clear the news had rattled Dekkar, he said, "I suppose we're on our own then," and threw up his hands.

Figg said, "It's the Prin. They do this kind of thing to keep people off balance."

"Why would they disrupt their own communications?" Dekkar asked. "Unless they want to isolate something on this side of the gate."

Figg was looking up at the sky. Another wave of aircraft passed overhead. "Those look like individual personnel carriers," he said.

"That's what I was thinking," Dekkar agreed. "Armored infantry, probably?"

"That's what Enforcement would use," Figg said.

"What else could it be?" Dekkar asked, as if he was considering this question carefully, and Kitra watched him for signs that he was using true language at the moment. He gave no hint.

"How long before we're there?" Nerva asked.

"At least six hours, provided I can keep up this speed," Kitra said. "You might want to rest."

Ten Thousand

V ekant called for the Fukate Choir to assemble as soon as he understood that what he and the daily choir of a thousand voices had seen was the launch of masses of aircraft from Ajhevan, from all over the continent, news that was confirmed by a call from Enforcement only a few moments later. The ten thousand, who actually numbered closer to eleven, were scattered over Jharvan continent, however, and would require time to return to the Citadel. For the early part of the attack, Vekant could assemble three thousand Prin or so, and there were likely another three thousand assigned to smaller choirs in the twin cities; those priests would return quickly to add their voices. As for the rest, Vekant made the call while in kei-state himself, and he could feel the impact of his words all along the local Oregal.

He felt a delicious thrill inside, giving the dramatic order for all members of the choir to return to the Citadel. The fact that he was already afraid was no more than was to be expected; he was often afraid, even in the pursuit of normal activities like a daily round of meetings or a session singing the Tervan Symmetries with real Tervan musicians.

A cantor held within the Oregal is a creature curiously between freedom and compulsion. There was no impulse to obedience, but always present was the will of Great Irion, implacable and persistent. As if Vekant stood in Great Irion's presence, he felt that distant consciousness, borrowed part of its strength, and made a call to all the Prin who could hear. The subsequent response from all the Prin sounded in his head like the rustling of wings, birds preparing for flight. He could feel the wave of the choir's concern and the throbbing of certain notes in the current song, "Seeing and Far," mixed with other odes. The drill of an emergency return to the choir had been rehearsed many times; orderly groups of ten and one hundred headed for their skitters or putters, dropping every other task. As if Vekant himself spanned the whole continent, he could feel them moving toward him now. Even from a distance they could add to the power of the choir, and so, in that sense, most of the ten thousand were assembled almost as soon as the trouble was seen.

The process that caused this to happen, that drew these voices together, had been called magic for generation after generation, until Great Irion opened the first gate to join his world to the world of the Hormling. The word "magic" had served as a placeholder, preempting even the idea of faith; for everyone born in Irion understood that magic sprang from God. But now that Great Irion had encountered science, his own faith was said to be shattered, and a word like "magic" no longer served.

The Fukate Hall was opened and staff began to prepare it for the coming work of the cantors.

The daily choir sang in an open air ampitheater suspended over Citadel Park (Shu Shylar, the Park of Blossom Everlasting) near the center of downtown Avatrayn along the river. The sound of the daily choir had become part of twin-city life, ringing in the stone canyons between the tall buildings; Avatrayn was an island around which the river Trennt flowed; buildings there had grown into the bottoms of the clouds. The sound of Prin singing was difficult to describe; the sound had a way of making the skin prickle, eerie at times, full at times, not words that could be understood but that plucked at the consciousness of the listener, causing every sort of reaction from confusion to hallucination. Not everybody in Avatrayn proper enjoyed the sound, and many a soul avoided the park at all costs; it took a brave person to walk near the choir, though it was not at all forbidden. Today a change of song soon came about, moving from the near-unison of "Seeing and Far" to a blend different songs and lines of chant, the three thousand voices breaking into component choirs, the singing and accompanying music harsher, more energetic, accidents of tonality colliding. This song was far more strident than anything the choir sang routinely, and people at the edges of the park were stopping to listen. Attendants were closing the park itself and moving crowds away from the choir. People near the park were looking up at the sky before any warning, as if, from the Prin singing, they heard an echo of what was to come.

Within moments, the sound of air raid sirens, unheard of

in Feidreh-Avatrayn since the earliest days of the colony, pierced the city and countryside, and alerts of every kind permeated the local Surround.

Vekant stood in his place as lead cantor at the pivot of the music and began to work. As always, when he rode the choir he felt its vastness, an expansion of himself, his hands reaching farther than anyone's hands ought to reach. Each of the Prin was part of a pair, a ten, a hundred, a thousand, and so on; each choir could take a separate function of the incanting, so that the total music was made of many songs, some of them more like dances, some of them unspoken but intoned within the kei-space, some played on instruments. Part of the choir sang to enable Vekant to find what he needed to find, the war machines moving toward Jharvan. Part of the choir sang to recall the rest of the Prin to the Citadel, part sang to maintain a link between them. Sometimes the collisions of music raised the hair on his head; sometimes there was a clash like the world was coming apart. All this was familiar, part of the job.

He should have had no room in this head-space for emotion, certainly not for fear, but it was there from the start. The music even in the early moments of the engagement had a quality of otherworldliness, impossibility.

What was unfamiliar was what the work of the choir had shown them all, and what it was showing them now. Here was an attack that was not a drill, that was real. Everyone had expected some kind of civil war to break out and here it was, fearsome and immediate. Vekant could feel the armies coming, waves of aircraft, sections of the choir naming each one, beginning the work of reaching for them all. Even though he had only part of the choir assembled, their voices should be enough.

The choir reached toward the airborne intruders in the most routine way, meaning to disable them and plunge them along with all occupants into the ocean; the core of this was a choir of a hundred who would disable the war machines in a single wave, once they were named. The only difficulty Vekant might expect was the music itself, which sometimes carried him too far beyond himself, swelling in every direction. But all at once within the chant Vekant was aware that the choir was opposed, not feebly as by the rudimentary Hormling anti-Prin devices but quickly and expertly by voices at least as powerful as the choir.

True language flowed forward from the approaching armada like nothing Vekant or any of the Fukate Ten Thousand had ever heard.

The impact was felt throughout the choir, and then beyond, through the whole local Oregal. The component choirs of the Fukate were staggered but their singing never faltered. Evars kept discipline over their tens, juduvars over the centuries, krii over the millennial groupings, and the various units split the drill of listening as they had all been taught. The choir faltered in the naming song and lost its image of the approaching air armadas. At the point at which they ought to have begun to bring down the invaders, the work had to begin again.

One need not always know a true language to defend against it, as Drune and Malei-Prin understood from contests with one another. A good ear ought to feel the intent behind the work of any cantor or speaker, and one kind of operator can often decipher the work of another. But this sound, this countersinging, protecting the airborne fleet as it approached, was bizarre, jarring, a rude cacophony, a jagged feeling in the mind, nothing like a true-word in it, and the choir managed to pierce the defending song only here and there, sending a few dozens of the airborne vehicles into the ocean. Already Vekant could feel the difference, that this was an engagement like nothing that had tested the will of Irion in centuries.

He could feel the bluntness of all he and the Prin were doing from the choir. What should feel precise, keen, un-stoppable was instead tepid and indecisive; where movement should feel easy he felt as if he were slogging through mud.

He left the circle of the choir, still in the kei-state, main-taining himself in the pivot of the many songs; he needed more information of the kind that the Hormling could tell him, and he needed to warn Commander Rui that the choir could not stop the armadas from reaching Jharvan. He hur-ried to the crisis command center in the Citadel with his Cleric of the Left, Shoren, and a fifth-rank operator carrying data equipment. He had been to the command center hun-dreds of times during drills and for other routine duties, but now a real crisis called him here, still so fresh he could hardly credit that it was real.

Representatives from Enforcement were already assem-bled when Vekant—his three lictors arranged prettily around him, and to his discredit he was aware of this—burst into the situation room and said, "Gentlemen, the Prin choirs are not able to stop the attacks."

Commander Rui was moving toward him.

The murmuring of the other groups of officers and staff ceased, and a shocked silence hung over the room.

"The rebels have an ally that can counter the Prin. We're fighting this enemy, but we know nothing about who it is and can't stop the air attack or any invasion that follows. There's a wave of flitters approaching as well, along the established routes and toward the isthmus. We're bringing down only a few."

Rui stood perfectly still, and he felt her uncertainty.

One of her junior officers moved toward her with a look of pale panic on his face.

"Launch counterattack, everything we have," Rui ordered, voice clear in the sudden quiet. "Get every soldier and every piece of hardware we've got in place for Plan Green Line." To Vekant, she said, "We'd been keeping clear of your people, trying to stay out of your way. That was a mistake, I guess."

Her voice snapped everyone in the room to attention and they set about their work, point nodes plugging themselves into their consoles and graphics operators starting to stream visuals into the tanks.

Rui turned to Vekant and gave him a searching look as the room moved smoothly into a new mode. She drew Vekant aside and lowered her voice. "Are you really telling me your Prin can't contain this?"

"Not until we learn who these speakers are and what language they're using."

"But nothing we've ever faced stops you people." She was attempting to control her shocked expression, to mask it.

"We stop one another quite easily and handily," Vekant said. "That's what you're dealing with here, Commander: a being, or a group of beings, like us, who've allied themselves with the Dirijhi."

"Heavenly fire," she said and looked at her hands, dark knuckles tight as she gripped the back of a chair. "I have to tell the governor. Maybe some of your own people? Do you have rebels in your ranks, too?"

He shook his head. "We'd hear their words, know their language."

By now the main approaching force had been identified as armored personnel carriers, some for individuals and some for groups, along with thousands of transport flitters that hugged close to the surface of the ocean. A fight escort of drones and manned craft flew alongside, and as soon as Enforcement got its own fighters aloft, fireworks began in the afternoon sky.

As the Ajhevan aircraft drew nearer the continent, some of the Prin singers began to have more effect, overwhelming and penetrating the strange countersinging here and there, dropping more scores of the carriers and their support craft. For a moment Vekant felt as if this might turn to victory, the kind to which he felt entitled, true words bringing down the war machines or disabling them with a thought, sweeping his hand through an advancing infantry troop and dropping them in their tracks. But the countersinging redoubled and the Fukate choir struggled to maintain any kind of perimeter, even when the invaders reached the shores of Jharvan and dropped their cargoes onto the ground.

The Enforcement tech operators were making use of all available media and commandeering satellites, public cameras, and any private ones offered up by the database, and reports of strikes were starting to come in from a thousand miles of Jharvan coast, all the way to the Isthmus of Fostine and Badrigol.

What emerged from the armada of flitters shocked Enforcement and made Vekant concentrate for a moment on the singing of the choir in order to steady himself. Construct troops appeared first, cloned organics married to machines, human in shape but with a patched-together crudeness. Hundreds of thousands of constructs came ashore in the first wave. Intelligence assemblers got to work classifying the types of construct soldier the Dirijhi and rebels had employed, while on the ground Enforcement armor and infantry began to meet them and try to drive them back.

Meantime the armored single-carriers were starting to drop, and what got out of those was hardly like a weapon at first. A carrier fell into the middle of an infantry battalion struggling to set up heavy automated laser fire; a thing unfolded out of the carrier on at least six legs, with two vicious arms like spikes, the creature's carapace looking like it was made of black metal, maybe pure carbon, a body like an insect trembling and pulsing. Lifting a snakelike head, it shrieked and knocked troops flat with the sound, started spearing them on its forelegs, dismembering them, tearing open human abdomens, ripping limb from limb, blood coloring everything except the creature's own pure, lightless armor.

Another single carrier landed in a public plaza, popped, and something flew out of it, a stream of wings; civilians started to shriek and go down, sliced to ribbons or frightened to death.

Minutes passed. Arriving now were pods filled with nanoweaponry, most of this launched into manufacturing zones and military bases; arriving now were automated artillery and flying drones; arriving now were members of the northern press corps with their inflatable communications centers.

More civilian reports streamed to the command center from the office of the planetary governor. Vekant heard bits and snatches of the texts as he struggled in the kei-space to maintain himself against the fear that came to grip him. He could feel a change in the farther choirs now, the ones closest to the invaders. Where any particular smaller choir was near the battle lines near the coast, it had a fairly devastating effect on the invaders at that range. Some of the decades and hundreds at the front were sweeping waves of killing-song through lines of the constructs; others were managing to drive the mantis-creatures back. A front was beginning to take form.

The Hormling data network, efficient and responsive as it was designed to be, flooded the intelligence processors and assemblers with data, which they sorted and compiled and began to use to paint a broad picture.

"Do you want to come into the quiet room with me?" Commander Rui asked, and Vekant realized she was repeating the question. He had lost himself trying to sort out what was in his head, the flutter in his stomach. Listening again to the uncertainty of the choir, he shivered.

He asked, "Do you have some better picture to share with me?"

"A completer one. Not a good one." The commander's quiet room lay off the main ward of the command center, a small data room, dingy-white walls, chairs for a dozen.

Vekant sat. "I can offer you what I know as well."

"Our troops barely got deployed, even with the warning you were able to give us. We're being pushed back all along the coastline except in the twin cities. It appears that the Prin are being somewhat effective in holding off the rebels here."

"That agrees with what I know," Vekant said. "The closer the fighting comes to the Prin, the more effective we are."

"We're facing construct ground troops designed to take heavy damage and using weapons at least as good as anything we've got. We knew the northerners had a big arsenal but I never expected anything like this."

"Can your troops hold?"

She shook her head. "My troops were never meant to hold off an invasion. My troops were expected to supply ground support for the Prin." She could hardly bring herself to meet his eye.

"We've all relied on the Prin once too often, it appears." Vekant tried to ignore the feeling of humiliation, of having let the officers down. "How long can we hold out?"

"I'm not sure."

"You have a recommendation?"

"Pull back everything to whatever kind of zones the Prin can defend. Pull the population back with the troops, call for the rural population to abandon their towns and homes and farms and come to the capital for protection, if they can."

The planetary governor was linked to the conversation and began to implement the commander's orders as soon as they were given.

"What about you?" Commander Rui asked Vekant. "What do you have?"

"Some of these enemy carriers have to contain local cantors. This much true language is not moving from a distance; somebody close to Jharvan is doing the countersinging against the Prin. We have to find out who."

"All right."

"I can give you a team of Prin for that."

"Won't that hurt the main choir?"

Vekant shook his head. "We don't have the main choir here. I have three choirs of a thousand and about three thousand more in smaller choirs in the city; the rest of the Prin are recalled, but I have no idea how long it will take them to get here if these attacks reach into the countryside. I'm ordering them to consolidate into centuries; anything less is defenseless. They're likely to do us more good if they're close to the invaders, anyway. I'm going to tell the smaller choirs to stay with your people in the field for now. We'll coordinate locations with your staff."

"Done. What else?"

"Lay in supplies and any needed ammunition for a long stay here in the Citadel, in case we're driven back here."

"And?"

"Call for help. Through the gate." Vekant gave her a simple, direct look.

"I suggest you do the same," said the commander.

"Understood."

At that moment a shuddering ran through everyone; the command center's equipment faltered; Commander Rui touched the back of her head, the base of her skull, and Vekant felt a moment of intense nausea, the whole choir pausing in its cascade of music. A moment later came the news that the Anilyn Gate had collapsed. Silence fell over the situation room. A whole world went quiet, and waited.

Million Mountains

I n the northern borderland of Iraen, beyond the Fenax Plain,
a single figure stood in the Fang of Gar, the pass leading
north, where mountain piled upon mountain; here one could
see the beginning of the never-ending teeth, Cundruen. The
mountains towered on either side of him and the flank of the
narrow pass swept upward. He wrapped his long coat around
him, pulling the head-wrap closer. Wind howled in the pass,
shredded on the rocks. Rank on rank the mountains marched
to the horizon. When he was a boy, he believed they went on
forever, to the edge of the land of heroes, Zaeyn.

He was dressed in heavy Erejhen weave, good boots and
thick leggings, and he carried a small pack on his back and a
long walking stick. A big-footed animal walked beside him,
looking something like a dog or a big cat. His sleeved cloak
was wrapped tight around his body, and his face was masked
with the head-wrap. "Coromey," he called, and the animal
trotted to his side, mouth neatly compressed, nostrils the size
of slits, narrow openings for the eyes, multiple ears heavily

fringed in fur, some of which could be closed and warmed while others were in use. Designed for the coldest mountains. "Here, fur-child. Sit. We need to think."

He had strayed farther north than this before, but this time meant to go farther still. This was a journey he would make in the body, risky as it was to take his original form out of Inniscaudra and chance its life in the depths of the Barrier Mountains. He had sent warnings where he could about the danger he felt, or, rather, the danger he now knew to be present, both far away from Iraen and very near it. His disappearance into the mountains at such a time would upset Malin, he knew, but there was no help for it. Without information, he had no way of fighting Rao.

The last journey he made in the north country was for the one of the recent weddings of the Great Wife of the Svyssn, who killed her king-consort every decade and took another. It was said one day she would run out of husbands; the sky would rain down on the world and collapse and all would then be night. She had many husbands still to pick from, the ten tribes of the Svyssn fat and snug in their stone houses and warm winter pits, happily scratching the fleas off each other's backs and watching Hormling vid-surround through the long winter. This trip he had traveled as quietly as possible, which meant silent and invisible in his case, even Coromey slipping along unnoticed by the mountain hawks and scry-owls. He had made Coromey for this use, for company on long journeys; he made the cat-hound partly through his own true-speaking but also employing the skills of his Hormling partners, scientists he had sponsored to come to Inniscaudra to live and study with him.

Here was Great Irion, Lord of Iraen and Binder of the Oregal, walking alone into the mountains just as Malin had always predicted he would. The thought made him chuckle. "Not quite for the reasons I thought," he muttered, lifting his face to the sharp wind.

He had often walked these mountains with Kirith Kirin, hunting or questing after some hint of what lay farther on in the peaks. Endless, jagged, inhuman they looked, worse the deeper one penetrated, but nothing had stopped the two of them in those days, far too long ago, and nothing need stop him now.

To present his consciousness as simple in this manner, as confined to his body, even his original body, would be deceptive. The physical part of him might no longer be the sum of him but it was of considerable use; a being without a body was not much good as a cantor. He carried many kinds of awareness at the same time: first of all of the tower over Inniscaudra, his home, the heart of him for too long to think about, and then of the Oregal, the hierarchy of priests, the choirs of Prin and Drune that he held in his train, whose presence he could feel from their appointed posts across the far-flung Hormling stars. He felt the gates, first the one that led to Senal, and then the other, the Anilyn Gate, the one that hung in space far above Senal, that led to a far, distant star, more remote than any of the Hormling had yet guessed. Just now he was keeping careful eye on the gate, since beyond it, on Aramen, was Rao; he could feel the choirs beyond, the Fukate millennium, his Prin in the trading stations as they wheeled in their long rush along the Trade Line, his Prin on all the worlds of the Hormling, each a separate strand of himself that he could pluck and engage or let alone to work as it would. He peered into places where copies of him stood, and he felt concerned about what he saw from those eyes as well as his own; he was in these other places as fully as he was here, in the Barrier Mountains, headed north in a direction he believed himself to have traveled before.

When he was a child, when people had called him Jessex rather than Great Irion, once during a hard storm while he was riding in the old forest Arthen he had been taken up by God's Sisters and carried to their fastness in these mountains, the tower and fortress Chulion. That God had three Sisters Jessex had never doubted in those days, since he had met them and been taught by them. Only now he knew more about God and suspected her Sisters were not sisters at all, but something else. Now he meant to find them again, to ask them some questions that had come up over the last couple of thousand years.

Above all, he wanted to know where she came from, meaning God, and who were her enemies, for at least one of them was here now, on the verge of causing a problem. The question of her nature had plagued Irion for a long time.

This world was her body, he thought sometimes, and at other times he thought her body was the words he spoke, the language Wyyvisar, which he had learned from those same Sisters, who claimed to be its only teachers. If there was a source for this language, they would know it, and might even be it. This language he suspected to be, in fact, the substance of God, the last evolution of some species that had once stood like the Hormling on the threshold of all real knowledge, the final collapse of all their technology, all their information, into Words. She had become a sentient language, a body that had shed the needs of energy and space and existed as self-aware quanta of meaning, words that changed reality without reference to sequence, independent of time. Words that caused the world.

Or maybe more than the world.

He made fast progress across and up the peaks, reconstructing in his head the feeling of that long-ago journey, what had felt like a flight across the sky, wind pouring over his body, the Sisters speaking true language over him to keep him still. He and Coromey traveled fast, not bound by ordinary limitations, Jessex cheating their travel using tricks he knew, sometimes scaling straight up the side of a peak, the big cat-hound following, agile, equipped to grasp any crevice in the rock, to lift and stretch one step at a time. For Jessex there was little danger; he could climb and feel the cold pour over him and feel himself scattered across the landscape, fragments of his consciousness changing every second as each copy of him and each facet of him fed the center, which was partly in this head, his original head, and partly in the tower at Inniscaudra.

So he camped for the night and listened and heard, across the gates, the murmuring of that voice he had known lurked there, in the forest of the green trees—the Dirijhi's Shimmering Garden, as they called it. He knew this enemy had come not only for him but for her, for YY, for God herself. This enemy had come to take the gate and make it his own, or learn to make another, or both. Irion heard the uncouth singing in a language that sounded hardly like words at all. His long peace was over.

That many would suffer and die could not be avoided; even the choir of the whole would not effect much of a change on such a strange singer using such an unsavory tongue. If this stranger who had come to Aramen were like YY, a being of her rank, what good could even Great Irion do?

He pressed forward, moving with more urgency.

Across the Anilyn Gate a long way from where he waited, but still within his awareness, Rao began to move. Jessex felt the vastness of him, this enemy, and understood that the long-feared day had come. Whatever troubles YY had made in her long life had found her here. So far from Inniscaudra, without his tower under him, Jessex could not longer defend the gate as he should, and so, without any fanfare, he closed it. Without warning to anyone, as if it were as simple as bringing two fingers together, and afterward a quiet rang through him.

When darkness fell he made a bonfire, gathering wood from a half-buried stand of pines blown mostly over in a storm. The roar of the fire soothed him, showers of sparks flying upward like summer insects. In the windless night the fire burned peacefully, and he watched the flame as an object for once, not as a device he might use to focus his Words. With the Anilyn Gate closed, with so much of himself focused within his flesh again, he felt a singleness that gave him a peace he had missed. If he was thinking of anything in that quiet, he was remembering Kirith Kirin during that other winter, long ago, when the cold was gathering and the world turned hard and there was nothing Jessex, the boy, could do about it except try to survive from one moment to the next.

A shadow stirred at the edge of the fire, and he thought it was Coromey until he saw the figure of a person, robed, step out of the shadow of the pines. The appearance startled Jessex deeply, since he had sensed no one near him and ought to have. "May I share your fire?" asked a voice.

Coromey rolled over from the shadow where he had lain, bared his teeth a moment, flattened his head, and stretched out his paws as if he meant to pounce.

A young, smooth hand appeared, a man's hand, ringless, traced with strong veins, skin clear, the color of ivory.

"Share the fire you may." Jessex studied the figure uneasily. "I'll allow that much."

"But no more. A person of caution." The voice purred. "May I take down my hood?"

"If I'm to see you, I suppose you must."

A handsome face appeared, brutally scarred across the center, a slash at a slant that had not healed, cutting from forehead to jaw but somehow missing both eyes; blond hair, a strong neck, thin lips. The man touched the edge of the wound and appeared a bit self-conscious. "If you find my mark distasteful, you may say so and I'll cover it again."

"The scar looks fresh."

"Maybe it is, in a way." He squatted on his boots near the fire. "I came a long way because of it. Someone you know gave it to me."

A hollow opened in the pit of Jessex's stomach. A first hint of something unfamiliar flooded him, a touch of fear.

"I mean you no harm," said the man. "I only came so far to talk. To fight at such a distance would not be practical for either of us."

"So I know who you are," Jessex said.

"I believe you do." The man gave his head an almost co-quettish tilt. His beauty had been extraordinary before the wound; one could see, at moments, the old face. "I thought we should at least sit eye to eye."

Jessex kept silent, watching the fire, deeply stirred. This body sharing the fire was not a physical copy or he would have felt its substance more clearly. "Will you offer me peace?"

The blond man went on reaching his hands toward the fire. "Will you offer it to me? I've done you and yours no harm."

"Not until now, no."

The face was earnest, the voice silken, and he opened his cloak dramatically to show his finery, his well-shaped form, chosen quite carefully. "Won't you hear what I have to say?"

"How could I deafen myself to your voice?"

"She is a betrayer herself, the one you serve. You think she has not killed her trillions? More, even?"

Jessex was silent, making a show of tending the fire, adding the biggest logs he had found, heaping the flames onto flames. Rao stepped back to make room, and Coromey stretched his paws, still watching the man.

Jessex asked, without turning his head, "May I offer you tea? I have no wine or brandy."

"You would serve me tea from your own supplies?"

"You're my guest, Rao." Jessex bowed his head.

He bowed his head in return. The gash was glistening; for a moment it was plain he felt the pain of it still. "Thank you for using my name. You speak it without rancor. Thank you also for offering hospitality, but this body doesn't require tending. I keep it for traveling."

"Is this your native form?"

"I have many forms."

"The cut on your face?"

He gave Jessex a grim smile. "Your mistress gave it me. To tell you when would make no sense to you, but a great distance from now."

Jessex bowed his head. "You've known her a long time."

Light danced across his features, glittering on a necklace he wore, a circle divided from the center by radius lines at regular intervals, the lines intersected by smaller, more delicate circles at irregular intervals, the gold very pure and heavy. He took off his outer wrap, a sleeved coat with a long panel of fabric in front to be used to wrap the head and body again. "Yes, I have. You show your longing too well, Jessex. You long to ask what I know of her."

After a while he faced the fire, his heart pounding. "I can't deny it."

"She rides you." He offered his hand, and now there was a gold ring in it, plain and unadorned. "Take this and she'll no longer task you so."

He had shaped his form well. He had a body something between Arvith, who had been gone a long time, and the King, who had been gone far longer. Jessex bowed his head. "I've no need of anyone's ring."

"Take mine and she has no more hold on you," he said.

"Then what would I do?"

He wet his lips, moved the ring to his other hand, stepped forward.

Jessex stepped back.

Coromey sprang to his feet, crouched.

"I'm as old as she," he said. "I can show you far more than you would dream."

"Better the master I know," Jessex said, averting his eyes.

"I'm far more gentle to my servants," he said, lowering his voice, stepping forward the smallest possible step.

"So you say."

"I can tell you so much about the ones like us, like your mistress and me. Primes, you call us. I know you're curious."

He listened to the fire, wishing the wind would blow, or that something would howl in the distance; but there was only crackle of the wood, the popping embers. "I confess it's true. I'd like to know who she is."

Rao wet his lips, held Jessex's gaze earnestly. "Hold the ring, then. Just hold it."

Coromey hissed when the avatar moved.

"Stay where you are," said Jessex.

"She's lied to you for so long, in so many ways," Rao said. "I can tell you the truth."

"The truth is a strange creature, forced to compromise herself to fit so many mouths."

His voice was honey-soft, as if he were speaking next to Jessex's ear. "You're lonely. You don't have to be."

Jessex looked Rao in the eye, one last moment. The wound had grown somehow more pronounced. The moment lengthened and Rao closed his fist around the ring, looked into the fire as if he were sad and lonely himself.

"Come, fur-ball," said Jessex, and the cat leapt to him, pressed closed to his sides. He bowed his head to Rao. "Good night to you, friend. Enjoy the fire. My cat-hound and I have a bit more walking to do before we rest."

"There's nothing to find where you're going," said Rao. "Plenty of reason to stay by the fire with me."

"Not a one that I can see, no offense, friend. But as I'm the one who built the fire, let's say I'm the better judge. My road's this way."

"They're coming," he said, advancing a few steps toward Jessex, still offering the glittering thing on his palm. "The ones like me and your mistress, the ones you've been fearing. They're all coming."

Jessex trudged into the dark, shadow lengthening, one of Coromey's ear-tufts brushing his hand.

"Your gates are a big draw. They're all going to want to meet you." The voice echoed. The wind did come up, blew some clouds over the nearest peaks, and soon enough the shadow of a ridge cut off his view of the pine stand and the bonfire. He trudged through the dark, wrapping his cloak around him.

Flat Head Farm

1. Fineas Figg

The flitter made the journey quietly and efficiently, not a sound from the mag-lev drive, only the wind rushing against the sealed chassis, buffeting the car slightly. Figg watched the weather, the skies clear now that the air armada had passed. The others in the cab were quiet, Dekkar sitting with his head against the headrest, eyes closed; Nerva and Keely collapsed into one another, breathing deeply and peacefully. Figg's link was still down; there was some news on the one station from Ajhevan that the flitter receiver could pick up through the silverfield, but the broadcasts consisted of jubilant repetitions that the revolution was under way and Aramen would be free, no details or real coverage.

Near the Ajhevan coast a patrol spotted Kitra and queried, and she gave her ID. Off the radio, she said to the others, "The flitter is registered in my name and I live on Ajhevan, so we shouldn't have a problem."

Circumstances proved her right, though Figg felt easier

when the flitter was cruising in one of the overland fly routes toward his farm.

He had bought land along the river David, a tributary of the Silas, one of the major river systems on the continent; the David began as a creek in the hilly part of Greenwood, flowed out of the forest and drained a goodly part of the Ajhevan hills, descending into the plain and flowing into the Silas about mid continent, at Arsa. The farm was called Flat Head and occupied most of a valley nestled between hills covered in conifers, big oaks and hickories, open meadows, plowed fields. The continent had long since been settled, though never as densely as Jharvan; treaties with the Dirijhi fixed population densities and growth rates, and had for the most part been adhered to; that and the Dirijhi policy of paying a generous bounty for Ajhevani teenagers to be turned into symbionts had kept the population under control.

"Is it true that the trees only buy northern children to become symbionts?" Figg asked.

Kitra glanced back at him with a flickering of interest that made Figg feel unaccountably pleased with himself. She was rearranging her heads-up display for better flying in the uneven country. "Yes. The trees claim that humans not born here don't taste right in the link; the trees and their syms are joined almost totally at times. A sym has to feed from its host regularly or it dies."

"Nonnatives don't taste right?"

"I know. It sounds rather parasitic. A person who's born here and moves away won't work, either. The flavor changes, apparently."

"Parents must sell their children fairly readily."

"Mine sold my brother. He begged them to do it, he fell in love with the whole idea of living with the trees, having them talk to him. He saw a lot of vids that were nothing but nonsense, but he was too young to know. He was too young to make the decision, too, but the trees pay a lot for a sym. The Dirijhi term for a sym is something like 'hands and feet.'"

"Your brother was sold."

"I divorced my parents because of it. The Dirijhi call it a bounty. The whole process is supposed to be voluntary. But the bounty is the price of a small farm. The money is coercion in and of itself."

"They have that kind of money?"

"The Mage long ago conceded that the trees actually own the planet, but since nobody intends to let them run the show here, the Hormling factions and combines pay a huge indemnity for use of the world, a royalty on nearly everything that's made or sold or imported."

"I didn't think you could own another person."

"You can't. That's why they call it a bounty. The volunteer agrees to be a sym for nothing. The parents or the family are paid for the referral. It's all strictly legal."

"So the trees had a vested interest in helping you northerners get your independence in the first place."

"What do you mean?" Kitra asked.

"To protect their supply of humans," Figg answered. "Just about now your people will be learning how free the Dirijhi intend for them to be."

Dekkar opened his eyes and looked at him.

Kitra said, "I believe that's your farm. That's the beacon I'm homing on, anyway."

"I'm sure that's it. I've never been here myself, you know."

Kitra glanced at him uncertainly; Figg watched her hesitate, then decide to speak. "I feel as if I ought to know you from somewhere. I'm monosexual, so that's not a pick-up line."

He liked her bluntness. As for her being monosexual, he took any such declaration with a grain of salt. "I'm a figure of some scandal."

Dekkar grunted and chuckled.

"Really?" Kitra asked.

"He's very famous, Kitra, at least on Senal," Dekkar said. "He's being droll with you, at the moment. Do you know what the Orminy is?"

"Or was," Figg said.

"Yes. I've seen enough vid for that." She was looking at Figg with suspicion. "You're one of them?"

"He's not just one of them, he's the eldest male of the eldest Orminy house. He's the one who killed that degenerate and set off the Common Fund Reforms." Dekkar yawned, affecting boredom. "Surely you heard about that."

"Oh, heavens," Kitra said, "I followed that whole thing on the vid. You killed Sade. Now I recognize you. So this is—" She stopped short, looking at Keely, who was still sleeping.

"Yes," Figg said quietly. "This is the girl's brother. I adopted him."

"You had that bug thing and it crawled all over that poor man." She shuddered, though the gesture appeared more voluntary than not.

Penelope nearly always knew when someone was discussing her and took the occasion to preen herself a bit on his head. Kitra glanced at the spider in surprise a couple of times, though she'd seen it before. She'd thought it was one of Keely's toys, perhaps.

"My family was licensed for a certain number of assassinations per year," Figg said. "I used one. It was perfectly legal."

"Under some law that's how many thousands of years old?"

Figg shrugged. "The old laws are always the best."

"At any rate, he's our passenger," Dekkar said. "And he's an old friend of mine and really not at all a bloody murderer, so do close your mouth before you catch something in it."

Kitra gazed fixedly ahead, jaw clamped, and set the flitter down at the edge of a parking platform. Her repressed indignation was more or less amusing to Figg, who understood her to be very young, not even a hundred yet.

Figg had bought a full-fledged working farm that grew protein meat-forms, a lot of soybeans, corn, two crops of wheat per year, and a few hectares in truck which were shipped daily to a local produce market; the farm was fully staffed by professional agriculturalists and had shown a good profit for the last decade or more. The former owners lived on the premises and ran the farm; Figg intended to follow their example in living on the farm but to see to it that somebody else did the managing. Reform had left him poor but not that poor. Figg had bought the place initially for the income from the farm and only later realized its utility as a place to live. The estate complex, while not elaborate, was large and comfortable, set on a wooded hillside on a place where the hill leveled out to form a kind of broad shelf that was the lawn and garden for the mansion.

The house was built as a series of pavilions joined by a series of covered walkways, surrounded by gardens, pools, and paths. Each pavilion had walls that were in fact sliding screens that could be pocketed nearly out of sight, leaving the pavilions open to the gardens on one or two sides. Galleries ran under deep eaves along the perimeter of each pavilion. Privacy inside was maintained with folding screens. The insect population near the house was damped by machine; the pavilions could be completely opened to the air in good weather, inviting the feeling of living in the outdoors but with all the comforts of a home. The climate in most of Ajhevan was mild, though weather could be sharp at times in the winter; the screens were made of a paperlike material that was nevertheless a good insulator, and translucent as well, so that light entered even when the screens were closed.

The central pavilion was spacious, all the internal dividers opened for the moment, making a large space where everyone could congregate. The house had a Hilda and a Herman as staff, and the Herman in its usual efficient way prepared a buffet table of food while Hilda set up a couple of newsframes near the pavilion at one end. Figg wandered in the pavilion, pleased at the look of the place and feeling something of his old self, a host seeing to the needs of his guests, perhaps somewhat less lavishly than had been his custom but richly enough, and with nothing but good intentions.

Nerva right away had to stop Keely from drawing pictures of a speaking tree on the wall. The boy was too large for the sullen, childish look on his face; at times Figg wondered whether this age regression was having any effect at all. "But it talks," Keely said, pouting darkly. "You didn't even let me draw the mouth."

"You have a slate to draw on, Keely. Why do you want to draw on Uncle Figg's walls?"

"Not a good idea, chum," agreed Figg.

"The crayon doesn't even stick good anyway," Keely said. "Poo."

"Poo? What's poo? That's no proper word."

"It is too a word," Keely said, and shrugged. "It means I feel poo."

Dekkar and Kitra were scanning the news-frames at a low volume. Figg went to listen, leaving Nerva to watch the boy. She was sitting on the balcony in the fresh air, watching the garden, where dappled sun played over a field of gorgeous plants, not one of which Figg cared to learn to name. Would his indifference to nature change as he lived here? Nerva appeared to be memorizing the garden already, tugging idly at the fabric of her skirt.

Hilda and Herman carried the hand luggage to the other pavilions to prepare them for the arrival of their occupants. The presence of the pair, which were identical to the Herman and Hilda he had used in his penthouse in the Marmigon, gave him a feeling of comfort; though these were, of course, updated models from the current line, with enhanced software and guidance features and with what was supposed to be more efficient AI.

Penelope crawled off his head and moved into the garden, most likely having located something to eat. She preferred hunting for herself to being fed; she was not a web builder but a stalker of prey—anything up to the size of a small elephant would do. Though for eating she preferred something much smaller and more suitable to her taste, like a bird or a large insect. She ran, legs flashing, along the top of the balcony railing, then leapt down into greenery and disappeared.

Dekkar, at the news-frame, said, "My lord. That doesn't sound like a war for independence, that sounds like genocide."

Kitra had turned away from the frame, pale and shaken.

With the Anilyn Gate closed, the only media available were local sources on or above Aramen. This news-frame was from a satellite news center, Pivotnet. An image of a town, or rather, two images side by side, one a wide shot showing several blocks of structures from an aerial view, the other close-ups of corpses in the streets, and one shot, horrific, of something glimpsed partially at an intersection near the limits of the camera's range: a thing eating one of the bodies, something like an insect head but huge, glittering, black as obsidian, showing no features and moving in a way that made Figg wonder whether the camera was functioning properly, moving in a kind of blur. The camera coverage focused on the eating thing, which was using something like a beak to snatch the meat off the bones of a woman, face partly devoured.

Figg tuned to the voice-over and heard that the village was called Flores, east of the capital; Flores served as a data

center and market for the local farms. Had served. As of today, the population had been wiped out by construct troops
from the north, aided by creatures like this mantis, which
was at present out of attack mode and eating the scores of
corpses that lay about. After a few more bites of the woman,
the thing's jaw expanded, unhinging grotesquely at the back,
wrapping itself quickly over what was left of the dead
woman's head and pulling the body into its ballooned throat.
The mantis then raised its head and sucked the rest of the
body down its gullet. The throat and abdomen expanded
and then sharply contracted, crushing and compacting the
body, moving it down the monster's digestive tract. The
mantis grasped another corpse in its forelegs, what looked to
be a child, and pecked at it, tearing at the flesh of the face
and tasting as before, as if this were a delicacy.

The images came from an automated floater camera that
had survived the attack and continued to broadcast footage.
Rebels were declaring the village to have been a secret military installation that had to be annihilated, but the camera
showed nothing of the kind, only ordinary dwellings smashed
to bits, quiet streets, and slaughter.

"Why are they doing this?" Dekkar asked Kitra. "Why
are they attacking ordinary people? You used to work with
them. Do you have any explanation?"

"I don't see any human troops there, do you?" Kitra asked,
making no effort to hide her complete discomfiture, her
upset.

"No. I don't see anything that looks like any troops from
our side, either, just constructs and this scavenger thing."

"That's a pretty vicious-looking scavenger," Figg said.

"This is pure viciousness," Kitra said. "This is nothing like any attack we ever discussed when I was with PFA."

Dekkar gestured to one of the folded icons at the bottom of the frame. "This is an official feed from a rebel outlet. It's claiming all the attacks are being directed against military targets. But there are a couple of independent stations from island settlements that are still broadcasting from the south. They're claiming wholesale slaughter of civilians and non-combatants all over Jharvan."

"You think it's true, it's not just propaganda?"

"These are rebel images," Dekkar indicated, the wide camera panning over another empty village, this one along the eastern coast. "I don't see any civilians alive here. Not a hint of one."

"Maybe they're terrified and staying inside."

"Nice try, but most of those houses don't have an inside anymore. This is complete devastation. Just watch."

"What about the Prin?"

"They're holding the twin city. There are some pockets of them in other places. The independents claim the Prin have left the Citadel and dispersed into the streets and that's kept the rebels out of the city. At first it looked as if the Citadel was going to be overrun. The rebels are claiming some victories in the outlying parts of the capital, and they've captured a couple of Enforcement bases."

"Minor ones," Kitra said. "Communications and coastal radar."

"This is astonishing," Figg said, and he was smiling in spite of the image on the screen. "Someone's finally giving the Prin a black eye."

"You think that's a good thing?" Kitra asked.

"Why, yes. I have to admit I do."

"All these dead civilians don't bother you? These people didn't all have to die for Aramen to convince the Mage to give us a local assembly, to elect our own governor."

Part of him was enjoying her outrage. "I suppose I have to admit it appears a bit excessive."

Dekkar snorted.

Kitra said, "Aren't you the least bit curious as to who this is who can fight the Mage and Great Irion and not back down? Don't you think that whoever this is may be even more dangerous than they are? And maybe a good bit less friendly?"

Figg scratched his head, looking at another horrific image in the frame, a smaller version of the shadow mantis ripping ribbons of intestine out of a woman about Kitra's age.

"It's a fact the Prin don't often eat their victims." Dekkar moved toward the fresh air with a bemused look on his face.

"Even I would have to admit that."

"You're angry at them because they took your money?"

"Understandably, don't you think?"

"No. Not really. Look at what you still have. I'll work all my life and never earn enough for this."

"You can always apply to the Common Fund," Figg countered, with something of a sneer.

She was getting more heated, her color rising. "Not for a life like this, not unless I invest my share in a business and make a mint."

"Which you're quite free to do."

She scowled at him. She was a handsome woman, strongly

built, not afraid to sneer back at him. "You talk as if you've done it yourself. I doubt you actually have."

He damped down his own reaction; he was old enough to know better than to argue out of anger. "I suppose you mean I never earned the money myself. That's true enough if you mean money earned independent of the family name. Under the new laws, I'd have no choice but find out what I could do for myself, since I'd have no matripart. I suppose you think that's just."

"It's certainly more along the lines of what I'd call a free market."

"I'd disagree with that."

"You still have a very prestigious name, don't you? You still have a lot of rich relations who can help you. That gives you a lot of advantages."

"You can't have an elite without elite wealth. You can't have a real civilization without an elite."

"Garbage," Kitra said.

"Maybe that's true," Dekkar said, mildly. "But there's no law that says the Orminy have to constitute the elite."

"That's clear enough." Figg ground his jaw and scowled.

"From the point of view of the Mage, destroying the Orminy is very sensible. No empire survives long at the center unless it periodically destroys its elite and replaces it."

"That's logic I understand. That's logic worthy of my mother." Coming from an Orminy, this was meant as high praise. Figg raised his glass of wine to Dekkar, and just then Penelope, having fed herself to the point of satiation, no doubt, came skittering across the floor and clambered onto his shoulder.

"So you think that's what the Mage is doing?" Kitra asked.

"I think she has a lot of motives. The reforms have destroyed what was left of the Orminy, there's no doubt about that. Or at least sent them packing." With a slight bow to his host, Dekkar continued. "Between them, the Mage and Hanson have annihilated the factions, the combines, and most of the major corporations as rivals of government. If the reforms are adopted all along the Trade Line, this will be a shakeup among the wealthy like nothing anybody has ever done."

"You're a fan of hers, I see," Figg said. "I hadn't realized."

"You have to admire this kind of panache. Who among you Hormling realized what a wolf you had already let loose among yourselves in the person of this Hanson? You don't mention his role in this, but without Hanson's control of Hormling data systems, there'd be no way to enforce these laws to begin with."

"I suppose I had been ignoring that part of this whole process."

"When did a ruler ever have the power to make such a declaration stick? When was the central government of an empire ever so secure?"

Figg amended the statement in his own way. "When did a ruler ever have the authority to order such a complete disaster of a policy?"

"Too much money in the hands of too many people to suit you?" Dekkar asked. "That's the real democracy, after all."

Figg was sincere enough to feel severely discomfited, particularly when his gaze lighted on Keely and he remembered the kind of squalor that the boy had endured in the Reeks. He had starved, had hardly known his parents, and had been pimped to adults for money or food, used as a courier for this or that illegal substance, and beaten—horrors so thick that his therapists had insisted on age regression as Keely's best hope of any kind of normalcy. Figg felt responsible in an odd way; at one point in his long life, he had traveled in the Reeks for pleasure, had rented children of Keely's age for his own use. In these darkest and lowest parts of the subcity lived nearly twenty billion of the thirty-odd billion who had crowded the planet before the Mage began to encourage out-migration through the Anilyn Gate. In the Reeks people lived in public spaces, jammed body to body with hardly a moment of privacy, let alone comfort or safety; this enabled the rest of the world to live in a state of relative spaciousness and provided fodder for any number of other appetites of the upper class.

"I never much cared for the Mage until she shook things up like this," Kitra said. "Now I find myself thinking she's not such a bad thing after all."

Further news from what was left of the Surround. More and more armor was landing on Jharvan; the armies of the northern rebels were now landing near the twin cities. Rebel leadership, all rather sullen, pinch-faced people, were listing demands that were being communicated to Governor Andrick at the Citadel Palace. None of the demands sounded much different from what one would expect, and none explained the slaughter of civilians or the indiscriminate destruction of nonmilitary targets. The rebel spokesman, someone whom Kitra claimed not to know, was Tosh Unrotide Fu Chong, a complex name that was likely part true-name and part proxy, an older Hormling with a weak chin. He took a question about the allegations of high noncombatant casualties and looked momentarily nonplussed. "We're hearing those reports, too. We can't confirm or deny anything at the moment."

"Is that all you have?"

"That's all I have."

"What about the reports that towns in the western part of the continent are being massacred and annihilated? Flores, Defarcke, Michnin, Rosewood, Cedar Hills. There's a long list."

"We can't confirm or deny any of those reports at the moment. We have not to our knowledge targeted any forces in those areas. Leadership is looking at the information and we may have a statement forthcoming on this."

"So you have nothing to say about the deaths of tens of millions of civilians."

"You have our demands." Chong drew a long breath, becoming impatient but governing himself with care. Figg felt rather sorry for him. His last hair-restoration had been rather badly managed and his scalp appeared patchy. He had an unpleasant, pursed mouth. The PFA might have chosen a prettier public face. "These are the conditions of the People for a Free Aramen to end the fighting. These are the reasons we started fighting in the first place. That's what you have. Aramen will be free today. Thank you."

Kitra had drawn close to the frames again, staring at his image avidly.

"I thought you said you didn't know him." Figg was having a glass of wine, careful to sip it slowly.

Kitra poured a glass for herself. "I don't. But that was an unusual little dance routine he just did, don't you think?"

"About the killings?"

"Yes."

"How?"

Dekkar was listening as well, leaning against the stone fireplace at the center of the pavilion, empty this season, covered with a filigree grate.

"They're hedging," she said. "They're shocked. They don't know what to make of these questions about the viciousness of the attack and they're hedging."

"So you think these images are real?" Figg asked. "You think the rebels are attacking towns and villages for no reason?"

"You heard what Chong said. The rebels didn't target those towns."

"Then who did?"

"The Dirijhi," Kitra said. "And this new ally of theirs."

"My God, what a disaster," Dekkar said.

No one responded. Figg felt the wine settle into him, found the sensation unpleasant. "I've had enough of the news, I think. I'd like to rest a bit after the trip."

"I'd like to do the same," Kitra said, having withdrawn to the balcony, where she stood looking out at the flowing pool of water lined with mossy rocks, a peaceful image, her frame silhouetted against the beautiful garden. "Assuming we're staying."

He found himself amused by her need to have her status confirmed and stepped toward her. "I've told Dekkar that you both are invited to be my guests as long as you like."

"We're heading north," Dekkar said, "I expect we'll set out tomorrow." He gave Kitra a questioning look, and she assented.

"I'll feel better the sooner we're under way," she said. "But we don't have a guide."

"I thought you were the guide," Dekkar said.

She shook her head. "I need someone who knows the river system better than I do. Someone with a riverboat license."

He looked her up and down. Without a word he turned away from her. "How do you propose to find someone like that?"

"I'll take the flitter and go to Jarutan. I'll super-sleep for a couple of hours. There are people I know down there who can tell me more about what's going on. Maybe tell me the best route into Greenwood, one that will avoid the war traffic on the rivers."

"You think you'll be back tomorrow?"

"With any luck. There are a lot of Erejhen guides in Jarutan. They don't like to live too close to the trees."

"Erejhen?"

"Yes. That's all right with you, I suppose."

Dekkar considered for a moment, then assented. "Yes. That's fine."

"You have problems with Erejhen?"

Dekkar answered with too smooth an air of unconcern; Figg was suspicious, even though this was not his conversation. "They're such snobs about my people. But I'll be fine. Get back here as soon as you can."

By then, Figg had sent Nerva to take Keely to the pavilion they shared, east of the main pavilion along a gallery of carved wooden beams, a roof of tile. Kitra was housed in a smaller structure down the western gallery, the Green Spring Pavilion; the Hilda escorted her. Figg rose long enough to see her off; he found her likable for all that she held such naïve economic notions.

He found himself much more comfortable talking to Dekkar with the pavilion empty. "So you're really going into Greenwood," Figg said, when he and Dekkar were seated near the teapot.

"Yes."

"That's a bit dangerous, in the middle of all this confusion."

"Maybe." Dekkar shrugged. "Maybe more dangerous not to go."

"Why?"

Dekkar looked at him. Figg felt the intensity of the eyes, as he had at times in the past, visiting Dekkar in Béyoton. Figg was too old to be unaware that his friend had secrets. "There's something in Greenwood other than the Dirijhi. I need to know what's there."

"Trees, my dear. Lots and lots of trees that have their own human servants and make nasty, poisonous gardens. Everybody who uses the Surround knows that."

Dekkar smiled. For a moment a silence fell between them, and Figg was conscious of how comfortable he felt in the other man's presence. Every time they talked, Figg felt the same sense of ease, of having spoken to Dekkar only yesterday. Figg said, wryly, "You know I'm over three hundred now."

"Yes."

"I feel old enough to say anything I want."

"Is there something you want to say?"

"Something I want to ask. How old are you?"

Dekkar looked away, amused, toward the balcony that faced east, where a small green lawn stretched toward a field of clean, raked pebbles. "A bit older than you."

"How much?"

"A few years." Because he kept his face turned from Figg, though, Figg never believed a word of it.

"Why do you need to go to Greenwood yourself? I didn't think you worked with the, the whatever, anymore."

"The Drune. They're part of the Prin, a separate order. No, I don't work with them."

"You're not here to satisfy your own curiosity."

"No."

"At least that's not a lie."

"You think I'm lying to you, Figg?"

"Yes. When you need to. I expect no less. You can rely on the fact that I would do the same to you."

Dekkar smiled, reaching for a slice of apple from a plate.

"You forget the kind of power I had," Figg said. "Having that kind of power makes you realize when someone else has it, too."

Dekkar shook his head quietly. "Don't say any more, please."

"Why not?"

"It does pain me to lie to you, Figg. Believe it or not."

They watched each other. Breezes full of the sunny smell of the garden flooded the room.

"One more question." Dekkar spoke easily, but the seriousness of his tone was plain. "Where did you find Keely's nanny?"

"Nerva? It's an odd story, really. I hired her from Sade's household after I killed him."

"The man you killed at your birthday party." Dekkar raised a brow. "Why?"

"She was taking care of Keely for Sade. She's the one who found Keely's sister to begin with. I believe she may have had something to do with getting Sherry licensed for a public suicide. I've in mind to ask her one of these days, when it won't feel so awkward."

Dekkar hardly reacted but considered the information with a blank expression, touching his fingertips to a carved napkin ring sitting beside the plate of fruit.

"Why the curiosity?" Figg asked.

"I'm always curious when I see an Erejhen in a subordinate position, like hers to you. It doesn't suit their character well."

"She's quite pliable and very good with the boy. She's handling this whole regression for him, with guidance of course, but she's watching him through the whole thing. Very competent."

"I don't doubt it." He appeared to leave that thought, staring into the sky, full of broken clouds.

Figg took the opportunity to catch up on what he could of his news queue.

◦1 A newsburst about the Twelfth Fleet, in the midst of maneuvers in orbit near Arsus, another planet in the Aramenian system: the fleet acknowledged orders to break off the drill and boost for Aramen to take up orbit for bombardment of the northern continent. No word from the fleet since, reported by several news sources, many of whom had journalists or proxies on the fleet's flagship, *Jurel Durassa*. Speculation continued that the closing of the Anilyn Gate had in some fashion caused the fleet to lose its bearings or that some kind of pulse wave or other energy blast had disabled both the gate and the fleet. Scientists had no explanation for the closing of the gate since they had no idea how the gate operated to begin with. As had been true in the many years now since the Mage came to power, nobody was listening to scientists with the same devotion as of yore.

◦2 Large portions of Feidreh-Avatrayn were without power due to the growth of a fungus in the power transmitter system; in some portions the fungus had spread to power receiver-receptacles and had begun attack anything with even a low-grade electrical system, including human bodies.

◦3 Chill-trees were growing in various parts of Jharvan, including three in Feidreh-Avatrayn, phenomenal fast-growers that appeared to break down a variety of building materials and organic substances to sustain their growth rate. Their outer bark was cool to the touch. Initial studies indicated the tree's increased rate of growth was partly due to associated nanobots that helped to assemble the tree's central bole using supersize components supplied by the organic molecules. The chill-trees were part machine, in other words, and every bit as much an engine of war as the mantises and construct soldiers. Much of the report predated the attack on the twin cities; it had been recently updated and re-released.

○4 No word on why the Anilyn Gate reamined closed or whether help could expected from that direction. No one in the government cared to speculate as to why the gate had closed, whether this was the act of the Mage or whether the gate shut down against her will. The office of the public voice of the Fukate Ten Thousand issued a statement that no advance notice had come to the cantor, Vekant Anevarim ap Kiram, of the gate's closing. He declined to speculate on any reasons the Mage might have for closing the gate without warning, or even to speculate that it was the Mage who did so. Similar appeals to local particles of Hanson received the same polite statements; no warning had come from the core of Hanson concerning a shutdown of gate functions. Local particles of Hanson denied that they were of insufficient critical mass to maintain Hansonian supervision in regard to the Surround.

○5 Rebel groups including the People for a Free Aramen were declaring a provisional government in Jarutan, headquartered at the New Marmigon. No provisional president had been named but a Council of Twenty appointed, names that meant nothing to Figg even as he took in the newsburst. The rebels continued to declare their limited aim of securing independence from the Hormling imperial government based in Avatrayn, of further securing the complete independence of the Dirijhi from Hormling imperial rule, and claiming that all control of this side of the Anilyn Gate must be ceded to the provisional government of the People of Aramen and the Dirijhi.

○6 A lone flitter outran rebel pursuit near Fentonmarch, a village east of the twin cities; this was a local report from a Jharvan news source, not widely circulated but drawn down from the Pivotnet database. The flitter had been rented from a paramilitary outfitter in the name of Fineas Figg, wealthy eldest clan member of the formerly powerful Orminy clan Bemona-Kakenet, most recently notorious for the murder of his best friend Sade during the broadcast of Figg's three-hundredth birthday party. Figg and his family had continued their practice of exercising their legal, hereditary right to murder; the ensuing scandal had led to the final downfall of Orminy privilege when the Mage imposed the Common Fund Reforms on Senal. Figg was known to have emigrated recently to the Ajhevan continent. There was no human reporter attached to this newsburst; an autobot had assembled the narrative from raw data, and Figg's own powerful search-protocols had brought it to his attention. The flitter had to be Zhengzhou following north with Figg's luggage and household goods.

∘7 The Grand Ballet of the Temple of the Good Woman was forced to cancel its presentation of *Pins and Palaver* in Feidreh's Kraken Imperial Arts Coliseum due to severe allergic reactions that had a number of the company in states of near collapse before they received medical attention. This was another minor item routed to Figg most likely because, when his plan had been to remain in Feidreh for a few days, he'd bought tickets to the ballet for this evening.

∘8 Reports of armies of constructs and massive artillery attacks continued to reach satellite news recorders from all parts of the heavily populated southern continent. Enemy troop estimates ranged absurdly into the tens of millions; some of the speculation was hard to credit. Enemy cantors and true-language operators were working unopposed in many parts of Jharvan, and the destruction they caused was worse than that of any of the creatures or constructs.

2. Keely

As far as Keely was concerned, the farm so far looked pretty much like a park. The pavilions of the house were surrounded by gardens and a forest; from most of the balconies, he could only see fields in the distance, over the tops of trees. He had seen no animals, not a single tractor, not even the hint of a barn. There was Uncle Figg's house, which was pretty but spread out all over the hillside, so that Keely could run along the galleries from one building to the next. He liked the walls because they were thin and made a bump-whoosh sound when he slapped his hand against them, which he did, over and over, till Nerva made him stop.

If she was his aunt, why didn't he call her Aunt Nerva? He thought about that for a few seconds, then wanted to slap the wall again, which would never break, as he knew, because he had asked and Uncle Figg had said so.

If he couldn't draw on the walls, which made no sense because the crayon washed right off, then why couldn't he slap the walls and make noise, since he couldn't do any harm? But it was never wise to disobey Nerva.

Because there was daylight outside it was all right to think that thought, but he had a dread of Nerva at the same time and wanted to slap the wall again.

"Come and study your numbers for a while," said Nerva, patting the chair beside her and pulling out the math machine.

Dull and gray, it had a flat surface, not the least bit shiny, and the headset made Keely's head ache when he looked at it. He felt a moment of fear. "I don't want to."

"Come and do it anyway. You almost made the shape come together last time."

"I know. It's boring." But his heart was beating harder.

"Not to me."

"Come and play in my Disturber fort with me."

"No. Keely. Do as I tell you, come and use the math box."

If he didn't obey, she would make him. She had a way of speaking that made him do whatever she said. Nobody else had a voice like that, and sometimes, when she used it, the jaggedy edges of the sound in Keely's head were frightening.

In the past he had tried to remember to tell Uncle Figg that Nerva scared him with the math box, but he always forgot. The fact that he could now remember having tried was a clear sign that something was happening, that Nerva was about to make those sounds again, that she might start to hurt him again. He tried to keep control of his breath and become very small.

She stepped toward him offering the box and the headset. He fixed his gaze on the box and avoided her eyes; he could tell by instinct, though, that her expression was stony but not dangerous. She wanted him to use the box so she could do something else. She wanted Keely out of the way for a while.

He could only think like this at times when his head was full of the bad memories as well as the good ones. At times when he could remember all the bad things that had happened to him, like his sister Sherry dying or like living in the Reeks or like the way Nerva treated him when they were alone, he felt older and stronger. At other times, he was only aware of the good memories, but that was like being half asleep. That was like being a helpless kid again.

He put on the box and she set the frame in front of him and the colors started to swirl. He was hearing numbers in his head and seeing numbers in the frame, very fast. The box had taught him how to speak the math in a way that was different from thinking about it, and he could now say functions of curves out loud and watch them appear in the frame. The hard part was to bring all the functions together into a shape in the middle of the frame—he had to speak that part really fast, and if he messed it up all the curves dissolved into a blob and Nerva made him start over. It was hard work and made him sweat now in the warm, fresh air of his room.

When he wanted to stop she used the voice on him and made him continue. She was more agitated than usual and checked the one open wall-screen over and over, stopping now and then to use the voice for something else. Keely had lately been able to hear the voice whenever she used it around him, though only if she were in sight. He never knew what the voice was doing unless she was using it on him, and then he could feel it. When she told him something to do in the voice, his head hurt but the rest of him did as he was told, without thinking. He wanted to tell Uncle Figg about this, too, but he kept forgetting, until he was alone with Nerva and she used the voice again.

When she finally let him rest he was hot and sweaty and lay on the balcony in the breeze on a pad of fabric.

The priest was on the walkway and stopped over Keely,

looking down at him. The priest had taken off some of his robes and was wearing more ordinary clothes, trousers and a vest. He knelt and touched his hand to Keely's forehead.

"What on earth are you doing touching that child?" asked Nerva, stepping out of the pavilion from behind a screen.

The priest straightened slowly.

Nerva used the voice without making any sound this time, but Keely could hear it in his head.

"He looked ill. I was passing by on my way to my own pavilion."

Nerva used the voice again, silently, but Keely could still hear it. Even though it was not aimed at him it hurt his head; his head was always tender after she made him use the math box.

The priest knelt and looked into Keely's eyes. "Are you all right, child?"

He nodded his head slowly, his heart pounding.

He should be losing his memories of bad things, he should be feeling like a little kid again, but none of this was happening. The priest kept his hand on Keely's forehead, warm.

"His stomach was unsettled from the trip." Nerva was speaking aloud, in her regular voice. She looked pleased with herself. She was trying to be the good Nerva, the one Keely could think of as his kindly aunt.

"How is your stomach now?" the man asked. His name was Dekkar. Keely brought the name to the front of his mind.

"Fine." He spoke the word and sat up and went into the pavilion again, feeling Nerva watch every move. "Better."

"You look as if you've been in some pain."

"He's quite all right, good gentleman, now do leave us in peace."

Dekkar smiled at her, as cool and distant on his side as she on hers.

Something about his placid manner must have made her angry, because she went on. "I understand you're a friend of Mr. Figg's, but I can't have you interfering with my management of the child. He is a responsibility entrusted to me." This was another of Nerva's voices, one that she used to address other adults. She sounded like one of the old volunteer school proctors who used to visit in the Reeks.

"I do understand. It's just that I'm quite sensitive to pain."

"Beg pardon?"

"I'm quite sensitive to pain. If someone near me is in pain, I often feel it."

"I don't have any idea what you're talking about. That sounds absurd."

"Does it? Try me again, and you'll see just how sensitive I mean."

She started to say something and he raised a hand. She stopped so suddenly it was almost as if it were against her will.

He said something to her in a language that brought a deep flush to her neck, and a look of fury. Turning, he walked a few steps away and said to Keely, "My room is just down this way, young man. If you need me at all, for any reason, come and find me."

Keely had dissolved his Disturber insect to goo and was fixedly kneading it into a ball in his hands, pretending to have heard nothing.

Nerva closed the paper partitions and paced the big room. Vividly colored and angry, she glared at Keely once, but he was using his ring to make a set of pieces of an action figure that he would have to put together. She was speaking to him in the voice again—she was trying to make him forget. He was aware he should pretend to be younger than his age, that he was not losing the bad memories this time, that he was re-membering the things he wanted to tell Uncle Figg about her. He had become adept at the art of watching adults while pretending to do something else and was on the alert for the moments at which Nerva stopped and glared at him, fierce, as if she wanted to use the voice on him more, or make him do the math box the rest of the night.

"That man said the rudest thing to me," Nerva said. "And in my own language, too."

She paced again as Keely started to put the toy together. She was thinking. Looking into her bag, she started to paw through her stat, jewelry, freshener kit, but Keely already knew what she was looking for. The brooch with the black gem that she kept in the silver box. She would open the box, take out the brooch, press it in her hands, lift it to her mouth, close her eyes. He had watched her do this many times when she was alone with him. Now she lifted out the silver box but held it in her hands without opening it. She walked to the sliding panel, opened one, then closed it again. She stood in the middle of the room, using the voice again, closing her eyes, turning slowly in the room.

"I don't have any choice," she said.

This was not a voice Keely knew, and he held perfectly still, heart beating.

She opened the box, did the ritual as he remembered it. Nothing happened. At one point she glanced at the sliding panels as if she expected to be interrupted, but no one came to the room. She held the ornament in her hand a long time. Though it was a pretty, shiny brooch, she never put it on her clothes like other people did with their jewelry. When she was done, she closed the box and put it in her bag again. After that she looked more peaceful.

She came and stood near Keely. "What do you think, young man?"

He hardly knew what she was asking and froze for a moment, then continued to put the toy together as if nothing were happening to frighten him. She would use the voice and hurt him. She had that kind of cool edge to her voice, a sound of danger.

"You missed a lot of practice with the math box. Do you think you can do more?"

His heart was pounding. It was no good to be afraid, now. He looked up at her and shook his head. "I'm sleepy."

"Sleepy? You're lazy."

"I want to go to sleep."

"You're lazy, and you'll never learn anything. I don't know why anyone wants to bother with you."

There was nothing in that sentence that required him to

answer so he kept still, an arm of the superhero he was putting together dangling in his fingers.

"You didn't think that priest fellow frightened me, did you?"

He shook his head.

"That's good. Because you should realize that I can handle twenty of him and not even think about it. Exactly the way I handle you. Do you understand?"

She meant the voice. She was getting ready to use it again, so he would know what she meant.

"Don't worry," she said, "I'll make you forget afterward."

"Please," he said.

"I won't let you make a sound, though you won't be able to help but try."

He was starting to shake, waiting for the first wave of agony.

She watched him tremble for a while, then sat next to him and put her hand in his hair, gently. "All right," she said. "It's enough to see you frightened. If I've done nothing else for your training I've taught you fear."

"Can I go to bed?" he asked.

"It's barely dark yet."

"I want to."

"Don't you want any dinner?"

"No." He shook his head.

"All right then. Go in the privacy and wash your face and ears and clean your teeth with the good solution, not that candy-tasting stuff you like." She was watching him indulgently now, even fondly, as if she had not frightened him out of his wits only moments ago. He did as she ordered immediately. He took a long time in the bathroom because he could be alone there but hurried to finish when he heard her stirring in the room. In his bed he pulled the covers high and tried to make it dark by covering his eyes. She hardly ever bothered him when he slept, though sometimes he heard her using the voice in the dark.

He was more tired than he knew and plunged quickly into dreamless sleep. The last thing he heard rang in his head. Her voice, crisp and hard, this time in the tone she used for talking to herself. "This charade only has to last till morning, anyway. Then I'll have a bit of fun with this Prin, maybe, before we go."

"Go where?" he would have asked, if he had trusted her, but instead the question slid away and he escaped, for a while, from fear.

Later, while he was sleeping, he dreamed of the voice of Father again, the kindly light hovering over him, illuminating the bed and the white wall of the pavilion. "Tomorrow will be a good day," Father said.

"Why?"

"Because I've sent my friends to find you."

"Me?"

"Yes."

"Friends?"

"Yes. Though at first you may not like them. You'll have to be brave."

Keely felt as if he were wearing the math box, he could hear the music that it made in his head, the sound filling out the dream, rhythmic, matched to his heartbeat, as if he were hearing inside himself. "I'm not brave."

"You'll be frightened at first, you won't be able to help it. But you're called to do something very important."

The thought of that made him feel warmer and maybe a bit safer.

"You won't be in any danger yourself," Father said.

"What am I called to do?"

"To serve your father. To offer yourself. The gift of yourself."

He felt uncertain, until the light brightened and flooded him with a feeling of love and warmth. After a while, he said, "All right."

"If my friends hurt some of your friends tomorrow, just try to remember that this is the way it has to be. It can't be helped."

He was supposed to be happy and to smile while the words drifted over them, he was supposed to say yes so that Father's voice would have permission to change him, to pacify him when the time came. Father's voice was like Nerva's voice, only stronger, capable of more delicate, more lasting work; but he always asked permission, in a way.

"I don't want you to hurt my friends," Keely said, but the love that was already pouring out at him was so strong.

"It won't be my plan to hurt anyone, but your friends will never understand how important it is that you come to me as soon as you can."

Keely could feel himself softening.

"I need to have my family near me," said Father.

To be needed, to be part of a family, flooded Keely with

a feeling that carried him away. "You have to do bad things sometimes," Keely said, "to get what you want."

"It's true," Father said. "You do."

3. Kitra

Kitra spent some time in the flitter looking for an open route to Jarutan, something relatively free of military traffic; she tuned in to the flitter traffic control station and routed herself on a flyway just east of Flat Head Farm. Certain routes had been commandeered for the military and were closed to all other traffic, so she picked her way carefully. She was flying late in the night; the trucking lane below was moderately filled but the passenger lanes were lightly traveled. She made good time, calling Shanes on the way, making a date to meet at Shanes's cousin's house in a suburb of Jarutan, Piney Haven. Most of the northern continent was rural, the larger cities clustered along the southern coast, the settlement pattern designed to keep the denser part of the human population more distant from the Dirijhi. Jarutan was a city of millions, but from above it was as green as a forest except for the skyscrapers in the city center and along the harbor. Kitra keyed the address of Shanes's safe house into the flitter, and it found her a public flitter pad only a few blocks away. She rented a putter for the rest of the trip.

Nobody was looking for her, so she made no effort to conceal her travel, using a credit chit to pay for the putter and parking at the flitter pad. The streets were crowded with military traffic. The house was nondescript, a box on a tiny plot of land, heavy with vegetation, a path leading through the wild growth to a door. Shanes greeted her with a furtive glance outdoors; she'd put on a few pounds at the middle and looked a bit thick. Her hair wanted combing, and her clothes were a bit of a mess, as if she'd been lying down.

"You'd think the Prin were after you, with all this business of a safe house."

"I know this seems kind of dramatic." Shanes opened the door and squinted a bit at the sun.

"Are you on the outs with somebody important these days?"

"I just don't think it's too smart for us ex-PFAs to be talking too openly right now." Her expression was grim. The tiny apartment had a grimy look, old-fashioned construction, cheap striped curtains pulled over blinds drawn and closed. Shanes led Kitra to a tiny sitting room crowded with electronics, a lot of it jamming equipment.

"Are things bad here?"

"The city's hot. People are mad as hell about the news they're getting, and PFA is scum here at the moment. People were prepared for some bloodshed, but what's going on in the south is slaughter. And no matter what you're hearing on the broadcasts, we all know it. Chong isn't fooling anybody."

"What happened?"

Shanes opened the curtains at the window, drew up the blinds. The window looked onto a tiny garden centered on a huge old tree—a sweet maple, maybe, a native tree named for another tree it resembled on Senal. She spread her hands at Kitra's question and shook her head. "The Dirijhi made fools of us. Exactly the way you told me they would, what was it, five years ago?"

"Ten."

She shook her head. Remembering herself, she offered Kitra a drink, but Kitra asked for water, nothing harder. The super-sleep pill had made her thirsty, and she would likely have to take another for the flight back.

"Did the PFA change the military targets?"

"No. And you're not seeing PFA troops anywhere except near Jarutan. But there are millions of troops heading out of Greenwood that we never knew anything about, and we're taking the blame for all of it."

"We hadn't heard that much."

"I think the PFA is going to have to pull out of its own war."

They sat in the quiet amid the calls of a cherub in the sweet maple. Kitra caught the flash of red wings as the cherub flew away.

"How soon?"

"Pretty soon. Whatever these monsters are that the Dirijhi sent south, they're killing everything that moves. There's not going to be anything left outside the twin cities in another day."

"You think the PFA are going to make a truce with the Prin?"

"Won't that be a sweet surprise to everybody?" Shanes was looking more awake now, smoothing her hair, sipping her tea, looking entirely satisfied. "The rebels start a war so terrible they have to turn on their own allies to stop a genocide."

"It would be a delightful irony if there weren't so many bodies on the vids."

She looked stricken, shook her head. "That did sound callous, didn't it? This will set us back fifty years."

"Maybe. Or maybe the Mage will see the mess that's left after this and decide she may as well let us govern ourselves."

"What, out of good-heartedness, or contempt? You have such a rosy view of things, Kitra."

"I didn't until she reformed the Common Fund. I'm on record."

"But now?"

"But now I'm willing to let her do whatever she wants for a while. If we had our own planetary assembly, would they have the guts to pass the kind of laws she just imposed on everybody on Senal?"

"You trust her too much. Besides, I have the feeling the Mage would always overrule an assembly if she felt the need. Who could stop her?"

They sobered, hearing the sentiment they'd just expressed, a commonplace among the Hormling for three hundred years; but somewhere here on Ajhevan was a match for the Prin, and maybe more than a match. Kitra said, "Does anybody know who these new allies are or what these things are they set loose on Jharvan?"

"No. Nothing. They're calling these monsters shadow mantises, the rebels came up with that name. But there are a couple of other things down south that we weren't warned about, according to Ruth."

"Your contact?"

"Yes. She was angry when I left, and she stayed in touch with me to tell me how bad things were getting."

"Did you see the footage of that one in the town? Flores?"

She nodded. "Everybody here was watching it. The bodies are their fuel, you know. They fight for a while and eat for a while. Did you see the footage of that big one shitting?"

"Oh, no. Please."

"It looked toxic. My God."

After a while, Shanes said, "I called Pel." Her expression was shockingly soft when she said his name.

"And?"

"He'll be here first thing in the morning."

"He'll guide us?"

"Yes. The only problem is that his boat is tied up at Dembut. So you'll have to go through there."

"Do you think it's possible?"

"Yes. Pel's good. He showed me parts of Dembut I've never seen before the last time we were there."

Kitra gave her a mischievous look. "You traveled with him?"

"Yes."

"Did you—"

Shanes stretched her arms over her head, looking pleased with herself. "I love Erejhen men. They're the only kind I can stand."

"I thought you hated men altogether."

"I do. I hate Aramenians and especially I hate rebels, at the moment. But Erejhen men are different. They can't make babies with you."

"You tramp."

"Careful you don't take to him yourself."

"You know I like girls, and only girls."

"Those were my famous last words. From what I've seen, you might find a spot in your heart for Pel. Go ahead. I don't mind sharing. It's a long trip up there." Quiet again. "So you're serious this time? You're getting Binam out."

"Yes. I have a way to feed him. That's what I never had before. I can keep him alive."

Shanes looked her in the eye, almost spoke, then shook her head. "I know it won't do any good to say anything."

"No. My mind's made up. I don't know what I'll do with him after I get him out, but I'll think of something." It was on the tip of her tongue to mention Dekkar, to mention that she had help. But she had no idea what kind of help he could be; the Prin who had accompanied her before had never expressed the least confidence in their own ability to deal with the dangers of Greenwood beyond a point.

"You're always presuming he's going to want to escape with you. What if he refuses?"

"That won't happen," Kitra shook her head. "You didn't see how unhappy he was."

"That was ten years ago."

"It doesn't matter." She set her jaw, looked Shanes in the eye. "Let's not talk about it anymore."

They settled down for quiet, for sex and a snatch of rest. About the time Kitra was looking for her super-sleep kit, her link unfolded with an urgent message and she was listening to Dekkar's voice in her subaural. "Are you there?"

"Yes. What's wrong?"

"I need you to come back to the farm as quickly as possible, we have less time than I thought."

For a moment Kitra was conscious of the warm body and warm bed that surrounded her. She took a breath, shook herself alert. "I can get under way as soon as I get hold of the river pilot. He was expecting to leave in the morning."

"Leave him if you can't find him. We'll go back for him."

"Dekkar, what's wrong?"

A sudden crashing noise, distant, chilled Kitra, and she waited with her heart pounding. Dekkar said, "Good lord, I have to go. Get here as fast as you can."

He broke the link and left her there, staring at Shanes wrapped in the sheets, skin moist, a breeze running across them both so delicious it was a sin to waste it, though she had no choice.

Citadel

1.

Vekant's apartment in the Citadel was tucked away in a corner of the inner cloister, in the Western Tower, the oldest of the twelve stone towers. The apartment was near the top, beneath the suites that were maintained for use by the Mage on her periodic visits. Vekant managed to seclude himself after the first hours of the fighting, after the initial shocks. For a few moments he sat in his favorite chair looking out the broad corner window at the winding of the river Nayal through the old city of Feidreh; the Nayal flowed into the Trennt at this juncture. The twin cities were largely built of red-flecked granite, including the skins of the skyscrapers that packed themselves along the riverfronts. It was as if the whole immense city were one vast, jagged building. Vekant had often sat here musing on the Citadel stonework he could see, the gargoyles on the eastern choir halls, the stone lacework along the colonnade leading into the park, the precisely pointed arches, overshadowed by the taller structures surrounding the Cloister and the Citadel itself.

He was numb from shock and filled with a pain that hit him acutely at odd moments. Prin had died under his charge. Few Prin had ever died in service, almost none during the Conquest; it was possible to kill a single Prin easily enough, a pair of Prin with some difficulty, but the common wisdom held that the choirs of ten or more could not be hurt except by one another. Since the Oregal was controlled by Great Irion, this eliminated any question of rebellion within the ranks, and so the Prin's aura of invincibility had never been shaken. Until today. A choir of a hundred lay dead. A dozen choirs of ten dead and three more missing. Other individuals killed while serving in the millennial choirs that were still in operation, when no Prin had ever before died while serving in one of the grand choirs.

A thing was here, on this world, a power that was more than a match for the Fukate Ten Thousand, more than a match for Hormling Enforcement.

Would the Mage come herself? Had she closed the gate, and could she open it again?

Where was Great Irion?

Vekant was in kei-state, meditating in the word-space with the Choir while seated in his body in the chair in front of his broad window. He and the Choir were defending the perimeter of the twin cities against further attacks from the northern armies, while at the same time allowing refugees from the surrounding countryside into the cities to take such shelter as they could find.

A fear had taken hold of Vekant and would not leave him. He had come to the room to sit with it, to look at it, this fear. Some voice, some cantor of strong ability, was searching for him through all the mazes of the Prin chorus; some thought was aimed at Vekant, knowing him to be the center of the voices that held the city closed against the armies that had overrun the rest of Jharvan.

"How many times did we drill and train for times like this one?" he asked aloud. "Why did I never believe a day like this would come?"

"It's hard to believe in trouble when you've had peace as long as we have," said Shoren, his Cleric of the Left, seated quietly in a dark corner. She was never allowed to leave his presence while he was in the pivot of an active choir; he often forgot her presence altogether. She must have thought Vekant was addressing her rather than simply talking to himself. She was youngish for a Prin of her rank, in her sixties, training to serve as juduvar in a century choir while assisting Vekant in his duties as chief cantor of the Ten Thousand.

"We felt nothing in the north on this scale. Did we?"

"No, sir. I've been in every choir with you, I've never heard anything like this."

"It makes my teeth ache, it's not like words at all."

"Did the cantor want me to have someone open Cueredon Tower?"

"No." He shook his head. He had a dread of the place. Only the Drune liked to walk on towers like Cueredon; they could imagine themselves striding the high place like the wizards of old times in Iraen, stirring the wind and calling storms out of the Barrier Mountains. "I'm no good on the high place."

"I could call for an operator."

"Do we have anyone qualified?"

"Eshen," she said. "She's uluvarii and fourth rank, she could stand there."

"I hate to put a solitary Drune on a tower."

"We have Seris and Faltha, too. They could go with her."

A pair of Malei-Prin and a fourth-rank Drune. Seris and Faltha were the best pair in the choir. He nodded. "I'll send the tower keys to Eshen, tell her to expect my personal Hilda to bring them."

Shoren went to find the data operator. Since the Prin were not able to maintain links with the Surround, they required the services of data specialists trained to avoid disturbing chant-work. Vekant failed to recognize today's young man, but he appeared steady and knew to keep himself out of sight until he was needed.

Vekant could see Cueredon Tower from the window of his bedroom; close enough that one could feel the mass of the stone, the size of a modern office skyscraper. The Mage had built this tower, bringing a team of Tervan out of Iraen for the work; the stones were fitted seamlessly, exactly joined, no mortar. The high place on top of the tower was a device of solo operators like the Drune, and from it they could have an effect equal to the Ten Thousand, since the towers borrowed from the strength of Great Irion himself. This was something of a fearful thought for Vekant, for whom the idea of using true language by himself was in some way alien. The assignment to stand in a tower was dangerous to give over to a Drune who might prove to be a rival to Vekant in terms of Prin politics afterward. What if Eshen should prove more effective from Cueredon than Vekant from the pivot of the Fukate Choir?

While he was watching, Cueredon came alight; the top was too distant for him to see any figure on it, but he could imagine tiny Eshen striding about in the wind, getting a feel for the place, waking up the stones, with Seris and Faltha waiting at the lip of the stairs, not daring themselves to stand directly on the high place.

With the tower active, the defense of the twin cities went better, and choirs working with Enforcement brought down some of the mantises that had entered the city. Construct troops were no match for the Prin at close range and kept their distance, but the frontline choirs were not able to press any advantage. The cantors among the rebel army, still unseen, were countersinging against the Prin very effectively. A line was established, on either side of which one kind of true language become too strong for the other. As this resolved itself around the twin city, the perimeter proved to be a remarkably regular circle with its center point on the Citadel; more specifically, fixed on the high place over Cueredon.

Refugees filled the city to overflowing, camped along all the streets, thick in every alley, most guarding a few precious crates of possessions or sleeping around a putter loaded with their household goods. Police were keeping good order, and where the Prin were on patrol nobody was thinking of looting. Immense as the city was, its population swelled to bursting with newcomers. The governor had his hands full trying to keep every mouth fed.

Another thousand Prin had returned to the city. More were in transit, but others were protecting pockets of survivors and dared not move from whatever sanctuary they had found. Mantises of all sizes and the flock-creatures of many configurations roamed the countryside looking for stragglers. As far as could be learned, most of the continent was in the hands of the invaders after only a few short hours of attack. Enforcement had been unable to provide air cover of any kind, and no one had heard from the Twelfth Fleet, the planetary fleet on guard around Red Star, or from the Ninth Colonial Navan' Fleet, which was assigned to protect the coast of Jharvan. The Prin were defending and had no means of making any kind of attack.

The Anilyn Gate remained closed, nothing moving through it in either direction, no transmission from Senal or from the other half of the Hormling universe since the first moments of the attack.

Vekant assigned a novice to attend Commander Rui, to give her a kind of wakefulness that left her more fit for what she had to do. The other option was to allow her medical people to drug her into wakefulness; in Vekant's opinion, an Erejhen herbalist could do a better job prescribing for people than most of the Hormling doctors, who were entirely too fascinated by their pharmacology. When the commander was more wakeful, they had a meal together in her briefing room.

"Their army appears to be all ashore now, there's nothing else coming across the Vad. But we're still hearing reports about armies in the east and west."

"I expect there are reinforcements waiting on the docks at Jarutan. Lord knows how many of these constructs they've got."

"Their transport flitters crossed back to Ajhevan hours ago, and there's no sign of them coming back."

"Numbers?"

"Two million constructs." She stopped to let the numbers sink in. "We had no intelligence that indicated anything like those numbers. Along with the constructs, about a hundred thousand human independence fighters, which was what we expected. Maybe a thousand mantises, no way to know how many of the flocks. We had no idea any of those creatures even existed. Untold numbers of botanical weapons from the Dirijhi. Hundreds of the black pits growing, most of them in the areas where the mantises are operating, so we know there's a connection there. We've counted about two hundred chill-trees within the twin cities perimeter, but we expect there are still a lot of seed around for those and we'll get more."

"Do you know what this black slime is?"

"We think it's some kind of eating machine, not quite as small as nanobots, but basically an artificial shit-maker—it eats everything it comes in contact with and turns part of it into black shit and part of it into more eater-machines. They can adapt to eat different materials. They only make a certain number of themselves, too, so they can go on eating efficiently. We have stuff like this; this is mass-destruction stuff, not people but infrastructure."

"The mantises?"

"Some kind of carbon construct. Powered by what it eats—like all the construct troops, too, by the way. A carbon mantis can smash through most construction like it's not even there. I just got this, too. Oh, mother." She looked at the window in the frame in front of her. One of the mantises was ejecting something from the rear end of what was apparently its digestive tract. "Media guys have footage showing these mantis things taking a crap, and they say the black pits start to spread after that. So the mantises may be the source for the eater-machines. They eat us and make these machines out of us."

"They'd need to eat some metal, too, wouldn't they? And other things?"

She shrugged. "They do. We've seen it. They can eat an armored tank and snack on the personnel inside for a couple of hours."

"The flocks?"

"We have no idea. The creatures look like some kind of special effect from the Surround; I've seen footage. There's a flurry of shapes, all colors; they fly into a funnel shape and get dense, and then you'd swear that it was a person in front of you, not some kind of multiple thing. They give off heat when they're assembled but not when they're a flock. In either form you can't shoot them; it's like trying to hit one of you Prin." She smiled at him. "From what I hear, I mean."

Over the past few hours Vekant had grown accustomed to new levels of fear, though at times his terror rose to a peak and he had to breathe deeply, like now. He pretended to be reflecting on the image in the frame and slowly got himself under control.

"What about the Mage?" Rui asked.

"You spoke to Hanson yourself, right? To what's left of him on this side of the gate, I mean."

She nodded, blowing out a breath.

"Then you know we won't get any help from anyone until the Anilyn Gate opens again."

From outside, from somewhere rather far away, a shock ran through him all at once.

The same shock had overtaken the Fukate Choir.

He was no longer seeing the room in front of him, not altogether; he was seeing from the pivot of the choir glimpses of a far battlefield and had a feeling of oppression, of something moving toward him.

After a few of these impressions the overall image came clear.

Coming ashore now was an operator, vast, engulfing. A song began that would not but be heard, no matter how ragged or sharp, no matter how the listener longed to turn away.

Here was a cloud of language to engulf him.

"Vekant? What's wrong?"

"Something just arrived." He faltered, his heart pounding. Touching his hand to his brow, closing his eyes, he was aware of his stricken appearance and wondered whether these other people would understand it.

Commander Rui looked at her staff, who fumbled among their frames. "You look as if this is serious."

Once Vekant had met Great Irion, when Vekant was invested as cantor of the Ten Thousand, a trip to the far north country of Iraen. The trip through the green landscape and the audience with the ancient wizard had carved themselves deep into his memory. Vekant had stood in Great Irion's presence in one of the stone halls of the House of Winter; his presence was vast like this, a tidal wave, sweeping over everything around him. Vekant looked at the Commander, feeling the huge presence moving over the city, feeling the fear of all his choirs.

"A single flitter just arrived, nothing other than scattered traffic is moving over the Vad," said one of the officers.

Commander Rui nodded.

"We're not going to be able to help you for very much longer," Vekant said. "The rebels have a third-level operator coming ashore. We can all feel it."

"Third level?"

Vekant shook his head. "There's no time to explain. We can't hold our perimeter against this cantor, Commander. I don't know exactly what this creature is, but it's going to take us all apart."

"One creature?"

"Commander. Great Irion is a third-level operator. This is his peer."

Then, blackness, a concussion like an explosion, a cringing feeling of terror, and Vekant dropped to his knees.

Neither Vekant nor the Fukate Choir had been called on to sing any of the serious fugues in the lifetime of anyone currently in the choir; few if any of the Prin had ever used the chant to kill, not for the generations since the Conquest, which had been peaceful. There were perhaps a hundred Drune in the choir and some of them had sung death songs in the Ildrune language; from them came the initial feeling of panic.

For Vekant the feeling was like a blinding light, or, if

framed in terms of noise, like a sudden cacophony filling his head. He had a feeling of outrage, almost petulant, that this was one indignity too many, that suddenly he was no longer master of his head-space. After the noise came a searing pain that dropped him to his knees, and he felt the shuddering through the whole choir as if it were a tangible physical event, as if the ground were shaking, the floor buckling under him. The Prin song faltered and stopped.

The sound of the enemy cantor was like a sawing along all Vekant's nerves. Not a syllable, not a word could he understand, but the intent, the taste of the power, and the stunned silence that followed among the Prin were all unmistakable. Vekant could feel the weight of the enemy as if he were bearing her on his back; she was amused at his fear and wanted him to know she was a she. She had in some way caught Vekant and held him and he could not get off his knees, could not rise, could not remember where he was.

Someone was trying to tend him, and he remembered, after the first panic subsided, that he was with Commander Rui and her staff; somewhere in his distant body he was knocked to the floor with these good people trying to help him; the hand of the new enemy was inside him by then, and the awful sound of her voice was all he could think about. No meaning that he could understand, just the scent, the taste of her intent, that she was singing many ways for them to die, that she was counting them and weighing them.

The Prin and Drune alike had faced only one another in such tests before; training was nothing like the savagery of the real thing. The whole choir was open to her; the whole Hormling army was open to her; the whole of the twin cities were open to her. The Prin had been fighting for control of the weather even before the war, but now all their control was stripped away.

She stood in front of Vekant in the room. No one else was there. The room had changed, a very white room, plain walls, dark floor, intricate black and while tile forming a mosaic that drew the eye toward her, the gray-wrapped figure gesturing, four spindly arms, body invisible, a face like a mask. She beckoned with one long, double-hinged arm and he approached though not on his feet; why was the floor so detailed whereas the walls were a blur, the ceiling a mist? The pattern of the mosaic shifted: fast, sometimes, as if streams of current were rushing through it; slow, sometimes, like a snake flexing its body in the sun. Vekant prostrated himself on his belly at her bark-covered feet; he assumed whatever posture she granted him.

She felt vast. She surrounded him in such a way that there was no question of struggle. With a shock, he understood. The Oregal of Great Irion was torn to shreds; there was only, here and now, her voice, whatever these sounds were. Again he felt the petulance, the irritation, the wish that he could sulk, insane impulses mixed with his panic. Why now, when he was so tired? Why him, when he had never done anything to deserve . . .

Was she looking at him? She must know that he was the pivot of the Choir, she must have brought him to her for that reason. She had shaped this space and trapped him in it. Did she mean to talk to him? On her mask he found no sign of a mouth, but this was the mind-space, anything could happen here.

She had to be a power of the third circle, like Irion, to feel so vast, to strip the whole Prin choir out of the Oregal, to shut down the song so quickly and completely.

Who are you? Are you the one we always thought would come, the one who wants to take the Anilyn Gate, or to take for yourself the one who makes it? Why are you here?

From her no feeling, no attempt to communicate, only the shifting pattern of black and white, nearly hypnotic, underfoot; no clear sense of her at all except her glee, her distinct pleasure that he thought of her as "she"; the distinct impression that he had gotten something right, though there was not a hint of a woman or of any female characteristic, or male characteristic, for that matter, in the form in front of him. She was like a spindly tree, in fact, tough in the bark.

For a while she ignored him and he could tell then that she was feeling some kind of opposition. Distantly he himself was aware that the tower Cueredon was her problem, that Eshen, Seris, and Faltha were putting up a better fight than the rest of the Ten Thousand. In fact, Vekant realized, with the same feeling of abstraction, there were no longer anything like ten thousand of the Ten Thousand alive.

She had come ashore south of Feidreh; that first taste of her singing had been the killing of the Hormling Eighth Army and the choirs of Prin who were defending that part of the city perimeter. Following her lead, the rebel armies and their creatures had begun to fill the twin cities and to destroy them.

She could reach her hand wherever she liked. Alone and unaided she could take the continent apart.

She showed him so many things. Time drained away so fast.

Construct troops lumbered forward, trundling behind the mantis-monsters, who smashed through buildings and vehicles and Enforcement defensive barricades. Ahead, where Enforcement divisions were trying to form a line, the swarms of bird-shades flew through them, swarmed around them, sliced the people and machines to shreds, tore the defenses of the city to dust. Not a sign of a single Prin left to defend even a city block, not at the perimeter, at least. Not the hint of the Prin chant or the voice of a single cantor.

Over the city, white-hot blasts ignited in midair, sometimes in mid building: shattering waves of ignitions, awful for an instant before the concussion ripped the city to shreds; overhead the sky serenely blue except where smoke was already rising. She was making explosions, ripping steel frames of buildings into tatters. She spoke that ragged language of hers, and the world convulsed with fire.

In the Citadel, construct troops poured into the building, bound the helpless Prin, most of whom were still knocked senseless in the choir hall; some were dead but many were alive, and she meant to capture all of them if she could. She felt glee at the image of her troops binding the Prin in some kind of hood and shackle, carrying them out of the choir to a column of transport flitters. Beyond them the twin cities burned, a column of black, the air full of debris.

Most awful of all was the silence of the streets, for not a soul survived now except the few Prin and Enforcement who were in the Citadel. She had not moved much ashore at all, she had simply planted her feet on the ground and reached out with those sounds she was making. She showed him this much, she wanted him to know. In what she showed him there was no hint of gloating or victory; the notion that any other outcome might have been possible had no place in her thinking at all.

In the mind-space she kept Vekant, the notion of time lost to him, but he knew it had been a long time. Without the Choir to support him he was humble as a rag, almost cringing. As for what had happened to his body, whether he himself had been hooded and handcuffed, he had no real notion. He felt so distant from his flesh he might have left it for good.

Numbers. She wanted him to know she was singing in numbers. Or, to be more exact, she was willing for him to know; the notion of "wanting" was not exactly the thing, she had no true inkling of desire. She was a creature of numbers making her chant in numbers; there was no notion of words in her. What she knew of meaning came from some other direction. She had no inkling of words, she found the idea of them curious, nearly useless.

The beaten magician in the stories struggles and rises and makes an attempt, at least, to fight. But a single Prin is hardly better than a poet for making things happen. This was too much for Vekant—he had felt it from the moment the gate closed and he was left to his own devices.

The tower gave her trouble for a while; she planned to leave the twin cities as soon as she had broken the back of the opposition, which meant she could ill afford to leave Cueredon standing. Malin had built that tower and the voice of

Irion was in it, even though the operators could not make much of it. Even she would have to take the tower in a body, no matter how weakly it was held. Were these her thoughts or his thoughts? She held him so close now, he could hardly tell where she stopped and he began; this was not a pleasant feeling, more like being digested than being loved; curious to feel engulfed by someone and to feel nothing of the expected intimacy. Even the bitterest human enemy would have felt warmer than she.

When she lifted him from the floor and the mosaic of the floor rose with him, streaming through his legs now, he understood he was with her in the flesh, that she was standing over his body somewhere, that he was hers. She had a mouth now and began to bite off pieces of his face. She kept the wounds from bleeding because she planned to eat the blood with all the rest, but she had no concept of pain and therefore spared him none; without the chant he could not hide himself from the agony, especially since she ate the soft parts of him only. He had no voice, not even in the body, certainly not in the mind-space, only the racking agony, the feeling of that razor maw ripping through him, her body quickening with the food in a way that was palpable to him. She ate him for a long time but not enough to kill him. Then she threw up paste onto him and it burned and clung to him; she smeared the paste onto his half-eaten surface. He had no voice, but he was shuddering. Some of him faded but some of him remained.

He was no longer sure who he was or why he was here suffering this agony. If he had a name there was no way to tell what it was or had been. Something was chewing through the top of his head now, that was all he could think about; he had combed his hair so carefully this morning and now some creature was eating through the top of his head. Funny that he had no memory of who he was or what kind of creature he had ever been but he had a clear memory of having combed the hair on the top of his head. He could not have pictured what the hair looked like or what any of the rest of him looked like but that was just as well now, because he was a snack for some kind of horrid creature. His nerves were so overloaded he could hardly feel anything. He flickered and vanished, not into death but into something else that came out of the paste she was spreading over him. She was eating away enough of him that she could replace him with herself; she was making a copy of herself. His feelings ebbed away and he understood what it was simply to replace wanting with something more like planning. He felt the way numbers shaped her, the way her thought was different, and that kind of thought filled him. He had no need to do anything or learn anything; he was simply a kind of carrier wave for her presence.

The pain had disappeared and the goo had hardened and he was feeling what she felt and seeing what she saw. He was standing with her on a devastated wasteland, a hell of fire stretched to the horizon, so much soot and ash in the sky that there could be no notion of anything but one long night. He was at the foot of the ruins of the Colony Bridge that crossed the Trennt River to the island of Avatrayn. She had eaten him at the foot of the Colony Bridge. Beyond, in Avatrayn, nothing stood except the tower, dimly lit.

The Eater would soon depart. The Eaten would walk

forward, still in the hand of the Eater, still under her control. The Eaten would enter the tower and take it in his body, but using her voice.

Wind was rising. One by one, she was bringing hurricanes ashore all along the coast. Soon she was gone in her flitter with the remnants of her army, and he was standing in the high wind, planted more firmly than he had ever been in his life, beginning to walk across the wreckage of the bridge toward the island and the tower.

Out of the Forest Comes a Rider

1. Keely

Keely woke with a hurting head and sore scalp, forgot where he was at first, then remembered. The new house with the paper walls. He sat up. He felt as if he had forgotten some things again. Last night was a blur, the way it was when he forgot things; he couldn't remember which toys he had played with or where he had left them, when usually he could see them exactly as they had fallen from his hands wherever they had landed. He remembered getting into bed early and pulling up the covers, hoping it would soon be dark. He had dreamed about the sphere with the tentacle arms again, but only for a little while. That was all.

Nerva had laid out his clothes for him and he pulled them on, looking around the sparsely furnished room. The hour was early and the light had a pink color, like dawn in Uncle Figg's penthouse windows at home on Senal. Keely pulled on the clothes and yawned and felt sore all over his head. Nerva had never made him use the number box last night, had she? He had no memory of it. But there was a lot of blur.

Once, in the penthouse on Senal, he had found a note written in his own hand that said, "I bet you don't remember writing this, do you? But you did. And guess what? There are a lot of things you don't remember." He had kept the note, then one day it had disappeared, too.

"Do you remember where you're supposed to come when you're ready for breakfast?" Nerva stood in the open panel wearing a gray dress over gray leggings and boots.

He shook his head. She was using her calm voice. Her eyes were placid. Had she been angry at him last night? Surely he would remember that. But if she hadn't been angry at him, why was his head hurting? Did his head hurt, as Nerva sometimes said, because he was defective, because he came from the Reeks, where people were all bad?

"Follow along this gallery," she said, gesturing. "Don't be long. We don't want to keep your uncle waiting."

He pulled on his shoes and fastened the straps. When he walked outside he saw his suitcase, closed and upright, next to Nerva's, standing at the foot of her bed. Were they packed again?

The pilot lady had flown away in her flitter, the pad was empty, and Keely looked at it forlornly.

He was feeling a kind of fluttering in his stomach. Something made him wish he could run back to his room and hide but if he did . . . if he did, what would happen? Why did he feel such dread?

Uncle Figg was already awake, as usual, standing at the balcony in his robe sipping coffee. The pavilion was mostly open to the freshness of the morning, the priest fellow sitting at a low table on a cushion, his legs crossed. He looked as if he was sleepy, a bit, the way Keely felt. The priest was drinking the dark stuff in a cup and said, "Good morning, Keely."

"Good morning."

"Do you remember my name?"

After a while, he nodded. "Dekkar. You're my uncle's friend."

He smiled, patted Keely on the head. Nerva was watching this and pretending not to. Keely listened but never heard her use the voice, as she sometimes would when she grew irritated in a crowd. She could use it silently so that other people were never aware of it, but Keely always knew; and she appeared to be wary of exposing herself to danger for the most part. Nerva must be afraid of Dekkar. Keely felt as if he ought to remember something about that, something that had made him afraid, too, and his head started to pound again. He felt all mixed up today; he was remembering some things when he shouldn't, and he had the feeling this was because the priest had spoken to him the day before, had touched his forehead. But if Keely said anything Nerva would make him regret it later. She was the one who made him forget, she told him so, and tried to make him forget that, too, but sometimes her tricks didn't work so well and Keely still remembered. Like this morning. He remembered enough bits and pieces to know that his fear of her was because of something real.

"I don't think he's feeling very well," Dekkar said, looking at Keely.

Uncle Figg knelt next to him, looked into his eyes. "Your eyes don't look right, Keely. Are you in pain?"

"No, sir."

"Are you sure?"

"My head was hurting a little," Keely said.

"Is it still hurting now?"

"No."

"You sure?"

"I'm sure he would have told me if it were anything serious," Nerva said.

Dekkar stood behind her, watching her. Keely felt Nerva still waiting behind him. "I feel fine," Keely said.

Uncle Figg was sitting on a cushion, reaching for a piece of fresh bread.

The side of the pavilion lay open to the morning. No one was in the house except the grown-ups and the new Hilda and Herman, who were even more grim and silent than the old ones. It would take Keely a while to invent personalities for these. The food was eggs and fish stuff that Keely hated, so Herman brought some cereal and Keely ate that. He took his cereal cup to Uncle Figg's bed platform and sat there to look outside.

A huge creature stepped into the garden, shaped like one of Keely's Disturber toys, one of the big bugs, but the one in the garden was much bigger than the toy, so huge it stood higher than the pavilion. When it moved there was hardly any sound at all. Behind it the trees were shaking, as if the bug had just stepped out of them, or over them. The bug monster had a black shell so dark it drank light and its tiny head swiveled back and forth, assessing the garden and the terraces leading to the house.

Another creature exactly the same as the first stepped into the grove of trees on the other side of the pavilion. That bug monster had forelegs like needles and was rubbing them together with a rasping sound.

Uncle Figg stood suddenly and looked stricken. Penelope fell off his head and collapsed to the floor, inert.

Nerva was using the voice on Dekkar and he was curling up on the floor, in pain.

The monsters in the garden were moving strangely fast, in blurs, with a sound that was sometimes like a buzzing, other times like a note of music. One of them was tearing away part of the house and the other was uprooting shrubs and trees in the garden. The sound made Keely's head hurt. Nerva was still using the voice. The black bug things slowed and stepped one jointed leg at a time toward the pavilion; they were looking into the pavilion, their big jaws snapping from side to side.

Uncle Figg huddled on the floor next to Dekkar, not moving.

One of the monsters moved out of sight of Keely and started to wreck the garden, slashing through shrubs and trees with its forelegs, raising two more legs off the ground and using them to heave whole trees out of the ground, roots shivering and raining down dirt. Keely gaped, drawing back against the nearest wall.

"Nerva." Uncle Figg could hardly get his breath, but she had not even used the voice on him.

"Don't worry about the pets," she said, indicating the monsters. "They aren't hungry right now. They just want to play with the house and the yard a bit."

"What's going on?"

"Isn't it obvious?" she asked.

She gave him a smile that Keely recognized; he could feel the words she was using, the language, the numbers spinning in his head. Nerva spoke the same sounds as he heard in the math box, dizzying. She was focused on Dekkar, trying to control him, having a hard time. Keely felt dazed himself, flooded with memories, from last night and all the nights compounded, watching Nerva, frightened.

"You brought these things?" Uncle Figg was gasping.

"Yes, I did. And I have more friends on the way. Here we are." She looked up, smoothing back her hair. She had an air of expectancy, like when she was talking to her friend on the communicator.

The priest, Dekkar, appeared to be twisted in the most horrid shape, and it looked as if his arms were broken; but there was something wrong with the space around him, and his image was not altogether clear. He was silent, voiceless, his face puckered in a way that made Keely queasy as he watched.

A lot of shadows flew into the room and took a form, first a funnel pouring down into a tight spiral, then a man with slick, dark hair, a wide mouth, and sharp teeth that looked like needles at the tips. He had a body like Keely's pop-together superhero, and he wasn't wearing anything, showing his privates like a jackass, the way Sherry used to say about naked people in the Reeks. Sherry was his sister, whom he could only remember at times and in pieces. But in the case of this toothy man, the teeth made him look hard and his eyes make him look harder, all black like buttons. "I headed south as soon as you called," he said. He was speaking a language based on the math box sounds; Keely could understand most of it, though it made his head hurt. The size of the man-thing's teeth made his voice sound funny. He was watching Nerva with a strange look in his eyes.

"You're a welcome sight," she said, speaking the same language.

The man-thing leaned over Uncle Figg and sniffed him with flared nostrils, slowly and carefully, all over the face. Uncle Figg held still as if he were in somebody's grip. Nerva was still using the voice on the priest, who was on the floor and looked like he was movie dead or vid dead, sprawled with his legs tangled, not breathing.

"You made good time," said the man-thing. "Your candidate is only the third to arrive."

"He's a good recruit, this one," Nerva said, running a finger through Keely's hair. He wanted to pull away from her but knew better. "He's up to level six on the math box."

"Six?"

"For his age, that's impressive."

"The God Rao will be pleased. I know I am."

The man-thing walked toward Nerva, touched her like he liked her. She moved toward his hand pliantly, and something sickening happened along her body, as if the skin had become unglued and her edges blurred. The look on her face was young like a girl. The man-thing looked down at Uncle Figg. Now the creature was speaking in Alenke, his accent heavy but understandable. "Which of my appetites do I satisfy first?" he asked, grinning, those needle-teeth splaying a bit, and Uncle Figg started to shake. "Do I eat you or do I have sex with my friend here? What do you think?"

After a while Uncle Figg said, in a forced voice, "Go for the sex."

The man-thing laughed and moved toward him, mouth opening. Keely's heart started to pound and he tried not to watch but could scarcely stop himself. The man-thing opened the mouth wide, impossibly wide and pressed those needle teeth partway into Uncle Figg's face, all around the edges of it, that's how wide the mouth opened. Blood poured down Uncle Figg's face and neck. He shuddered, his legs thumping the floor. The man thing drew out the teeth again and licked the blood with a long, pointed tongue. The blood slowed then, but continued to ooze. Uncle Figg was shuddering and shivering. The man-thing drew back. "Just a taste," he said.

The priest was still. He looked dead. Nerva was standing over him. Now the man-thing caught his scent, stood over him, nostrils flared.

"Shall I get our bags?" she asked.

The thing was pacing around Dekkar. "Not so fast. This one. What is he?" He had switched to the other language, which appeared to be more comfortable for him. The switch made Keely's head ache again. For a moment the man-thing blurred and his body appeared to rearrange itself; he was suddenly taller, looming over her.

"It's better if you stick to their language," Nerva snapped. "I'm fixed in this form, remember, it hurts my head to speak otherwise."

"You were speaking Erlot against him. Is he learned?"

"I don't know what he is. He's not one of their Prin and he's been stripped of his Drune, I already checked that part."

"He does not feel properly bound to me."

"I bound him," Nerva said, running her hands over Dekkar, doing something that made him flinch. So he was not dead.

"We were not expecting one of their incanters this far north. Why have you traveled here with him?"

"He brought us here by flitter. Without him I'd have been stuck in your war in the south."

"Yes, but you've allowed him to be close to the child."

"The damage was done when he met us. What did you expect me to do?"

The man thing was gingerly leaning down toward Dekkar as if compelled; the nose started to sniff and ran over Dekkar's face, his hands. "I cannot leave him here and I cannot take him. I will not eat him myself. But if I let the eaters have him and Rao wants to know more about him, I will regret it. You would be far better off, my dear, not to have presented me with so grave a problem."

"Don't threaten me. I'm a foster mother to Rao once this child goes into Greenwood."

"Yes. You are. Then. Not now." He advanced on her slowly, opening that wide, wicked mouth again. In spite of herself she backed away. "I will have to speak with the source. We will likely have to bring the incanter with us."

The smell of Dekkar drew the man-thing back again. Keely closed his eyes when the thing began to press its teeth into the priest's dark face.

When Keely looked again, Dekkar's skin was oozing blood, same as Uncle Figg's, and the man-thing was looking blissfully down at him, carefully cleaning the teeth with that sharp, long tongue. "He is the better taste of the two by far."

The pavilion shook on one side as the huge monster mantis uprooted trees and destroyed the outlying pavilions of the house. Keely found himself watching the monster's dark eyes, which looked like a lot of glittering beads; it had captured some kind of small animal and was holding it in forelegs, tearing the flesh into its maw. It had reached the pool of water and stood there with water flowers tangled around its legs. The bug monster on the other side of the pavilion was standing quietly with its huge jaw hanging over the balcony railing. The inside-parts of the bug's mouth looked moist.

The man-thing reached into a pouch that hung at his waist and pulled out the same kind of brooch Nerva carried. He took it in both hands, held it above his head, and closed his eyes. Nerva watched him. With his mouth closed he looked almost like a person, his skin a sickly gray-green, his naked body gleaming. A few of the shadows broke off from him and flew around him in short loops.

Keely was sitting on the edge of Uncle Figg's bed. He still had his cereal bowl on his lap, empty now. Carefully he set it on the floor.

The room went suddenly dim and Keely froze. More of the shadows had broken off from the man-thing and were whirling in the air around him. Sometimes their wings brushed Keely's face and made him shiver. He stared at Uncle Figg, who had frozen completely still with his eyes open, fixed on nothing, lying on his side on the floor. His face had stopped bleeding but the puncture marks were blue and swollen.

The priest, on the other hand, looked as though nothing had happened to his face at all. He looked more present in the room, less sickeningly twisted than before, and his eyes came open.

He started to move, sat up, watched the man-thing. Nerva, who was standing still herself, holding her own brooch, flung it down and hurled herself at Dekkar.

By the time she moved, he had stood, and she stopped in front of him as if he were holding her and looked him up and down. Her expression slowly shifted from the meanness that Keely knew so well to a first wave of fear. The flying shadows, looking more and more like dark birds, were whirling around them all, and a darkness covered Dekkar's skin, like an oily shadow, and then a kind of popping sound burst out of him and the shadows fell, collapsed. The man-thing stood watching Dekkar as the fallen shadow birds flopped aimlessly and tried to use their wings to drag themselves.

Dekkar was watching the man-thing for a while and closed his eyes. Light wove itself over and through the surface of his skin, colors shimmering, and Nerva shrieked and fell to her knees. The man-thing broke apart into the flying shadows all in an instant and they attacked Dekkar, flew at him from all directions, but some passed through him, sliced through the walls of the house, and then their shapes changed and they slammed into the walls or the floor or the ceiling and were stunned. After a moment it was clear Dekkar was taking control of the shadow-birds one by one, and he went on standing there until the shadows started to form the man-thing; then he tore them apart again; and they tried to form and he ripped them separate again, over and over. Nerva was shrieking, blood leaking from her ears and nose, from the corners of her lips, a trickle. Uncle Figg was on his feet backed blindly against a wall, touching the wounds on his face. At his feet Penelope was starting to move her legs.

Keely moved to sit at Dekkar's feet all in one motion, suddenly, holding his breath. The shadows tried to touch him and failed. Finally they clotted all in front of Dekkar for a moment and the man-thing formed again and froze. Dekkar opened his eyes and said, "Shut down your constructs or I'll kill you this moment."

"You know all I have to do is wish it and they will destroy this house and everyone in it."

"If you want to test my limits, friend, please feel free to try. I'm likely to tear you to pieces, though, while I'm in the process of making rubble out of your toys. Tear you to pieces permanently, I mean. So make your choice."

"You'll kill me one way or the other."

"Maybe."

"So why should I help you do it?"

Dekkar closed his eyes again, and the light along his skin darkened, deepened, till the whole pavilion was gloomy. The insect-monster nearest the pavilion shuddered and shook and moved away. It took on a defensive stance against the hillside. The other, the one that was presently destroying Figg's compound systematically, gave an unearthly piercing shriek that made Keely fall back trembling on the carpet. Uncle Figg looked like he'd been knocked to the floor.

"I'll shut down the one that's left," the man-thing said, trying with all its needle teeth to look contrite.

Dekkar nudged Nerva with his toe. Keely was watching the look of pain on her face with a feeling of warm satisfaction. "Who is this woman? Where did she come from?"

"I will die before I answer," the man-thing said. "I am a high servant of a high master."

"Yes, I know. The God Rao."

The creature looked discomfited.

"You should not have said his name for me to hear," Dekkar said. "But that was only one of your mistakes. You should never have bit me. I tasted you as well, you see. You might have had a chance to keep me bound until then."

The thing was whimpering, as if Dekkar were using a special voice himself, but Keely heard nothing.

"You made contact with Rao or one of his subordinates, too. That was another of your mistakes. So now I know where he is."

The man-thing was breathing with effort, stretching his lips across those teeth.

"Now you are mine," Dekkar said, and his voice was not at all nice but it was still just a person's voice. "For the record, you said earlier that you would die before you answer. In fact, you will die after. Now, who is she?"

The man-thing fought for a while, mouth moving, those needle teeth out of control, piercing his cheeks and lips. When he could no longer control himself, he answered, gazing at the ceiling. He looked as if he were in agony. "She is one of the envoys. Sent to select from your race ten candidates to learn the Erlot."

"Say that again."

"Erlot. The numbers of Rao."

Keely had heard this name before today, in the math box. It made him cold, and he shivered.

"Ten candidates?"

"It was the box," Keely said in a whisper.

"What?" Dekkar asked, not moving his gaze from the man-thing even for a second.

"That was a word in the math box. Nerva made me use it every day. To teach me numbers."

"Keely is one of your ten?"

"Yes," the man-thing hissed.

"What was to happen to him?"

"One of the ten will become the body of the God Rao on this world. The others are taught to be ipocks, speakers of Erlot."

Dekkar made him say that again too. The man-thing did everything Dekkar told him to do.

"Who are you?" Dekkar's voice hardened.

The man-thing flinched, bit his needle-teeth into his own gums, his face running with brown-red blood. He spoke even more obviously with the strain of resistance. He made a sound that might have been his name. "I gather the ten for Rao. Nothing more."

"Why this child?"

"He has a gift for numbers. They all do. She searched for him and found him and brought him." He indicated Nerva, senseless along the table where she had fallen.

"You were coming to take him away today."

"Yes. I was sent to bring him into the north."

"You meant to kill the rest of us."

"Yes. The calcept would eat you and shit you out and your farm would be a ruin."

That time Dekkar repeated the word, *calcept,* and Keely knew it meant the big bugs with the maws like black saw blades. "Why? The northerners aren't even your enemy."

"We are Rao. We have no friends or enemies."

"What kind of creature are you?"

"Chalcyd. Ipock. I speak Erlot at the fifth rank."

He had to repeat all that, and did. His eyes were streaming with yellow fluid, more viscous than tears.

"I am Dekkar," the priest said. "I speak three true languages at a level you will soon learn all too well. This is your lucky day," and the priest made the man-thing's name sound, exactly the way Keely heard it the first time. "You live to go home. Tell Rao I'm coming."

"Rao will not need to fear so small a one—" His words choked off and his features wrenched as if in agony.

Dekkar said, "No more foolishness. Go and give my message to Rao. I won't give you back your calcept pet— it's mine now. And remember this while you're on the way. When you finish this last task for me and carry my message to the God Rao, I will withdraw my hand from you and you will drop dead where you stand."

The man-thing made a low shriek and spat fluid from its shredded mouth, pink-flecked saliva. Its lips hung in tatters, the teeth retracted inside.

Dekkar opened his eyes and smiled at the creature as if he were its best friend.

A moment later in a burst of black wings it was gone, and Dekkar knelt to Nerva. She flinched, to the degree that she could move at all, and tried to move away from him. He glanced at Uncle Figg, who was starting to get his breath under control. "Are you all right, Figg?"

He nodded, nostrils flared, eyes big as if he were still seeing that mouth with all its teeth close over him, prick him. "I need to clean these wounds."

"You'd better not touch them until I get a chance to look at them. How do you feel?"

"Numb." He drew a sucking breath, ran a hand through his hair. "I swear, Dekkar, if you don't kill her I'm going to."

"No, you won't. I need her alive for the moment."

"Who is she?"

"At the moment she's more or less Erejhen. The copy is far from perfect. That's what I was noticing last night when I questioned you about her. I have no idea what she is originally. One of the chalcyd, maybe. Those flock-creatures. They appear to able to change shape."

Figg moved to sit beside Keely, embraced the boy, who was stiff and frightened still. It was hard to have anybody close, but this was Uncle Figg.

"What has she been doing to you?"

Keely shrugged. The question closed up his throat.

Dekkar released her partially so that she could talk, but otherwise kept her as she was. He said, "This voice of yours is troublesome. Be careful how you use it."

She made incoherent sounds, trying to move.

"Did you enjoy tormenting me a few moments ago? You appeared to."

Her hair was sliding into the remains of her breakfast, pudding on her face, and sausage grease, and gobs of sticky rice.

"I want you to know I opened myself to you in order to give you joy," Dekkar said. "I allowed you to cause me pain. I want you to know that. But, you see, in taking advantage of my offer you've made a grave error, and you'll pay a grave price. I'm going to keep you with me for a while till I've learned all that you know, and there is nothing in this fold of space and time that will prevent me from finishing my work with you. Do you understand?"

Her toes were curling out of her shoes. She was still making that whimper noise; she was trying to make the voice.

"Figg, do you want to ask this creature any questions?" Dekkar asked.

"Yes. But I'd rather Keely weren't here."

"All right. I can leave her with you in a way that won't permit her to harm you as she's been harming Keely."

She was sitting up now, food sliding down her face and dress. She looked funny and Keely snorted.

Dekkar laughed, too, looking down at Keely. "You want to know what I'm going to do right now, Keely?"

He nodded, too shy to speak.

"I'm going to take her voice out. Not her whole voice, just the part that hurts you. Would you like that? And I'm going to wipe her brain so clean of all those words that she'll never get them back. Would you like that?"

Keely understood the first part but not the second; he nodded anyway. He could tell that was what he was supposed to do. He felt old inside, wasted. All the memories he had lost came flooding back. Whatever Nerva had done to him to keep the old memories away, Dekkar put an end to it.

Nerva shrieked, a ghastly sound, and Uncle Figg walked Keely to the porch where he could not watch her crying. So Keely stopped and said, "No, Uncle Figg. I want to see." His heart was pounding.

Uncle Figg spoke with effort, his face so swollen he could hardly make words. "I had no idea she was hurting you," he said.

Keely shrugged and smiled to make Uncle Figg feel better. "I don't remember much of it," he said, though in fact he remembered all of it, now. But for some reason the lie didn't make Uncle Figg feel better at all. His face was all cloudy with sympathy. In the pavilion, though, Nerva continued to wail, and Keely's heart brightened at the sound.

2. Fineas Figg

Figg toured the wreckage of his compound, the garden shredded along one side of the house, two pavilions still standing, the dead mantis collapsed under what was left of a tree, its black carapace decaying at an ominous rate and sliding into the ground with a toxic sheen.

His face ached. Dekkar had cleaned the wounds and said it was better to leave them be until he knew more.

The Herman and the Hilda were stirring, cleaning the mess that had been made of breakfast. The bodyguard Zhengzhou, who had arrived last night with the rest of the party's luggage, crept out of one of the intact pavilions and stood dazed in the bright day.

Figg had talked to Nerva, not that she gave him much satisfaction. But it was easy enough to piece together the story. In her guise as an Erejhen she had lived on Senal for many decades. She had come to Senal to find one of ten pupils for her master and had located a group of candidates, all gifted in their potential for mathematics. She selected Keely as the best of them, visiting him in the guise of a social worker from the upper levels of Kinahd, the city beneath which Keely had lived. Nerva had used Sherry, and later Sade, in her bid to get legal control of Keely; since she needed to emigrate with him, she did not want to risk simply kidnapping him. Nerva had convinced Sherry of the advantages of a high-profile public suicide. From that point she had simply waited out events and at some point during the whole preparation for Sade's now-infamous party, she had helped Sade purchase an option to adopt Keely, and the two of them had seized the child.

Following Sade's death, Figg had proven ideal in the bond he felt with Keely, in his sense of obligation, and above all in his irreproachable family connections. She had used this voice of hers and her knowledge of true language, likely the same Erlot that the man-thing had mentioned, to get Figg to do what she wanted, to hire her.

At times Figg had suspected her of using the child to get into his own good graces, due to his wealth, which was still considerable. Now he understood that Keely had always been her focus.

In exactly the same way, this morning, when the monstrous mantises first crashed into the garden, he had thought they had come for him, because of his family name. Even in disaster he was still living in the past, in the old, dead world of his importance.

Sherry had obtained a license to commit public suicide in order to sell herself to Sade as entertainment; Nerva had helped Sherry with the arrangements. The girl might never have wanted to die, in fact, and the realization sickened him. Sherry might have been under Nerva's influence all along. Sherry might have been listening to this creature's voice, might never have wanted to sign those papers, to consent to her own death, at all.

"You can't make it any different by brooding about it," Dekkar said, stepping up behind him.

"Where's Keely?"

"In your bed. I took Nerva to her room. She won't be bothering anyone."

"What do you intend to do?"

"Listen to her. Until I know what she knows."

Figg laughed, softly. "I told you I could spot you for what you were. The fallen Drune is not so fallen after all."

"I'd never have blown my cover if it could have been helped, but I draw the line at letting monsters eat my friends."

"I've never been so frightened. I didn't know a person could feel so much fear." He looked at Dekkar, the man's hard, dark eyes. "So what are you, really?"

Dekkar had a face that could be described as neither gentle nor harsh; he had mastered a kind of blank draw on all expressions. This was one of his charms for Figg, who was very old and easily wearied by the shallow and easy. "I work for the over-mage in Iraen."

"You work for Great Irion? I met you all those years ago when I traveled to Iraen and tried to meet him."

Dekkar laughed at the memory. "Yes. I remember. You know, in all these years, I've never asked you what possessed you to think you could simply walk into Iraen and ask for an interview with Great Irion himself."

Figg shrugged. "I heard a story once when I was a child, just after the Conquest. When my mother brought me to your country for my first visit. As the story goes, any villager there could ask for a meeting with Great Irion once in his or her life, once upon a time. I don't know whether it's true or not."

Dekkar smiled. "I wouldn't know. I spent most of my time in the deep south. That would be a custom for the northerners, maybe."

"But you know him. Irion."

Dekkar shook his head. "Not well. I work for him, that's all."

"You've never even given me a hint in all these years."

"It would limit my usefulness for people to know."

"Then why tell me now?"

His face went into its mode of tight control and he turned aside from the wreckage of the pond to view the crater where the mantis had collapsed and died. "Who knows how much longer I'll be of any use to anybody?" he asked. "I'm in the mood for the truth, I suppose. This crater is getting bigger. What is this black sand? Don't touch it."

"My God, what a foul smell."

"This thing turns into something else when it dies."

"I'll have to have someone dig it out of the ground when I rebuild, I suppose."

Dekkar looked at him and shook his head. "This crater is still getting bigger, Figg. There may be more to dig out than you're reckoning."

He knelt and saw what Dekkar meant. The layer of black was seething, eating the topsoil and the remains of the garden and creeping up one of the support posts that remained after the mantis demolished the pavilion.

"You and Keely ought to get ready to come with us," Dekkar said.

"What?"

"Kitra and I will be leaving very soon. I spoke to her a few moments ago. She should be close to the farm by now. You should come with us."

He was looking around in a daze. He knew that what Dekkar was saying ought to make more sense than it did. "I can't think right now."

"Figg, they'll be back for Keely if he stays. If you come with me I can at least try to take care of you both."

"You want us to go with you to Greenwood?"

"I don't see what choice you have. These monsters are all over Aramen, now, and if they're looking for Keely using the kind of tricks I know, they'll find him wherever he is. If you stay with me there's a chance I can protect you until this is over, one way or the other."

"Those things are in Greenwood," Figg said, shuddering.

"Those things are everywhere. As far as we know, they may be on Senal, too. Or maybe they're the reason Great Irion closed the Anilyn Gate."

Figg shook his head. "The God Rao. Who is that?"

"I don't know. But I do know he's north of us, and I do

know he can't be allowed to stay here. I have to go north, I don't have a choice."

The puncture wounds on Figg's face were sore and aching suddenly. He almost reached fingertips for the tenderest, which felt as if it was oozing, but he forced himself to resist the impulse. "I was so frightened of that thing that tried to eat me. I don't want to go."

"Those wounds will make you sick. I don't have time to purge them now." Dekkar paused. "If I leave you here, do you really want to face one of those monsters again, alone?"

A flitter was crossing the distant hills. It was only then that Figg looked through the gash in the forest near the house, saw the ruined fields below, the smashed wreckage of the distant management building. The destruction had the look of caprice; some of the buildings in the distant management campus were intact, others smashed to bits, a couple burning slowly, sending up thin trails of smoke.

His heart sunk low. "We'll go. Are we taking the Nerva-thing, the woman?"

"Yes. We have to. I want to know what she knows when we're inside the forest. I want to know what she is."

"Keely will be terrified."

"I hope not. I mean to have a long talk with her now. If I'm successful, she won't look much like herself when I'm done."

Figg felt a kind of breaking inside, a rush of emotion like those he had known when he was young. The ache of it shook him. "Can you tell what exactly she did to Keely?"

"No. And I can't tell if it's over."

"But I thought—"

"She faked his regression. She used it to hide what she was teaching him."

"Right under my nose. What was she teaching?"

"True language," Dekkar said, quietly. "The kind she was using to control you all. He was learning it from the math box he talked about. Were you listening then?"

Figg nodded. He had heard Keely dimly, through his own immense terror.

"It's a teaching device like the ones we use in Prin universities. I have it from her bag. If my suspicions are correct, he's well on the way to becoming a novice operator of a true language. He won't forget what he knows unless I make him, and I think he's been tampered with enough."

Figg shook his head. "I can't believe what I've done."

"I don't think you should blame yourself."

"I thought I'd rescued him from poverty, and what I brought him into may be worse."

"She engineered most of this, Figg. She lured both of you into it. You weren't acting out of choice. There's no question that what she did to Keely hurt him badly. You can feel his terror. But she'd have had control of him one way or the other, Figg, with or without you. She's like me: she's single-minded. When she sets herself to a purpose, she marches to it."

Figg tried to listen. He was thinking of himself more than Keely. There was a need he had to do right for Keely that had nothing to do with the child at all. But that wouldn't work anymore. "All right. I'll do whatever I can to protect him."

"We'll have to watch him. He may need the math box again—he may have no choice but to keep studying it. And you have to be aware of something, too. We're taking him to the place where this Rao creature wants him to go. I have to go to Greenwood because that's where Rao is, and I have to come as close to Rao as I can."

Figg stood in the ruins of his house, the wreckage of his new life, looking Dekkar in the eye. "Things can't get much worse."

"Don't tell yourself anything of the sort. Things can get much worse for all of us." He started to say more, then shook his head. "Let me go and do my job with this Nerva creature. Keep your eye on Keely while I'm in there."

Kitra had landed the flitter and came into sight at the edge of the garden. She was walking toward what was left of the house with a look of awe. Someone followed her, a tall, broad-shouldered man with an easy swagger. He studied the wreck of the garden and the many piles of lumber and paper that had once been a house, his expression, if anything, be-mused.

Kitra pulled off her sunglasses and looked at Figg, and he was conscious of the swellings on his face, their tenderness. "What happened?"

He told her quickly and briefly. Her companion was Pel Orthen, a riverboat pilot from Jarutan, an Erejhen, a strapping fellow with long red-brown hair and a heavy, square chin who looked more like an actor playing a rugged river naviga-tor than like the actual article. Figg showed them the mantis that had survived, deactivated in the backyard, folded into a tight knot of needle-sharp legs and razor-sharp mandibles and teeth, looking so lethal that they studied it only from the distant balcony. "I've seen bits and pieces of those things in the news-frames," Pel said, his voice surprisingly musical and mellow for his bulk. "How big is it when it's standing up?"

Figg shuddered. "Big. Too big to think about."

"What killed the other one?"

"Dekkar."

Kitra looked surprised. "Then I suppose his secret is out."

"Which is?" Pel asked.

"That he's not really an ex-Drune at all."

Figg almost said, "No, he works for Great Irion," but caught himself and let her think what she wanted.

They had paused near the gallery that led to Nerva's room, the last of the pavilions standing other than Figg's central one. Figg could hear nothing of what was going on inside the paper walls. He had asked the Herman to pack him a bag and went to the room to check to make sure the drone had not lapsed into stillness between tasks, as sometimes happened. The Hilda was sitting next to Keely on the bed. Zhengzhou was on the balcony outside, wary eye on the pile of the deactivated mantis and on Keely, for whom she had a liking. Keely had his pale hand on the Hilda's artificially warmed skin and lay there with his eyes closed, breathing deeply and evenly. Penelope sat in his lap, still stunned by whatever Nerva had done to deactivate her. She was a cyborg with an enhanced brain for a spider and without emotion, as Figg knew; but he would have sworn she was taking comfort in her nearness to Keely, who petted her back tenderly at moments.

"How will we travel?" Figg asked.

Kitra looked at him in surprise. "You're coming?"

"We have to. They'll send another one of those things after Keely if we stay here."

She frowned. Pel stood with his arms folded.

Figg said, "I'll pay. Whatever it takes."

"It's a big boat," Pel said, scratching his head, looking indifferent.

"You do know how far we're going?"

"Yes," Figg said, feeling suddenly weary, wishing for nothing better than to crawl into an empty bed himself, to lie there peacefully wrapped in some nice sedative. "There's no help for it."

Kitra still looked suspicious. She was thinking about her brother, most likely, about her chances to find him and how this new angle figured into that. He studied her without much interest. "I'll talk to Dekkar," she said.

You do that, he thought, and felt unpleasant. One more moment passed in which the clear morning settled into its deceptive calm.

Suddenly the roof of Nerva's pavilion exploded upward and shade-birds flew out of it in a whirling funnel. The sound was enormous, like a charge of dynamite, and the dark things were shrieking, changing color, some deep hues of red, a few a dirty white, shimmering from hue to hue.

Zhengzhou leapt into the pavilion at Keely's back, and the Hilda hovered over him as if she would ward off any attack with her own body.

Keely kept still as if he heard and saw nothing.

The walls of the pavilion burst outward in a boom, revealing Dekkar defending himself at the center of the platform.

Figg watched, heart thumping, as the flock of black-wings dived at Dekkar over and over, beating him to his knees. His face and arms and torso were covered with blood. He bent for a while and then straightened, and the things lashed at him and sometimes appeared to slice into him or fly through him; the funnel convulsed and shook. The flock collapsed hard into its center and took form again, a sharp crack like a whip and then a shriek from the thing that was standing in front of Dekkar. His bleeding had stopped and most of the bloodstains had vanished, but he looked a fright. He was breathing evenly and calmly, and the thing in front of him— the Nerva-thing—resolved to a form that looked like a middlewam, almost; there was no means to determine gender, and it had a mouth full of the same teeth as the man-thing. The Nerva-thing fell to the floor and lay there. Dekkar looked over his shoulder, curiously, at Pel Orthen. Some charge passed between them, as if they knew each other. "I need rope or cord for a binding."

Pel registered only a moment of surprise, then nodded his head once, sharply, and loped off through the pavilion and into the garden.

Dekkar was still standing over the Nerva-thing. "We have come to an understanding, she and I. She's mute. She's forgotten her own language and she can't speak ours without reeducation into this form of hers."

"My God under heaven," Kitra said.

"Hello, Kitra. You made good time."

"I see you weren't joking."

He blinked mildly, inclining his head. "We'll need to head north immediately. We'll have more passengers."

"We can get eight in the flitter," Kitra said. There was no trace of argument in her at the moment, no doubt due to her having seen the Nerva-thing's mouth. Watching the creature stretch its mouth and flex its teeth made Figg's face ache more. "Nine, if someone holds Keely."

Figg said, "We're only seven, eight if I take the Hilda."

Kitra looked at him sharply.

"For Keely," he said. "The Hilda at home could always calm him down."

"I don't think he'll be afraid of this thing, not as much as he was of Nerva," Dekkar said. "The river man and I will bind it and put something over that ghastly mouth. At any rate, we can tell him truthfully that Nerva is gone."

"This was her?" Kitra asked, aghast.

"Yes."

"I don't know whether I want to travel with that thing."

"You don't have a choice," Dekkar said. "I can't release her, and I won't leave her here—she'll only escape and come after us. I won't kill her until I know as much as she can teach me."

"How do you propose to make her do that?"

Figg felt as if he was overhearing an argument he shouldn't. Dekkar looked at Kitra sharply. "You don't get a choice in this. Get that through your head. Go or stay." He wiped the blood from his face. Pel was loping across the garden with a cloth bag. He walked coolly onto the platform that was all that remained of the pavilion and knelt and started to bind the Nerva-thing, starting with a complex of knots to keep the jaw closed. Then a network of cords to bind the hands at the back, not a single loop of cord but an elaborate weave, knotted carefully to allow circulation but still to bind her, without much other regard to comfort. Dekkar touched each of the knots as Pel worked, fingers moving quickly.

"I need to clean up a bit and then I'm ready to leave," Dekkar said, when they were done.

"I'll watch this pretty bit of monster," said Pel, and sat in a chair near the bundle of the Nerva-thing.

Figg was surprised to note their ease with one another. He had never thought of Dekkar as having any kind of sexuality.

"We should load whatever we're taking in the flitter starting now." Kitra shook her head as if to free herself of what she had seen and moved off the balcony with a determined step. "I need to get a clearance for a route to Dembut."

Penelope climbed out of Keely's lap onto the balcony railing, taking in the sun. Figg stood near the big spider and stroked her back fur with his fingertips. She clambered onto his head and flattened herself there, slipped her legs into their sockets, embedded in his skin. The contact gave Figg a low rush of pleasure, a sense of well-being that soothed him. His hair was false anyway and adjusted itself to the spider-cyborg's contours. He'd paid a fortune to the capilliologist for this particular kind of wish-configurable hair.

He woke Keely and sent him to the car with the Hilda and the bags. Pel and Kitra were loading the Nerva-creature into the storage compartment of the flitter, at the back, where Pel would keep an eye on it.

The black pit where the garden used to be was still growing, getting deeper, spreading along the wreckage of the nearby pavilion and up the remains of several trees. It was as if a shadow were eating the garden and house.

Dekkar went out to the garden once he'd cleaned himself up, stood beside the heap that was the shadow mantis, unfolded it, let it stretch those needle-limbs, and sent it gliding silently down the hillside.

Figg waited for him by the car, watching.

"Did you think to pack food?" Dekkar asked, walking up as the mantis moved easily down the road. "I never ate much of my breakfast."

"Yes. Herman put together what we had."

"We'll get real supplies in Dembut," Kitra said, settling into the pilot's harness. "Everyone in?"

Keely sat in front next to Kitra, holding himself stiff as if he was still frightened; Figg had hoped it would make the boy happy to sit next to the pilot. Keely looked back at Figg and tried to smile. "You like your seat, son?" Figg asked.

Keely nodded. He looked his age again, the younger behavior completely vanished. His calm eyes resembled those of his sister, whom Figg had briefly known.

The flitter sealed itself, rose, and swooped in a curve over the shadow mantis, which lifted its head momentarily as it slid into the river David and disappeared from sight.

"What did you tell that bug-thing to do?" Figg asked. He had slid into his own seat next to the Hilda, who was sitting still as usual, running a protocol that enabled her to simulate looking out the window.

Dekkar had clambered to the back pair of seats with Zhengzhou; beyond them was Pel in the cargo space beside the Nerva-thing, still motionless. "I told it to wait for us in

Greenwood." Dekkar shrugged. "We'll see. If my control doesn't hold, it's just one more of the monsters to deal with later. If it actually comes to Greenwood and waits for us, we may find some use for it."

"Here we go," Kitra said. "We're off to see the wizard."

"Beg pardon?" asked Dekkar.

"A reference to a fairy tale. Something from pre-Transit."

"Then we're off to see the wizard," Dekkar agreed, and Keely giggled as Penelope crawled onto his lap off Figg's head. The spider sat there in pleasure as Keely rubbed its back and belly. Outside, the peaceful landscape streamed by, and Figg did his best to catch his breath.

◦1 Movements of the allied heavy artillery ambient called "chalcyd" and flocks of the airborne allied units called "calcept" have been sighted throughout the Ajhevan continent, in contravention of the treaty between People for a Free Aramen and the Dirijhi Collive. Allied troop movements are restricted by treaty to one corridor along the river David. Protests have been lodged with the Dirijhi consul at the edge of the forest near Dembut. The two known types of allied support for the rebellion are extremely volatile and will attack on very little provocation. The names are those which are currently in use by northern media, said to be borrowed from the Dirijhi symbiont dialect.

◦2 Tens of thousands cheer progress of rebellion in Jarutan's Freedom Plaza, celebrating the early success of the rebel armies in shaking up the colonial government in Feidreh-Avatrayn. Chong Tosh addresses the crowd from the statue of Kraken the Great standing at the feet of the old Hormling hero of the Faction Wars. "We will see our children and our grandchildren as the respected citizens of a self-governing world," Chong declares. Secondary school bands and parades of schoolchildren and youth organizations fill the plaza afterward, and fireworks light up the city along the river Silas.

○3 Fans of *The Adventures of Little Agnes in Monospace* were heartbroken when the new episode failed to air on the familiar Airy-Fairy Stream in the Surround. The shutoff of all new entertainment from Senal has Surround fans upset at missing a lot of new installments for popular serials like *Don Ameche Speaks from the Dead* and *Southside Reeks*. Other forms of popular culture are also suffering. Music fans have missed the spray-release of the new Shaptown Boys recording, and S-Boys' fans are known to be violent when they can't keep up with the sweet, sweet harmonies of their adolescent heroes. Coverage of the investiture of Ess Haven as a Node of Hanson in Grand Wheel was interrupted at the time of gate closure; no ships were in transit at the time, or at least none is known to have been in transit. All communications with Grand Wheel and Home Star have been interrupted. No word from Gatekeeper Station as to when gate services will be restored from the Aramenian side.

○4 The Hormling Eighth Army continues to hold a strong defensive perimeter around the colonial capital twin cities, Feidreh-Avatrayn, and the Prin appear to have found an effective means of preventing further encroachments on the city. What appeared to be the first serious defeat of the Prin may be turning in their favor, as has been the case in all other conflicts since the Conquest. Some media outlets in Feidreh-Avatrayn continue to function.

○5 Edenera Sade, proxy name for the daughter of the deceased media star Sade, released a protest to news outlets in the twin cities today upon learning of the emigration of her father's murderer, Fineas Figg, to Aramen. Figg, scion of the Orminy House Bemona-Kakenet, is known to have fled Senal due to recent setbacks to the family fortune under the Common Fund Reforms; he is rumored to have settled in an underground estate far to the north of the Ajhevan continent, in a facility in which he has secreted much of the fortune he hid from Hanson and the Mage. Figg invoked his house's right to murder when he and Sade became embroiled in an argument over a young woman at Figg's three hundredth birthday party, ironically thrown for him by Sade. Edenera Sade is the newly adopted proxy name of his biological-natural daughter, thought to be seeking her own status as a celebrity in the Hormling pantheon.

°6 Debris from an explosion which destroyed at least part of the Twelfth Fleet has been detected by Hargirs Station in orbit around Arsus; the debris field is several million kilomeasures wide, indicating some broad scale disaster within the fleet. High levels of radioactivity in the area are making further reconnaissance difficult. No communication from any of the ships assigned to the fleet has been received in nearly two days.

°7 Skygard Aramen has taken the unprecedented step of suspending pulleypod service to and from the surface. Surface-to-space cables are being withdrawn into Skygard to prevent station destabilization should the war in Feidreh-Avatrayn escalate. No Skygard station has ever attempted to reel in its ground cables, and engineers involved in the project remain uncertain as to how long the process will require.

°8 A candy tree has blossomed in downtown Jarutan, near the Ordinance Park entrance. Candy trees bloom once a decade or less and are increasingly rare, even in their native habitat along the

Ajhevan coast. A candy harvester is in place and a squadron of militia has the tree under guard. Candy-tree addicts are gathering but there are no signs of violence to report. The candy tree is considered to be an endangered species by wildlife groups, but there are no efforts under way to preserve them. Candy trees are protected under the terms of the Treaty of Silas Ford, which governed relations between the Mage and the Dirijhi until the recent rebellion.

Unto Greenwood

1.

Kitra flew the flitter north into the Silas valley along a familiar route parallel to the track of the river, a low path with not much traffic, guide-planes visible in the heads-up but not in reality. She was fretting about the number of people in the flitter, all of whom would be in the riverboat heading into Dirijhi country without any papers, all of whom would have to be hidden, each one of whom lessened her chances of getting Binam out this trip, a goal that urged itself on her more strongly as the war in the south unfolded.

As if he were reading her mind, Pel said, in his mellow voice, "I can get papers for a private excursion upriver, provided the trees haven't closed the river traffic."

"There's been no news about a closure," Kitra said. "And that would be news, up here."

"There'll be a lot of frightened southern tourists stranded in Dembut," he said.

Dekkar nodded, glancing at the thing tied up in the back compartment.

"How's that thing in the back?" Keely asked. "Can it get loose?"

"No," Dekkar said. "I have it safely under control."

Sitting next to the boy, Kitra could feel some of his tension. She was more acutely aware of Penelope, however. The spider thing was still sitting in the boy's lap, and every time it moved, Kitra's gaze flew to it.

Pel had opened a frame with a map of Greenwood, the one he had used when she told him her brother's location. "Are you sure?" Pel was asking. "Because that's almost too good to be true."

"Yes. I'm very sure."

Pel met Kitra's eyes in the mirror. "Your brother's tree. It's very close to where we need to go."

"The place where you expect to find—"

"Yes," Dekkar said, quietly. She could see him in the mirror again, looking behind at some movement in the back.

"Who's your brother?" Keely asked.

"His name is Binam."

"Is he your little brother?"

"Yes."

Keely had to think about that for a minute. "Is he little like I am? Does he like to play with toys?"

"He used to. There aren't a lot of toys where he is now."

"No toys?" Keely gave that serious thought.

"The trees don't play with toys, and my brother has to do what the trees want him to do."

"He does?"

"Yes."

"Why?"

"Because he belongs to a tree. He works for one. It's his job."

From the second row of seats, sitting next to the quiescent Hilda, Figg asked, "How long to Dembut?"

"A little over an hour. I'll park the flitter in one of the big public lots near the airway terminal."

"My boat is at the commercial dock," Pel said. "I keep some provisions on board but we'll need more."

"Buy whatever you need," Dekkar said. "I have cash chips. I'll need to lie low in the city while we're there."

"We'll take you to the dock," Kitra said, "and you can wait with the thing in the back."

"Do you think they're looking for you?" Figg asked.

"They'll be looking for someone who feels like I do to their senses. I could hide from most of their operators, but there's at least one who'll find me unless I take precautions."

"One?" Figg asked.

"They have a very powerful cantor with them. She feels female to me, but she has something to do with the trees. She's returning from the southern continent at the moment, a good number of hours away."

"Hours?"

"Yes."

"She'll be pursuing us?"

"I expect she's coming up from the south to deal with me, yes." Dekkar spoke mildly, without any hint of arrogance; Kitra studied his face in the back-view mirror, which gave her a good look at the whole passenger compartment.

He had known this was coming when he hired her in the first place. A sudden instinct told her this was true. He had been sent here. Maybe even by the Mage herself, or the one that the Hormling called Great Irion.

The cabin fell quiet after that and remained so until the flitter reached Dembut. There was a public flitter pad near the riverboat docks, and Kitra landed there. Traffic in the city appeared much the same as usual, though these days Dembut grew so fast she found herself recognizing less and less of it, other than the old village at the center, which was now too posh a location for any but the most wealthy residents. River and tourist traffic had moved into new development upriver toward the forest, which loomed green and verdant over everything.

She went to the market on her own to buy supplies. Pel was to wait while Dekkar worked on Figg's wounds and healed them; afterward he and Zhengzhou would accompany Figg to apply for papers for a private expedition into Green-wood, as far as the Capital, the usual tourist route. The trees would expedite a request of that sort if the supplicant was willing to pay the large fee required; the trees had a great appreciation for money. Dekkar planned to remain behind on the boat with the Nerva-thing and Keely, in order to control the former and hide the latter. That left Kitra to buy supplies for the journey.

She wandered in the market to listen to the talk, at the same time eyeing shops where she could order what she needed. She had brought the Hilda for help with portage, and the drone followed at her elbow with a bland expression. Pathfinding with these creatures was chancy out in the open, so it was best simply to keep close to it herself.

People were subdued here, even in the taverns. She heard

a lot of muttering about the docks, the war traffic flowing through. Heads clustered close together. News-frames in the bars carried the rebel media, that bimbo blond man Nars Federson chanting about the coming of independence, Aramen to be ruled by local assembly. In the tavern where she paused to watch, some people were jeering at him openly.

She was about to leave the bar when the frame switched to a survey team send by one of the Jarutan independent telecasters, stunned faces milling about a heap of wreckage, the camera rising and panning back to show a field of ruin, smoking husks of buildings interspersed with dark, shadowed craters eating deep into the earth. Silence fell over the bar. The images were being broadcast from remote cameras in Rarnak, a city on the northern coast of Jharvan. Some of the faces around her were obviously listening to the voiceover on their link. She was glad to have none.

In Dembut, merchants maintained a tradition of selling face-to-face from physical inventory; Kitra always found it a pleasant change to purchase from a human being rather than from a machine interface. This was what she was used to from her girlhood, after all; she had grown up on this continent, she and Binam and her parents living on an algae farm until Binam was sold to the trees. That gave the parents enough money to rid themselves of the farm and move south; Kitra divorced them and refused any part of the bounty for Binam in the settlement.

She went to the only outfitter she had used here, a shop that kept a good deal of inventory. Ard's Overland Supply had a big showroom and a lot of stock for cross-country parties and river travel. Kitra bought sleeping rolls in impossibly tiny

Jim Grimsley

and hygiene; she bought a large store of food of the survival
variety—dehydrated meats and nutrient-soaked cakes, foods
that they could carry overland—and canteens and packs, along
with a lightweight set of cookware and a couple of tents. She
bought adjustable biosuits with one-pass hoods, transparent
over the face; she bought a dozen kits for fitting them properly, in case she ran into trouble. The store owner showed her
a portable covered cooker that made no light or smoke and
she added it to the smart-cart that the Hilda was leading about.
She paid for all this with a cash chip from Dekkar and rented
the smart-cart, too, to carry her purchases home.

Since the riverboat had a galley, she bought fresher, more
palatable supplies at an open market, on top of the more
portable supplies she'd already purchased. She shopped in a
rush, planning for a long journey: better to stock Pel's kitchen
for a month and let him keep the surplus than to run out of
food in Dirijhi country.

Behind her trotted the Hilda with the smart-cart at her
heels. They headed through the crowded market along the
riverfront, the gray-brown waters of the Silas flowing fast,
swollen with rain. Dembut attracted Ajhevan farmers, militia,
symbionts on break from the consulate or in town to make
purchases for their trees. To most people the syms would have
looked very much like one another, male and female hardly
distinguishable, but Kitra had worked with syms a long time
and had learned to see them both for what they had become
and for what they might have been before their transformation. She studied the few she could see now, wishing that one
of them might be Binam.

Ten years ago she had passed through Dembut on her way into Dirijhi country, a revolutionary freshly returned from a fact-finding trip to Paska, one of the Hormling colonies in the Cluster. She had been a different person in those days; the decade since then felt longer than all that had come before. Too long, in fact, for she spent it knowing that Binam still languished in service to his tree.

The market crowd thinned at the riverfront, and she and the Hilda made good progress toward the boat district. Pel's boat had just come in sight when Kitra heard a boom so loud it stunned her and felt a concussion that knocked her to the ground. The Hilda had kept upright and managed the smart-cart; the market behind them was framed in orange flame and a cloud of black.

Out of the river, dripping, rose three of the big black mantises, the things that had destroyed Figg's compound. Calmly they walked ashore, black legs smashing through boats, docks, piers, kiosks, and buildings, the lead bug raising its head and bleating, the most awful, shrieking sound. Kitra shivered and her skin knotted to bumps. The Hilda closed a hand around Kitra's shoulder, heaved her upright, and forced her to trot toward the boat; the smart-cart's engine whined.

Pel and Figg rushed down the wharf, took Kitra by the arms, and hurried her on board. Figg was giving her a look of such concern that she almost liked him. His skin had lost the gray tinge and the wounds around the edge of his face were almost invisible. "Are you all right? What happened?"

"I don't know." She shook her head, stooping to clear the doorway, hurtling into the dark of the boat's interior while, after them, Zhengzhou followed, leading the Hilda. "There was an explosion. Then those things came out of the river. I thought they were coming after me for a second."

"They're attacking the town," Pel said, from outside.

"Bring the cart on board." Figg stood at the open hatch for a moment, watching. "We don't have time to unload it."

The cart started to alarm when it left the dock; Pel ripped open a panel and poured bleach on its organics to stop the shrieking once he jostled it down the couple of steps. "Where's Dekkar?"

"Here," the priest said, stepping out of the shadow of the interior. "You'd better get us under way."

Kitra jumped when he appeared, stepped away from him, her heart in her mouth. She was rattled by the explosions, the mantises that had stepped so close, the fires on the docks. She sat stupefied on something, a chest with a cheap cushion tied to the top.

"Why are they attacking their own allies?" Pel headed to the pilot's station; Figg was already taking in the mooring lines along the dock.

"Allies don't always get along. Though they could be looking for us, I expect."

Figg slid into the boat, closed the hatch expertly, signaling to Pel, who backed the boat out of its slip and carefully eased into the river.

On the shore, chaos, and then, behind the boat, another trio of the black mantises walking out of the river, smashing into the boat slips. Some of the fleet attempted to escape into the river; the creatures went after each of these with especial ferocity, smashing carbon-hard forelegs through the hulls, ripping their head crests through each craft in the same motion, stem to stern, the composite hulls shredded, occupants ripped to pieces. Overhead, a flock of dark bird-shapes appeared, streaming down toward the town.

Quiet shock overtook everyone on the boat; Kitra had to will herself to breathe more slowly. She moved to the glass walls, stood there watching the cloud fall over the town.

"They don't see us," she said.

"No." Dekkar moved beside her; Figg, beyond, was kneeling by Keely, arms around the boy. "If our luck holds and none of them blunders into us, we may make it into the forest."

She watched him carefully, trying to control her new fear of him. Having studied with Prin, worked with Prin and Drune, she knew them well enough to spot the signs of their work; in Dekkar she found no tell-tale look of distance, none of the partial distraction. He appeared to be completely and fully engaged in conversation with her, to the degree that he was not absorbed in the chaos along the river-bank. No sign hinted that he was engaged in any other activity, but it was impossible that the creatures would have missed the lone boat leaving the dock when they emerged from the river.

Further explosions rocked the town; there was no apparent source, no bombs or missiles falling from the sky, only the clouds of black birds that looked so odd and angular as they flashed in twists and dived in arcs, many of them puncturing the sides of buildings. The center of Dembut started crumbling and collapsing. A group of syms stood at the edge of a patio on the town side of the consulate, built within the shadows of the edge of the forest; they were watching calmly as their allies took the town apart.

"Can't you stop this?" Kitra asked quietly, voice aimed toward Dekkar.

He gave her a cold look and shook his head. "Not without revealing where I am, no."

"But all these people are dying."

He simply blinked at her, impassive. "Yes, they are. By the hands of their own allies in a war they helped to start."

She ground her teeth and glared at the grassy riverbank, the deep shade and gloom of Greenwood closing around them.

After a moment, he spoke quietly in her ear. "If I'm to do any good here, including for you and your brother, I must be circumspect about how much I display of myself. I could stop this attack now and very quickly find myself and us attacked in turn all the way to our final destination. That would greatly lessen the possibility of finding Binam. Is that what you want?"

Flushed, jaw locked, she shook her head fiercely.

"Then leave me to decide what my business is, if you please." His even tone infuriated her all the more because he was correct, as far as she could see. He found a reason to go to Figg, the bodyguard spider skittering to the side as Dekkar leaned down to look at the wounds on Figg's face; she stood at the plates of glass staring at the deep dark of the river.

Boat traffic had been halted just up-current; a group of patrol boats crewed by armed syms sliced up and down the center of the river. Pel quietly pulled to the riverbank, cut the boat's impeller, and they waited beside a tourist boat where a young woman with a short skirt and a young man in shorts were serving beer to a few frightened guests. "I want to a put on a bit of clothes," the young man was saying, "if there's to be shooting and such."

The patrol boats were directing the rest of the traffic to moor along the riverbank in order to keep the center of the channel clear, the traffic a mix of tourist barges, cargo scows, couriers, and private dinghies and dories; a couple of the symbiont patrol boats started searching the craft one at a time as they tied up along the bank on either side. The searches set off confusion among the crews and the passengers, who could see the plume of dark smoke rising from the direction of Dembut. On the *Erra Bel*, Pel's boat, everyone was watching and whispering to one another, even though Dekkar had never asked them to keep quiet. Once a patrol boat drifted close to the *Erra Bel* and passed farther downstream; the syms looked past the boat and the passengers without appearing to notice them at all, an eerie sensation. Kitra kept an eye on Dekkar as well; never a sign from him, never a sound or a movement.

"You think they're looking for Keely?" Figg asked at one point, when the boy, still unnaturally quiet, appeared to be sleeping. Penelope curled up beside him, keeping watch.

"Yes, I expect so." Dekkar was looking at the back of the riverboat, the motionless bundle that was Nerva. "At any rate, we can't sit here forever."

"You think they'll find us?"

"Not for a while."

He headed to the front of the boat and stood with Pel. They conferred in voices too low to hear; the boat began to ease along the bank, a speed just above drifting. Kitra moved to the other side of the boat, near Keely, who was lying on one of the low bunks with his eyes closed, hands tucked under his chin. He was small for his age but appeared far older than when she first met him, maybe in the set of his mouth, the furrow of his brows in sleep, or maybe the careless way his feet hung off the bunk. In the confusion of leaving Figg's farm, she'd heard someone mention that Keely had been under psycho-regression, but apparently no longer.

She sat carefully, and Figg sat near her, close enough to keep his eye on Keely. The Hilda squatted on the floor unpacking the smart cart, movements neat and measured. The *Erra Bel* was drifting farther from the center of the current, barely making headway, gliding just beyond the moored boats near the shore.

Tense moments passed, the acrid smell of smoke drifting with the wind, mingling with the dank smell of the river. The Hilda was making food in the galley, same neat motions, perfect economy. Figg watched her and then watched Dekkar at the prow of the boat. "Unfathomable. No one sees us, no matter how close they come."

"Prin mind tricks," Kitra said. "They're always impressive the first time you see them."

"It's a bit eerie, really." He watched Dekkar soberly. "All these years I thought he was out of the priesthood."

"What?"

"Dekkar. I've known him for a long time. I thought he was a fallen Drune. I thought they lost their abilities with the chant when they fell." He looked as if he wanted to say more, then closed his mouth.

If Dekkar's senses were as acute as most people with his kind of training, he was listening to every word. Kitra studied the erect posture of his back, the easy way he compensated for the bobbling of the boat on the chop thrown up in mid river by all the traffic, knees bent, adjusting his weight in small, precise ways. The *Erra Bel* was heading to the center of the river now, getting clear of the crowded riverbanks. "As long as he keeps the patrol boats from stopping us, whatever he's doing is fine with me."

Figg gestured to one of the patrols. "What are those things on the boats? They don't quite look like people."

"The tree syms? Symbionts. You've heard of them, I'm sure."

"They talk to the trees," Keely said, eyes open, sitting up to look out the windows. "Where are they?"

"Over there," Figg pointed. "Keep quiet, now, son. You see where I'm pointing?"

"He looks green."

"Yes, he does."

"You think it's a he?" Kitra asked. "I'd have said she."

"Does it matter?" Figg wanted to know.

She shrugged. "Only in vestigial ways. You can usually tell what sex a sym used to be, but they're not sexually functional anymore, one way or the other. I used to help transform people into these things."

"Symbionts?"

"Yes. I used to help regrow them and blend the plant organics with the human stuff." On the patrol boat Keely was watching, the pale figure of the symbiont was silhouetted against the dark hull, looking more or less human, though its joints appeared a bit stiff and its movements a touch languid; tree symbionts were in fact legally human, one of several hundred legal variants from the normative range of human DNA.

"You're a geneticist?"

"No, a technician."

"But still," Figg spread his hands. "What are you doing out here?"

"I gave up the tech work. I don't even know why I chose that field to begin with. Maybe because of my brother."

He was watching her. His face was no longer swollen; the wounds were still distinct but appeared to be less inflamed. Neither was his expression any longer impassive or patrician, qualities she had found in his manner and attitude when she first became aware of who he was. Because she had been born on Aramen, she had less presupposition about how an Orminy prince might behave or exactly the kind of status he might possess, but she had seen enough movies, read enough novels, to have an idea. Figg appeared not so much humble as humbled, as if he had undergone a cataclysm. His eyes had a gentled look, a peace that had cost him. He lay his hand in Keely's sandy hair, touched the boy with affection that appeared real.

The boat was moving more swiftly upriver as the boat traffic thinned. Dembut was visible still, a glow at the bottom of a plume of smoke that reached dark and heavy to near the center of the sky. As the *Erra Bel* drew farther upriver, the forest canopy thickened and the sky was harder to see. The acrid smell lessened; one caught scent of the perfumed auras of the Dirijhi gardens along the banks.

"We'll lose what's left of our links pretty soon," Kitra said. "No matter what kind you have."

"The forest?"

"Yes. We're entering the Dirijhi preserve. From here north, we're under the jurisdiction of the trees. There's no Surround in here."

"There's not much more than local stuff on my link anyway, since the gate closed. You've traveled here a good deal?"

"I grew up near here. I've traveled into Greenwood four times now. That doesn't make me a river pilot, but it's more trips than most northerners make, unless they work on the river system."

"Kitra's brother is a tree symbiont," Figg said, trying to draw Keely back into the conversation.

The change in the young boy was remarkable; the quality of childishness vanished, and he appeared somber, hardly even boyish, so grave was his manner. "Does that mean he can talk to the trees?"

"Yes." Talk about Binam made her anxious in the pit of her stomach, especially now that she was so close. "He can talk to one tree. His tree."

"Does he like it? Does he like living here?"

The question drew her to watch the trees again, the arch of low branches along the shore, for any glimpse she might catch of a tree-servant at work in the gardens. "I haven't heard from him in a long time. The last time I saw him, he wasn't very happy here, no."

"Why not?"

"Symbionts aren't really free the way you and I are, Keely. Each one of them is biologically tied to its tree. They have to be fed by their own tree or they die."

The thought made him big-eyed, younger again for a moment. "I still think it would be okay," he said after a while, but he no longer sounded convinced.

Erra Bel turned her nose toward the north and rode smoothly against the current. The Silas was hardly a gentle river, flowing swiftly at the moment, so broad at points that the canopy from the riverbanks no longer joined over the center. Through the glass roof of the riverboat Kitra saw darkening sky, low clouds, the red moon becoming more and more visible as the day waned. The sudden sky brought a feeling of vastness to the journey; she wished the boat might sail free of the canopy all the way north.

For a while she was lulled by the feeling of the current pressing along the riverboat's hull, the silken feeling of motion; Pel's boat, for all its shabby affect, rode the water like a dream. Peaceful to think of herself heading upriver again. But the channel narrowed, the forest closed in, and the river traffic settled into a normal pattern. They had come some dozen or so kilomeasures into the forest; did anyone sailing this far north on the river know that Dembut had been attacked?

She stirred, headed to the smart-cart, saw that it was unloaded and found the biosuits laid out on the galley table. The Hilda caught Kitra's purpose and moved to help her; she gave the machine suits to carry to everyone. She had even brought a suit for the thing that had once been Nerva, who (or which) lay along the wall on one of the built-in cots. Now she realized what a pointless move it had been.

Zhengzhou, the bodyguard, was keeping an eye on the creature; she acknowledged Kitra's nearness with a short lift of the chin. Another butch girl, Kitra thought; a type she knew pretty well. Zhengzhou had elaborate face art along one side of her jawbone and sported several piercings, ear and lip. The hardware might be part of her weapon systems; she was Figg's bodyguard, after all, and could likely afford expensive gear. Like a lot of younger people, she sported a scar on her face as a kind of decoration. She knelt beside the gray-skinned thing on the floor, its mouth expanding as it—she?—breathed.

Kitra handed Zhengzhou a suit, showed her how to wear it, and helped adjust the shoulders, elbows, and wrists. The woman stripped down to her underwear with no ceremony; she had a nice, firm body, but for some reason Kitra founded herself disinterested, regarding Zhengzhou with clinical detachment. "You can keep on your underwear," Kitra said. "Just don't layer too much under there or you'll be hot this time of year."

"This thing have face protection?"

"Yes, pass-through netting, tucked behind the head in the pouch."

"You know what it's rated?"

"There's a smart tag on it somewhere, read out the specs for yourself."

Zhengzhou frowned, holding the flimsy fabric in her hand; she was looking at it skeptically. "You ever wear one of these into the forest here before? I saw what some of those bioweapons did in Jharvan—"

"These suits aren't military grade but they're close, if that's what you're asking. If you don't want to take your chance with one, you can swim back to Dembut, I guess."

The chill that settled over Zhengzhou's features pretty much ended the question of any attraction between them. "Just asking."

"They're rated for filtration down to some ridiculous level that nothing can get through. But this is Dirijhi country. I have no idea what the trees have come up with lately."

Zhengzhou's scowl relaxed a bit. "It's better than my civvies. Thanks. You did a lot of shopping fast, back in that market."

"I've been to Dembut before. It's familiar ground."

At the front of the boat, Pel was sliding into his suit, wide shoulders freckled across, firm and thick. Dekkar helped him adjust the joint fittings.

Figg had no trouble with his own suit; he sat distracted, as if paying attention to his internals. Kitra found herself watching him.

Outside an early twilight was falling, the smoky sky filling with clouds, the pale bright patch where the sun was setting tinged with red, barely visible through the trees. The *Erra Bel* showed her outboard running lights for evening, but inside dark settled over her passengers.

Keely had struggled into his suit but the fittings were baggy. He flapped his arms a couple of times and the suit made a swooping noise. Kitra carried one of the fitting kits to him; she was showing him how to use the straps when Figg leapt up in alarm and stood in the center of the boat. He gave Kitra a long look, full of terror. "Good lord."

"What's wrong?" she asked, heart pounding, and Pel turned from the bridge at the sudden movement.

"I was reviewing some newsbursts that were in my queue. Those cities we were in when we landed, the names—" He was agitated, running hands through his hair as if he was feeling for that spider-thing of his, which was tucked into a ball at Keely's feet.

"Feidreh and Avatrayn."

"They're gone." He looked at her. "They're destroyed."

"What do you mean?"

"The cities are gone. Satellites showed a series of small nuclear explosions." He had that momentary nearsighted quality familiar as the look of someone reading from internals. "Your satellites—I mean, the ones from Ajhevan."

She thought he was going to say rebel satellites; she bit her tongue. The thought was too big. There were nearly fifty million people along the coast and around the twin cities, including her parents; most of them would be refugees in the city by now. Her heart was pounding. "You're sure?"

"The burst is from a few minutes before the attack on Dembut; I queued them up to review them when I had time."

"What's wrong?" Keely asked, struggling with his one-pass hood.

Zhengzhou was standing over the Nerva-thing, looking at it.

Pel turned to the river, then back to Kitra for a moment.

Dekkar kept his back to the boat, said nothing. She had the strong feeling that he had already known.

"The Prin choir is dead or captured." Figg was stunned, still relaying information from the newsburst. "The Citadel is destroyed. There's not much standing in the city."

Vekant, she thought. The poor silly man.

Dekkar spoke very calmly, without turning. "The tower is still standing," he said. "There's a high place there. It'll be harder to take down than these creatures imagine."

"Is that supposed to make us hopeful?" Zhengzhou asked, and everyone turned to look at her.

Figg had moved to Keely to help him with the suit. He checked Keely's handwork carefully.

"No," Dekkar said. "Not hopeful. I don't know what, really."

"You people call this a war for freedom," Zhengzhou said, the bitterness on her face so tentative, so against her reserve, that it was all the more evident and painful. She was speaking to everyone on the boat as if they were all part of the rebellion, as if they were all northerners.

"I'm the only one here who's ever had anything to do with the PFA," Kitra said, watching Zhengzhou evenly. "The rest of these people don't have anything more to do with this war than you do."

"But you do," she said, scowling, lip trembling.

"Not really. I quit the group ten years ago. I work for the Prin. Or I did."

Her face was falling to pieces.

"My parents live in Feidreh," Kitra continued. "I expect they're dead."

Zhengzhou nodded, trying to get herself under control. She knelt beside the cot on which the inert Nerva-creature was lying. She kept her back to them all for a while, maybe in embarrassment at her inability to restrain herself.

"The thing that destroyed the Prin in the south is on the way here now," Dekkar said, his tone still maddeningly calm. "We're not going to get very far without a fight."

"Is it Rao?" Keely asked. He was sitting very erect and still, looking solemn, averting his eyes from the vicinity of the Nerva-thing. He kept Penelope in his arms, scratching her fur; the spider appeared happy there.

Dekkar shook his head after a minute. "No. It's his ally,

probably something like a priest or a servant. It's related to the trees, I think."

"Something like Great Irion, you said." Kitra watched him.

"Yes."

"Then what chance do we have?" she asked, almost to herself. She sat down on an empty cot, put her head in her hands. Her skull was pounding.

The boat was quiet. The deception of peaceful surroundings helped her breathing to ease, and the fact that no one else spoke was a relief. She found herself staring at the pack she had brought on board, her equipment for collecting sap from Binam's tree. She wanted to ask about him; she knew she would feel better if she did. But she was becoming more afraid at the same time. This trip was not like the others. She had only to look downriver at the glare of burning Dembut to remind herself of that. What if there was never any way to find Binam, what if the war had uprooted him, too?

She could just hear the whine of the impeller, the sliding-slapping sound of the river.

"You might as well get some rest while you can," Dekkar said, after a while. "There's some time. She can't fly here herself, a flitter has to bring her."

Instead of sleeping, though, Kitra lay with her eyes open and watched the others settle into resting posture. Keely drifted to sleep quickly, and Figg slept on the floor beside him. His trousers were covered with dust at the back and his overshirt had creases running along the length of it, caked with mud from some accident during the day. The sores on his face were throbbing-big. Kitra found herself watching his shadow in the dim interior, feeling a fondness for him that was unfamiliar, a bit disarming. He snored lightly and Keely's breath was deep and even, untroubled.

Later she would realize that, when she spied on Dekkar during what followed, she did so because he permitted it. At the time she had no real inkling of who or what he was, except in the vaguest terms, but later it was clear that he could have caused her to sleep, as he possibly did the others. For everyone else very quickly dropped off, but in her case, it was as if she were stilled but conscious. She had no sense that he was holding her, only that she could not move. Perhaps because he had engaged himself to her, or wanted to reassure her, he allowed her to see the bundle he drew out of the boat chest, untying it near the pilot's wheel where Pel was standing.

"Do you have to do that now?" Pel asked, and his tone was familiar, as if he had known Dekkar for a long time.

"Why?"

"I thought we could talk a bit." Pel turned to look at him. "They're all dead to the world, right?"

"Yes." He answered after a bit of hesitation.

Pel was giving Dekkar a wry grin, all the while checking the pilot wheel and the heading. "Did you know I had come back before you saw me?"

Dekkar was standing over the bundle, no longer moving. "No. But that doesn't mean Irion didn't. I'm only a copy of him, you know."

"But you knew me when you saw me."

"Yes."

They were looking at each other. Pel said, "You don't seem surprised. I'm back from the dead."

"I don't know what to say, to tell the truth."

"Well, you might ask me something like, 'Pel, how did you come to cross the mountains again?'"

"All right. But I'm not him, you see, I'm a copy."

"Pretend."

"Pel, how does it happen that you crossed the mountains again?"

"She sent me back."

"She?"

Pel scowled, stepping close to Dekkar. "Don't pretend you don't know who. She's very real, you know. She's watching your every move."

Dekkar stood there.

"Aren't you going to ask me about Kirith Kirin?"

"I told you, I'm not Great Irion. I'm a copy. He doesn't copy that part of himself."

"But aren't you curious?"

Something pained revealed itself in Dekkar's stance, something indescribably lonely in the pinched set of his shoulders. Kitra breathed carefully and felt herself still unable to move, though likely it didn't matter. This was a quiet of Dekkar's doing, too.

"Yes, I am," Dekkar said.

"He's there, across the mountains."

"Doing what?"

Pel shrugged. "It doesn't matter. You could say, waiting. You could say, not. You could say, being dead." He shrugged. "It's hard to explain until you've been there."

Dekkar nodded. "So she brought you back here for what?"

"To get killed again, I don't doubt. Otherwise I don't know. Haven't a clue."

Dekkar laughed, nodded.

"You're not him, you said. Just a copy." Pel was speaking quite low.

"That's right."

"You're a friendly one."

They were very quiet then, standing close. When they separated, they came apart slowly, as if they had touched each other in some way. The room was full of the charge; it made Kitra ache.

"That's enough," Pel said.

Dekkar looked, suddenly, much younger, though only for a moment; pale and dark-haired, taller by a hand. The illusion faded then, and he was himself.

He knelt by the bundle, which glittered when he opened it.

Onto each finger he slipped a ring. He stacked several bracelets on his wrists. Into his earlobes he fastened earrings.

He was beginning to sing, a song so harsh and cold it pierced Kitra through. Her heart was pounding. She was hearing because he wished it. Why?

He stood and turned his palms up and the gems made a sphere around him, and then they began to shine and to move, slowly, orbiting in shells.

Pel had pulled the boat ashore and moored it next to a thick tree root.

"As soon as I'm aground, pull up under the bank, there

ahead where you see the overhang." Dekkar pointed out the pilot's window.

"You don't have to tell me my business, I was keeping clear of your like before you were ever a dream."

Dekkar glided through the hull as if either he or it were not altogether there, calling back, "Our friend the mantis will be in the river to keep the debris off your boat."

"Your friend? That thing from the farm."

"Yes. It's a long story. Don't be alarmed when you see it."

Sick with fear, finally able to move, Kitra hauled her mattress near Figg, then lay next to him, and he embraced her as if he knew what she wanted, even though he was fast asleep.

When she was a child, she had dreamed that she was Kraytl and her brother Binam Hanzl and they were lost in the woods where a witch wanted to eat them. Now she felt that same fear coming from the trees all around her, as if everything ashore wanted to eat her, and as protection against that Figg was warm and welcomed her. Beside him she lay through all that followed; the sphere of light that was Dekkar rising through the trees as the *Erra Bel* took shelter under an outjutting of the riverbank. From near the boat came the shriek of the mantis, and her skin went to bumps. She envied Figg his deep unconsciousness; even when she tried to wake him there was no way to do it. So she settled against him and lay her head against his back. Let me sleep, too, she prayed, and soon enough, she did.

Embers Floating into Dark

1. Keely

A t first it was as if he were dreaming fireworks after a circus, like at the first birthday party Uncle Figg gave for him, when he was acting like he was a little kid because he was under regression. Now that he had all his memories again, he remembered the state of age-regression as being something not-quite-him and not-quite-not. Tonight he felt the rocking of the boat, the lullaby that made him sleepy echoing in his head, and behind that sound the numbers, the constant stream of what he had learned from the math box, which more and more preoccupied him.

For a while he did sleep and dreamed of the sphere again, the machine that unfolded, membranes sliding out of it like long tapes, tentacles circling his neck, wires shoved deep into his skin, and then the thing filled the inside of him, the voice, his father. The voice sputtered but could not speak. The machine, frustrated, kept trying for a long time, while Keely drowsed.

Lights, a light show, wanted to wake him, wanted to draw

him out of sleep. He too wanted to waken, felt that he should. Was it the numbers that were insisting so, edging him out of sleep, nullifying the lullaby? Or was it the desire to watch the priest alight in the trees, his spinning lights and then the storms he and the other singer threw at each other?

First Keely passed through the quiet night and distant thunder and then, all at once, a blaze like a thousand bombs in a million vids on the Surround, the boat full of light, and he was awake and sitting against the hull sweating, looking down at Uncle Figg. Uncle Figg and the lady who flew the flitter were lying side by side with their eyes closed, sheltered against one another; it was as if they knew they were there together but at the same time were somewhere else, were unconscious. Keely's senses felt more acute than he could remember, so that he could tell the difference between unconscious and asleep. Even Penelope was unconscious, nested near the top of Uncle Figg's head, legs curled under her.

Outside on the riverbank was confusion, at least on the bank that was visible; with the boat sheltered against one shore only the opposite could be seen. Where there had been trees and their orderly gardens was a nightmare of twisted trunks, fires collapsing branches to embers, crashes sending explosions of embers upward like showers of stars, as far as the eye could see. The boat was safe because the priest was making it safe, but nothing else in the landscape moved.

Outside in the river one of those mantises strode back and forth in the current, sweeping debris away from the *Erra Bel*.

Keely felt as if nothing else were moving except the mantis and him; then out of the corner of his eye he saw the boat pilot slouched against the railing outside. A narrow plank walkway ran around the edge of the riverboat, and the pilot was standing on it, just beside the hatch, illuminated by the fires from across the river and by the flashes of light from overhead. The shadow of a tall tree was visible slanting down over the river, light in blues and violets, in white light and red; a single tree still standing.

For the first time he heard the voice of Father while he was awake.

"They tell you lies about me," said Father. "I'm not attacking you or your friends."

This time he was able to control himself, unlike when he had been dreaming, and he said nothing, kept his eyes fixed on the windows.

"None of this would be necessary if they had given you over to my couriers in the first place. You could be with me now. You could be learning all that I want to teach you."

He fixed himself on the thought of Uncle Figg, his kindly face, the way he flushed purple when he had to yell at somebody, like when he yelled at the Herman back home in the apartment on Senal.

"I'm very old, Keely. Do you have any idea how old? If I were part of you, you would know everything that I know. There are so many things we could do."

Sherry hovered in front of him, or he pretended she did, dressed the way she'd been the last time he saw her, in the gown that looked so old and adult, and Sherry getting sick suddenly and falling to the floor and that was that, she was dead. The memory hurt but the hurt kept Keely focused on what he ought to be doing.

"No one around you can teach you the things that I can teach you. You have a rare gift, Keely. You're called to this. It's what you're meant to do."

Keely shook his head, refusing to answer.

When he crept away from the wall it was over; a silence fell where the voice had been and he knew Father was gone. He felt only dizzy, the numbers in his head like a roaring, louder than the thunder or the wind. He stepped over Kitra and Uncle Figg, both motionless; he chanced a look at the thing that had been Nerva tied up on its bunk; Uncle Figg's bodyguard asleep on the bunk across from it, curiously still. Pel must have heard Keely because he stuck his head in the door, smiled, and nodded. "You're awake."

"Yes, sir."

He looked a bit surprised. "Can't sleep?"

"No, sir. Can I stand out there with you?"

The pilot made a gruff sound. "Stay close to the hatch," he said. "Mind, the boat rocks a bit when a chunk of tree falls too close."

Across the riverbank the last remnant of a tree went crashing over, this one falling away from the river into blazing underbrush. Heavy smoke blotted out the sky. Light flashed on the undersides of smoky billows, what looked like distant clouds. The canopy that had covered the river from both sides had vanished, as had the visible forest.

"What happened?"

"The wizards are fighting," Pel said. "Same old story."

"Wizards?"

"Yes. You know that's what Dekkar is."

"He's a priest. He works for the church."

The pilot had a nice smile, steady and safe; Keely felt better standing in the open air next to him, no matter how eerie the lights or how sudden the sounds. "You can think of him as a priest, I guess."

"Do you know him?"

"Yes. For quite a long time."

"Who are you?"

"Pel. This is my boat."

Keely understood that part, started to say so, then a flash of light and wind rushed over the river, rocking the boat, so that Keely hung onto the railing. "My stomach," he said, clutching it.

"You're smart to keep your hand on the bar, no need to try to prove anything."

"Are we tied up?"

"Yes. I lashed us tight to a tree root; we're okay as long as the tree holds. You can feel the impeller kicking in, too, holding us steady in the current."

Once he said so, Keely could feel the boat doing its work to keep itself in place against the river's motion. They were sheltered, close to the shore, and the mantis was still moving in the river clearing the debris; he kept reminding himself because it comforted him. "Did you see the bombs?" Keely asked.

"Bombs? You mean the fire."

"Weren't there bombs?"

"Not exactly." Pel shook his head. "Wizards, you see. It's what they do, make fire where there's none. The fellow you call Dekkar is from very old stock."

Dekkar was the priest's name. It kept slipping from Keely's mind, but this time he tried to remember. A cascade of lights washed over the river; along the distant horizon were other lights, dim. "Where is he?"

"Up in the tree."

"Who is he fighting?"

Pel nodded to the lights on the horizon. "That fellow way off there. Or, most likely, that woman way off there."

"It's a woman?"

"I expect so, yes."

"How do you know?"

Pel shrugged. He spit something over the side of the boat; he was chewing a sliver of wood idly, tattering the end in his mouth, biting off bits and toying them on his lips, then spitting. "I'm old. I've been around a while."

"You don't look old."

"People don't always look as old as they are."

"My uncle Figg is three hundred three. Is that old like you?"

"No. Your uncle's a young squirt. All these people are young squirts, except you. You're not even old enough to be called a squirt."

Keely was smiling a bit. "I am, too."

"You can't be more than, what, twenty-five years old?"

Keely giggled. "I'm only eleven."

Pel snorted, scratching under his chin; he had dirt under his nails, and his fingers were blunt at the end. He reminded Keely of some of the pleasanter people who lived in the Reeks. "You're barely a sprout. I shouldn't even be talking to you."

Keely stared at the distant lights, rainbow colors along the undersides of clouds. "How old are you?"

"Too old. Never you mind about the number, you wouldn't believe it anyway. I'm so old I could have dated your great-great-great times twenty grandmother. Or grandfather, either one."

"Why are they so far away?"

"Who?"

"The wizards—why are they so far away from each other, if they're fighting?"

"That's how wizards fight. They don't come close to each other until they're nearly finished."

"How long?"

"Till they finish? I don't know. Sometimes they fight for years and years."

That was a sobering thought. Keely was always concerned that the Hilda would get tired and quit working; what if the priest got tired and quit fighting? "I don't think we have that much food," Keely said.

"Could be we don't," Pel agreed, stroking his chin again. His face was bristly; most men stopped their beards growing, so the sight kept drawing Keely back, the funny stubbly stuff on Pel's face. "Likely these ones won't fight for so long, though. It's the wizards in towers can stand up to you forever and a day."

"You must have been around a lot of wizard guys."

"And women, too. Don't forget the women, they don't like it. I've known more than my share, I think. Gods on top of it. When you start mucking about with gods, you're in for a deal of trouble in your life."

Keely felt the wind on his face, stronger, rocking the boat. "I don't think you're supposed to say stuff like that."

"About gods, you mean? Oh, no, let me tell you, they like it. A god likes it a lot when you spit right in his face. Or her face, as the case may be. Minding the women again, naturally."

Keely cocked his head doubtfully. The wind was gusting, throwing up whorls of sparks from the fires, fanning some of them brighter. Wind blew his hair in his eyes and he pulled it out and tucked the longer strands back of his ear.

"Weather blowing up," Pel remarked, smirking at the haze as if he could see through it to the real clouds. "And that's another thing you can look for when your average— let's call them true-language priests for the sake of cor- rectness, I suppose—start to have a knock-down-drag-out. Storms heaving hither, thither, and yon. Wind blowing like Emmen-go-home."

Keely giggled. "What's Emmen-go-home?"

Pel shrugged, grinning at him. "Just a saying, back where I come from. Once upon a time it was the name of a storm that happened in the late summer."

"Where?"

"You ask a lot of questions."

He felt abashed for a moment, till Pel chucked him on the shoulder.

"No harm in questions, boy. You'll never amount to much if you don't ask. But you know, in my case, the ques- tion of where I come from is just too deep to answer."

"Too deep?"

"Too many ways to think about it. Let's look at the storm instead."

Distant rumbles might be thunder or might be something else. At times Keely felt as if he could feel the distant one, the voice of the enemy singer in the flitter; he could hear the echo of the sound of the river of numbers, of values, of the math box. A break in the smoky mess showed the undersides of low clouds and a bright patch of light overhead, the place at the top of the lone tree where Dekkar was doing his priest-work.

"How come the fire stuff never falls on us?"

"Dekkar won't let it," said Pel. "He's a cunning devil, that one. These lot will be sorry to have tangled with him, these trees."

By now Keely had an inkling that Pel's jovial tone was meant to be reassuring, but Keely felt better while talking, regardless, and he hardly minded having company, since he could not sleep. Again he wondered that the others could in all this noise and confusion.

The ache in his head was less, but still behind the rest of his thinking ran that stream of music, that place where his brain was putting together what he had learned from the math box. For instance, as time passed he came to have a clear feeling for where Dekkar was, too; not so much an image of him atop the standing tree as a feeling for his relative location. There were currents of sound flowing from Dekkar but these sounds were nothing at all like the numbers in Keely's head; still, there was some connection. These were feelings inside Keely, not thoughts; he was aware of some disturbance in himself but could not have articulated it. Nor was he concerned about it; his mind was taken up with the fire, the lights in the distance, the dull pain in his skull.

Rain began to fall, and the strong wind sent it straight along the river against the current for a while. The overhanging bank protected them at first, but as the wind changed Pel was doused in the face, since he was tall. He shook his head and guided Keely inside the boat, closing the hatch.

When they turned from the hatch, Dekkar was behind them, smelling of wind. Water dripped off the cloak he was wearing. He had a palm full of colored stones that he was pouring into an embroidered pouch. He studied Keely in the dark. "You didn't sleep?"

"For a while I did, but I woke up." He was thinking that Dekkar looked more like a priest than anything else, no matter what Pel said. Beyond, through the portals, the big bug monster was still sweeping the river.

Pel shook out his rain cloak. "We had a nice chat on top until the rain started."

Dekkar considered Keely another moment or so, saying to Pel, "We should head upriver, as fast as this boat will go."

"You're finished here?"

"My opponent is reconsidering her options, since I made it clear I'd destroy this forest down to the last tree in it if she continued attacking me."

They were making no attempt to hide the conversation from Keely. The back of his neck prickled.

Pel was steering the boat clear of the bank, picking his way into the center of the current through the clog of debris. The mantis vanished beneath the current and Keely wondered whether it would follow. Pel asked, "The trees matter to it?"

"To her. Yes, they do. I'm pretty sure she's one of them." From his cloak he drew out something familiar, the math box, the thing Nerva had used on Keely night after night, the sound of which the boy still heard in his head. Dekkar held it for Keely to see. "This was very helpful."

Keely nodded, not quite understanding. He wasn't sure how he felt that Dekkar held it.

"Do you want it back?" Dekkar asked, kneeling in front of him. "I took the box from Nerva but it may be you want it for yourself."

Keely looked at the flat box, dull in the dim light. "No. You can have it."

"She used it to hurt you, I think."

After a while he nodded his head. He refused to look up from the deck, where Uncle Figg and Kitra were still lying side by side, breathing deeply.

"It doesn't have to hurt, Keely. It's just a teaching box. If you want to put it on again, I can see to it that it doesn't cause pain."

He looked up at Dekkar, confused. "You're going to make me use it, too?"

"No. But you may find you need it. You've learned a language from it. Not really words the way we think of words— a language made of numbers. You've learned a kind of math that Nerva also knew how to use. She was using it on you to control you. That was the part that hurt. But you may find that you need more information from the box in order to understand what's inside your head now. I can't make that go away."

The river of numbers in his head, that had been so present before, chose this moment to diminish to a trickle, hardly a concern. But he understood what Dekkar was talking about, and he nodded his head.

"Thank you," Dekkar said, but Keely wasn't sure for what. He stood. "Anyway, it was a help to have this while I was up in the tree dealing with our pursuers."

"More than one?" Pel asked.

"Oh, indeed," Dekkar said. "Heading up from the south and down from the north. Whole armies." He chuckled quietly.

"Careful."

"What, you're worried about Keely? I don't think I'm frightening Keely, am I, son?"

Keely shook his head. He felt himself smiling, he didn't know why. Overhead, rain drummed heavy and hard on the roof of the boat; outside the world had gone to a wash of gray rain, flashes of light occasionally illuminating the shores of the river.

"Are the trees dead now?" Keely asked.

"These ones burned up on the riverbank are dead for sure," Pel said.

Dekkar was watching the river ahead, torrents of water over the glass.

"The syms are dead, too, then," Keely said.

"It's not a very nice thing, is it?" Dekkar asked, then answered himself, his voice softer, more tired-sounding. "No, it's not."

After that Keely sat on the bed, kept his back to Dekkar, watching the lights along the southern horizon, dimly visible behind the curtains of water.

Uncle Figg and Kitra woke up at the same time, Kitra rolling away from Uncle Figg's back, standing, shaking out her hair. Uncle Figg sat up and watched her. Uncle Figg's face was swollen again, the sores from the monster-teeth inflamed. He touched them as if they were tender, looking at Keely. "You're awake."

"Yes, sir."

Penelope clambered to the window ledge, balanced there looking out. At the back of the boat, Zhengzhou was stretching.

"My God, what happened along the shore?" Kitra asked, leaning into the glass.

"We've had a bit of a struggle while you rested." Dekkar glanced at Keely with a glimmer of a smile, and Keely bowed his head, feeling warm and pleased inside. "We're glad it didn't disturb you."

"The place looks flattened."

Dekkar was staring at the bank; if he heard, he decided not to respond.

Keely touched the math box, which lay heavy on the bunk, partly covered in a fold of bedroll. "The trees are dead."

"Apparently."

He put the headpiece over his skull, turned on the box. In the math-space in his head he was watching functions change, curves propagate, space form, knots untie. At other times, though, the streams of equations repeated in less regular ways, and he had understood for a while that some of these number sequences served a function like words, the numbers carrying values that were more like meanings. He was listening for this, and when he heard the sound, when he understood what was being said, the feeling of tension in his body built. This was the language called Erlot, the words Nerva had spoken that had forced Keely to do this and that. When he heard Erlot, he had a hard time separating the language from Nerva's voice using it. His stomach fluttered, and as soon as he could he took off the headset, put the box down again.

Dekkar was watching.

Penelope climbed into his lap and he petted her fur till she settled down, content as a cat. She put out a vibration that he found comforting.

Now he could feel some of what Dekkar was doing; Dekkar himself, even while standing here in apparent quiet, was speaking a language of his own. The river of Erlot in Keely made it easy to fathom part of what was happening near Dekkar; near him not in any visible way. Shades moved, silhouettes twisted, ghost images flickered, lights danced, and, on occasion, the flash of pin-lights, bright and variously colored, moved fast in a sphere around him; but none of this was happening in the world of Keely's eyes. There was another world behind his vision, and while he was sitting still he could feel the presence of Dekkar in that world, distinct as a lighthouse in a crashing sea.

Pressing them from behind was another presence, very strong, overwhelming. Erlot words, not a song but a ribbon of musical values, odd sour harmonies, a feeling like fingers along Keely's spine.

For a moment Keely could feel all of them: Dekkar, the other singer, and himself, all locked in the same drama, the riverboat in a sphere of glass riding against the current of the river and a hand pressing down, behind wind and rain, driving the sphere and the boat forward. The pressing of the hand made Keely's head ring with pain. He tried to stifle the echo of Erlot, and it was in fact already fading; the feeling that he could see the hand, hear the speaker, sense another aspect of Dekkar, ebbed away. Rain beat down on the boat, wind rocked it, but nothing from the sky touched them and they sailed steadily upriver unopposed.

For a long stretch of the journey the land was flattened, and for a while after the trees were increasingly intact but blown out of the ground all in the same direction. The rains doused the fires and left charred bodies of trees at a tilt— somehow disquieting, when he remembered that each of them was living and conscious as he was. When they were ripped out of the ground like that, were they still alive, at least for a while? Were they suffering? The *Erra Bel* passed a lot of boats with the tree-people on board; the cluster of boats massed at the point where trees reappeared, beyond the smoldering line of fires doused in rain.

After they were upriver from the fires, Zhengzhou gestured to the glass canopy and said to Uncle Figg, "Some of those boats are following us."

"They see us now," Dekkar said. "I'm not hiding us anymore."

Keely reached for the math box, held it against him.

Into darkness the riverboat sailed. A few tense minutes passed, and Zhengzhou announced, "They're not gaining on us, they're hanging back."

Uncle Figg walked toward her and then stepped back

suddenly, not from Zhengzhou but from the bench where the Nerva-thing was confined.

It sat up in a quick move like a snap, the Nerva-thing, ropes fallen off it as if they'd collapsed through its body, and Keely's heart pounded and he leapt out of the bunk. Penelope was reared up on the blanket where he had been sitting as if she meant to protect him. He ran to Dekkar as fast as he could and hid behind Dekkar's boots; Keely's legs were crossed and he was afraid he would wet himself, but he had the math box in his lap. Dekkar touched a hand to his head.

The thing was like Nerva again, with Nerva's face and not the face of the needle-mouth, but she had changed, as if pieces of her face were missing, as if she had been wounded. The teeth were shorter but still hideous. Her skin was colored a clammy gray that looked wet, and under the skin pulsed a wave of dark color, a thin line, that passed through her top to bottom. She tasted like the math box, the quality of her, across the boat, and Keely wanted to look away but was afraid to take his eyes off her, especially when Dekkar started to move.

The Nerva-thing stretched its mouth and made a shrill sound. Its eyes flushed red as if shot through with blood. It spoke in words everybody on the boat could understand. "If you're coming upriver to find me, it may amuse you to know I'm already here with you on the boat."

"Great Rao," Dekkar said, bowing his head.

"You know me by name."

"Yes, I know your name. Not much more than that, really."

"Humble."

"Practical."

Nerva's face shuddered, fluttered in the most sickening way. The thing fanned that mouth again, its breath wet, the body not altogether under control; it was struggling. After a spell of this, unable to move from the bunk, it drew itself upright and still. "You have not told me your name."

"Dekkar up Ortaen."

"False. That is not who you are."

"That is my name."

"But not who you are. I know who you are, what you are."

"Do you?"

"Yes. Release me and I will show you what I know."

"Better I should hold you." He had drawn near to the end of the bunk and stood there; she, the Nerva-thing, sat facing him on the bunk, wounds oozing on her face and arms, her eyes the color of burning embers.

She struggled suddenly, looking more like Nerva than before, that wave-pulse still passing through her, the occasional shadow or burst of shadows fluttering like bird wings out of her, then subsiding. Dekkar stepped back and the Nerva-thing hissed.

Keely pressed the math box against his ribs, remembered what Dekkar had said, that the box had helped before. He would have to walk very close to the Nerva-thing in order to give it to Dekkar.

"If you can hold me, you mean," said the Nerva-thing. "But why should we struggle when we could speak? May we not treat as friends? You are a creature of many talents."

"What you are is an open question."

"Not a question for the likes of you, you mean. Humble soul that you are."

Dekkar made some sign, some gesture. His hands were moving too fast to see. But it was a threat; Keely felt the impulse in the part of himself where the Erlot he had learned was beginning to stir.

The Nerva-thing spoke without any hint of concern. "I could make a creature like you feel so greatly appreciated."

"I seek only to feel serene," Dekkar answered.

"Practical."

"I like to think so."

"Perhaps it would be best for me to break these bonds, then, and eat you all."

The creature lunged, not with any movement of the body but in some level that made the fabric of the riverboat interior ripple, as if the world were simply a broadcast being adjusted, or, in this case, contested. Keely took a deep breath and walked across the cabin, planting his feet firmly, pressing the math box into Dekkar's hand.

Dekkar looked down at Keely and blinked.

The next instant so much happened that only later could Keely sort it out. The math box was so welcome to Dekkar that it unsettled him, Keely could feel it. The intensity of the math-music pouring through Keely himself had grown so strong his head was pounding. Dekkar faltered and the creature lunged, physically moved off of the bunk for the first time, grabbed Keely by the shoulders. The Nerva-thing shrieked and Keely glimpsed that hideous mouth opening and unfolding, striking at him, covering his face. Strong hands held him in place when he kicked and struggled. Burning and blackness followed. The needle-teeth entered his eyes, and they burst and drained wetness down his face. Convulsions wracked his body and he felt himself struggling but still the arms held him firmly and the teeth raked him. A burning like acid poured over his skin.

He heard the Nerva thing scream, an awful sound full of a terror Keely had not heard since he left the Reeks. Commotion followed around him; he had an instant of panicked breathlessness and then blacked out completely.

2. Fineas Figg

The child a dead weight in his arms, Figg sat on the floor, numb, Kitra behind him.

The thing was on the bunk again, fastened there, Dekkar standing over it, Penelope prowling the length of it, now and then rearing up as if she wanted to fight it again. The thing was palpitating more than breathing, no longer resembling Nerva so much as a kind of soup in which pieces of Nerva's face and torso were floating. Whatever Dekkar had done to it had hurt it and stunned it, though the voice, when it returned, was as placid as before.

"You may hurt this corpus as much as pleases you," the Nerva-thing said. "What happens to it does not reach me to the slightest degree."

"You should kill it," Kitra said, "before it attacks one of us again."

Dekkar was standing over the creature, which began to smile. "He can't," it said. "He tried."

Quiet on the boat, and Figg felt a hollow in his stomach, fear settling there.

Kitra knelt behind Figg, starting to whimper. The Nerva-thing partly opened its mouth again, expanding those teeth, hissing.

Dekkar stepped toward it and that look of vagueness, of parts floating in relation to one another, happened again, and the thing squealed—a smaller, weaker sound this time. Dekkar looked strained, though, his body somehow more physical than before, more present. They were fighting each other, clearly.

"Starting from this moment you are dying and dead," said the voice, matter-of-fact. "You are abandoned."

"So you hope," Dekkar said, his voice strained.

"Your master has closed his gate. He is afraid of me."

"To confine you," Dekkar said, making an effort even with so few words, but he was shaking his head, and the Nerva-thing was coming to pieces, the dark wings appearing and now and then one of the flock careening out, fluttering, shattering, dissolving.

"Your master will never reach you. The farther north you come, the stronger you'll find me."

"You need a body," Dekkar hissed; he was flushed, veins standing out.

"I have one," Rao said, and the body of the Nerva-thing collapsed, dissolved into wraiths of smoke, as if the hand that had held it released it and no longer protected it.

Dekkar, for once, was making sound, singing, a sound so

eerie Figg wished it would stop, and he covered his ears with his hands, looking down at the bloody mess of Keely's face.

But the thing was gone now and they were all right. Silence, quiet, overtook the *Erra Bel*. Pel set the boat heading along the center of the current again, as far from both shores as possible. Penelope clambered onto Figg's head, set her legs into the sockets there and flattened against his skull. Zhengzhou stirred from her hiding place, behind a counter in the galley near the stern. Kitra stood behind Figg, a hand on one shoulder, then faced Dekkar, her arms folded.

"You should never have brought her if you couldn't control her."

He gave her a look so dark she stepped back. He knelt, peering into Keely's ruined face, the glistening of the liquid from inside the boy's eyes still draining onto his acid-burned cheeks. His lower lip and chin had been spared; the rest of his face was a charred burn. The smell was nauseating. Dekkar studied it, closed his eyes, drew in a long breath, and the familiar look of serenity settled over him. None of the eerie singing from moments ago reached Figg's hearing; Dekkar took on the quiet, removed look that had been his only mark when doing his work, using his true language, or whatever he called it. Keely murmured, and a wave passed through his face.

"Is he in pain?" Figg asked, looking at the pitted skin.

"No. He has some kind of control of it."

"What did that thing do?"

"Injected something into him. Not just acid, something else."

Figg's own sores were swollen again, painful to the touch. "The same thing the other one did to me?"

"No. Different viruses from the ones they put into you. The viruses you got were to kill you. The ones in Keely are carriers. They're delivering some kind of cargo. And the acid is deliberate; she wanted to maim him and blind him."

Kitra crossed her arms and paced to the pilot's wheel, standing behind the pilot, shaking her head. Her terror was plain; Figg could feel it. He had become, without warning, sensitive to everything Kitra was feeling, ever since he woke to find her lying next to him, frightened, taking comfort from his warmth—certainly not from his courage, since he was as shaken as she.

"They're preparing Keely to meet the God."

"What God?" Zhengzhou asked, timid, emerging from the back of the boat, crawling over the folded form of the Hilda, which had deactivated itself.

"Rao. The thing that's here. The thing that was speaking through the creature's mouth."

"You call him a god?" Zhengzhou tittered nervously, glancing out the window at the rain and the river, running fingers through her hair.

"They call themselves gods. I don't know what to call them." Dekkar knelt again, touched Keely's face; the boy sighed in his rest, turned toward Figg, breathed into his middle. Figg felt warm all through, anchored to the real world by the fact of Keely, the weight of Keely's head. Some of Figg's fear left him.

Pel announced, from the pilot's console, "There are boats blocking the river ahead of us."

"They'll let us pass," Dekkar said.

Sure enough, after a moment, Pel said, "You're right. They're parting to make a lane."

"She doesn't want me to kill any more trees than necessary," Dekkar said. "She knows it will be easy enough to finish me when I'm farther north, closer to Rao."

"Is that true?" Kitra asked.

He stood motionless in the center of the boat, still in the same spot as when he made the Nerva-thing dissolve and vanish. Now he appeared more shrunken, maybe even a bit stooped. "Yes. It is."

"They'll kill you?"

"Most likely."

"What about us?"

"I don't know. Pel will try to take care of you, I suppose."

She glared at him, trembling. "That's it? That's all you have?"

He gazed at her somberly. "What do you expect?"

"Why are you going north if it's going to kill you, why aren't you talking about destroying this thing, Rao? I thought that's what you had in mind."

He shook his head. "No."

She was stupefied, and made something of a show of it. "Then what?"

"I'm here because it's where I was sent. I never expected to live through this. I don't know whether you will or not. Probably not. I brought you here because there was nowhere to leave you. There aren't any people alive on the southern continent, and pretty soon the northern population is going to be enslaved by these Dirijhi allies of theirs."

"Enslaved?"

"Breeding stock. For tree symbionts. And forced labor for the Shimmering Garden. That's what the trees call this place, you know. The Shimmering Garden."

Kitra looked irritated. "Yes, I know. I grew up here."

"Quite right, you did. I'd forgotten."

She blinked at him. Maybe she was remembering, as Figg was, the sudden attack on the river town. "You forget how long I've worked with the Prin. On your own you can't know anything of the kind."

He looked at her. Pel, behind her, was shaking his head.

"I know what I know," Dekkar said.

"You're no good to anybody unless you know how to get Great Irion himself to come here."

A light poured out of Dekkar, the wind picked up, the boat rocked, and suddenly he was difficult to see, covered with light, appearing to rise, in some fashion, through the glass of the ceiling, as if he were riding on the column of light that he had partly become. An instant later there were flashes of light, concussions, explosions on both shores, a firestorm of wind, fires raging in the broken trees flattened on either side of the river. The terrifying noise, the booming, went on and on, a moment so frozen and endless that Figg thought it would never be over. His heart pounded, the light of the explosions filling the cabin. Everyone inside instinctively ducked except Pel, who stayed at the helm and kept the boat headed upstream.

Figg backed against the wall, pulled Keely with him, huddled there. He tried not to watch the column of light that moved with the boat; something about it made him nauseous. At the stern Zhengzhou rose up on her knees to peer out the glass, her shadow framed in bright fire, in what might be more explosions. "The boats are scattered," she said. "They're not really following anymore."

"Merciful Am," Kitra said, and she crept beside Figg, sitting close to him.

"It's a wonder to watch the wise ones work," Pel said, voice booming. "There's no mistaking it. Dangerous business it is, too, to be as close as we are."

"What choice do we have?" Kitra asked.

"Damn little, you're right about that."

"He should never—" Her voice trembling, shaking. Figg pressed against her, and she fell silent.

"No use muttering and moaning," Pel said. "Because, you see, it's bad enough to be this close, but if we were any farther away, we'd like to be dead by now, sure."

A long time passed. The boat was moving quickly, no lights along the shore, no traffic to speak of, the southern sky lit with flickering orange and red, the northern sky dark and featureless. Under the canopy of trees, the light of Dekkar echoed on the undersides of branches, dimming. For a long time he was absent from the boat, silent, until suddenly he appeared on his hands and knees in a shadowy part of the cabin near the galley, breathing deeply and evenly.

He found his feet slowly, as if he was feeling pain. Zhengzhou tried to help him and he tolerated it a bit, looking around the interior of the cabin as if not entirely sure where he was.

He stepped toward Figg, at first uncertainly. It was Keely he was watching.

"Put him on the bunk," Dekkar said, glancing at Figg for a moment.

"Why?"

"I think I know something I can do for him. I need to try it now, while there's time."

"Do for him?"

"To help him when he wakes up," Dekkar said, lifting Keely out of Figg's lap.

When Figg stood, Kitra followed. The Hilda had also unfolded, and it obeyed Dekkar's instructions to bring water. The priest found his own pack and brought out a sack of leaves; he took one in his mouth and chewed it, put another to Keely's wrecked mouth. The pitted face moved a bit, the leaf sliding inside a little at a time. Penelope, who had been lying near Keely like a bodyguard, skittered anxiously around his head before drawing away.

Dekkar stood over the boy; sometimes it was difficult to see what he was doing; sometimes Figg heard a phrase of singing, a clear tenor voice that was overwhelming. Sometimes Dekkar gestured: precise, small, dancelike movements of the hands. His features blurred, as if he were behind a veil. Most of the time, though, he simply stood over Keely, his eyes closed. Keely breathed peacefully, mouth working as though he were chewing the leaf.

One by one Dekkar covered Keely's face with the leaves, pungent, a musky sharp scent, hard to put out of the mind. He wet the leaves and placed each one carefully. Each stayed in place and soon the whole mass started to dissolve, a deep green salve that looked soothing, whether it was or not. At

one point Keely giggled, though Dekkar had finished placing the leaves and was nowhere near. The sound of the
laugh, even for a moment, lightened Figg's sense of horror.
The boy looked as though he was trying to smile.

"You used the math box," Keely said, and his voice was as
clear as if nothing had happened to his lips.

Dekkar turned to him, stood very still. "Yes. Thank you."

"I should have thought of it sooner."

"You did right." Dekkar swallowed, stepped near. "She's
gone now, for good."

"Where are we?"

"Close," Dekkar said. "I'm helping Pel to move us along
as fast as possible."

"The tree-woman is after us," Keely said.

"I know."

"Do you want me to tell you what I see?"

Dekkar knelt beside the bunk. His hair was thinning at
the top, the pink scalp showing. Keely's hair was plastered to
his head. The green stuff of the leaves adhered to the burned
skin and flesh, smoothing it out. Figg had an impulse to
touch the child's hair, or his flushed cheek; he had come
close to Keely, too.

"Hello, Uncle Figg," Keely said.

He swallowed. "Hello."

"It's all right. You can sit down."

Figg sat carefully, laying a hand on the boy's shoulder.
"How are you feeling, Keely?"

"Better."

Figg looked at Dekkar, cocked his head. Dekkar said,
"Himmel leaves, and thuenyn."

"What does it do?"

"I can't stop the changes that are happening to Keely, but I can adapt them."

"What does that mean?"

Keely answered. "I can hear the math in my head all the time now, Uncle Figg. From the math box. I can do all the levels in it."

He must have looked puzzled. After a moment Keely said, "You're making a face, Uncle Figg."

"You can see?"

"Yes."

Dekkar nodded, touching a fingertip to the leaf-stuff. "What were you going to tell me, Keely?"

"She's coming closer again. She's still in the flitter."

"What does she look like to you?"

"Like she's made of bark, like she has tree branches for arms, like she has the insides of a person, like her face is not for making faces."

"That's very good."

"She's talking to my father."

"He's not your father, Keely."

"He says he is."

"He's not. He's no relation to you."

"You remember your sister Sherry," Figg said, heart pounding. "She was your family."

"Sherry." Keely said the name; one of his hands was visible, fingers making small, hesitant movements. He was trying to smile again. He sat up.

The leaves were changing texture, smoothing over his skin, nearly but not quite the shape of a face with the proper contours, a dark patch, green and shiny, smooth over the eye sockets, the lower lip intact, the upper smooth and green. He touched his fingers to his face. "That feels better."

"So, do you remember Sherry?"

He was smiling. The green membrane made expressions; made them plain if not detailed, at least. "Sherry was my sister. She was my real family."

Figg ran a hand through the boy's hair. "That's the fellow."

"Remember that," Dekkar said, standing.

When Keely tried to stand, Figg said, "Don't take it too fast, sport. Hold still."

"I'm all right."

"You can be all right sitting on the bunk. The boat's moving pretty fast. We should all stay still." He was looking at Kitra when he said that.

He had come to feel close to her, for some reason. He could tell she was afraid now, and ashamed of herself for being afraid. She must have always considered herself to be the stalwart type; at seventy or so she was young enough to have held onto such illusions. Sooner or later everyone came face-to-face with something too terrifying to endure.

She moved quietly to Figg's side without the least hesitation or discomfort, laid her head on his thigh, sighed, and watched Keely. Dekkar was standing with Pel at the front of the boat. Zhengzhou, hesitant, moved toward the bunk, maybe needing a bit of comfort herself. Figg nodded to her, and she sat across from them against the wall.

Kitra's voice was somber. "He said—Dekkar said—everyone's dead in the south."

Figg wet his lips. "I heard."

"How many people is that?"

"Two or three billion. Jharvan is a big continent." Figg felt a sinking in himself. "If it's true. For all we know it's just a rumor."

The Hilda, on whatever internal schedule governed its behavior, unfolded itself in the galley and prepared food. At Figg's side Keely sat quietly, holding the cyborg spider in his lap. Beyond the glass slipped the dark river, shadowy trees hanging over the banks in the gray light, slim figures slipping among them. They had come through the night into some kind of day.

Billions of souls in the dark fluttered up like fireflies, or else cascaded upward like the showers of sparks along the burning river, dying to dark after a short flight.

The possibility began to occur to Figg—he was on a boat sailing north from the wreckage of his farm to a war zone, or worse, out of one disaster into another—that he might soon die himself. He had collided with a scale of thing, a catastrophe like something out of fable. A whole world was being destroyed. Or, rather, a whole people was being wiped off the face of the world. One race was being supplanted by another. Somewhere in that process he might vanish, too.

From his feeling that he was responsible for Keely had flowed the rest of his part in this. How had he ever got caught up in anything but his own pleasure? Why had turning three hundred changed him so drastically?

"We're close," Keely said, face turned toward the front of the boat. The green film had grown regular, almost symmetrical, to simulate the contours of his old face. The texture was like calloused skin. He touched it again, reverently.

"Close to what?"

"To the place where we have to leave the boat."

Dekkar was looking back at them, listening. "He's right."

"Are we not going to my brother first, then?" Kitra asked.

He watched her for a long time. "He's here, too. Quite close."

"He can't be. His tree's not in this part of the river system. He's along an interior canal."

"No." Dekkar shook his head. "You'll see."

"I'm telling you, I've been there—"

"His tree was moved, Kitra. Some time ago." He spoke with certainty, not a sign of hesitation.

"You can't move a tree that far."

"Yes, you can. If you're Rao."

That quieted her, at least until it sank in. "What does my brother have to do with Rao?"

"I don't know."

"But you know his tree is here."

He looked at her.

She flushed, angry. "Answer me."

"No, I won't. You'll see for yourself soon enough."

"Dekkar, I swear—" She tried to get to her feet, found herself suddenly too dizzy.

"Save your strength," he said, turning his back to her. "You'll need it. I know I'm sure to need mine."

Figg lay his hand on her shoulder, drew her against him again. He watched her face, and for a moment she watched back. Her confusion made him tender. He touched the back of his hand to her cheek, light and quick. She closed her eyes.

A few moments later breakfast, or something like it, was

ready. Outside the riverbank rushed by at such a clip they might have been riding in the flitter instead of a boat.

By now, with Figg's link down, his newsburst queue no longer received its updates. He was reaching further into the queue, the sorts of items that he rarely attended.

○ **1193** Since the opening of the Anilyn Gate, the population of the Reeks beneath Béyoton has declined so drastically that city officials are speculating on what to do with the open space. Nearly two hundred million citizens who lived in the Reeks have migrated from Senal in the past two years, most of them claiming support from the Common Fund and investing in a place in a colony along the Conveyance. Béyoton is estimated to have lost nearly thirty million inhabitants of the informal city-beneath-the-city population. Other Reeks citizens have migrated to other locales within Home Star or have simply moved upstairs to open shops closed since their owners sold their stock and migrated in the early years of the Conquest. Compiled from bot-search protocols, this item is not an official news broadcast newburst.

○ **1206** Miss Destiny FormiCon was crowned at a recent Speculative Surround Convention in Deep Rahd, an underwater city off the coast of Nedai Protectorate. Destiny's Divine is a beauty pageant in which middlewams and neuters compete to determine who makes the most convincing example of a gendered phenotype; Miss Destiny was won by a costumed, hormone-riddled middlewam from the capital while Mr. Destiny was a neuter pumped up on steroids and testosterone to resemble any number of vid action heroes. This item was compiled from bot-search protocols along with a notation that these protocols were scheduled to expire on a date within the next twenty days. The expiration date was a sign of

Figg's passing interest in the sudden fashion in male body hair that had swept parts of Senal over the last year. This was an offshoot of constantly changing trends in retrograde fashion.

○1211 Date-stamped. The Imperial Colonial Experientiarium in Feidreh reports that much of the physical art on display in the Magus Malin Gallery was found to be covered by fungus when early staff arrived to prep the museum for opening. The fungus appeared on all artwork overnight but by time of discovery had already done substantial damage. Several types of fungus were identified, each adapted to consuming the particular material to which it was attached. The designer fungi are thought to be the product of a bioterrorist either attached to the northern rebel movement or else a lone radical wishing to make a statement about the current state of art. Some experts speculate this could be the work of an artist whose medium is bioterrorism. This was a news bite logged in the twin cities several days ago, rebooted into the queue due to the recent upsurge of interest in strange fungi reports throughout the Surround.

○1228 The Dirijhi consulate in Dembut has stated emphatically that the Earnest Council remains fully committed to the independence of the north. The Dirijhi are aware of reports of atrocities committed in the south and the Earnest Council states unreservedly that it does not consider any atrocities to have been committed. The agreed-upon subjugation of the south has taken place. Allied infantry herds are grazing in the ruins of the enemy cities and the continent will be scoured, cleansed, and prepared for northern use. A new item improperly placed low in the queue by the last link server Figg had passed, in Dembut.

○1232 The Dirijhi consulate in Dembut announced that allied infantry herds would move into cities on the border of the Dirijhi preserve in order to protect the trees from unwanted incursions by southern retaliatory units. A partial transmission from Dembut, improperly placed in the queue due to the confusion at the time of the attack on the town.

○ **1241** The marriage of EdgeNite to Ruthy Feely was annulled in the Marmigon today, in the Empire Throne Room, the site of so many celebrity divorces and annulments over the years. Feely remarked to the press afterward, "The Marmigon is not the same place now that it's publicly held. The old families knew how to do a few things right." But she confessed there was still no grander location for a star looking to bring an end to a tortured public marriage. Weeks old, retained by trash-bot due to Marmigon quote reference including the term "family."

○ **1257** Fineas Figg and his boytoy Keely File, infamous younger brother enriched by his sister's public suicide at Figg's three hundredth you-know-what, are fleeing to a farm on the Ajhevan continent of Aramen, all the way through the gate! Figg, a well-known pederast and purchaser of young boys from the Reeks in his days as a tweenage scion of a powerful Orminy clan, claims to have reformed after a term of imprisonment during his second century, but MarvaMaven wonders about his sudden attachment to the young, tender-delicious Keely; we hear the boy's even been age-regressed, a sure case of gilding the lily, shame on Figg! From a Surround data-girdle, currently under legal injunction by Figg's attorneys, placed this low in the queue because he'd already heard about the slander from his attorneys and because, really, there was always plenty of slander in his life.

○ **1266** The Council of Orminy recently awarded Mage Consort Jedda Mermartele a further letter to her name, the postpendant "z." Her status now placed her among the very highest of Orminy houses, should she choose to found her own mother-line, either by propagation or adoption. Further additions to her name were felt to be unlikely due to the unpopularity of the Common Fund Reforms with what was left of the Orminy houses. The item was gathered by news-bot search and tagged to expire in another day. Figg had a fascination with the Mage's consort, the Lady Jedda.

○**1267** A young math prodigy recently vanished from Qons Quilyan's inner cloister; the neophyte, one of a handful of Tervan allowed to travel abroad from Iraen, had apparently fled the cloister in an attempt to emigrate off Senal. The young Tervan was a master of the Tervan-derived art of singing mathematics that is taught to all Prin; his specialty, in this case, was Tervan choral subparticle physics of the neutron. The item was footnoted with a text link that informed Figg that the Tervan were a people who lived in the north of the country Iraen, thought to be responsible for much of the stone architecture and construction throughout northern cities there.

The Way to Chulion

1.

Coromey traveled as fast as Jessex and hunted well enough that Jessex need not bother; even high in the mountains there was game: snow-fowl, hares-a-whiting, high deer, fastlings, feasels, plain mice. During snow melt grew quickfix and thrush, bitterberry and comb, other scrub stuff, in carpets along the ridges and peaks. Most animals dug into the snow or found shelter under rocks or in tunnels where they could be snug and sleep through the winter on their fat; some of the predators stayed active and lived on the fat, too, though in their case, the fat of others. Coromey was adept at digging out a plump hare-a-whiting, chewing his half raw while Jessex roasted his hot over a fire.

Jessex had been trained by God's Sisters to economy and therefore built the fire from wood he gathered, mostly scrubby stuff gleaned from shrubs and small trees; sometimes he used a Word to start the fire and a Word to slow it but otherwise gathered more wood to fuel it instead of sustaining it with true language. If there had been fuel in plenty he'd have used no Word at all.

He moved toward a destination that he could feel. Somewhere deep in the mountains they still existed, his teachers. He meant to find them. If they were truly God's kin, they could answer his questions about her, about God herself.

He had long since passed any named peaks, or at least any peaks with Erejhen names. So high he was that there should have been scarce vegetation, though there was more than Jessex remembered: twisted pines and other woody evergreens along the friendlier slopes, scrubby brush throwing finedrawn shadows onto the snow, tough spindly grasses that took hold in any crevice of rock. Where he built his fire he was sheltered by a cove of rocks shaped a bit like a farmer's lean-to. Coromey stretched out beside the fire, splaying his toes and showing his fine, sharp claws, scratching them in the tough mat of thorny grass to clean them. He watched Jessex between slow, sleepy blinks.

While the cat-hound slept, Jessex walked the peaks, counted stars, blinked at the sharpness of the wind. Between one step and the next he had crossed out of his own time into another, or so it felt. He was no longer the master of towers and devices; he was a simple body moving toward an end. For the moment he had put aside the role of Great Irion, had stepped out of his office, abandoned the whole hierarchy of true language choirs, of Prin singers and Drune operators. He had fled the Oregal. For the moment he had only himself with which to concern himself; he had his journey to find his teachers, to find a path back to God, or not, once and for all.

When Coromey was rested they moved forward along

the mountains faster than should have been possible. Even so, not all the distance to Chulion could be covered through mere travel; at least part of finding the place would be out of his hands.

It had been a long time since he humbled himself or was humbled by anybody else. Whatever his crisis of faith, he understood the hierarchy in which he took part; in his world, the one that he had recently left, he was unmatched. But in the greater worlds were powers that outranked him. He was a true-language operator of the third order, but this was his own parlance, meant to shield him from the uncomfortable notion of magic, a more difficult word for him to compass with each year that passed. In the parlance of his teachers, he was a wizard of the third circle of power, a great achievement for the One who had brought him into being. He was a magician who moved power through Words, the same Words that had been used in the creation of all the worlds. He had learned those Words from God's own Sisters, three of them, a long time ago, along the shores of a placed called Lake Illyn. He had told this story himself; his people told this story about him; some version of this story was venerated in the Church of Irion beyond the Ocean Gate. But so much time had passed, he had only the merest shreds of belief left, and hardly any memory he could trust.

He had no doubt that the Sisters existed or that he had been taught by them. His doubt was that they had ever told him the truth about who and what they were.

Soon enough he entered a country where all was starry night and none of the stars were the right stars. He suspected that the country in which he had lived his life, whether one called it Irion, or Iraen, or Aeryn, was no more than a vestibule, that beyond the mountains lay many other places, more than anyone had ever guessed. Somewhere in this far country was Zan, the land of the dead; somewhere here was Orloc country, and far below lay the territory of the Untherverthen; maybe in some other direction was Earth, from which the Hormling had come in the long, long ago. Elsewhere beyond the mountains were places of which Jessex had no inkling. As wizards go, he had been no great traveler, at least to this point.

Coromey hunted and ate and they pressed onward. The peaks rose around them, jagged as the edge of the world, yet endless, reaching as far as the eye could see, heavy with snow, except to the east where a vast wall of ice rose nearly to the top of the peaks, obscuring everything.

"There," he said, and Coromey heard him.

Weary of travel if not weary in the body, he made a fire within sight of the glacier, in a cluster of rocks that surfaced through ice, sheltering him from the wind. A moon hung heavy in the sky. It was a moon he had seen before, a long time ago, under the Old Sky of Aeryn before the Ocean Gate was opened. This moon was called Familiar because it returned only occasionally, recognizable from the pitted design on its surface, like a person's face, almost.

"What sky is this?" he asked Coromey, scratching the animal gently under the chin. The hound lifted his head with pleasure, eyes heavy-lidded; he made a low cat-purr and stretched the chin toward Jessex's hand. "You don't much care, do you? Then why should I?"

Long ago, God's Sisters had taught him the game of waiting. As he sat before the fire, this one burning from air, charmed by his Word out of nothing, occasionally needing his attention lest it devolve, he remembered the long era in which he had worked with them, under their thumb, doing as they bid. Time when they were training him passed but in a different direction from real time; they could confine him to their timeline for as long as they chose and had often done so, teaching him, as they claimed, the art of patience. At the end of each training session they returned him to his own timeline, to the precise second after the one from which they had taken him.

Their names were not to be said, and no one had ever revealed them; but one was Plump, one was Thin, and one was Young.

"For patience certainly is an art," had said Thin, by the serene shore of that blue lake.

"One we all hope you'll learn one day, sister," said Plump.

Young shook her golden hair. "No fighting, elders. Please. We have so much to show this petulant child."

Though at times they took their time to such a degree that he wondered whether he were really learning anything at all.

So here at the foot of the wall of ice at the roof of the world he sat, protected from the piercing cold by the Words the Sisters had taught him, knowing that his presence and his use of Words would stand out like a beacon in the mountains. What convinced him, in the end, that at least one of them would come was the fact that they kept him waiting.

At some point, maybe in the instant between one footstep and the next, maybe as long ago as when he felt himself leaving his old world, he had entered their variety of time.

He withdrew from all the use of Words in which he himself was employed. For the first time in an era he withdrew into his body, stopped his kei-meditation, shut down his insinging, and was silent. Since he was no longer in real time, none of that would do him any good.

Under clear stars in the dark he wandered over the sheet of ice, searching for nothing, feeling a peace settle into him. He had not been so single, so unified, in such a long time; he had not been engulfed in anyone else's magic in so long. Clouds came, formed low, and dumped snow in bales over the landscape. Moons passed overhead, even a blue moon, pale and crepuscular. Winds that would have cut him, frozen him to the bone, passed through him without effect, and Coromey, tough as he was, needed the same protection.

He had brought the slightest of packs: a blanket, a water bottle, a bag of gems, a cup, a supply of tea in efficient Hormling pouches. He found better shelter in the shadow of a cliff, a dry cave, and on his walks gathered any brush or shrub he could find for times when he wanted a fire. He stocked the cave with bits of branch and tree; even this high, there sometimes came a spring, and maybe even the light of day.

A blizzard blew in, mountains of snow on top of oceans of ice, and afterward broke a thin daylight. Wind had calmed but during the storm had shaped the fresh snowfalls into waves. Jessex and Coromey walked atop the waves of snow in the white world of winter.

In the evening, eating the bit of snow hare left from the

fire, hearing Coromey's contented breathing, he realized he was happy, and a moment later realized he had been otherwise for a very long time.

He found another camp, what looked like the outer room of a mausoleum or the entrance to some underground dwelling, a small doorless room in the face of a mountain all but consumed by the glacier. Stone writing that might be old Untherverthen, Orloc, or Tervan decorated the lintel, made of a flat, shaped stone, fitted stone columns on either side. Inside, the small space was unadorned except for two raised platforms bracketing the door. Each of the platforms was big enough for a tall person's bedroll. For a moment after he found the room, heart in his mouth, he thought he had stumbled onto a hidden entrance into Chulion.

Days and days went by. He grew to have no worries, no thought of the future. He could feel himself close to the Sisters by now; he felt one or another of them pass nearby sometimes. Plump, he thought, or Young, or, rarely, Thin.

One day when he had been out walking he returned to camp, this time to the circle of rocks open to the sky. By then there had been no night for so long he decided to move back to the cave, because he was tired of the brilliant light reflecting off the snow. Once Coromey knew which of the camps was their destination, he loped off in the proper direction, and Jessex followed, almost as fast as the cat-hound.

Since he was not using his Words or any of his inner senses, he mistrusted what he saw at first. Near the cave waited a tall figure wrapped in white. Once convinced she was real, he walked toward her with his head bowed; she had pulled part of her robe across her head, her face obscured, and the volume of the cloth, blowing in wind, hid her body. She stood by a gnarled, twisted pine, a few stubborn needles clutched about the height of her shoulder; Jessex had admired the persistence of the tree and spared it from burning.

Which of the three Sisters was this one? They were all quite tall from a distance, no way to tell from that. Sometimes the body looked plump, sometimes thin; sometimes the hand, holding the edge of the robe in place against the wind, looked old, sometimes young.

Wind roared up, blowing powdery snow, as clouds covered the sky. Her wrapping-robe whipped around her, the border edged with elaborate embroidery, vivid colors, very fine tracery. The colors shifted, the Words shifted.

"Is this your cave?" she asked.

"Yes, lady."

"A fine cave, too. Very snug."

"I've laid in a good bit of wood, if you want a fire."

"You need wood for a fire?"

"No. But sometimes I like it."

She held the hood to shadow her face but he thought he saw her smile. "If I asked for tea, could you make it?"

"Yes. A most agreeable tea, in fact. Though I am fresh out of lake water and I have only the one cup."

"Never mind your cup. I travel with my own. The snow will do for water, though you'll need a deal of it. It's as pure as lake water, I expect."

She built the fire at the mouth of the cave while Jessex gathered snow. He pressed two cups of water from a pure white drift and brought the cups back. "You may as well heat them yourself," she said when he drew near. "The fire won't be hot enough for a while. And I'm impatient for my tea."

He did as she asked and dropped the tea filter into the cup.

"What's this?' she asked. "I ask for tea and you give me a bit of rag."

"It's a paper filter. There's tea inside. Good southern scuppling."

"I prefer a pekoe."

He shrugged. "I brought the tea to suit myself."

She sniffed.

"Besides, a pekoe is a Hormling tea. When did you ever taste it?"

"You act as if you think you know where I'm from and where I've been."

He stirred his tea with his finger, heated it a bit. Coromey stretched near the fire, wanting to put his head in the woman's lap. Perhaps it was the soft appeal of the fabric of her wrap, shining white, drawn up around her head against the wind, that charmed the cat-hound.

She was Thin. The tapered, long bones of her hands caught the firelight, casting graceful shadows as they moved. Her cheeks were hollow, her face long, her eyes dark. Wind occasionally lifted the hem of her wrap, showed her face more plainly, and she made no attempt to hide herself.

"Beg pardon," Jessex said. "I meant only that out here, so far in the mountains, I wondered that you would have tasted pekoe."

"I might have tasted it long before you did, obtained from an entirely different direction. It's a small universe, af-ter all."

Jessex was too cautious to look her in the eye. "Now it's you who sound as if you know who I am."

She snorted, laying her tea pouch onto the paper cover from which she had torn it. "Who does not know Great Irion? Who has not heard the name?"

"Now you're making fun of me."

"Quite right. At least you still have sense of humor enough to recognize it."

He studied the fire, added a bit of wood, said a Word to guard the flame from wind, which blew strong.

"Go ahead, drink your tea. It's a fair blend. Scuppling, you call it?"

"Yes. A mix of green mint and redberry. From near where the marshes run up to the mountains, in Karnes."

She looked up at the bright sky, which had started to fade, running her fingertips along Coromey's tufted eartips. "Dusk. We'll have a spell of night, now."

"Why such long days and nights?"

She spoke more sharply; her voice had changed, but now he recognized it. He had called her Commyna when she was his teacher. What her real name might be he had no idea. "The scale suits us, that's all. Surely you don't think you're in real time, in a real country."

He shook his head. "No. Or else I'd have been frantic."

"Why? Because we've kept you waiting so long?"

"You haven't kept me waiting."

"Then what did you mean?"

How long had it been since anyone spoke to him so sharply? Since he had to bear it? His pride ached, but there was something necessary about it. "In real time, I don't have days to spend preparing. I have hours."

She sipped from her tea as the sky darkened. After a while, she said, in her driest tone, "Once upon a time you were a very modest child."

He flushed. "If I'm less modest now, maybe it's because I've been left on my own too long."

"Long? What is it? Three millennia? Not even. And you already feel sorry for yourself."

"I don't feel sorry for myself."

She mocked his tone of before. "You have hours. Really, Jessex."

"It's true."

She blew out a breath, derisive. "When were you ever given less time than you needed to do what you have to do? It would seem to me you've often taken a good deal of time you might have done without."

"You mean the long sleep. That's very cruel. As if it were my fault I slept a century."

"Well, if it wasn't your fault, it was certainly your choice. Never mind," she held up her hand. "That's ancient history."

"It was the first war you got me involved with, in fact."

"I got you involved?"

"Who else?"

She stared at him, and he felt a warm glow in the pit of his stomach. "You have the cheek to sit there—well. We'll see about that." She sipped her tea and said nothing at all.

For a long while, under the stars that glittered, a moonless night, scattered flights of cloud, they sat together around the fire. He added wood when the fire burned low; he used most of his stock to make it bright and cheery. "So I suppose you blame us for this current disaster." She spat the words.

"I don't blame anyone. But this is more than I can cope with on my own."

She gave no reaction except to hold her cup in both hands near the fire.

"You know I'm right," he said. "This creature is another one of her kind."

Thin scowled. She drew down the wrap from her head and showed her dark hair, piled in a bun behind, wrapped with pearls. Her ears were covered with fine chains and precious gems, and her hair was bound in a golden net. Her eyes were gray in the firelight, though at times another color pulsed through them. "Creature. Her kind." She nearly spat. "What kind of language is this?"

"You know what I mean. If YY is a god, then so is this one. Whatever she is, this is another."

"She is the mother of your kind. That is what she is. She is the one who made you what you are."

"Does that make her a god?"

Thin's face darkened to a deep scowl. "Careful, boy."

How long since anyone called him "boy"?

"I mean the question seriously. I mean no disrespect. But is she a god?"

"She is herself. Whatever that is, that's enough for me."

"But it wasn't always," Jessex said.

She glared at him, as behind her head a puff of snow swirled in a twist of wind.

The fire crackled and he added more wood. "You rebelled. You betrayed her. You told me so."

She turned down her empty cup and looked at him. He fetched more clean snow and made water of it, heated the cup in his hand, gave it her with a fresh pouch of scuppling. She dropped the pouch into the water. "I do like these Hormling friends of yours. They have the most ingenious ways of packaging things."

"They're very clever."

"Cleverer than we?"

"The Erejhen? Or you?"

"The Erejhen. No one is cleverer than my Sisters."

"No. I suppose not. There are so many of the Hormling, it's astonishing to contemplate. But we Erejhen hold our own."

"Then how does it come about they've made you doubt yourself?"

"Myself? No. It's God. It's she."

"But how can you have any doubt when you've seen her?"

"I don't doubt she's real. I doubt what she is."

"What do you mean?"

"I don't think she's a god at all. I think she's something very old, left over from an ancient race of people like the Hormling, but much older and much more advanced."

Thin smiled, swirled the water in the cup, pulled out the pouch and sipped. "Suppose that's true. How is that not God?"

"I don't understand."

"Given who she is. Given what she can do."

"God should be more than that—God should be—" The thought felt as if it ought to be clear, until the time came to utter it.

"God should be God," Thin said. "Of course. And to most people she is. But to her priests? To you?" She shook her head. "The priest has to explain God to people whom God hurts. The priest has to explain God to herself. The mage has to move God's power in Words. God can come to seem quite commonplace to her servants."

He was gritting his teeth, flushed. "But we could learn the truth about her, about everything we do if we only studied ourselves—"

"What do you hope we would learn?"

"Her nature. The nature of Words."

She smiled at him very gently. "You really have come just in time, I think."

"What? You were expecting me?"

She sat there looking pleased with herself. The statement might be true; on the other hand, she might simply like to have it appear so. "I'll take you to Chulion. My Sisters will be happy to see you, in their way."

"Will you?"

She looked in his eyes. She had always been the hardest of the three, the most exacting, but also the most tender. "I already am, child. In my way." She stroked Coromey's long neck, and the cat-hound's purr was audible in the stillness. For a moment there was not a breath of wind and the sky was completely clear, studded with glitter like a jeweler's vault. She stood. He packed his things. The fire burned low and winked out. Pulling the wrap over her hair again, she began to walk. He followed, covering himself with a cloth the Sisters had given him a long time ago. Coromey stretched on his back, fanned his front paws out, showing his claws, then leapt to all fours and trotted after them, wet tongue licking the top of the snow.

2.

They walked along the top of the glacier after climbing a long, criss-crossing stair of ice that appeared in the ice wall as naturally as if it had always been right there, not even a full kilomeasure from the cave. They were headed across the waves of snow along the top of the ice, traveling in a clear night, the wind strong sometimes but never so much so that their walk was impeded.

"What is the nature of a Word?' she asked after a while. "Is it here, or not?"

"Here?"

"Yes. And now. Here and now. A thing must always be both, though not necessarily at the same time."

"Is a word here. Or do you mean, a Word?"

They were speaking Wyyvisar, the language she had helped to teach him long ago; parts of conversational Wyyvisar had merged into the formal language of literary Erejhen. The distinction between "word" and "Word" was unmistakable.

"I believe you know the answer to that question."

"No. A Word is not here."

"Then where is it?"

"Beyond. Always." In the logic of Wyyvisar, this conclusion was inescapable.

"Exactly. Then why do you doubt my Sister? Because she is my Sister?"

"No, not—"

The wind blew up gusts like ice fire in their faces, and even through their cloaks they were cold. Long ago she had taught him how to live with cold, what to do with the feeling, how to keep the body warm enough, on walks like this one, though not so deep in the mountains.

"You mean, do I doubt that she's God because I've seen her? Do I doubt that she's God because she has a story?"

She was watching him for a moment, snow blowing up from the drifts. Everywhere, on every side, white waves of snow lined the landscape to the horizon. They walked on for a long time, his fingers playing in Coromey's fur. The cathound stepped steadily as if there were no wind blowing, no whipped-up flurries and fogs of snow.

"Suppose it's true, suppose I do doubt her because she has a story. It might help to know what the story is. You see?"

"Do you think a question as big as that can be answered? Your head could not contain the answer. No, you want to ask something much simpler, I think."

"Leaving out the size of my head—"

She gestured to him impatiently, as if he were still the gangly boy by the lake, as if he were still fresh off the farm. The thought might have made him angry but instead it made him laugh, and an instant later he realized it might as well be true, he might as well still be that child. That boy had felt clean and new like this.

"You want to ask me whether she is the leavings of some wise old ancient race of beings. You want to ask me whether she is one of the First of this universe, one of the Primes. You want me to tell you whether who she is and the Words she inhabits are gifts that can be explained."

She went on. "I can answer part of the question. The creatures you describe do exist and this Rao who has come to visit you is one of them. We call them Primes because of their knowledge; some of them are individuals and some are not and some are neither-nor. But God is not any kind of First. God is God."

"How can I know for sure?"

"Is a Word here?" she asked.

"Tell me what you mean."

"If the Universe dies, do Words die with it? Do Numbers die with it?"

When he tried to ask another question, she shook her head, rearranged the wrap to hide most of her face, and led him forward into the snow.

3.

In his childhood memory of traveling to Chulion, there was only the fortress, an impression of a flight over tall towers, high walls, a forbidding reach of mountain—fleeting glimpses, since he was supposed to have been asleep and had only barely managed any sense of where he was.

Even now, knowing what he knew of Words, he had no way to fly. Today, crossing the ice, Thin had shown no signs of helping the crossing to go faster.

Around Chulion was a city. They arrived in it down another long flight of steps that led to a crowded market, the settlement carved into a crevasse between the glacier and the mountain. "The house is buried beneath the glacier," she said. "We'll climb down through the steps."

"In the ice?"

"Yes. You'll be fine, but you'll have to help your animal to manage."

The market was tiers of stone platforms and colonnades, some open to the sky, some under cloth roofs fastened to the side of the mountain tight as sails on a ship. He saw Orloc and Untherverthen, Smiths and women from Svyssn. A few of the stalls looked as if there were Anin or Erejhen working the merchandise: cloths and foodstuffs, craft work, saddles, bridles, clothing, even some Hormling gadgets. A few working forges belched smoke higher along the mountain. He saw no buildings, only the maze of platforms and colonnades.

"Their houses are below the platforms, in Undertown. This city used to be located at the foot of the gate to Chulion, but when the glacier covered us, we had to move it higher onto the mountain."

"Does the city have a name?"

"Middle of the Mountain," she said, and she led him through an armory selling weapons and a bazaar for raw gems and then into a public plaza and down a long causeway. This led, eventually, to a stair leading down through the glacier. Light glowed softly from the steps, hundreds of them, carved of ice. Jessex followed the Sister and helped Coromey, who whimpered a bit at the slick surface.

For a while there were cross tunnels leading to the residential quarters of the city, but soon enough there was no more traffic, only a bit of breeze coming up the steps. They climbed down, and down.

"Here we are," she said, stepping through an arch into an open courtyard, and there, suddenly, was the night sky.

They were in another pocket not filled by the glacier, a cove of the mountain from which rose a sheer, vertical fortress, walls of fitted stone in the Orloc style rising high, partly hiding the taller towers beyond them. The wall of ice that the stone barrier faced was far taller and higher still, casting a deep shadow over the vale. Gloomy firepots lit the walls, and some of the tower windows gave off a dim glow. Torches lit a causeway from the broken flank of the mountain up to the gate of Chulion, and he followed her toward it in the dark; behind them the road descended, broken by the ice. Maybe the ruined city lay that way, where the road had once led.

"When did the glacier come?"

"Over the last two thousand years, give or take."

"Might you not have stopped it?"

She had drawn down her head-wrap and turned to him, lips pursed. "Whyever? Easy enough to live with ice. Better to take the world as it comes, sometimes."

At the gates stood Orloc guards, spindle-legged, ice-blue, their heads shaped like winter squash. In the lower house, many other Orloc were living, and the rooms were strewn with their worktables, hard benches, straight-backed chairs;

in the upper halls, however, there was no one moving, not a soul. "We don't like visitors, or company, or servants, or any sort of bother with other creatures," explained Thin, removing her outer wrap altogether, draping it over her arm; a beautiful, shining cloth that was the equal or better of any Erejhen weave. The bright embroidery gleamed. "Though you and your cat-hound are welcome, to be sure."

They had crossed two empty levels of the main keep, hollow stone rooms echoing around them, and had ascended a dark wooden stairway into a high-beamed hall that occupied the entire floor of one of the towers. Windows opened on all sides, some looking out on the mountain, some on the ice, all on the night. What a view these windows must have offered before the glacier came! She led him around piers of stone and abutments from the outer walls that carried the weight of the tower upward. The stones were flat-joined in the Orloc fashion rather than round-joined in the Tervan style. Inside would be a metal skeleton to bear the weight of the stone, also in the Orloc style, to allow the tower to soar as high as the peaks.

At a circle of couches she stopped, near a series of doors that led outside, where a balcony looked onto the sheer blue-gray of the glacier. She opened the doors but seated him on the couches inside. Behind, chimney vanishing into one of the stone piers, a fire burned in a fireplace.

"How much of this place do you remember?" she asked. "We brought you here when you were a boy."

"I remember bits and pieces. It was during a storm."

"You were supposed to be asleep but you were not."

"I woke up on a stone slab, I think."

"We were trying you."

"Trying?"

"With this and that. Trying you. So you don't remember this room, these couches?"

"No."

"Well, they're new, anyway. We get new furniture, too, you know. So you wouldn't remember these couches." She chuckled, her shoulders shaking. "It was a test, just a bit of a test, but you passed, you did. Would that they were all so easy."

"You look old, Sister. Why? You need not."

She smiled with one side of her mouth. "How do you know what needs I have and what needs I don't?"

"I know you don't age."

"We are in a winter phase, here. We are old." She cocked her head, touching a jewel at her throat, a dark blue gem, on a thin, glittering chain, held very close to the hollow above her collarbone.

"Have you built yourselves a true language tower?" he asked, gesturing to the mass of the place that weighed down on his head.

"You can't bring yourself to call it by a proper name. You can't bring yourself to say 'wizard's tower.' "

"My name for it is very proper. It's a tower for use of true language."

"Which is a silly term you made up yourself. You'll pay for it, one day. At any rate, no. We have no need for your toys."

She found Drii brandy, the smell unmistakable, and poured it into delicate snifters. The couch was warm, though a cold draft blew in through the open doors. Coromey stretched out by the fireplace.

"Drink," she said. "It's from the time of the King, when there was real Drii brandy to be found."

"You find the present day stuff to be faulty?"

"I can't say I've tried it. Why should I?"

"We live in diminished times," Jessex said.

"Surely it can't be that we agree so well."

He inhaled from the snifter, drew in the warm brown. "You had this from Evyynar Ydhiil in the days before the war. How did you keep it so long?"

"Why would I not use Words for such a worthy preservation?"

"True." He held the glass to the light. "Though it never works so well for me. It was a worthy time, that time. But long ago, and finished."

"You need not tell me."

He set down the glass on a stone table; he watched her tall figure as she turned back from the window, settling onto a couch across from him, her image silhouetted against the night. He said, "You asked me a riddle on the way across the ice."

"Not a riddle, really. But go on."

"Now I have one for you."

She gave him a wary tilt of the head. Had her voice changed as much as her appearance? How could he trust his memory after so long? "Go ahead."

"How do you know which is a fortress and which a prison?"

At first she simply blinked, then her expression soured a bit. Behind her head a bit of tapestry rigging was rattling against the stone, its eyehook ringing. "Not a very good riddle."

"No?"

"Really too easy. One would look for the way the guards were facing."

He was quiet and still—waiting, though in no obtrusive way.

She said, "There need be no nonsense between us, Jessex. Why don't you say plainly what you mean?"

He spoke carefully, watching wind blow through potted trees on the balcony. "This world is meant as a prison. Not a fortress."

"Why should this world be meant as either?"

"YY made this place, just as we were always taught. I've always known this to be true. But she made nothing else. No other world. She made only this one. Why?"

Her face had suddenly changed, stiffened, as if she were preparing herself for something unpleasant. "Pardon me, child, but who are you to ask?"

How long since anyone called him "child"?

He answered quietly, his posture deferential. She was his teacher, after all. "You know very well who I am. I'm the one who keeps watch at the gate."

"Do you really think she cares a whit for your gate?"

"I know that she does, without doubt."

"Why?"

"Because of the kind of creatures it will draw here."

She stood very still. The night had lightened a bit. At the fireplace, Coromey rolled onto his back and stretched his paws upward.

"Say more." Her face had become more difficult to see, as if it lay in shadow; she was protecting herself in veils.

He fought an impulse to protect himself in the same way. She was a power of the second rank; he could not defend himself from her in any case. He took a deep breath. "She intends the gate to attract beings like you, Sister, or me."

"Why would she care to do such a thing?"

He shrugged. "She is who she is. Perhaps she will eat them. Perhaps she'll imprison them. Perhaps she'll learn their languages. Maybe some of all. I don't know."

She stood and stepped toward him coolly, stopping some distance from him. So far she had not reached any of her Words toward him, but her figure was indistinct, a kind of cloud. "You first had these thoughts when you went into the underworld with the King?"

"Yes. A long time ago. When I went to find him."

"But you've waited a very long time to ask the question."

"It was not my place to ask."

"Now it is?"

He nodded, curtly. "Yes."

"Why?"

"You know very well why, Sister."

"Still, I want to hear you say."

Now that the time had come to say the words he felt heaviness in himself, sadness, even an edge of fear. "One of them has come, one of the creatures she's baiting. He's an operator of the second order, at least."

"You know his name?"

"Rao."

"What language does he speak?"

"No language. He speaks a mathematics. His helpers who speak the Hormling language call it Erlot." He tried to keep any hint of resentment from his voice, staring at the patterned flower in the carpet beneath his feet. "I'm sure you know this."

She hesitated so long that he looked at her, in the end. She was watching him. Her face was now clearly visible, her eyes calm. "We only knew his name. You've done well to learn the rest."

He acknowledged this with a bow.

Wind howled in and blew the tapestries, sent sparks from the fire; she moved serenely to close the doors.

"Does YY know more?" Jessex asked.

"We haven't asked her."

"Then I need to find her and ask her myself."

She gave him a long look, neutral in every way, and walked around him to stand at the fireplace. Behind her was a painting of YY walking in Illaeryn in a floating-in-clouds style, all grays and browns. "Why?"

"To learn how to fight him."

"Why do you think you need to seek her out? If she intends to help you, she'll simply come to you."

"When?"

She waited patiently, Coromey rubbing the top of his head against her ankles. The cat-hound paid no attention to the true language she was using. "Do you think to hurry God?"

The heaviness weighed on him again, the knowledge that he had been keeping back through the long, serene journey in the mountains. "I'm a guardian who is failing his task, Sister. My people are dying. Billions of people are dead. She can come to help us and does nothing. Why?"

The look she gave him was nothing like the Sister he re-membered. For the first time he could see, could feel, her age, even a trace of her weariness. "Do you really think you're strong enough to ask her yourself?"

"I have to try."

Glistering Phaeton

W hat pleased Vekant most, his precious, puttylike self safely tucked inside the machinery of the Eaten, was that he no longer felt any fear at all. As a human being he had experienced constant apprehension of one sort or another in nearly every social or personal milieu. But no longer. The little that was left of him witnessed all that followed with glee, as if the actions of this altered body were still those of Vekant himself, as if he were the powerful Word-wielder attacking the tower, all his fears shed, all his doubts removed.

The Eaten was in charge now, and all the other cantors across Jharvan answered to him; for Vekant it was as if he were the master himself. They laid waste to every city, flattening the buildings with nuclear fire, killing the humans in waves. Orderly and quick, grid by grid, a plan unfolded. The Hormling died methodically, quickly, and completely.

The work of taking the tower fell to the Eaten and to Vekant, or so it felt to him. The body he shared with the Eaten was crossing the blasted place that had once been the island city of Avatrayn, shattered rubble from temples to Ama and Mur, flattened ruins of public plazas, fires on every side, a sky so filled with smoke and ash there could be no question of day or night. Mantises roamed the streets grazing on corpses, shitting piles of stuff that ate the city into dark ooze. Other creatures were taking shape out of the ooze: rodents with spidery legs; clouds of flies that laid eggs in more of the corpses, the eggs each hatching into a different kind of insect, some burrowing into the ground, some crawling into the ruins, some taking flight. Two-legged rats with long, thin arms skittered through the empty streets. The waves of explosions had destroyed the chill-trees but new ones were sprouting, a dark forest taking shape out of the city, visible on every side. Where the trees met the black ooze the combination made twisted shapes, some of them taking root like plants, sprouting leaves of various kinds, putting out a foul smell.

Ahead, untouched, the tower Cueredon stood amid a small circle of intact buildings at its base.

He was walking through the wreckage of the Fukate Choir, and some of the corpses being gathered into the flanged throats of the mantises and crushed by those lurching constructions, swallowed head-first, were Prin. Some of these were the bodies of people he had known. The thought that some of them were "friends" no longer occurred to him, since that concept had been gnawed out of him by the Eater. A small herd of mantises was feeding here, some tearing at the explosion-cooked bodies bit by bit, others taking the body by the head and swallowing it whole, its legs jostling aimlessly, silhouetted against the smoky sky. Wind was coming up, as if a storm was about to blow over them.

Vekant felt nothing but a vague satisfaction, watching the destruction. He was riding inside the Eaten and nothing could harm him. Fear was a thing he remembered but no longer felt.

What he could feel was the Eaten, its consciousness flooded with concepts, numbers, curves, knots, cascading patterns repeating themselves endlessly; this rendered into a sound that had no resemblance to any music Vekant had ever heard. If he had still been able to fear anything he would have been afraid of that sound.

The Eaten would not be able simply to approach the tower. From inside, Vekant could understand the creature's thinking. The creature did not entirely understand how the tower functioned or what needed to happen to bring it down. The tower was being held by inferior operators, but it belonged to an operator of the same order as the Eaten, and therefore the taking of it would require time. The creature had already begun its work, circling the base, trying to find a gate or a door, and at the same time reaching upward, to the top of the tower where the lone Drune, Eshen Arly, and the pair of Prin, Seris Annoy and Faltha Menonomy, were directing its defenses.

The Eaten knew all that Vekant knew about the operators on the summit, along with the little he knew about the tower itself. A tower was a structure that enabled its handler to evoke true language very fast; it was a kind of macro-generator of Words, enabling large-scale feats like weather control and surveillance over large areas. The inner core was lined with runes, written phrases and sentences of the three true languages, the runes as effective as spoken words when evoked, and they could be evoked very quickly by the tower's handlers. Cueredon's current handlers were in possession of two of the languages that ruled the tower. The third, the one known only by Great Irion and the Mage Malin, was reserved for their use. No one could gain entry into the tower without taking it from them.

The question was, could Great Irion defend the tower with the Anilyn Gate closed? Vekant, in knowing the question, transmitted its consequent uncertainty to the Eaten, who was very satisfied with the idea of a weakness.

When the work of breaking into Cueredon began, Vekant heard the voice of the Eaten as if it were his own; in fact, it had been his own until only a short while ago. But what the voice was singing, and whether this could be called singing, were not apparent. He had heard some use of Tervan Symmetries that had this quality; the Symmetries were the Tervan way of recording mathematics as music, taught to the Erejhen long ago. The most talented Prin and Drune trained in the Symmetries, and choirs with this training were among the most powerful. This was information that the Eaten had not found useful but that Vekant himself pondered, to the degree that he remembered and understood it, while bathed in the sound of the Eaten's voice.

The tower being closed, sealed in a way that disguised the entrance, the Eaten circled the base over and over, probing. Vekant's body, now the property of someone else, had grown a middle set of spindly arms, each ending in a slender hand of two fingers and a thumb; these touched the air as if tasting it as the Eaten canted and listened. To a degree, just as the creature knew what Vekant knew, the opposite was also true, so that Vekant could feel the creature's puzzlement, which was Vekant's own puzzlement, at the hiding of the door. Words were strange for the Eaten, it did not entirely know how to digest them; it had more success in absorbing what Vekant knew when he was simply aware of a fact than when he put it into language.

The Eaten rose up in an erect posture, arms out, and suddenly the sound of its voice trebled, grew vast; at the same time, like a concussion from an explosion, something from the tower struck the Eaten and flattened it, pain rushing through Vekant, through the creature. Vekant felt the body reach for breath, nerves afire. It struggled to its feet.

It began again circling the tower, as close as it could come, nowhere near the stones of the foundation. The sound that raked Vekant's nerves recommenced, and so did the feeling of a hand constricting them, Vekant inside the Eaten, neither able to breathe; but for a true-language operator this was not much of a challenge—the body was trained to compensate. The pain, though, was never-ending, and Vekant, since he was not in charge, was obliged to feel most of it; even the remainder of Vekant's own knowledge of true language was useless now that he was never the one in charge of speaking. Prin were strong in groups, sometimes in pairs, never alone.

The thing was patient. It circled the buildings, reached, was pressed back, regrouped, did it all again.

A wind had begun to build. Underfoot, a spongy fungus had begun to overlay the black sludge. The chill-trees were crowding the ruins now, an infant forest, corpse-white branches twisting out of pitch-black trunks. Some were beginning to leaf, papery pale or dark leaves, dripping shapes, or else sharp needles, or fans with jagged edges. Overhead, amid a mix of smoke, ash, fallout, moved the dark shapes of flocks and stingers, rushings of wings, clouds of flies.

He had some capacity for sadness; he could feel its echo as he looked around at what was left of Avatrayn and Citadel. Almost nothing remained intact, not a building standing, hardly three stones together anywhere in sight. Even now as the mantises grazed, they leveled any standing fragment of a building in their path as if by instinct. When he looked farther out, as he could now, easily, he saw the same: the explosions had raised a cloud of dust and debris that blotted out daylight; everywhere was gray sky and pulverized terrain, fires belching more debris into the gray, roads wrecked and ruined, cities unrecognizable, as far as his eye could reach.

Circling, probing, gradually drawing nearer to the base of the tower, the Eaten, at last, laid fingers on the foundation stones, those strange slender digits probing. Another sending from the tower flattened it, pouring such agony through Vekant that he very nearly forced the body to cry out. For a moment he was almost inside himself once more. But the Eaten reasserted itself and fought and after a while was able to move again; it touched the stones, probing deeply, then was flattened by the massive hand again, more agony. How many times?

The forest grew. Packs of man-rats rustled through the new undergrowth. Some kind of spindle-bird appeared, with a long thin beak like the proboscis of a mosquito; now and then it caught a rat and squeezed it in sharp talons, sucking the animal dry. Dragonflies flittered over gray-petaled flowers and round, red-spotted mushrooms. As hours passed, a new landscape appeared, as if its seeds had been planted in the mantis shit, as if the black ooze were a wave of transformation. All the while the wind grew and the heavy sky grew heavier.

The Eaten circled the tower, fought off pain, rose to its feet when knocked flat on its back, struggled against the enemy's Words. Each time it managed to touch the stones of the tower for a while and each touch gave it more knowledge of the stone. The Eaten was patient. There was a door here, and the creature would find it, only a matter of time.

Conflagration

1. Kitra

The worst of the terror had passed from Kitra and she was trying to control herself, huddled against Figg's legs and looking out at the devastation along the shores of the Silas. Her heart pounded and her head ached. She was watching Dekkar in loathing, averting her eyes whenever he appeared to be watching.

Stunned, whichever way her thoughts landed, she found no comfort except in the thought of her brother. The priest had told her she would see Binam soon. Only that thought made her want to stay in the boat; the fact that she might be with him soon kept her from screaming and jumping out of the *Erra Bel* to take her chances in the river.

She was as afraid of Dekkar as she was of anything chasing them. She could only have explained the fear as an instinct— she had never before seen a Prin who did his work so easily. He ought to show more sign of effort after having fought the thing chasing them, after having put fire to kilomeasures of riverside. She had watched Prin of all kinds do their jobs at one time or another, but what Dekkar could do was beyond anything she had seen. Her dread of him grew worse as he paced the boat, watching.

Day should have come hours ago but there was very little light; she felt as if a hand were constricting her chest, as if the shadows were closing in on her.

In the forest, the mantis creatures were rampaging and flocks of the shadow birds were diving and looping, visible when they passed close to the boat. The creatures appeared to be attacking the Dirijhi gardens, the cultivated zones at the base of each tree, tended carefully by the syms. These days, many of the gardens had become habitats for toxic or flesh-eating plants or even laboratories for experimental growths of various kinds; the rampaging mantises were carefully avoiding contact with the great trees themselves.

She could see well due to a filmy light that clung to the boat and spread out from it; she realized soon enough that this light was something Dekkar was making, that he was not only watching the riverbanks himself, he was making sure that the others could see, too. For a moment she felt as if he were showing this to her in some particular way, just as he had allowed her to be awake when the others were sleeping, as if she were his witness. He made no sign of this, neither speaking to her nor taking note of her at all, so perhaps the paranoia was only an offshoot of the fear. But she did watch, heart pounding, as the creatures wrecked the Shimmering Garden.

She drew a shivering breath. "There's some kind of disagreement between the trees and their allies." She was talking to Figg, who had a hand in her hair to keep her calm.

"Excuse me?"

"Look along the riverbank. The mantises are destroying the gardens."

"Those are gardens?"

"Yes. They're cultivated by the trees and the syms."

"You think it means there's a problem?"

"The creatures aren't hurting the trees, see? It's a demonstration of force."

"That's right," Dekkar agreed, speaking quietly, his voice making her shiver, though it sounded like his ordinary voice. "This is one ally keeping another in line. He's showing his hand with the trees as well."

"Rao?" Figg asked.

Kitra could no longer bring herself to look in the direction of the priest's calm voice; she was staring fixedly upriver, where a burning boat hurried toward them, lighting the landscape as it rushed downriver with the current. The mantis that was following the *Erra Bel*, the one from the farm, nudged the flaming wreck away from the boat. Keely had pointed the mantis out to them a while back, and now she was watching it, too. "Or it might be an ally helping another with an internal enemy," she said.

"That's even more likely." Dekkar paused in front of her; she felt him watching and shivered.

When he was close like that, at instants she heard some sound, the briefest possible snatch of music, so overwhelming; her skin went to bumps and she hugged herself. These moments were like the glimpse of him she had gotten when he reached into his pack, or when he was talking so earnestly to Pel. She said, "I doubt the trees all agree with each other about this war." Her voice sounded much calmer than she felt; speaking soothed her, in fact, and being answered by Dekkar in his easy tone soothed her more, though she was still trembling.

"Perhaps some of them feel tricked, as your rebels did."

"We're near our landing point." Pel spoke without turning to face them; the boat was moving much too fast for him to take his eyes off the river. Their speed slowed and Kitra felt the lurch of the impeller beginning to brake. Along the riverbank distant fires flickered, and the underside of the smoky clouds glowed overhead.

Through her ran a sensation of sinking, as if she should already be in tears; the whole landscape reeked of terrible events, from the lights in the sky and the fires along the southern horizon to the crashing of shadowed marauders along the riverbank. The gentle disk of light still radiated from Dekkar, more obvious now, serenity in the glow, but he at its center still fearsome, forbidding. She drew closer to Figg, who put an arm around her, a hand on her shoulder.

She put out of her head any need to think about what she was doing, what it meant to feel such affection for Figg without questioning it.

Ahead, at the prow of the boat, was a fork in the river and a series of docks and buildings along the promontory of land; a few scattered boats floated at the docks, lit by rows of globe-shaped lamps. She should recognize what part of the river this was—she had sailed very far up the Silas on her second journey here—but her head was foggy. Maybe this was a fork of the Silas around an island or maybe the place where one of the tributaries fed into the main river. The buildings were clearly one of the trade posts the trees maintained; they frowned on cities inside Greenwood but allowed settlements of a certain size. Pel drew up the boat and backed the impeller to stop; the *Erra Bel* drifted in the water, and Pel turned to look at Dekkar.

On the docks stood formations of syms, a hundred or more, staring through the muck and the dark at the riverboat. A few leaned on canes or crutches and some were bandaged or splinted. Some were helping other wounded out of boats on stretchers, carrying the stretchers into the buildings near the docks.

A pair of the syms stepped out of their formation, walking down a long pier into the river; the boat was holding its place some meters off the end of the pier, rocking a bit in the flow.

She found herself staring at one of the pair, only gradually seeing the shape of the head, the familiar features in the alien face: her brother, wrapped in that altered skin of his, his body half plant, half animal, but clearly he and no other, waiting at the end of the pier. Heart in her throat, she stood, walked to the glass. "That's Binam," she said. "That's my brother."

"Which one?" Figg asked, stepping beside her.

"The taller one. The other one is a female—used to be female, I mean."

"You're sure?"

"You think I wouldn't know my own brother?"

"He's here to greet us," Dekkar said. "He's here because you're here, Kitra, because they think we'll trust him enough to let him on board."

"How do they know I'm here?"

"Their allies know a good deal about us by now, I suppose."

She looked at Dekkar's face for the first time. Distant he did look, but he knew her and she felt for a moment she had nothing to fear from him; she knew the panic would return, but for the moment she breathed without a feeling of constriction. "Then will you let him on board?"

"Yes."

She felt her eyes filling with tears and nodded. Her heart pounded and she covered her mouth with her hand, leaning against Figg, getting her breath.

"Are you ready?" Dekkar asked.

She nodded quickly, wiping her eyes.

Pel piloted the boat to the end of the pier, backing the impeller while he opened the cockpit and threw out a mooring line. The woman sym tied the boat to the dock and Kitra opened the side canopy, a ladder sliding up.

Binam stood there, watching with no emotion she could read. The only sign of agitation he showed was in his mouth; the corner of his mouth quavered a bit until he saw her. He tried to smile, glancing at her friends, at Dekkar in particular. "May we come onto your boat?" he asked.

Kitra looked to Pel, who nodded, swallowing. She reached a hand to her brother, flushed with the moment, uncertain what expression she was offering him, whether happiness or uncertainty.

His skin had the same cool, smooth texture she remembered. He showed no sign of having aged; his weight was the same, his grace, his care in movement, placing each foot as if there were some delay in the sensation reaching him, placing the next step with the same caution. The other sym, the woman, moved with no such hesitation. "We welcome you." He was shivering as he spoke. "We welcome you in the name of trees who did not wish this harmful war on your people."

"What's happening along the shoreline?" Kitra asked. "We saw the mantises destroying gardens, expensive plantings."

He glanced at his partner, and she cocked her head. "What you call mantises we call feeder-breeders, which is close to what their masters call them."

"They were attacking the gardens."

"To punish us. Because we don't want this war."

"Though it's too late now," said his partner.

"Excuse me," Binam said, "This is Kowon, for whom I am second. She's here to treat with you."

She stood considerably shorter than Binam, her skin mottled, the color of an elm leaf, whereas Binam was a darker green, more the shade of a water oak. Bowing her head a bit, she stepped toward Dekkar. "Honored Prin," she said. "Welcome to Lower Land of Flowering Silas."

He studied her, and Kitra kept hold of Binam's hand, kept him well behind Kowon, afraid of what might happen, of what Dekkar might do.

Binam, following her gesture, drew her to the back of the boat, away from the others.

Two realizations came to her when he embraced her, comforted her. First was that she felt the absence of Figg keenly, that walking away from him caused her a sensation of loss; this was remarkable not only because of his age but because he was a man. The second was related to Binam, that in his presence she felt less of a flood of emotion than she had expected. She felt glad, but not ecstatic; she felt relieved, but not overjoyed. She loved him, but she missed the feeling that she was about to rescue him. He hardly appeared to need her. In fact, he had sought her out.

"Is it true the Dirijhi moved your tree?"

"No. The Earthlings did that. The chalcyd creatures, the flocks. With sym helpers."

"Earthlings?"

He nodded. "These allies of ours. They come from Earth. At least, that's what they claim."

"Rao?"

"Yes. He's their God."

"He's here?"

"We think so. They claim so, the chalcyd."

She remembered Nerva, mouth open, sinking those teeth into Keely; she shuddered. "Those things are here, too?"

"Yes. I suppose they're our bosses now." He spoke in an even tone, almost lightly. The makeup of his body was familiar to her from before, the feeling of muscles in the wrong places, of his chest not quite moving as it should when he breathed, which was rarely, since only a portion of him relied on animal respiration. Stoma on his shoulders and arms opened and closed at intervals. "They killed my tree when they moved us. He lived for a while in new ground, but he got root sickness that the others couldn't cure. It killed his brain completely."

Her heart was pounding. "He's dead."

"Yes. That makes me a widow."

"A what?"

"That's what we call a sym without a tree."

"But how do you eat?"

"His tree body still grows for the moment; he still makes sap."

"But you're free of him. Are you sorry?"

He cocked his head at her, looked at her quizzically, lips pursed. "It's been a long time since I thought about freedom."

"What do you mean? You remember how we parted last time, don't you? You told me you were a slave and I told you I would come back for you."

"Yes, I remember." He hung his head a bit. "That was a long time ago."

"I've come back twice since, but not to your part of Greenwood. I didn't have any way to get you out."

He shook his head. "It doesn't matter. I wouldn't have gone."

"What?"

"There's no need to think about it anymore. I wouldn't have gone with you, anyway."

"Why?"

"Things change. The trees and syms had to pull together when the invaders came." He released her, listened to the quiet voices near the pilot's console, watched the others. He tried to shrug, the movement not quite right. "I would have had to stay and fight."

"Why?"

He gave her a wistful smile now. "This is my home."

She was confused: to feel her long-held image of him change on top of all the turmoil of the past few days was too much. She ran a hand through her hair, took a breath. On the docks, some of the syms were milling about. From one of the lit buildings beyond spilled a group of syms in a rowdy mood, a rare sight; it appeared they had been drinking a bit, so maybe the building was a tavern. Groups were keeping watch on the river and others on the trees. "Why did they move your tree?"

"The Dirijhi bred for him a long time. I told you. He was created to be a prodigy with numbers, with their form of mathematics."

She looked at Keely, who was holding his math box in his hands again. He liked to keep it close; he and Dekkar appeared to trade it back and forth. "For Rao. To serve Rao."

"Yes. He was brought here to be part of a group of trees rooted specially together. Part of making that thing in the sky that chased you. As far as the trees are concerned she's a monster, but she's one of them, in a way. My tree was in the first planting to try and make her, and a lot of them died."

Pel was tying a second mooring line to the pier, and Kowon moved toward the steps as if she was ready to climb them and exit the boat. She signaled with her hand and Binam acknowledged. "We should head to council now. Are you coming?"

"Council?"

"Yes. The trees want to talk to the Prin master. That's what Kowon was asking for."

"He's not Prin, exactly."

Binam cocked his head, arched what remained of a brow.

"Never mind." She shook his head. "Yes, I'll come. I'll be glad to be off this boat."

"Do you have a hood for that biosuit? Pull it up if you do."

She reached for the hood, slid the one-pass netting over her head, sealed it. The others were doing the same. "Where are we going?"

"Not far. To the dumb-tree grove."

"The what?"

"The dumb-tree grove. Made of trees that don't have a brain. It's our version of a public building."

Keely was standing beside his bunk, Zhengzhou kneeling in front of him to help adjust his one-pass hood. The Hilda had come to life and was waiting behind him. He climbed out of the boat, the patch of green stuff on his face gleaming in the harsh globe lights; it looked supple but somewhat like Binam's skin, a stiffer texture. Keely moved as if he could see well enough, but he held his head perfectly motionless; his seeing had nothing to do with his eyes. He carried himself with the same distant air Dekkar had. Just now he ran up and handed the math box to Dekkar again. Dekkar petted his hair a bit, knelt in front of him, said something nobody else could hear. Keely nodded, ran back to his keepers, walking hand in hand with Zhengzhou and the Hilda.

Kowon led, Dekkar at her side, Keely after, and the rest followed, along with all the syms loosely in formation as if they were a bodyguard.

"What happened to the child?" Binam asked, staring at the membrane, so as they walked she explained, quietly, that Keely, too, was a math prodigy, brought here to fulfill some purpose related to Rao. She told the story of what had happened since the war broke out, including what she knew of the attack on the farm.

He told, in his turn, his own story, that shortly after her visit ten years ago he had learned of the Dirijhi's allies, that they taught a way to fight Great Irion, a way to win back the world from the Hormling and make the Dirijhi masters of it, if the Dirijhi joined with them. "They claim they can take control of Heaven Gate," Binam said.

"You mean the Anilyn Gate?"

"Yes. We call it by the other name. But that's what we mean."

Up a long path they walked, past intact gardens and immense old Dirijhi, some of them multitrunked, supported with buttress roots, virtually groves. Syms kept the walkway carefully maintained, clean round stone bordering slate tiles set in earth; between the tiles grew moss, chamomile, creeping jenny, green creeper, lichen, mouse-grass. On either side, living trees grew twisted together to make vaults, colonnades, arbors; farther along, older growths of dumb-trees, started by the oldest syms and carefully tended all the decades since they came, climbed toward common points to create vaulted chambers, each more spectacular than the last, one after another mounting the terraces of the hill.

The uppermost terrace was tall and narrow, walls woven of living evergreen, carefully groomed and pruned, the smell of cedar and pine pungent in the air. At the center of the chamber was a hot-stone hearth, no flame burning since the Dirijhi did care for any form of smoke; the rocks were heated using microwave technology provided by the Hormling; pots of water among the rocks provided constant moisture, pleasant to the syms, and there was also a larger pool for bathing. Some of the injured syms had been brought here for nursing, their pallets lined at the edge of the pool on the rocks or the grass.

The syms who had accompanied the party from the docks seated themselves in a pattern, groups of six or nine alternating in a ring, eleven groups in all, and the rest stood behind. Kowon stood in the middle of the circle with Dekkar; Kitra took her place near him with Keely and Figg. Binam patted her hand, touched his cheek to hers, and walked to Kowon's side. The two of them sat together near the focal center of both groups.

"We'll link with our trees now," Binam said to Dekkar. "Then we'll all join together, in order to talk to you. Since my own tree is dead, I'll be the channel for the rest, with help from Kowon. My sister has seen this happen before, if you have any questions." He closed his eyes, slow and languid.

For Zhengzhou, at least, the fact that Binam was Kitra's brother came as news. There had been no time to talk to her about any of that part of the affair at hand, given all the events of the night. Perhaps this was news for some of the syms as well, though this would have been difficult to discern.

Dekkar beckoned for Kitra to join him. She felt an edge of the apprehension return.

"What does he mean, you can explain this? You've seen a conference of this kind before?"

She nodded. "Once. The trees are linked to their syms and to one another. They can conference with one another without the need for speech as we know it; the trees communicate in long, complicated protein molecules. It's a slow process, though they've used Hormling technology to speed it up a bit. The trees will speak to each other and to their syms in that language. My brother and Kowon will be the voices through which the trees speak to us. Since the trees make words fairly slowly, Binam and Kowon will be speaking for more than one tree."

"Welcome to the Hall in Lower Land," said Binam, eyes only partly open. "We are the living grove around you. We would name ourselves but our names do not translate well into your speech. For instance, my name is She-He-Who-Of-The-Sap-Tartly-Rising-Fills-The-Sky-Leaves-With-Bronze-Veins-Juice-In-The-Morning-Dove-Nest-Maker. This is only part of the name. You see? Therefore you need only try to hear what difference you can in our voices."

"Perhaps if we let the translators share the work," said Kowon.

"Agreed," said Binam, though in a different voice.

Binam again, tone lighter. "So, we are come together with the Hidden Master to speak in Earnest Council."

Dekkar nodded his head. "You give my title correctly. How do you know?"

"Some of us were servants of Rao," said Binam.

"In the early days," Kowon said. "Before we saw him clearly."

"We have no quarrel with your people," Binam said, almost hurriedly, agitated. "Pardon me. I should not interrupt."

"No, indeed, you should not," said Binam in another voice.

"Excuse us," Kowon said, "we must reinforce our protocols."

They were silent again, their eyes closed. The day or night had got still, no wind at all. Overhead the intricately woven branches of the dumb-trees reached toward the peak of the chamber with something near symmetry, bands of diamonds spiraling away from a point. One lone sym was high above them, pruning or grooming the evergreen branches, hanging on with one arm and both legs and pruning with the free arm.

"Once again, we apologize," said Binam.

"The intrusion will not recur."

"In Earnest Council with animals of your kind, we speak as a collective in a pattern so that those of us who are not actively speaking may listen or collect their thoughts," explained Kowon.

"We are not as swift as you in speech, though we have learned to become more so." Binam adjusted himself. The voice changed again, a slight tick up in pitch, then down again, and a variation in cadence, to mark the change in speaker. "First of all we express our understanding of your feeling of loss, which is like our own feeling of regret at the burning of our sister-brothers along the river shore."

"The difference being that I contained myself and my anger against your people along the shore." Dekkar spoke dryly, almost sarcastically. "Whereas your people and your allies have wiped out the greater part of a continent. Had I been so merciless, there would not be one tree standing."

Binam sat calmly, hearing and waiting, a half-smile on his face, vacuous; he was elsewhere, himself subordinated to the conversation coming through him. Kowon sat with her head bowed. Binam said, "There is justice in what you say. We are not here to argue the case for or against the grievances the Dirijhi have presented in the past. We are here because we do not believe a war was necessary to achieve our ends. Our allies have used our anger to make us a tool. Those of us who have come to know this have spoken out in this hour. You've seen the result along the shore." A tick up or down in tone between each sentence; many trees speaking a part of a thought in order to keep the conversation moving forward.

"We are here to make recompense for some ill-conceived actions," said Kowon. "We're here to do what we can."

"Which is?"

"We can guide you to Rao. All of us." Binam paused, this time for effect. "Not that you need us. He'll come to you in any case."

"The forest has changed so much north of Lower Land, we hardly know it ourselves anymore," Kowon added. "We can't do much to protect you from the Earthlings. But we can help keep you safe in the crossing through hostile trees."

"You can send all these syms with us?" Kitra asked. "What about their trees? Don't they need to feed?"

"They're widows," said Binam. "They're being weaned."

"Many trees have died in our preparations for this war," said Kowon.

"Far too many." Binam nodded, facing not Dekkar but Keely, as if he was seeing Keely, studying him. "Is this child for Rao?"

Dekkar turned to Keely, scowled. "I prefer we do not discuss that."

"We prefer that we do. If this child is one of the vessels, you must say so."

Figg drew Keely against him, covered his ears, as if that would do any good. Kitra leaned into them both, feeling how Figg's heart pounded. Pel had stepped toward them, knelt behind them.

"Yes, he is."

"He must stay close to you as we travel, or any of the Earthlings could take him. Why do you bring the child to Rao?"

"I have no choice but to go to Rao myself," Dekkar answered. "The child must be near me, as you said."

"And when you reach Rao?"

He spread his hands. "God knows."

"Indeed. Though which god? Who knows that?" Binam smiled; then the smile faded and he blinked very slowly. "This one tires. There are many of us to carry. We have said what we can say."

His voice faded away. Kowon had already stopped speaking. A moment later the other syms stood, waiting patiently. After a while Kowon stood, shaking her head, rubbing her eyes. She dipped herself into a pool of water, then sat, dripping, on the heated rocks.

After she did this, many of the others did the same. Binam stood near the last, stepped into the water, floated there for a while, then stood, shivered, and walked to the rocks.

Next moment the world turned white with light, too bright to see, and Dekkar was rising over them through the netted branches of the dumb-tree roof. Kitra shrank to the nearest wall and her friends followed.

It appeared that the syms understood what was happening as well as anyone else. They watched the lights and one another and occasionally one of them crept to the edge of the dumb-trees and looked out. Kitra sat between Binam and Figg, cradling Binam's head in her lap.

"The one in the flitter is not so good against Dekkar," Keely said. "When he has the math box, she can't do very much."

"How do you know?" Figg asked.

"I can see. She's trying to attack him here because she doesn't care whether he attacks the trees here or not, but she's not able to do much. He's singing this song, like—"

"Countersinging," Pel said.

Keely turned his face toward Pel. "Yes."

"I know a lot of the right words for what you're seeing," Pel said. "I've worked around these people before."

"They never come very close to each other," Keely said.

"They won't," Pel said, "until the end."

"The end?"

"When one of them is ready to finish the other off."

Figg gave Pel a warning look, but Keely said, "It's all right, Uncle Figg. I have to know."

"Why, Keely? Why do you have to know?"

"Because this is what the math box is training me to do."

What Figg said next was drowned out in a howl, a chorus of shrieking, a sound so shattering it stunned Kitra, sent her flat to the ground, panicked. She waited for a concussion to follow but there was only more of the shrieking, and she realized she had heard the sound before, from the mantises when they attacked Dembut.

"He's killing the monsters," Keely said. "Don't be scared. The noise is almost over."

A sound followed, unearthly, glass breaking, something like the pop of a cheap lightbulb blowing out, magnified by a million. Keely laughed, clapped his hands to the green membrane that simulated the movement of his upper lip, delighted peals of laughter. "They popped," he said. "Every one of them. Into a million pieces. You should have seen it!"

Dekkar became visible on the ground again, and for a moment Kitra had the impression he had always been there, that the image of him rising into the air like some kind of star afire had been an illusion, that all the while he had been on the ground with the rest of them, hidden. All the true-language types liked to hide their work, especially from one another. He was pocketing stuff in his robe again, something that he appeared to catch out of the air; gathering in his equipment, or at least some of it. She was meant to see this moment, she had the feeling, or even this much would have been hidden. He paid no attention to her at all, but she was aware of him, peculiarly.

The syms formed up in orderly ranks. "We're going farther north now," Dekkar said. "I wish I could leave you behind; you would be safe with these syms. But that thing is following us."

"We think we'd rather stick close to you," Figg said, looking down at Keely. "Wouldn't we, son?"

"We'll need a few minutes to organize supplies," Pel said, nodding to Kitra.

"I bought a lot of transportable stuff," she said.

"Hurry." Dekkar looked almost tired—or maybe thin, stretched, was a better way to put it. "We'll go back to the docks but we can't take much time. We have a long walk ahead."

"The syms are coming with us?"

"Yes. They're more valuable than trees, it seems, especially widows. Once they're weaned they can be fed from any tree. Even Rao won't like to destroy them."

"You know more than me, if that's the case," said Kitra.

"Your brother told me. I suppose he's reliable?"

She was watching Binam in the distance. "Yes. I'm sure he is."

Binam walked with her when they trudged north, leaving behind the *Erra Bel*, heading out of the Lower Land of the Flowering Silas. Some of her pleasure must have shone in her face, because he asked her, after they were settled into the walk, "What's the matter?"

"Nothing. I'm happy, actually."

He averted his eyes, nodded his head. Lips pinched together to keep them still, like when he was a boy. "Me, too."

"Things have changed for you since the last time I saw you."

"For some of us. Not for all." He met her eye. "I won't lie to you, Kitra, I was miserable when I saw you, I wanted to die."

"What happened?"

"The tree changed, for one. After he was moved, he understood pain a bit better; and when he learned he was dying, it gentled him. When we began to see what was happening, what the invaders planned, he lost his sense of superiority. Some of us understood we had something larger to fight for, tree and sym alike."

Beyond the dumb-tree halls stood a long road, vaulted over by the Dirijhi, raked and smoothed for walking and for transport by truss, though use of the pack-birds was dying out in favor of the riverboat and the inland scooter. Neither of these was available at the moment, however, due to the war; nearly everything mobile had been taken south. The party headed north along the road, moving under the cloudy sky in the calm, windless day; once, for a moment, the sun peeped through and threw down frames of light onto the murky river. For a while the road ran along Silas, then turned a purer north.

"All these years you've worked to come back for me," Binam said. "I wrote to tell you I was well, but I couldn't say much more. Mail from here is censored."

"I never believed you were well, no matter what you wrote," she said. "I knew you were hiding something."

"I can leave anytime I please once I'm weaned," he said. "As long as I can find tree sap. I'm not tied to any particular place in Greenwood anymore."

"But would you leave Greenwood altogether, if you could?"

He thought for a while, the look on his face serene, so unlike the image she had carried for the past decade. He shook his head. "No. Like I said before. This is home now. I've given up too much to make a life here, I won't live anywhere else."

"Do all of you feel that way?"

"All of us who aren't treated like slaves, yes."

A moment later, Figg's eyes on her from up ahead, she had an impulse to run forward; she took Binam's hand and led him along. "Let's walk with Figg," she said. "I want you to meet him."

"Your friend?" Binam raised an eyebrow. The gesture made it a boyfriend question, like when they were telling secrets on the algae farm long ago.

"Not yet. But maybe." She smiled, feeling herself blush a bit, but looked him in the eye again. "I don't guess you've stopped to think about your parents."

"What? Why?"

"They're probably dead, Binam. They lived in Feidreh. Everybody there is gone. Those are the reports."

He looked somber and slowly shook his head. "I suppose I did know it in a way. But I don't feel it."

No reason came to mind to cause her to press him for more. Neither of them had been close to their parents in decades, not since Binam's sale to the Dirijhi. She touched his hair and nodded. "When I get south again, I'll find out what I can and let you know."

"All right." He nodded, more sober than before.

"Tell me one more thing. Do widows ever get linked to another tree?"

He laughed, the most open sound he'd made since she saw him. "Yes, sometimes."

"Would you consider it?"

"If it were the right tree, yes." He smirked at her, looking himself up and down. "I mean, after all, what else am I going to do? Open a vegetable market?"

2. Fineas Figg

After a few hours of walking, the party stopped to rest. Sometimes Figg carried Keely himself, sometimes he let one of the others take a turn, including the Hilda. The boy was easiest to carry piggyback, and severely small for his age to begin with. He walked on his own when he could, but he was weak from the burns to his face.

As for Figg, his own wounds ached and throbbed, swollen so that his face looked ungainly and awful. So far the wounds stayed dry, but at moments he felt as if bolts were being driven into his head.

During a rest, Dekkar looked them over again. "I have no more thuenyn or himmel leaf," he said, "I used all I had left on Keely's face."

"I have a pouch," Pel said. "Good fresh stuff."

Dekkar examined them, Keely sitting by his knees. "You have to cut them off," Keely said.

"I see. Yes. They want to grow into him, don't they?"

"Yes."

"I'll give him patches like yours, Keely, how about that? Smaller ones. What do you think?"

"He'll look like he's in my family," Keely said.

"I am in your family," Figg said, tugging the boy's ear gently.

Keely giggled—like a small boy again, for a moment, but in a healthy way. It pleased Figg no end to hear Keely laugh.

"Is that what you're going to do?" Figg asked. "Cut them off me?"

Dekkar nodded. "I won't cut them, of course. But that's the essence of it."

"What are they trying to get inside me to do?"

"To kill you, I think. Or else to change you into one of those flock creatures. I'm not sure which."

"With the teeth, you mean? Not a becoming look for me."

"I daresay not."

"Do what you have to."

"In your case, the skin will grow back and the patches will fall off. I doubt you'll even have a scar. Though old as you are, who knows?"

"Bastard."

A few moments later his skin burned and for an instant he felt the pain of it, before Dekkar sent that away, too. "I let you feel the pain for a moment so your body will know it's there. But no more." He had put silver hand-chains over his hands; he lifted the swollen, pus-filled sores off Figg's face, set them into a clear, filmy sac. Even glimpsed in transit, the lumps of flesh were putrescent and lurid; Figg's stomach lurched. His face felt raw, as if the breeze were touching it inappropriately.

One by one Dekkar placed his leaves and powdered stuff onto Figg. Where there had been a feeling of rawness there was now soothing, a skin of balm. As Dekkar wet the leaves they softened, ran together. At first Figg felt the dry cool of the leaves as separate from him, and then there was a melting, merging, a light fragrance as if he had breathed in mint. Keely was laughing, clapping his hand to his mouth. If he had been using his eyes to look at Figg, he would have been facing the wrong direction, but he was seeing in some other way.

"You look like a Disturber toy, Uncle Figg."

"Thank you, son. I'm sure that's a good thing."

He giggled again.

For a moment the boy sat oddly still. A shudder passed through him. Figg pushed Dekkar away, looked at Keely, who wanted to put his hands to his head but appeared afraid to touch himself.

"My head hurts," Keely said.

"Do you need the box?" Dekkar asked.

He nodded. Dekkar gave it to him, helped him with the headset. After a while the aura of pain around him lessened, but still they sat there. "What's happening?" Figg asked, nodding toward the boy.

"She injected him with some kind of code. The Nerva-thing did, I mean. I would guess the code is to build something in his brain, some kind of programming or knowledge, or maybe something else. I don't know. But something to do with Rao needing to inhabit him quickly. Keely's going to start to change, he probably has already."

"To what?"

Dekkar shook his head. "I don't know. He doesn't know either, do you, Keely?"

He shook his head. Figg lay a hand in his hair, and after a moment the boy leaned against his side.

"I've mucked with the code a bit," Dekkar said. "We'll see what happens."

Keely listened somberly, keeping very still, the math box headset on his head.

"You lie down if you want," Figg said. "Rest your head while you're wearing the headset."

"Are we walking again soon?" Keely asked.

"Soon," Dekkar said. "But the syms need to rest, and so do we."

"You don't."

"Yes, I do, sometimes." Dekkar settled into the carpet of

leaves, legs folded under him. He smiled, looking up at the clouds. "See?"

Keely lay down then, closed his eyes. Figg spread the bedroll over him like a blanket, touched his hand to the warm green membrane.

Figg lay his head in Kitra's lap and drowsed for a while. She was talking to her brother. Her voice was easy, peaceful. She stroked the leaf patches on his face with her fingertips, gentle strokes. The smoke and the haze cleared for a few moments and Figg thought he opened his eyes and saw stars, the red moon, the broad flatland of the northern forest, but then he thought he was dreaming, because he was drowsing.

"Wake up, it's time to walk some more," a voice said—a woman, Kitra, who was the first person he saw, offering him a cup of morning tea. He shook his head, sat up, took a deep breath. Keely had rolled into a ball at his back; when Figg moved, Keely made a sound, sat up and took off the headset. He had worn the math box all night.

Zhengzhou knelt near Keely, adjusted his face mask, the set of his biosuit. They had all slept in the suits, those who had slept at all. "You look fine, sport," she said.

"So do you."

She laughed. "Ready to walk, you?"

"Is Hilda up?"

"A Hilda doesn't sleep," Zhengzhou said. "Don't make fun of it."

"I'm ready. Where's Dekkar?"

"Walking the line."

"What line?"

"That thing is close to us." She glanced at Figg.

Figg sat up, shaking off the heaviness, the wish that he could go on lying still. He gave the skies a worried look, heart in his mouth. "The other magician. The other operator."

"Yes. He brought down the flitter it was in." Pel sauntered near, chewing on a sliver of wood again. "That means it's on the ground. There's nothing nastier than one of that kind on the ground."

Keely was standing, facing first one direction, then another.

Zhengzhou kept a hand on his shoulder.

Pel said, "It's a bit angry, a bit roughed up. The syms want us to move."

"That sounds like good advice," Figg said, a sinking in his stomach.

"Dekkar's staying behind. He and the creature are trying to encircle each other." Pel waited behind Keely, watching the top of the boy's head.

"It's the finish," Keely said, finding the direction and becoming still.

The syms formed up in walking ranks, the humans at their center. The Hilda and Zhengzhou led Keely again, Figg and Kitra walking behind him, Pel at the rear of the formation watching the southern sweep of forest.

"It's like he's making a fence," Keely said. "Then the tree-thing tears it down."

"Do you see where Dekkar is?" Figg asked.

He shook his head. "I see where's he's reaching or what he's doing. Sometimes I hear."

The country around them turned strange, trees and underbrush planted and trimmed to different heights in a grid pattern that reached as far as Figg could see. Mist mingled with smoke in the damp twilight, one cloud rising and the other hanging low, obscuring all but the lights and sounds. Some of the syms were carrying lanterns in the shape of spheres that lit the fog, made it appear solid.

They were moving toward a new light far ahead over the northern horizon. The road stretched toward it. Beyond the arching Dirijhi branches, beyond the galleries of dumb-trees along the road, beyond the haze and smoke, a white light glowed steady and true.

"Milkly the Blossoms," said Binam. "It's the country where we're headed. Rao made his settlement there."

"He's moving toward us," said one of the syms.

"So we don't have to find him." Pel shrugged, throwing away the rest of his sliver of wood for chewing. He carved another with his knife off the chunk of cedar at his belt. "He'll find us."

Behind, a new shrieking tore through the twilight, and the syms doubled their pace. A light burned over the forest, shimmering colors, growing brighter. The Hilda scooped Keely into its arms when he threatened to fall behind; at this pace, she was the best choice to carry him.

Why go any farther north when they were only drawing closer to a danger greater than the one that chased them? The thought came to all of them at the same time, once they heard what Pel said and repeated it, one murmuring to another. A moment later the party turned aside into a green pasture, roofed by smoky haze, surrounded by twisted columns of dumb-trees that trailed weeping branches along the border of the meadow. "A willow-wait," said Binam, turning to

Figg. "We leave them for travelers to rest. There's clean water, a rock hill, and heated stones."

The grass stood knee-high, mixed with other plants, some flowering, none brightly. A gray ash or soot had fallen over everything, particles fine enough to cling to the leaves. The syms were wandering, touching fingertips to the ash, speaking softly to one another, confused. Figg sat on a group of flat stones, not the heated variety, near the water and the rock shelter, which was big as a hill, as its name suggested. The Hilda set Keely down near Figg and the boy quickly stood, green face glowing in the soft light that filled the willow-wait.

Kitra sat against Figg's back. He felt grateful that she stayed so close and easy with the warmth to share. He should have damped down those feelings hours ago, but now it was nearly too late. The emotion was for the moment, anyway, and nothing more; it was the excitement; otherwise what would she want with an old man like him? Still, it was nice to feel this comfort. "You think we should wait here?"

"It's a better place than the road," Figg said. "I like having the rocks close."

Pel was kneeling nearby, watching Keely. "We don't want to get too far ahead of Dekkar and his business." He was checking the status of a shoulder-mount gun, getting ready to belt it over his deltoid. Behind him, Zhengzhou was arming herself, too, one gun mount already strapped to her shoulder. "That bugger up ahead is the one I'm worried about, now that it's moving toward us."

"He has to kill this one he's already fighting or else he

has to fight against two of them at the same time," Keely said.

"Sensible," Pel said. "But this new one's still got me worried."

Light, and now wind, rushed over them, something near a cyclone at moments; clouds darkened overhead; after a while a smattering of rain began to fall.

They found shelter in the rocks, pitched some of the tents as awnings to keep the storm off their heads. The syms paid no mind, some of them dancing in the rain, spinning, even in the gloom.

"Remind me why we're doing this to begin with," Kitra said, into Figg's ear. "Heading north to meet the very thing we ought to be running from."

"Run anywhere you want," Pel said, sitting down to adjust the calibration of the shoulder mount, to which he had attached a line-sighter. The sighter-targeter moved this way and that. "You won't get very far."

"Why isn't Dekkar thinking about running? Why isn't he thinking about saving himself, and the rest of us? He told us he can't kill this Rao thing, he already said so." She was speaking intently, and Figg drew her closer. Binam knelt next to her, hearing the fear in her voice.

"He came here to get as close to Rao as he could." Pel took the sighter off one shoulder, hooked it to the other. "To find out what language he uses to make magic. They all use language, you know. Every one of them."

"That's all? He knows that, now. He found out from Keely's math box."

"He may know the beginnings, but he'll need more."

"What, he has to have a sample? What about us? Why do we have to go with him?"

"Where else do you want to be?" Figg asked, looking her in the eye. "On my farm? You were the one who begged to come to Greenwood."

"That's right," Binam said, stroking his sister's hair.

She blinked as, to the south, one light and then another streaked upward, like rockets taking off. Two towers of light stood side by side, burning in the smoke, pale and colorless; then at the top the lights thinned and twined and the two points hurled themselves apart.

Again, in a different part of the south, the towers of light sprang out of the ground; reeling upward in tight spirals, faster, hurtling apart, vanishing.

In another place, and then another, the towers fountained upward, sparked, and split into arcs.

"He can't be patient, he has to pick a fight," Keely said.

A howl and a light like a cold white star shone in the center of the willow stand, and suddenly the wind blew Figg and everyone near him flat, left every person clutching the grass. Figg's heart pounded and he gripped Kitra's hand and watched her face, frozen in terror.

Keely was standing, no one else; quick as a blink he hurled the math box at one of the lights. The box arced and was caught. Keely knelt on all fours, watching the dance in the clearing.

Two lights nearby streaked upward, spinning, but this time a soundless glare of light and a booming followed, shaking the ground like a dozen fallen trees.

"He moves so fast," Keely said. "Look."

But Figg saw nothing at all, only the cloud of dirt erupting upward, a crater dug up by whatever had fallen.

The sound that followed tore at his ears; he thought about no one else, nothing else, other than the sour music going wrong in his head in every possible way, excruciating sound sliding out of hearing, saw noises and grindings, insane shattered chords, a rhythm that maddened him because at times he almost understood it, had almost heard it before.

Keely was chanting, following the sound, but what Keely said made the other sound easier to take.

"Oh, good lord," Kitra said.

The tree-thing was bound in some way, trying to get out, a cloud of dust and fire around it, and for a time a whirring of wings like the flocks of shadow birds. It moved more slowly, or had weakened, or in some way that was hidden from Figg's sight was bound. A dark, spindly creature, built like the skeleton of a Hilda, a small head, emitting that noise without the appearance of any sort of lung. Four arms, two legs, but still reminding Figg in some way of the mantises.

"My father made it from a tree," Keely said.

"He's not your father," Figg said.

Keely faced him that time, almost as if he still had eyes. He looked at Kitra then, with the same affect. "I had a sister," he said. "Her name was Sherry."

"That's right," Figg agreed.

The thing in the clearing was audible again, and they clutched at their ears; Dekkar was invisible to everyone but Keely, who watched quietly, seeing whatever he saw. "The thing is fenced now," said Keely. "It can't break out this time."

"How can you tell?" Kitra asked.

Keely was kneeling, hiding his face.

Figg had a sudden urge to turn away, he could not resist, and he saw Kitra, Binam, everyone, doing the same.

Light like a small sun filled the willow-wait, lit the whole sky far up into the roils of smoke and ash. A concussion sounded, loud, and Figg covered his ears and curled tight into a ball. A queasy wave of nausea passed through him, and in the midst of the terror, he felt as if some hand were shading him from the worst. The flash of horrific light burst quickly into utter darkness, and then there was only the plain light of day, which looked dim enough after the sudden burst of fire.

"She's dead," Keely said. "She's gone."

Figg decided to stand. He was looking into Kitra's eyes, smiling. They were alive. He got to his knees, then to his feet, and saw, across the green, Dekkar, perplexed at something on the ground. Figg was happy, he was alive, looking at Keely, at Kitra. Nothing else moved in the clearing. Dekkar was about to rise. He looked as if he had been hurt, clutching his side, and Figg took a step toward him but for some reason looked down again, at Kitra, who was about to say something, about to scream at him.

Figg heard the whirring of wings, louder. The first bird sliced through him almost in slow motion, so fast it was a blur, a thud that set him back a step, the slice keenly through his abdomen so neat he had yet to feel it when the second, the third, the first dozen birds zipped through him.

He was falling into slices through the air; his body slid into pieces and he was astonished and still alive for a moment or two, hearing the cries, the beginnings of cries, before he blacked out and waited in darkness a few more moments, even pain absent in the last moments. He had wanted to look at Kitra for longer, he liked the sweetness of her face now that she had found her brother, and he wondered what would happen to Keely, and it looked to him as if Dekkar was nearly dead, too, so that would soon be a problem for everybody. But it was too late to think about any of that now, he had this turn he was making, he was about to find out about dying, you know, and that had to be the most important thing, uppermost in his mind.

These were the final newsbursts queued for his attention. He managed only three before he died.

○**387** Keely File's ninth birthday party was held at the Marmigon in high security and complete secrecy as the investigation of Fineas Figg on charges of illegal child procurement is completed. No charges are expected to be filed. It is known that Fineas Figg, when known under his Orminy moniker Finian Bemona-Kakenet, was prosecuted for illegal child procurement when he was a teenager . . . An item nearly two years old, this had remained in his queue only because of the mention of Keely; the reference to his early-life troubles took him aback at this last second of life. Had he atoned at all?

○**388** The Mage Malin is known to have read and enjoyed the young people's story series *Oaney Oakley and the Magic Temple,* says a source close to her consort's inner circle. The Mage Consort is known to be an avid reader of many kinds of literature and does all she can to promote literacy among the children of the Reeks. Queued here because he, like everyone, enjoyed odd tidbits that humanized the Mage and the Consort, and because of the reference to the Reeks; the item was years old. No one read *Oaney Oakley* anymore.

○**389** Hanson declares it possible that the Common Fund may eliminate the overpopulation of the Reeks to the point that the Ministries will be required to provide incentives to draw settlers to the unused space beneath Senal. The Common Fund may eliminate poverty as it has been defined for centuries. A newer item queued low because it was praise of the Common Fund, which was never a priority for Figg. The last thing he appreciated before he died was this item, precisely the last, a microsecond of attention, and then he was done with the news.

3. Keely

He had been glad to have no eyes when Uncle Figg fell to pieces in front of him; it was enough to know what had happened, to feel the sudden approach of the bird-things, and then to know afterward that there was no hope of any mending. They carried Keely away as if that would keep him from knowing. Dekkar stopped the bird-things but the effort brought him to his knees and he was hurt himself, sliced along the arms and face, bleeding red blood like anybody. He was tired, clearly, after the hard fight.

In Keely's head Uncle Figg was still following next to Kitra, and then the next second Keely would remember it wasn't true. Kitra was holding him close. Zhengzhou was staring back in terror. The syms had fled in panic but returned. Penelope had vanished altogether.

The bird-things had destroyed the Hilda, too. Her leg chassis was still standing, the skirt hanging off, the torso crashed over, cut to ribbons. Nobody was thinking about the Hilda.

"Will those bug things eat him?" Keely asked.

Dekkar knelt beside him. His face was stained with sweat. "You want me to burn him? And we can say good-bye to his ashes?"

Keely nodded after a moment. Dekkar gave the order to pile up the dead. Someone carried the Hilda to the pile at the last second.

No one asked why Dekkar lit the fire. Around them the shadows of the mantises were moving in the trees, closer now that Dekkar was weaker. That was why the bird-shades had reached as close as Uncle Figg in the first place.

Everyone stayed at the fire till it was strong, till it was clear it would burn the bodies. The wind tore away most of the smell. Nothing could eat Uncle Figg this way, burned to ash.

Now the southern sky was dark. The northern light, though, was closer.

"He'll send more flocks," Dekkar said.

"You'll hold them off." Pel spoke intently, and Keely listened.

"I don't know how long. She nearly wrecked me."

"You don't have any choice," Pel said.

"I do." He wiped his face. "I can fail."

Pel's face flushed. He was about to say something. Dekkar undercut him. "Don't say it, friend. You see that light's coming closer, don't you? It's Rao."

"What does it matter?"

"Creatures like us only come close when—" he took a long breath. "He's out of my league."

"Don't say this."

"You have to know it. He's out of my league. It's Keely he wants."

"Why?"

"To become embodied. To bring himself into focus here. Strong as he is now, he'll be even stronger after that. The bodies he's tried so far have failed. Keely's close, so he has to try again. He won't wait. It's what he came for."

"You think that's why he's moving now?"

"Why else would he come to us? He knows I have to find him one way or the other, he could have waited for me."

"Why are you telling us this?" Kitra asked. "What do you think we can do?"

"Stay close to Keely. See what happens."

"Wait here?" Pel asked.

"It won't matter where."

"But it won't hurt, either."

"Then you should move to the rocks," Dekkar said. "The bugs are going to come out of the woods in a few minutes. I can't hold them back."

"Fine." Pel ran a hand through his hair. "We'll move to the rocks."

"But he'll come to you there. I'm telling you. It's Keely he wants now. He knows I'm beaten."

"Then why did we come here?" Kitra asked, voice broken. "What was this for?"

"Either help will come and find you or it won't," Dekkar said. "If it doesn't, it won't much matter where you are."

Keely was numb. He could feel the frightened bodies, could place them, outline their contours. The river of numbers had merged with his thinking but had not overwhelmed him; he was himself, could still think for himself, both in words and in not-words. "You're going to fight my father?" he asked.

Dekkar faced him directly. His hair was damp and limp and he cradled his bleeding arm against his side. "Yes."

"You have to burn yourself up."

He smiled, close to exhaustion. "That's right. It's what I was made for."

"I think it's going to be all right," Keely said, fixed for an instant on something in front of him, a shape he had never seen before, which formed and vanished as quickly as he recognized it. "But not for a while."

Dekkar was watching him, touching him in some way. He pressed the math box into Keely's hand. "I think you're telling the truth," he said, kneeling. "Keep the box with you from now on. All right?"

Keely reached, slid his arm around Dekkar's warm neck. He lay his face against Dekkar's for a moment.

A moment later someone else was holding Keely's hand—Kitra—and he could feel Dekkar wheeling away, hidden again, to face the mantises.

"Back to the rocks," Pel said. "Orderly, now."

At first they moved toward shelter with the syms formed up neatly. But they had only gotten as far as the pool of water when the black-armored creatures emerged from the dumb-trees at the edge of the clearing. They ran then, a scrambling mass. Keely moved surefooted as a cat and climbed the rocks with his heart pounding, Kitra following, the syms all scrambling up. Dekkar stayed below, near the front, with Pel and Zhengzhou, whose shoulder guns hummed and purred. Keely could hardly breathe, a hand squeezing his chest so tight. He ought to be able to do something to help, he thought, but the numbers would not move for him, the sounds clogged in his throat.

Pel guarded the approach to the rocks while most of the syms clambered up. Dekkar was partly stooped, his voice audible at times, a sign of his weakness. For a while he held back the mantises, but Father was close now—Keely could feel the weight and size of him coming near. Dekkar would have to turn to Father soon, to try to stop him.

One of the mantises lunged at Zhengzhou, her shoulder weapons firing at it, plasma packets lighting it in blue haze and flashes of fire; she leapt out of its path, guns tracking it, and Pel turned his guns on it, too, but a pack of chattering things, rats on legs, almost like cartoons, swept over her, nearly knocked her down before her secondary started to pepper them with metal shot. The mantis speared her through the meat of the thigh and lunged at her; she tore her leg free, blood gushing, but the mantis caught her with its beak, opened it wide, shoved her whole into its mouth, reared up, her legs flailing; the throat expanded, crushed her, and Keely made himself watch, the fire still smoldering.

A shriek, almost human, piercing, distant, reached them all. Around the rocks waited the mantises, too many to count, stopped at the edge of the pool of water. Others took up places behind the rocks out of sight in the dark. When the road lit up like day, Keely pointed them out to Kitra. "See down there," he said. "They're waiting."

"In case we climb down that way."

Keely felt himself pulled toward the light on the road. Father was close, like a shadow rising over the clearing. Dekkar gathered himself, vanishing from sight, managing, for the moment, to mask his singing.

Zhengzhou was dead. Uncle Figg was dead. Now the only people left were Pel, Kitra, her brother, and a handful of the other syms. Kowon was nowhere on the rocks.

Keely put the headset over his ears and the ache in his head eased.

Father stood at the edge of the clearing.

Dekkar flew toward him. That was the image. They clashed like fire and fire, as the dark sky lit up; after a while Dekkar could no longer hide his voice and Keely could hear every word of his song, clear as water, so fresh it made Keely feel heavy and dull in comparison.

Dekkar began the battle weak from fighting the tree-thing, and Father was far too vast, too strong. He allowed Dekkar to live for a while in order to hear his song; maybe he admired the music as much as Keely did, or maybe he wanted to learn what he could about it. Dekkar hurt him, though, hurt Father, at one point, and the ground shook and all at once it was over.

"They go to light or fire when they die," Pel said. The flash was over by then. Keely no longer heard the singing or saw the lights. Dekkar's voice had stopped. Everyone was stunned. Kitra's eyes overflowed. She was shuddering, hugging Keely against her, but he was seeing nothing in his head other than the light fading, Dekkar going out of the world. Dead he was, like Uncle Figg and Sherry and maybe soon like Kitra, Binam, Pel, and all the rest. Father was angry. He had been kept waiting. But here he came now, darker than the dark.

God's Holy Love

1.

If the idea of a wizard as a guest makes the ordinary host think twice about her valuables, the notion of providing hospitality to a wizard in the midst of a spiritual crisis might make her think twice and then twice again. On the other hand, if the host need fear no repercussions from failure or even breach of custom—the host-guest relationship being, in many ways, the foundation of all relations, all civilization— the wizard himself might take pause. He will need to understand his place in the local hierarchy. How long has it been since he needed to fear for himself, for his safety? How long since he felt anything like the dread others felt in his presence?

Without Words he felt naked, but he dared not use them.

Thin gave him a room and food, and Coromey had a fresh joint of something dead and sat tearing at it by the fireplace. Jessex stood in the open doors looking onto the stone terrace outside his room. A garden of leafy shrubs and small trees whipped this way and that in the wind, growing in the center of the terrace paving stones, likely elegant in good weather. The same wind gusted through the room, which was equipped to withstand it: the tapestries triple-hung on sturdy frames and lashed at the corners like sails, the tables and surfaces bare except for sturdy, heavy implements like water pitchers and basins, towels anchored by carved stone weights. The fireplace was screened and set at an angle to the terrace windows, heavy iron tools hanging in a rack, a linked-chain screen to pull over the flames. On each side of the fireplace was carved a stag in relief, animate enough that Coromey had a hard time to leave off sniffing them.

It was one thing to remind himself that time here had no relation to time in his own world; it was another to leave off impatience and apprehension. While he was resting in comfort a war was being fought. As long as he was in company of the Sisters, while he was in their hand, the passing of real time was irrelevant; he was moving on a timeline at an angle to his own, and when the Sisters chose, they would loop him back to the moment from which he had departed. But he could hardly help but be anxious. He did the prudent thing, changed his clothes, bathed in real water, rested in a real bed, ate solid food of the sort that true-language operators needed after a long journey: savory organ meats of odd animals, bits of steamed or raw vegetable, the odd rancid cheese or bit of salty clay, bites from a variety of these, a little of a lot, as they say, and not a lot of a little. He drank glass after glass of water. On the bed on his back he folded his arms across his chest and waited as if he were dead, as if he were sleeping on a slab in a room under the a tower, the sound of the sea in his ears. . . .

The Young Sister came to fetch him when they were ready to talk to him again; he felt as if he had slept and had a clear head at least. Young stood wrapped in a silky robe, panels of cloth flung over each shoulder, shining white fabric of a quality that a north-Erejhen woman would wear for mourning. She waited for Jessex with a small purse of the lips, watching him as if she had never seen him before. "Welcome, traveler."

He pulled a thick robe over him, wrapped it around his head. The fire had burned low; he had never tended it. The room had the chill of the glacier in it, pleasant to feel on his skin. "Many thanks, Sister."

"When you are ready," she said, and bowed her head.

The show of modesty, the restraint, these were far from the Young Sister he remembered. When he was a boy, she had taken him riding in the mountains, showed him his first glimpse of Illaeryn, carried him around the walls of the Hidden City in the old woodland. She had taught him Words for travel, as she had termed them: how to move hidden and how to move fast. Now she stood cold and stiff as though she never knew him, a deliberate distance.

He had removed his gems—now he reached for them, rings and hand-chains, loose gems in a pouch, but before he could touch them, Young said, "You may leave those where they are."

"Even if I prefer to wear them?"

"We prefer that you do not."

"Why?"

"As we recall, you were a difficult pupil."

The words stung him, made his heart sink. He nodded,

stiffly, and left the jewels on the bit of yellow lace where they lay.

Leaving Coromey shut up in the room, asleep by the hearth, he followed as she led him, not downstairs but up, several flights, step after step. Galled by what she had said, he noticed little at first, but after the climb had begun he paid more attention. The last flight of stairs rose in a spiral along the outer stone wall of the keep, windows open on the jagged mountain, shaggy with ice and snow, wind pressing the glass, sprays of snowflakes and crystals of ice making a pepper of sound.

At the top of the stairs lay a broad hall, not as big as the entry hall in which Thin had first interviewed him but much taller, three tiers of colonnaded balconies surrounding it. The far end was all glass, opening onto a vista that overlooked the length of the mountain ridge against which the wall of glacier traced its route. The windows were as tall as an oak and as broad, three of them, and there, framed in those windows, the Sisters waited in a nest of cushions between three fireplaces, stone flues for which arched overhead to a single chimney. Beyond the windows was nothing except air, a sheer drop as far as the tower rose; before the coming of the glacier, to fall from here would have meant a tumble deep into the valley. Young Sister led him to the windows and they walked along the thick panes of glass. "Under there is the old town beneath the ice," she said. "On a warm day when the ice melts a bit you can see the old wall."

Thin waited at the side of Plump, who was sitting on a stool, wrapped in a plain white shawl, her dress and veil of fine brown wool stuff, woven by experts, maybe by Plump herself. Thin wore pale green fabric, almost olive colored, wrapped over a pleated shift and around her head and shoulder. Each of them wore two rings on each hand and many bracelets on each wrist.

So far as he could tell, none of them were touching him with their Words; but they would work without letting it show, while he had no capacity to hide from them and dared not try. He was in their hands, there was nothing he could do. He had hoped for a kinder reception—at one point the Sisters had appeared fond of him—but a long time had passed since then, in his terms; in their terms, who could gauge how long?

Plump said, "Well, he does look older, doesn't he?" She studied Jessex over, head to toe. Her face had grown more florid but less expressive, as if the cheeks and jowls had stiffened. She wore the face as if it were a costume, and he wondered whether it might be. "The years do pass, after all, more and more of them. Especially when you're in our business."

"Trouble everywhere," Thin said, pinching a grape from a cluster on a table near her, gesturing to Jessex to come and pour tea for himself. "Help yourself. We've no servants here, we don't like them."

"Pesky. Troublesome. Irksome, often." Plump folded her hands in her lap. Her cup of tea hovered nearby, awaiting her. This startled Jessex; the Sisters were never given to display, or never had been. She sipped the tea and let it hang, watching him. "Servants are apt to be spies. Friends, in fact, are apt to be spies. Strangers are nearly always spies." She refolded her hands and waited.

"What she wants to know," Young said, taking a seat on a cushion behind him, so he had to turn, "is which kind of spy are you?"

"What did you come to learn from us, in other words?" Plump was smiling, a bit toothy, as if she thought he might be tasty.

"Answer carefully," said Young. "She's anxious to trick you if she can."

He took his own tea and sat with it in his lap, pulling the wrap from round his head. It shimmered and caught the light, and, as he had hoped, Thin saw the cloth and her eyes softened.

"Sisters—"

"Oh, my," said Plump, blushing to the roots of her white hair.

Young had stepped up from her easy lounging near the fire and had taken the edge of fabric between her hands.

They watched him a long time. In the room was a tinkling sound, like glass chimes.

"We made this," said Plump, "we gave you this." She spoke as if she barely remembered.

"You've changed the shape," said Thin.

"Many times over." He kept his voice quiet, stroking the fabric with his palms.

Young was watching it as if she would have liked to take it from him, shake color into it till it went white, and use it for her mourning.

Thin gave him a sour look, veiny hands folded in front of her.

Plump looked pleased and vexed at the same time, as if she could not decide which to feel. "You kept our gift."

"You kept it well."

"We should never have given it in the first place," Young said.

"You're bitter," said Plump. She took a bite of muffin, chewed it, swallowed it, pinched off another bite, threatened to stuff it into her mouth. "Why blame him for that?"

"We wove it for him and we gave it to him," said Thin, shrugging and turning her back, which was hung with a thick rope of pearls and gold weighed down in the fabric of her wrap.

"But I want it back," said Young.

"You can't have it," said Plump, "it's given."

"You'll be cursed," agreed Thin. "You'll be more cursed than you already are."

As quick as that, a touch long since prepared, Jessex put the fabric out of sight, finger to the center of his palm. He bowed his head, earnestly studying the griffon pattern of the carpet.

"You needn't think she couldn't find it if she wanted it," said Plump. "There's only one way to keep it safe, if she decides to steal it from you."

"What would that be?"

"Pleasing us," said Thin.

"Yes," agreed Plump, and added more. "Pleasing us, and living through this conversation."

"That would be essential." Thin was standing by the fireplace, arms folded.

In Wyyvisar Plump said, "Speak in our speech, little brother."

"That way we can tell if you're trying to lie." Young had sprawled on one of the cushions near the third fireplace, a posture more like what Jessex remembered from long ago, as if she had come in from a ride and flung herself down for a rest. After a moment the pose became more demure and the brittleness closed over her face again. She was watching him keenly, he could feel it.

"As the Sister wishes," he said, bowing his head.

"As the Sisters wish," corrected Thin.

"Remember there are three of us," said Plump. "That's what she means."

"Thank you very much, all of you, for the correction," he said.

"How very self-effacing."

"Entirely agreeable." Plump folded her arms over her bosom, pinching up her many necklaces of gold and silver.

Young made an unpleasant noise, scuffing one white boot onto one another, as if they chafed.

"So," Thin advanced toward him, taller or appearing taller, or else having rearranged the folds of her green mantle, "you are here to learn the story of creation."

"Am I?"

Plump nodded. "We're quite sure it's time."

He paused, breathing calmly. One of them had brushed him, touched him, in the quiet, with Words. Likely they were making sure he was saying no Words of his own, after the trick with the cloth. His heart was pounding. "Then tell me the story."

"The story begins at the end of time. Once upon a time," said Thin.

"So it begins," said Plump.

"One dark and stormy night," said Young.

"A Word formed the universe, and since that Word was uttered the first time, it has never again been said." This voice he failed to recognize, since by then he could no longer move and the discovery disconcerted him; one of them had stilled him; the actor was easy to mask, now that they were all speaking Hidden Speech.

Their voices blended; he was only intermittently aware of the speaker from that point.

"After the universe started, it ran itself pretty well."

"Your friends, the scientists, they've figured it out exactly, in fact."

"They're telling you the truth, that's the way things work."

But life was far more rare than it should have been and nobody knew why. Worlds that could sustain life on their own, with no intervention, were few and far between, and nobody ever understood what happened. There should have been many more than there were.

Even so, there were still quite a lot of sentient races, and they grew, and some of them became so advanced they could make themselves increasingly intelligent, and so they did, and merged to the point that they could no longer be spoken of as a race of individuals. Some of them developed technology that took them beyond physical limitations. In some of them, all their technology collapsed to pure information, to language; a single Word became a complex machine.

He no longer heard the Sisters' voices—he simply understood, as he was held in their hands, what they wanted him to know. Still, sometimes, the words came as speech.

"A long time passed," Plump said.

"The end of the universe came."

"Some of the races, the most advanced, had survived and were still alive," said Thin.

"They had agreed to die," said Young. "All of them. But in the end, none of them wanted it, none of them cared to come to an end."

You see, there was all that empty time in the past. All those worlds on which no one had ever lived. Like a new green country into which they could go, all that emptiness awaited them. They had vowed, each of them, never to tamper with the past, and, in fact, it took them nearly till the end of time to learn how to do it. They had vowed to die when the universe died, to end with it, gracefully, like a light fading at the end of day, like a star dwindling to dark. But there was all that past, empty, in which they could still live, and all they had to do was go back.

"So they are coming back," said Thin. "Or they have come back already, depending on your point of view."

"Rao is one of them."

"There are many, many others."

"She wants them here," said Young, and he was looking in her eyes, and saw she was angry. "She wants to bring them here. As many as possible."

He became more present in the room, aware of them, talking to them, no longer sharing in that mind-space created by the Wyyvisar. He was stilled, breathing calmly. Whichever of the Sisters had been holding him had let him go. How long since anyone had managed him so easily? He felt small again, like the boy he had been when they gave him the cloth they had woven, when they named him Yron and taught him Hidden Words.

"So my gates are the bait to bring them," he said.

"A good trick you learned. But for most of these creatures, she herself is the bait." Plump was reaching for her cup again, looking down at him with ruddy cheeks and chubby hands.

"YY-mother?"

"Yes."

"Why? Is she one of them? Are you?"

Thin answered, pouring herself tea again. "Are we Primes? No, indeed not. My sisters and I are Singulars. As you are. We are individuals who have been trained to transcendance. True Primes are much larger than us. They are nearly like her herself."

"Then she is a Prime."

"If she is, she was the first of them all." Plump spoke with a prim tuck of the chin, her bosom heaving and necklaces whispering.

"You don't know who she is?"

Young answered, "They claim they don't. They always have. They're older than me, they keep secrets sometimes."

"For your own good, baby Sister."

"Indeed. Look at you now, pouting because we won't let you take back that scrap of cloth we gave him." Thin was playing with a ring, a third one, an opal; she slid it onto her hand.

"Oh, I'm not thinking about that anymore," Young claimed, but Jessex was watching her and found it impossible to trust her. She had glided to one of the windows, shining white, erect, framed against the dark rock of the mountain.

"I don't believe YY-mother is any sort of Prime," Thin said, sliding off the ring again, examining it.

"I know very well what you believe, but what do you know?" Young asked.

"I don't know what you believe," Jessex said, watching her.

"It's her own little fairy tale." Young knelt by the fireplace, adding logs, stoking the glowing embers.

"Maybe. But, as you said, Sister, I am older than you. I may know a bit more."

Young said nothing, poked at the logs, smoothed the shining fabric of her gown, and stepped languidly to the fireplace where Plump was basking in the flames.

"Tell me," Jessex said again.

Young answered for her in a surly tone, as if repeating nonsense. "That YY was the one who spoke the Word that started the universe in the first place."

Thin flushed to the roots of her hair.

Plump had grown very still.

"I'm sorry, Sister," said Young, blithely. "I should have let you tell."

"Yes, you should have."

They were reacting as if she had interrupted some script that they had rehearsed and agreed on. He looked at Young, who was busy stirring up Plump's fire, gaze carefully averted.

"But that's the essence of it," Plump said. "My Sister believes YY was the first Word. For myself, I believe at the very least that she was there to hear it spoken."

"Then what is this place? What's this world she made for me and for my people?"

"You and your people have always been quite vain," Thin said. "No one ever made any world for you."

Young gave him a careful look. "I thought you had already guessed. Elder Sister said you had, with your riddle about the prison guards."

He was aware now that they meant to manage him, for some reason, to some end. While he dare not use true language, he could use his wits. "If this place is to be used to imprison Primes, there must be some reason."

"Very simple, the reason. Those great green fields of the past into which the Primes intend to move—she feels very proprietary where they're concerned, YY-mother does. She considers them to be her province. She does not want them inhabited. She does not want the original running of the universe changed, unless she changes it." Plump had drawn an apple into her lap and was peeling it with a knife, not touching either.

Thin looked at the display with a curl of the lip. "Really, middle Sister, you've become a bit of a show-off."

"You'd have me jumping up and down off my comfortable parson's bench half the day, fetching this and that." Plump spoke mildly, as Young moved to tend the third fireplace, the one where Thin was standing. "I don't see why I should bother."

"It would do you good to move."

"Perhaps I will, sometime." Plump complacently adjusted a cap onto her head, pulling her shawl tighter, as if she were cool, though the fire roared at her back. "I'm as spry as anybody," she said to Jessex very directly. "Don't let appearances fool you."

"He's not a child," Young said, "don't talk down to him."

"You want to be his friend, do you?"

"I was his friend," she said, and watched him. "We were all of us his friends, and he ours."

"Times change." Thin's tone was brisk.

"He's stood guard a good long time now." Plump spoke into her hands, which were suddenly busy with needlework; she had drawn a basket to her side and picked her embroidery out of it. She was working gold thread into shining cloth-of-cream, a pattern like a winding vine stem of elgerath. This work she did with her hands, concentrated. "Perhaps he's done his job too well."

"What do you mean, too well?" Thin snorted in derision. She was measuring out flowery stuff from small sacks; some herbs Jessex recognized, some flower scents he knew.

"If you defend yourself with the very best defenses, then the person who finally overcomes you will be the one with the very best weapons. The consequence flows naturally from the cause."

"So perhaps we should be worse defended."

"I'm simply trying to piece out why YY-mother stands by and does nothing." She was watching Jessex with a mild smile. "More tea?"

"No, thank you."

"Do you have any more questions?" Plump was smiling now. "It appears you're doing rather nicely in terms of surviving our talk. Really, we thought you might be more imprudent. You were such a problem when we were teaching you."

The words stung almost as much when he heard them the second time. "I hadn't realized."

"Speak up. We're almost done. What more will you ask?"

"Where do I find her?"

"You don't," Thin said, arms folded, staring into the distance, clouds sweeping over the sky.

"Why doesn't she help us? I understand she means to do what she pleases with me, but so many people are dying."

"Hormling people, you mean."

"Yes."

They were quiet for a long time.

"They are a special case," said Young. Her voice rang out so very clearly; Plump was visibly perturbed, and Thin set her jaw in an angry line.

"That's all, I'm done," said Young, with a show of meekness.

"That's enough, I'd say." Thin's voice cracked like a whip, and the room dimmed as clouds grew heavy over the mountain.

In the silence Jessex held himself very still, kept his mind open and clean.

"Very good," Plump said, smiling at him. "You passed all your tests. You'll live to leave Chulion."

But she told him nothing about where to find God.

2.

At least part of a wizard's wakefulness is mental discipline, which Jessex could practice without recourse to Words. Still, he found himself surprised in the night when Young Sister came to his room and told him it was time to leave, that she had come to escort him to the borders of Unyurthrupen, the Orloc name for Middle of the Mountain; it had been their city at one time, according to her.

"I thought Thin was escorting me," Jessex said, wary at the way she paced the room, arms crossed. He tried to tell whether she was using Words on him, found he had no notion, his senses befuddled. That alone was a bad sign.

"No. She's occupied."

"Really?"

"This Rao fellow," said Young, picking at the brooch pinning her undercloak, shining it a bit with her head-wrap. "He's troublesome for us, too."

"Then why don't you do something—"

She shook her head firmly. "We may not intervene in your world. That fact has not changed since you were our pupil. Only YY can do that."

"Why?"

"Old as you are, you're not ready to know that yet." She signaled Coromey to come to her hand, petted the cat-hound, knelt to look it in the face. "Are you ready?"

"Yes."

"Well, then. Be very quiet, and stay close to me."

"Why?"

"Do as I ask, Jessex."

She spoke in a tone he remembered, or thought he remembered. Her white robes were changed to dull gray before his eyes; day had become night again, darker than any night he could remember since he had left his own country.

Down stairs they descended, beyond the entry gallery, hurrying from one staircase to another, Coromey loping along beside. They passed a room where Thin was slumped over a desk, lamplight slanting across her face, asleep. Young paused to approach the desk, dim the lamp, unhurried. She led him down through the empty floors of the tower into a narrow, dark stair that wound down for a long time, and he realized, after a time, that they were far below the Orloc barracks, far below the main gate and the path that led to the glacier stair. Young Sister led him down into the dark.

"You put Thin to sleep," Jessex whispered, when they had been descending for a long time, Coromey gliding ahead of them, stopping now and then to look back, amber eyes glowing.

"Yes."

"How?"

She smiled back at him, never breaking stride. "My secret. Beyond you at the moment."

"Where are we going?"

She reached for his hand to move them along faster; her grip was warm but filled him with apprehension. "Don't be afraid, I only mean to hold your hand."

"I'm sorry."

"It's natural," she said, shaking her head. "Creatures like us never come close to one another without thinking twice." The touch of her hand made him tingle with fear. She smiled at him, and they were watching each other; she was moving them both now, a device running along the stair similar to the climbing-runes of a tower. "I'm taking you where you wanted to go."

"To YY."

"Yes."

He felt very quiet and very still. After a while he sighed. "Will your Sisters be angry?"

"Of course. I'm intervening, in a way. Disobeying. But I'm due. I'm sure I've paid the penalty for their disobedience long enough."

He wanted to ask the question this suggested but thought better of it. There were only so many questions she would answer, even in a good mood, which this might not be, entirely.

"She may kill us both," said Young. "But for once I don't care."

"Why not?"

She shook her head. "It doesn't concern you yet. The business of your betters."

He set his jaw, feeling the way he had felt at fifteen when the Sisters refused to answer one of his questions. "Tell me."

She watched him. They had come to the bottom of the stairway; he carried his full weight again, a sluggish change. She had made light around herself; he still felt constrained to use no Words of his own. Through old chambers, treasure rooms shut tight, empty prison cells, through large chambers with fresh air blowing, though by now they traveled far underground, they hurried deeper in the pale light Young Sister cast. Through rooms lined with casks of brandy and wine and rooms lined with chests of all sizes, down a broad stair, he hurried as quiet as he could to follow her, Coromey sometimes behind them, sometimes ahead. Young Sister passed through the doors at the end of the stair without opening them and pulled him through in the same way, a freezing chill passing through him.

"She rebelled herself," Young Sister said. "YY did."

"When?"

"Many years from now. When the Primes first agree that none of them will travel in time, she will be the only one of them who knows how. She will come back in time and break her vow."

"How do you know?"

"Because she's already done it. Because that's why we're here."

She stood in a long tunnel, damp, ringing with dripping water, roomy enough for one of the Hormling vehicles. The tunnel ran straight in either direction, as far as he could see when he stepped into it himself. Coromey prowled the darkness in one direction. She took his hand again and smiled and began to run, Jessex falling into stride beside her, the cathound following. Soon they were moving effortlessly fast, watching each other.

"What do you mean, that's why we're here?"

"She came back here, she made this place, after she broke the agreement with the other Primes."

"Why?"

"I don't know. Maybe because she really isn't one of them. Maybe because she didn't want any of them to learn how to move in time. Maybe because she knew they would all break the agreement in the end, and she wanted to find a place to defend herself."

He was realizing what she had said. He was staggered. "What you mean is that it's all happened already. It's all over."

"I didn't say any such thing. All over?"

"YY already broke the agreement and came here. The rest of them all waited till the end of time and did the same thing. Everything's already happened."

When she answered, the moment drew itself out, then and in his memory. He thought he caught of glimmer of fear in her face. She drew her hood around her. They were still running, in terms of physical effort, but because of whatever Words she was using, the velocity was much greater; they might as well have changed into wind and howled through the tunnel, the effect was much the same. She kept them balanced and steady as if they were flying. He could taste the rune lines along the tunnel walls.

"What's happening here to us is new," she said. "And none of the rest may come out the same because of us, all of it may split into a thousand timelines, or collapse, or too many other possibilities to count."

"What's happening to us here—"

"She came back. She changed the past when she did. Not just because she came back."

"How else?"

"She made Aeryn. After that she made the rest of this place."

"A prison and a fortress at the same time."

"And more. A nexus. A way to reach a lot of different places. But there's more."

"What?"

"The Hormling. You know their legend, that they were brought here by a colony ship, that they came from Earth."

"It's true, as far as I know," he said. "The ship is really as old as they say, I've walked on it."

She gave him an envious look. "I wish I were as free as that." But her expression changed. "You're quite right that the legend is true. The *Merced* did come here from a place called Earth, the ship did establish a successful colony that grew to cover all of Senal. But not in the first running of the universe, and not without help."

It took him a moment to hear. The flood of emotion was intense; he felt nearly breathless. "There were no Hormling?"

"In the first running of the universe, the *Merced* was lost."

"But she rescued it."

"YY did, yes. When she broke the pact, when she came back herself, she found the *Merced* and brought it here. She tended the Hormling as patiently as she tended your people."

"Why?"

Her expression was grim. "To make targets."

His stomach lurched; he closed his eyes. He wished he could speak Words that would make the meditation-space in his head in order to rid himself of this feeling of helplessness, but he shook off the impulse.

"She wanted to draw the strongest of the Primes, which required a true prize. Eventually she plans to draw them all here, to tempt them with something they can't resist. The combination of your gates and the wealth of the Hormling is the lure. As is she herself."

"I don't understand, why my gates? She could have made them herself."

"Could she? She never has."

"But surely you Sisters can."

"Not in your world."

"But the other Primes?"

"To make a gate, they have to know Wyyvisar. Teachers are hard to come by. And even you don't know all that it means to speak that language. Not yet."

He was beginning to understand. "You said the Hormling are part of it, too."

She grimaced. "The truth is, no one expects the Primes to settle themselves in uninhabited stars when they head back into the past. They'll head for one of the inhabited worlds, for slaves or diversion or what all. So YY made a big puddle of sentients and added your gates as soon as she had you ready to make them."

"Bait," he said. His heart was sinking.

"And now she means to destroy your Oregal."

His heart was pounding; he felt certain now that Young was attempting to ensorcel or ensnare him in some way. But he also recognized the truth when he heard it. "Because we do our job too well."

"You were always a bright lad."

"Rao's here," he said. "The trap worked."

"And where Rao goes, others are sure to follow."

"What don't I know?" he asked.

"About what?"

"What you said before. Wyyvisar. What don't I know about it?"

He expected a teasing look, but what he got was sadness, even an edge of pity. "You'll learn sooner than you like. Don't rush it or try to foreknow it. Nothing helps prepare you."

"You're trying to frighten me."

"I would if I thought I could," she said.

You can, he wanted to say, a knot in the pit of his stomach.

"God lives in the Words." At the time he thought only that she was expressing a spiritual belief, bringing that part of the conversation, and the journey, to an end.

3.

Before, she had carried him at a speed he could comprehend, but now they moved faster still. He was no longer sure whether Coromey was with them and he had no way to ask, he had no voice. There was no question of talking; he had to balance himself, in an odd way, which was easy to do but which required concentration. He was blind, feeling only the balance of himself, wondering whether Coromey was near, feeling Young Sister around him, encompassing. Where were they going?

Did she warn him he would become blind and stay that way for a while, before it actually happened? He remembered a warning in her voice. He remembered suspecting that she was using Words. But he was nervous at the darkness, not only his eyesight but all his internal senses blinded, so that he truly saw nothing for the first time since his child-hood.

Without any sort of ceremony he came to a white place; he was surrounded with whiteness, light, and nothing else, perfect blankness in every direction. Any sense he had of himself began to dissolve in the glare. He was no longer traveling, he had arrived. Where was Young Sister? She had said she would take him to YY, to the place where YY was embodied in this world. But why had he wanted to go? What was his urgency?

For a long while, no telling how long, thoughts spun round in his head; though, indeed, as far as he could determine, he had no head anymore. He was hanging in a white light that washed everything blank, nothing at all around him other than the white emptiness, nothing but his thoughts that chased themselves. . . . All that Young Sister had told him drifted through him, all that Plump and Thin had told him. . . . He was a Singular, created out of the Erejhen race. . . . Primes made a compact to die with the universe when it died, a long time from now, but it had already happened. . . . A Prime was neither individual nor race but something beyond either. . . . YY had been the first to break the vow, a betrayer like the rest. . . . She claimed she had said the first Word, the Word that started the universe. . . . Where had Young Sister taken him?

He had arrived, but who was he?

Waiting, with nothing around him, he went over it all again and again.

God was here somewhere. After a long time he became convinced of it. She would come, she would talk to him, if he did what she wanted. But she had all the time in the world, so she insisted he had to discover what she wanted. What could he have done to make her angry, to make her refuse to talk to him when he had come so far?

Maybe years passed. He had no way of knowing. He neither slept nor moved. She could keep him waiting as long as she liked, even if he were lucky enough to discover something he might do, something he might change, that would please her.

If God had a wish of him, what would it be?

A specific moment returned to him. He had been standing on his tower, listening, when he had finally understood what Rao was. For a long time he had been hearing this new voice among all the voices he heard from his tower; for a long time he had been expecting some creature to come who would challenge him; and then Rao made himself understood, declared himself, on Aramen. This was clear, a memory etched in the space around Jessex, tangible as if he were creating it again. He stood outside himself and watched himself.

When he had understood what Rao was, that he was old beyond any point in measuring, that he had traveled here from an incomprehensible distance, that he had come because of the Anilyn Gate, Jessex immediately set off for the mountains and, when he could no longer guard the gate directly, he closed it.

He was sitting in the mountains with the animal, Coromey, feeling Rao begin his war; and he made the decision to close the gate rather than go through it himself to fight the war. The moment echoed, he closed the gate, over and over.

The memory returned to him so clear, and for a moment he remembered his own name again, could hold onto it, while he contemplated this problem, this memory that had come back to him, a few moments of awareness, and then he understood.

She wanted the gate opened again. God she might be, but she could not open his gate.

So, after a while, and maybe a little reluctantly—because his memory of his name would fade again, and he would be lost again—he did what had become so easy for him: he touched that gate he had made, which was no more than a place inside himself, and opened it.

God was pleased, and shone the bounty of her love on him.

4.

He found himself stripped naked in a circular room, a domed roof overhead, a pattern of tile on the floor in green and white, three thin circles of black marble on the floor, columns of black marble ringing the perimeter of the room. Windows on all sides looked onto treetops, as far as the eye could see. In the distance the notched shape of a mountain stood silhouetted against farther peaks; he should know this range by name, but there was something between him and the knowledge. He ought to know this forest, too, but his mind was stripped clean of many nouns. He had come for a good reason, he had been holding onto that thought, but what was the reason? Someone had journeyed with him here, and there had also been an animal on the trip, Coromey. That name was clear. Coromey, a cat-hound, had traveled with him. Maybe someone was letting the animal run about in the park or the forest, among all those trees.

Something felt wrong with the landscape, the when, not the where.

The wind felt like the weeks before winter, fall sharpness growing fierce, a pinching cold; but the trees were green as summer. He closed the window and fastened the frame again, his skin flushed, gone to bumps. He was sure he had been wearing clothes but on the other hand he was certainly naked now. Maybe he would have been less concerned with his state of dress except that he had also lost his name somewhere and that concerned him more. He had the name again for a while and lost it again. He possessed several names, in fact, and had misplaced them all.

She kept him in the room for a long time in order to make him forget himself and everything else; she did this to prepare him for something, to kill him, maybe; she had told him she might. God kept him here in the windy room in the icy nakedness of his body, she kept him here to wash him clean of everything he had come to say.

"I believe he's ready," said a voice, a woman's voice.

She was waiting at the center of the room. Near her was a bright light that moved at odd moments; her figure was silhouetted in the light, sometimes distinct, most often merely outlined. She might have been young or not. The shape was a woman's but he could not pinpoint why he thought so, perhaps the lower set of the hips, or the waist, or the suggestion of curves in the outline. When he tried to come nearer to her he found himself instead beside one of the windows again, and had to make his way back to the edge of the black columns.

His voice sounded weak, thin. "Who's here?"

"Who, he asks. Who. He might ask, whom did I come to see? Seeking whom did I walk across the ice and snow?" She appeared to be sitting now. More than one light glared at him, obscuring her, sometimes illuminating a part of her, as, at this moment, her hand, skin silky brown, covered with rings, bangles on the wrist, hand-chains and finger-chains studded with gems, nails pierced with tiny stones. The whole hand glittered, encrusted, fingertips painted ochre. "Here you are."

"I came to ask——" He said that much and stopped.

"Go on. I've come to hear you."

"I can't remember." He did remember, though, that he was naked, and he was ashamed and covered himself. "Where are my clothes?"

"We took them. What do you need them for?"

"I'm cold."

"You don't need to be. You know ways to manage cold, you've done so before."

He thought about it, knew it was true. He knew a lot of things, he could do a lot of things that other people couldn't. At the moment, though, he failed to name a single one, and the only thing he knew how to do was to shiver. "I can't anymore," he said. "I don't know why."

"You don't?"

"Someone must have done something to me."

"Yes. I suppose so."

"Why?"

She was smiling now. He could see her teeth, her red lips, her chin. A gem pierced the flesh beneath the center of her lower lip; it gleamed bright as a star. He closed his eyes. She said, "Perhaps you've failed someone who holds you very dear. Do you think you might have?"

"Failed?"

"Yes. You."

"What did I do?"

"It's what you didn't do. You came here, when you should have gone somewhere else. You came to see me, when you should have gone somewhere else, to fight and die for me. Do you understand?"

"I did that."

"Yes."

"Whom was I supposed to fight?"

"Rao."

The name had a familiar sound. He formed it in his mouth. "He killed a lot of people."

"Yes. You were supposed to fight him."

"But I couldn't."

"But you were supposed to anyway. Impossible odds and all that. Never stopped you before. But this time, instead, you came to seek me out."

He was watching her closely and carefully again. What she was saying was all true, and, as she spoke, windows of himself were opened and he glimpsed what he ought to remember. Awful, the picture that formed. Doubt, ignorance, laughable pride. But he refused to feel any shame. "Because I don't know—"

For a moment he almost touched the thought, almost found it.

"Don't know what?"

"Who you are."

There. He had said it. He smiled, clapped his hands, naked as he was; he knelt onto the floor, lay his cheek on the cool stone.

"I don't know who you are," he said again. "Tell me."

"You know very well who I am. You've known since you were a child."

"What you are. That part." He spoke dreamily, eyes cold, smelling the cold stone.

"Now we're getting somewhere. What I am. You want to know what I am."

He laughed, a perfectly delighted, childish sound. "Not just me. Everybody wants to know."

The lights dimmed and darkened; the room, without any warning, but what was more peculiar, without any change, became larger, the dome of the roof reaching high, the light less, the colors dulled. The column of light in which she stood or sat or waited imposed itself, was taller, more daunting. Now he could see the hand again, or maybe the other hand, blue tracery over the fingers, blue stones in the rings on the fingers, a fine blue netting adhering to the skin, graceful as a swan, the hand. "You're very clever." She spoke with a sullen tone. "Then tell me this. Why am I angry with you?"

"What? I don't—"

"Come. You really must answer all my questions. What has made me angry with you?"

"Confused," he said, but he was standing up, onto his feet.

"Never mind that. You were confused before but you found your question."

"You never answered."

"But I am. I am in the process. Tell me. Why am I angry with you, what is my reason?"

"Because I came here."

"No. No. I realize I said that, but really, I'm not angry about that, not in the least. You had no choice but to come here sooner or later."

The voice had become quite kindly. She was seated in a chair. Gripping each arm with the gem-encrusted hands, the painted hands, she watched him and calculated what his answers would be. The image was so vivid he could see it.

"What is true language?" she asked. "Who invented the term?"

"Words." He was breathless, freezing, his feet a blue that looked unnatural, his legs trembling so much he went to his knees. He should have known how to pass this sensation through him to some other place, should have known how to keep the warmth of his body protected even in the cold.

"Words that do what?"

"Make things happen." Ringing sounded in his ears; he pressed his hands against them.

"Make what things happen? How does true language work?"

He was making inarticulate sounds, hissing, reaching for a word with a hissing sound.

"Be careful," she said.

He said, "Science."

He slammed to the stone, face forward to it, and felt bone break in his face. Stunned, wheezing, spouting blood from the wreck of his nose, he flooded with pain, his front teeth aching, his lip torn through, tasting salty. He lay there, sweating in the cold, his body trembling. Struggling to his knees, he steadied himself on a hand, rose on weak ankles.

"I won't call it magic," he said, flooded with fury and pain.

That time he slammed into a wall, and then a column. Because the room had grown so big he reached a high velocity. Broken in more places than he could feel, he crumbled to the base of the black marble, lay there trembling. His jaw was broken badly, his tongue bitten in half. So when she spoke to him now, there was no longer any option of talking back.

"That statement raises a question as to your faith," she said.

Two jeweled feet appeared where he could see them, gold chains, gold chimes, gold bangles, gold filigree, the skin delicately painted with tracery of dusky red. She lay her toe gently against his broken nostril. She smelled like flowers.

"Who I am, well enough, that's clear. You said that very well, I thought. But what I am. That is my secret."

She drew back the foot and kicked him in the face, viciously, blood spraying over the marble and over her chains and bangles.

"Thanks for asking," she said.

Helpless to move now, he lay flat on the freezing stone, the sound of his breath a broken rasp.

Her robes, her chains, her gems, hung over him, moving

as she moved. Pulling him flat onto his stomach, she spread out his wrecked arms. She brought a firepot, set it on the floor. She moved carefully and allowed him to be aware of her, in his mind's eye, since his own eyes were crushed. From her waist she drew a long, thin dagger. In the fire she heated the needle-sharp tip. He could feel the movement of her clothing, the weight of her gold chains, her pearls, her gems, on his back; but he could hear no breathing, no heartbeat, no other sound. Silent, careful, she burned signs, runes, onto his back, the pain relentless. She covered him slowly from head to toe. He screamed like a child, slobbered like a child, and would have thrashed except she held him still; soon enough he weakened, made less sound until she turned him over and the raw burns pressed onto the marble. He screamed again, hoarse, his voice broken. She carved on his front, working patiently, the knife red-hot. She stopped at times to heat the tip in the firepot, as if she needed the fire. By then he was fading. His face was so broken that when she had turned him to write on his front he could no longer breathe, had no steady airway, feeling only the agony of her markings, and even less and less of that as he died.

Near the end he glimpsed someone else in the room, a woman in a white robe like someone in mourning. The pain had brought his memories back: he knew his name; he knew who it was carving signs in his skin; he knew where he had come, and why. Young Sister had brought him here. She was watching as he died, a bright piece of cloth folded over her arm.

When his breathing stopped, YY straightened over him a last time. She was a crone now, wearing only simple stuff, a shift and a long fabric panel to wrap around her head. She arranged it carefully over her gray-brown hair. "Are your Sisters coming?"

"Yes." Young Sister had drawn her own hood over her face. "It's done then? He's gone?"

"Yes." Her hands, the hem of her skirt, were covered in blood. "You're sure they're coming?"

"They were following me the whole way here."

"Good," said God. She gestured to Jessex, corpse broken and sprawled on the floor. "Bring the body, then. It's to come with us."

Last Word

1. Vekant

When Vekant was a child he had wanted so badly to become Prin, he had no memory of any other ambition. He had heard the music the local choir made in the town where he lived, Arsk, where there was a cloister of monks and nuns. His father took him to the cloister to listen from the time he could walk. The celebrants sang for themselves at all hours but no one could hear that music except them; they sang for the public on holidays and Vekant listened, the first time clinging to his father's skirts, enthralled by the fullness of the sound.

Later he volunteered to be a novice, attended the long sessions of singing open only to acolytes, and learned he had a gift for the Malei, the language of chant.

This was a scrap of memory left to him, as a child listening to the Weather Chorus from the Cloister of Saint Cuthru son of None, his father beside him, fat and warm. The memory remained only because of the accident of what had been eaten away from Vekant and what had not, back when the Eater transformed him.

For a long time he had been riding the Eaten around the base of the tower as the creature touched the rock so carefully and patiently, thinking itself to have all the time in the world.

When the gate to the tower blew open, Vekant thought the Eaten had won, that it would now begin to climb the winding stair to the top one step at a time.

He could feel the concussion against his face, the blast of heat and wind, as liquid metal splattered toward him from the overheated frame. Where there had been stone was a blasted place, part of a metal gate glowing, twisted on a hinge.

The Eaten was surprised; Vekant could feel the creature's reaction.

After that was something else, fear escalating to terror.

Figures walked out of the tower; the Eaten could feel them before he could see them. Women, three of them, leading a pack animal, ears like a mule, with a bundle across its back.

"Bring the tower down, Sister," said the plump one, who pulled on the mule's rein. "We won't be going back this way."

"Consider it done," said the tall one, and Vekant heard a crack, sharp and clear.

"Shall I kill this thing?" asked the young one, gesturing to the Eaten.

"The tower will blow in a moment and that will be that," said the plump one. "Anything hereabouts will be dead. We need to be moving."

"Well enough," said the young one, and they vanished, including the mule.

A moment later, shattering the quiet, Cueredon Tower broke apart in a ball of fire, to the momentary but tremendous surprise of the Eaten; and even then, to the last millisecond, Vekant felt no fear at all.

2. Keely

Father was a putrid child, a little girl with a rotted face. Even Keely's green face was nicer. After Dekkar was dead, Keely could see Father a long way off, riding on something immense, a huge creature, though the creature Keely could not so clearly see. First into the willow-wait were mantises, followed by flocks of the dark birds, some of which swirled in columns over the mantises, while others formed into the creatures like the one that tried to eat Uncle Figg on the farm, or like the Nerva-thing that sprayed stuff into Keely. There was never any question that the creatures would harm Keely's friends after Dekkar was gone. Keely decided he would be angry if this happened, and Father gave in. Tall, with folded arms, the needle-mouths stood as if they had clothing and as if they had faces, arms, and legs; now that Keely could see better, now that he was more used to thinking within the river of numbers, he could see that they were each one creature in fact, even when the creature took the form of a cloud. But at the same time, each of the shadow bird components of the cloud had awareness of its own.

His face was aching, his head aching, but when he put on the headset and played the math box he felt better. Lately he could play the hardest level and still focus on the rest of the world at the same time. He had the feeling this was not supposed to happen, in the same way that the bites from the Nerva-thing were not supposed to heal. Dekkar had done something to Keely to change him. So when he saw Father so clearly he had a feeling he was not supposed to; he had the feeling he was supposed to see something altogether different.

The mantises came up to the rocks with their jaws clacking, rubbing two legs together to make another sound that ranged from rasping to screeching. The needle-mouths walked among them, sometimes touching the mantises as if with affection. Other needle-mouths stood closer to the rocks, where Pel had disabled his shoulder guns. What use were two guns against so many?

Soon the rocks were surrounded with other creatures—more needle-mouths; stingers with wings; something like rats on two legs, packs of them—and lumbering through the host one lurching step at a time came a mantis big as a hill. Father was there, on that queen of mantises, or, rather, inside the glowing light it carried in its pincers. The mantis brought the light close to Keely, set it lightly onto the rocks, held it steady.

Inside the light was the shape he had seen in his head, the thing he had dreamed so many times, a globe of metal membrane, tentacles of metal, wires of light, inserted into the decaying flesh of a child's corpse. What he understood, watching, was that it was a machine, that it carried data inside it, that the data was not Rao but how to make Rao inside a host body, which it had tried to do inside this host. But this attempt had failed.

Still, the machine that carried Rao preferred to be housed inside a body, even a dead one.

Kitra drew back from the light in fear, as if she knew what it was. Pel was standing below Keely, watching. Something invisible snatched the guns from his shoulders, sent them skittering down the rocks. Something else took Kitra, quieted her, stilled her on the ground.

The syms were cowering or could not move. Binam lay face forward on the ground near Kitra's feet.

A voice said, "I haven't come to harm you, child. Whatever you've been told."

The voice sounded sincere, truthful, earnest. Keely tried to smile through the green face, as if he believed, but behind it he was seeing the truth, that the figure within the light was a child harnessed to the machine he had seen in his dreams, tentacles wrapping the neck, wires inserted into the skull and abdomen, the child putrid, its flesh dark, skin flaking off in patches, membranes from the machine sliding into the nose, mouth, ears, into a slit in the neck. The body was so far gone in decay it was not possible to see what gender it had been.

"Welcome, Father," Keely said, feeling fear in spite of himself, but facing the light and the thing inside it.

"Welcome, child," the voice said. "You're only the fourth to arrive."

"Yes." His heart was pounding.

"But we don't have time to wait to test the rest."

Keely nodded, swallowing.

"You see I've already tried the third vessel," Father said. "She had not been prepared to the proper level and could not sustain me."

The tentacles slid into a new configuration around the

wasted throat. Keely swallowed. He was afraid now. Through the green face he breathed, trying not to shake.

"I believe I'm the right vessel, Father," he said. Remarkable, he thought, that his voice sounded easy. Inside the light cage he was glimpsing other shapes, what looked like a console, other kinds of machinery. "I've been trained and prepared."

"I believe the same, child."

The sphere-machine was withdrawing its parts from the body. It was compacting to that sphere from his dreams, wires licking into its core, membranes wrapped around them, tentacles compressing to a hard shell. The corpse of the little girl collapsed; the mantis's jaws opened, flanged around the meat, swallowed it and crushed it with a few motile waves of the metal esophagus. The sphere was no longer visible, it had grown so small.

A hand knocked Keely flat, close to the dirt and patchy grass between the rocks. The light grew brighter. He heard Pel's voice, Kitra's, then silence.

Keely could taste Rao's greed. He had used up the girl-child's body in the fight with Dekkar. He hardly examined Keely at all. Metal slid down his head, around his throat, fine wires piercing; Keely's body shuddered and wrenched. He felt it enter him from all orifices, not pain but the sweetest pleasure, tendrils of Rao inside him, and he started to tremble, rose on his hands and knees.

It was as if he were being threaded through with light; at moments such an ecstasy coursed through him that he could hardly be still. The voice of it was inside him now. He had no more need to speak to it; he knew it from inside.

This code was what had come to Aramen from somewhere, from Earth; this device was all that had traveled to Greenwood. From this tiny sphere had come the maps to make all these other creatures.

Was Rao inside, too, or simply another map? The answer came back simply as puzzlement at the question; what difference could there be?

He stood, the green membrane pulsing over his ruined face, the tentacles of the machine shifting from one position to another. For another moment he was erect, conscious, himself, Keely, high on windy rocks looking over a sea of monsters, clacking jaws and rasping wings.

Then he was Rao. He was so old, so many. Voice after voice of him cascading, that river of numbers, of the sound of numbers and relationships, that music of the math box, grew large and engulfed Keely but never entirely swept him away.

Rao could never be killed. This piece of him was only a piece of him. But it was the piece that mattered; it was all of Rao that had come to Aramen.

Keely felt numb, distant, but still aware of his body, and Rao appeared surprised at this. Keely could, in fact, still move his body, and Rao was very disturbed. A pain went through Keely's head.

"Kitra," he said, and looked at her. He blacked out then, and slid to the ground.

For a moment the triumphant thing inside him felt its weight, relished the moment.

A crashing sound began, amplified, became thunder; around Keely and the rocks the world began to shake. Glass shattered, a screeching deafened him, and someone pulled him to the ground.

3. Kitra

Keely collapsed in Kitra's arms just as an immense shrieking rose in the distance, setting all the mantises close by to skittering and seething. Keely's head and torso were encased in wires and flexible arms that had appeared out of nowhere; he was motionless, lips moving aimlessly. She checked his forehead, (warm), his breathing (regular), his pulse (strong). Binam bent to watch her. "Is he all right?"

"I don't know. He's got this thing inside him."

"What is it?"

"I don't know."

Something happened in the distance, some commotion that made itself felt like a wave through all the ranks of Rao's battalions. The huge mantis raised its head and turned. It carried the light-cage hanging from its jaw; the cage swung back and forth. Keely was barely breathing, pieces of that metal membrane hanging onto him; if he was supposed to take Rao inside him, was that what the machine wrapped around his head was for? Was it Rao she was protecting?

From the rocks below, Pel gestured.

"Help me," Kitra said, and she and Binam lifted Keely.

The mantises shrieked and the needle-mouths shattered into their component flocks; something was attacking them or they were attacking something. Kitra and Binam clambered down the stones as fast as they dared; Pel gestured them to follow as the mantises began to climb over one another in their haste to move forward; Pel led them into a man-made cave a few measures deep. The mantises, the flocks, the packs of man-rats, all avoided coming too close to Keely as they carried him; some of the other syms who straggled were cut to pieces.

As if the sun had gone out, the sky darkened suddenly.

Kitra sat with Keely in her lap. When he shivered, hands moving as he were using a keyboard, she pulled him close to warm him.

"Is he cold?" Binam asked.

"He doesn't feel cold to the touch. But he's shivering."

From shelter they watched the chaos, mantises leaping, the sky clouded with winged shapes. In the distance no flashes of light, nothing at all to mark the battle.

"Cover your ears," Pel said, "this lot is loud when they die."

She covered her own, figuring Keely had the Rao-thing to take care of him. The shrieking sound tore at her nerves, even with her hands to muffle it.

When Dekkar had fought with the other true-language operator, columns of light had been visible for kilomeasures.

Now even though she had a view of the dumb-trees and the forest, even though her eyes adjusted to the new darkness, she saw nothing like light, not a glimmer. Leaping mantises, stingers in swarms, packs of the ratlings, other shapes less recognizable she saw once her eyes adjusted to the dark, but nothing of what was fighting what.

His army was acting as if it had no leader, she thought, and she looked at Keely and wondered whether this were true.

He had come into the clearing to take Keely as soon as he had killed Dekkar. He thought he had finished with his enemies.

Keely trembled, mouth open, eyes open. He grasped her arms and looked at her. "Kitra," he said.

"Yes, Keely."

"What's happening? He wants to know what's happening. He can't see."

"There's an attack," she said. "What do you mean, he can't see?"

"He's blind inside me. He's panicked." Keely broke into a sweat, wiped his brow, face flushed. When she touched his forehead, he was piping hot.

"You be still," she said, "you have a fever."

"It's him. He's fighting for something. I don't know what it is." His eyes were glazing. She shook him a bit, made him keep his eyes open, watch her. She moved him to the edge of the cave where the air was better, next to Pel, who was watching the dumb-trees and the forest beyond. The shadows were still moving, but there appeared to be fewer of them.

"That's better," Keely said. "I'm cooler."

"What does he want?"

"Me. He's supposed to have control of me."

"How do you know?"

He focused on her, managed to show impatience in spite of the blind look of his face. "I know," he said. "What that needle-tooth thing tried to inject into my face, that was to change me for Rao. But Dekkar altered it."

"He protected you."

"Yes. It can't control me yet." He was sweating, trembling.

"Take a deep breath, try to be calm," she said, and he did.

"The thing can't come out of me," he said. "It's too soon. It can't risk wasting me. What's happening?"

"Should I tell you?"

"It can't know what I know unless I tell it. That scares it, too. I can know what it knows, but it can't know me."

"Something is attacking. We can't see anything. Can you?"

After a moment he shook his head. "I can't see much of anything other than him. Father."

She started to correct him, faltered.

That sound again, unearthly.

Flocks and flocks of the shadow birds spiraled in and around the rocks, never close. Suddenly, like a cloud dissolving, they were gone.

A form took shape like a shadow whirling inside a shadow, one dark and one darker; another form took shape the same as the first. The willow-wait had grown still. The black hung over them like night gone solid, but even in that ink the shadows were darker.

A third shadow formed near the first two.

"Come out of the rocks," said a voice, a woman.

"You might as well," said another.

"Nothing to be afraid of now," said a third. "Wretched creatures they were, but they had no one to drive them."

Pel bowed his head.

Three women stood near the water, one of them leading a mule with a pack on its back. In the smoke it was hard to see them, but they were distinctly women, heads wrapped, long gowns, brown or gray or both, veils pulled back but faces still masked by shadow.

"If you're afraid, we certainly understand," said one of the women.

"You've been through quite a lot, I expect," said another.

"But you can trust us, at least, not to eat you," said the third. "Quickly now, before the creature takes hold inside the child."

Pel gestured with his head. "Can Keely walk?"

"We can carry him," Binam said.

"Are you sure?" Kitra asked. "Should we? Do you know them?"

"What choice do we have?" Pel asked, but refused to meet her eye.

Keely stood on his own, however. Kitra took one hand, Binam the other. "Are you sure?" Binam asked. "You don't have to walk."

"I'm fine," he said.

Kitra touched his cheek again. "You're cooler."

"It's them," he said. "They're helping."

"Who are they?" Kitra asked, but he was carefully stepping from one grassy stone to the next.

Pel had reached the clearing by then and stood there, blood on him from Figg or Zhengzhou, clothes torn, pony-tail twisted out of shape.

"Light, Sister," said one of the women.

"Certainly, Sister," said another, and the clearing filled with light.

The light somehow failed to render their figures more

distinct. They might all have been the same woman, wrapped in brown-gray stuff, faces hooded and difficult to see. Pel stood there, blinking, and waited a moment. He looked from one to the other, a bit defiant by the end. "I take it you're not surprised to see me."

"No. Should we be?"

He shook his head, after a moment. "It's just it's been a while and I came so far."

"You were called back," said the third woman. "You have no idea why, I expect. But you will."

"Where is the child?"

"There, Sister. Plain as dirt in front of you."

They stood as if guileless, barefoot, as if they were Keely's country aunts come to fetch him home on the back of the mule one of them was leading.

"What's that thing on him?" asked one of the women.

"Never mind what it is. Get it off."

"Not so easy," said the third, and they took each other's hands and one of them scratched the mule's ear and suddenly the tentacles fell away from Keely's neck.

One of the women gestured to Kitra. "You, there. Take those wires and pull them out of him. He won't feel it."

"That's a good idea," said another. "She has a steady hand."

"She's nervous."

"She'll be able to do it."

Keely was watching her, took her hand for a moment. "Do what they say. It's all right."

She took a deep breath. Tears stung her eyes, maybe fear or maybe because she was beginning to understand. Taking the wires in hand, she pulled; each slid easily out of him, skin closing up at all four points of entry.

"There'll be no escaping now," said one of the women.

"Not likely."

"Rao will have to learn to live with you, young man," said the third woman. "A neat trap."

"Clever of the boy to set it."

"I didn't set it," Keely said. "It was Dekkar."

"We don't mean you, don't be vain," said the tall woman. "And no, it wasn't Dekkar. Dekkar was only a copy, you know."

Kitra felt a sob rise in her, from so deep it made her shake.

"A copy?" Keely asked.

"Yes. Of him." This was the tallest of the women. She let go the mule's reins, reached for the rope on the bundle, pulled it to loose the knot. Like some magic trick the rope uncoiled.

A corpse slid to the ground, a man, naked, badly beaten, face crushed. He was covered with bruises and what at first looked like scabs.

The stiff tarp that had wrapped the body slid to the ground.

"Who is it?" Keely asked.

Pel made a low sound, once, brief.

"Great Irion," said the tall woman.

"Pity," said another.

"We enjoyed his company at one time. Much as we shall enjoy yours." The tall woman was speaking to Keely directly.

"Did you kill him?" Keely asked.

"Good heavens, no. He was our friend."

Hard to believe, Kitra thought, the way the body had tumbled so carelessly off the horse.

"Then who did?"

The women looked at one another.

Kitra could see the scabs more clearly now. Covering the corpse, head to toe, was some kind of writing burned into the skin.

"May as well say he died here fighting Rao," said the tall one. "It's as close to the truth as anything."

"Agreed," said another.

"It can't do any harm," said the third. "It's what he should have done."

"Setting such a clever trap as this, he might even have won," said the tall one.

They looked at each other in mild surprise, as if this was a new thought.

Pel went to his knees beside the body.

"Come, Keely," said one of the women. "It's time to go."

He started forward and Kitra grasped at him, Binam stepping in front of him. "What are you doing?" Kitra asked.

"Going with them," Keely said, that green membrane pulsing on his face.

"Why?"

He became very still for a moment. His voice no longer sounded like a child. "Rao's still inside me. I can't live around other people, I'm not safe for them."

"Very true," said the tall woman. "You said that very well."

Kitra searched Keely for some sign, brought her face close to where his face should have been. He had the body of a ten-year-old, frail and thin; he'd lost his family twice over; he'd been through the same ordeal she had. She spoke earnestly. "Keely, I don't know you at all, but there's nobody else around to ask you. Is this really what you want to do?"

He giggled, a sound that was gentle, but tinged with cold and distance. "What would you do if I say no? You can't keep me if they decide to take me."

She watched him. She turned to the women. Her heart was pounding so hard it left her faint; she thought she would sink to her knees but refused to give way. For a moment she glimpsed their faces, frozen as marble. Later, she wanted to be convinced she had seen peace and serenity in their countenances. Later still, she decided she had. "Where are you taking him?"

"To our home, to live with us."

She wet her lips. "Is he a prisoner?"

"No, he's not. But the one he carries is."

Keely stepped around Binam, slid his hand out of Kitra's. He walked over to the mule, which nuzzled him with its lips.

"I wish we could stay to help you," said one of the women, to Kitra.

"We can't see you on your way to where you're going, she means," said the tall woman. She was stooping, speaking to Pel directly. He knelt over the wreckage of the corpse's head.

"We have to take Keely with us right away," said the third.

Pel was controlling himself with effort and managed to nod, head bowed.

The tall woman went on watching him. "You might thank us, at least."

"For what?" he asked.

"For saving you."

He looked at her then, his face blank and ancient. Kitra felt tears streaming down her own face. "He was my friend," Pel said.

"Who's to say he's not still your friend?" the tall woman asked, her voice cold and dry. "Perhaps you'll run into him when you cross the mountains again."

"As you wish, Sister," he said at last, his face set as stone.

"Time to go," said one of the others.

"This took longer than we planned. All this talking at the end."

"It can't be helped," said the tall one, turning away, lifting Keely, setting him onto the mule. "These are good people, after all."

"You're always making new friends, Sister."

"It's my nature," agreed the tall one.

As the three of them headed into the clearing, the one walking at the flank of the mule asked, "Shall I kill the rest of the forest?"

"I rather think not."

"Enough waste," said the third. "Though what we did was necessary, of course."

"God's will be done, Sister," said the one at the flank of the mule.

The tall one looked around at the twisted stumps of trees, smoke rising from fires in the distance. "Amen, Sister. God's will be done."

Binam stood beside Kitra and they watched as the women vanished, Keely sitting upright on his mule, facing forward.

At the last moment Figg's spider leapt onto his shoulder, into his lap, folding its legs there. Keely lay his hand on the spider, sitting confidently, feet in the stirrups as though he'd ridden a mule before. Kitra shivered, chilled to the marrow. Binam pulled her against his side, tried to warm her. "I can't stop shaking," she said.

"It's all right." Binam lay his cheek against her forehead a moment. They stood quietly, breathing, and her heart was starting to slow.

Pel was still kneeling beside the body, touching one of the scars, a spiral inside a square.

"Who were those women?" Kitra asked.

He shook his head, big-knuckled hands touching the scar.

"Pel," she said, and he looked at her. Pain in his eyes joined to something darker in the set of his mouth, his jaw. "Who were they?"

Voice a husk, he said, "We have to cover the body."

"We can wrap it with the stuff they left when they threw it off the horse." She took his face in her hands, made him look at her. "Tell me who they were."

He spoke with effort, eyes half closed. "His teachers."

"Whose?" But as soon as she asked the question, she understood.

"Help me," he said.

Binam had fetched the stiff tarp where it had fallen beside the pool, and he started to flatten it in the grass beside the body. Pel was arranging the limbs; the arms had already been crossed over its chest and tied.

Pel took the cold, wounded shoulders in hand and looked at Kitra. She knelt, gathered its feet in her arms, tested the weight. The body looked pitiful and small, even fragile, an ordinary person.

"Are you sure you know who this is?" Kitra asked, wanting to let the body go. "There's not even a face left—"

He looked at her coldly, and she fell silent.

They swung the body onto the tarp. A moment later he knelt, and he and Binam wrapped the body carefully, covering, finally, the ruined face and dark hair. Pel stood and looked at her. "You and your brother can come with me if you want."

"Come with you?"

"I have to take him home," Pel said, looking at the tarp. "I could use the help. And you can't stay here, after all."

She was still kneeling, touching the stiff fabric. As if unfolding came the memory of the scene she had witnessed when Dekkar was first taking out his pack, finding his bag of gems, preparing to fight on the river, and talking to Pel so frankly. She found herself unreeling all that she had seen of Dekkar these last hours, every glimpse.

She looked at Binam. He smiled and said, "I can travel with both of you as far as the south end of Greenwood, anyway."

"That's a start," Pel said.

He made a litter to carry the body on the walk, and some of the syms helped him. The sky cleared more, though it looked as like to cloud over again with debris or smoke or weather, and wind was blowing warm from the south. A tear in the cloud cover dropped a shaft of daylight through the forest, a light between amber and brown falling through the haze, but still light, and she could see the sun was low. Binam and Kitra sat together as if it were the most natural thing in the world, as if they had been sitting together at sundown every day since they were children, as if the world had not changed. She wondered whether it was all right to be happy, even so, a little.

"Careful," Pel said when the bearers lifted the litter and the body shifted under the ropes. "He might wake up. You never know with these folk."

But if he was asleep, he went on sleeping. Kitra stood in the shelter of the rocks, looking out at the clearing, the grass beaten down, patches of the black ooze visible, a wasteland made out of a forest. A few more of the tree-widows were emerging from cover, and when Pel was ready with the litter, they stepped into formation as before. Maybe it was a gesture of respect, or maybe the syms did it to comfort themselves with some sense of order. Out of the willow-wait the party marched, perhaps a score of them beside the litter-bearers, beginning the long journey, carrying the body of Great Irion home.

Glossary

Includes character names

TERM	LANGUAGE	REFERENCE
Aeryn	Erejhen	Old name for the country Irion; used in sources before the departure of King Kirith Kirin.
Ajhenus Cluster	Alenke	The cluster of stars adjacent to Aramen in which there are an unusual number of worlds friendly to life.
Ajhevan	Aramenian dialect of Alenke	The dominant northern continent of Aramen, home of Hormling colonists and the Dirijhi; stronghold of the Arame-

TERM	LANGUAGE	REFERENCE
		nian independence movement.
Ama	Alenke	Mother goddess, generic; worshiped under many other names (Ma, Am, Mur, etc.).
Anilyn Gate	Erejhen	Gate from Home Star to Red Star, from Senal to Aramen, opened and maintained by the Mage Malin and Great Irion.
Aramen	Alenke	The principal world of Red Star, home world to the Dirijhi, a race of sentient trees; gateway to the Ajhenus Cluster.
Arsa	Aramenian dialect of Alenke	City where the river David joins the river Silas, near the middle of the continent Ajhevan.
Arsus	Alenke	World in the Red Star system around which the Twelfth Fleet is stationed.

Glossary

TERM	LANGUAGE	REFERENCE
Badrigol	Alenke	City that spans the Isthmus of Fostine along the Iriwak Canal.
Binam	Aramenian dialect of Alenke	Brother of Kitra; he was born a human but elected to become a tree symbiont; he has been a resident of Greenwood for many years.
calcept	symbiont dialect of Alenke	Shadow mantis, one of the creatures brought to Aramen by Rao.
chalcyd	symbiont dialect of Alenke	A group of creatures that takes composite form as a human or humanlike variant predator but that travels as a flock of component beings.
Chulion	Erejhen	The house of the Sisters to which Jessex/Great Irion was taken as a child; his destination at the time of the Ajhevan Rebellion. Far in the northern mountains.

TERM	LANGUAGE	REFERENCE
Collive	coined word	Legal category of a living being made up of closely connected, but still individual entities; the trees of the Dirijhi form a Collive.
Colony Bridge		Bridge that crosses the Trennt River from east Feidreh to Avatrayn.
Coromey	Erejhen	Jessex/Great Irion's cathound, trained to accompany him on the journey to Chulion.
Conquest		The defeat of Hormling Enforcement by the Prin and the subsequent takeover of government by Malin and Hanson.
Corvad	Aramenian dialect of Alenke	The ocean south of Jharvan.
Cueredon	Erejhen	High place over the Citadel in Feidreh-Avatrayn on Aramen; built by

TERM	LANGUAGE	REFERENCE
		Malin; has a central shaft of configurable metal allowing easy change of the tower's ruling language.
David River	Alenke	A tributary of the river Silas, the river David begins in northwest Greenwood as a small creek in the hill country there; the David links with the crossing canal system. The David drains a large part of northwest Ajhevan, including the area near Fineas Figg's farm.
Dekkar up Ortaen	Anin	Fallen Drune priest, a friend of Fineas Figg.
Dembut	Aramenian dialect of Alenke	Last village along the river Silas at the edge of the Dirijhi preserve; a main entrepot into Greenwood.
Dirijhi	Aramenian dialect of Alenke	Race of sentient trees on the north continent of Aramen.

TERM	LANGUAGE	REFERENCE
Disturber toy	composite	Name of Keely File's goo-toy set.
Drakkar Air Station	Alenke	Air base near Feidreh and the Jharvan coast.
Drune	Erejhen	The subset of the Prin who speak the true language, Ildrune, rather than Malei.
dumb-tree	coined word	In usage among symbionts speaking their dialect of Alenke, a dumb-tree is a tree without a brain. Symbionts sculpt immense structures out of living dumb-trees.
Eighth Army		Army that defends Feidreh-Avatrayn.
Erlot	symbiont dialect of Alenke	Numbers of Rao, the true-quantum system of manipulation used by Rao and followers.
Erra Bel	Erejhen	Name of Pel Orthen's boat.

Glossary

TERM	LANGUAGE	REFERENCE
Eseveren Gate	Erejhen	Gate from Senal to Irion, located in the Inokit Ocean, maintained by Irion; in Alenke it is called the Twil Gate.
Eshen Arly	Anin	Drune operator of the fourth rank assigned to Cueredon Tower.
evar	Erejhen	Cantor of a Prin choir of ten.
Faltha Meno-nomy	Erejhen	Prin member of pononter couple assigned to Cueredon Tower; a pononter couple is a couple practiced in the use of the Malei language together.
Fang of Gar	composite	Pass leading north from Svyssn Country into the Barrier Mountains; Jessex takes this route on his walk to find Chulion.
Fenton-march	coined word	Village east of Feidreh-Avatrayn, site of a small Enforcement airfield.

TERM	LANGUAGE	REFERENCE
Fineas Figg	Alenke	Eldest son of House Bemona-Kakenet; Figg is his proxy name.
Flat Head Farm	composite	Farm of Fineas Figg on the river David, where he grows protein meat forms, soybeans, wheat, truck.
Flores	Alenke	Farm-support village in Jharvan Western, located east of Avatran; destroyed in rebel attack by shadow mantis and construct troops.
Fukate choir of Ten-Thousand	Erejhen	The Prin choir of ten thousand stationed on Aramen; named for their victory in the Fukate rebellion early in the history of the colony. A well-armed armada of former Orminy loyalists went through the Anilyn Gate and landed marines on Jharvan in an attempt to take over the colony; the rebels came from Fukate,

TERM	LANGUAGE	REFERENCE
		the second-largest planet in the Home Star system. The Aramenian Prin defeated the armada and marines handily, with no loss of life on either side.
Gate-keeper Station	coined	The independent station in orbit around Aramen; it monitors traffic through the Anilyn Gate on the Red Star side.
Grand Wheel		The government complex that surrounds the Anilyn Gate on the Home Star side, including a Prin choral facility and a residence for the Mage and her staff; takes advantage of proximity to Senal and the gate (and Aramen beyond) for communications efficiency.
Hanson	Alenke	A very successful aggregate consciousness made up of several hundred individuals; Hanson ended

TERM	LANGUAGE	REFERENCE
		the most bitter phase of the Metal War by merging his organic components with some of the central machinery in the deeps of Senal.
himmel	Erejhen	Leaf chewed for its sedative properties; also used in certain kinds of Prin medicine.
Hormling	Alenke	The name for the human race on Senal that has also populated a number of the neighboring stars.
ipock	symbiont dialect of Alenke	Operator in the Erlot language; the ranks and levels are the same as for the Prin.
Iraen	Erejhen	Name for the country beyond the Twil Gate (Eseveren Gate), though the country is also often called Irion or Aeryn. The new name, Iraen, came into official usage

TERM	LANGUAGE	REFERENCE
		during the fourth century after the Conquest in order to distinguish between the country called Irion and the person called Great Irion.
Irion, Great Irion	Erejhen	Name of the over-mage who governs the Oregal from deep within the northern part of the country that bears his name. The original name of Great Irion was Jessex Yron; in the age after the departure of King Kirith Kirin, he became more commonly referred to as Irion, and later as Great Irion. In time his name merged with the name of the country over which he ruled. The most common earlier form of the name of the country Irion was Aeryn; this name is most commonly used when referring to the country

TERM	LANGUAGE	REFERENCE
		under the rule of King Kirith Kirin. The inconvenience of the blurring of these names led later politicians and scholars to adopt the name Iraen for the country, though the term Irion continued to be used as the name of the country for many decades.
Jedda Martele	Alenke	Former linguist who was consort of Mage Malin.
Jessex	Erejhen	Birth name of Great Irion; name by which he is called by his teachers. Later he was given the honorary second name Yron; this took place in the era before the passing of King Kirith Kirin. In later ages, he was better known under the name Irion or Great Irion, the over-mage who ruled the Oregal during the classical era.

Glossary

TERM	LANGUAGE	REFERENCE
Jharvan	Aramenian dialect of Alenke	The southern continent of Aramen, divided into eastern and western zones connected by a broad isthmus; the eastern zone is largely desert; the western zone is the site of a very large Hormling population composed mostly of descendants of immigrants from Senal.
juduvar	Erejhen	The cantor of a Prin choir of one hundred.
Keely File	Alenke	Fineas Figg's adopted son, though Feely refers to Figg as "uncle."
Zhengzhou	Alenke	Fineas Figg's bodyguard.
Kinahd	Alenke	City from which Keely File comes, though most city jurisdictions don't extend as far down as the Reeks, which underlies most cities on Senal.

Glossary

TERM	LANGUAGE	REFERENCE
Kitra Poth	Aramenian dialect of Alenke	An Aramenian employed by the Prin who is asked by Dekkar up Ortaen to escort him into Greenwood; she is on a mission to rescue her brother Binam from his tree slavery.
Kowon	Alenke	A tree symbiont; conegotiator in the Lower Land of Flowering Silas.
Lower Land of Flowering Silas		Land where the river Russ runs into the river Silas; the land between the rivers bears this name.
Malei	Erejhen	The name of the true language developed by the old Erejhen priests and spoken by the main body of the Prin. Malei is the easiest to learn of the known true languages.
Malei-Prin	Erejhen	The body of the Prin who speak and chant in the true language named Malei.

TERM	LANGUAGE	REFERENCE
Malin	Erejhen	Mage of Senal, niece of Jessex/Great Irion.
Marmigon	Alenke	The entertainment complex lost to Fineas Figg in the Common Fund Reforms, including his penthouse, his main residence as the former prince of the chief Orminy factor.
Milkly the Blossoms	coined word	Country north of Lower Land of Flowering Silas.
Nerva	Erejhen	Keely File's nanny.
Oregal	Erejhen	Aggregate of all Prin, including Malei-Prin and Drune-Prin and all other speakers and cantors, controlled by Jessex/Great Irion and kept working toward the same end by his efforts; Malin shares in this control.
pekoe		Name of a tea from beyond the Gate, Senal.

Glossary

TERM	LANGUAGE	REFERENCE
Pel Orthen	Erejhen	River pilot on Aramen familiar with the Silas and tributaries.
Pel Pelatheyn	Erejhen	Hero from the older tales of the Erejhen, a companion of Jessex/Great Irion and the King during the Long War, and the center of many old hunting stories in the land of Irion.
Pivotnet	coined word	Satellite news center serving Aramen.
Plaza of Two Worlds		The plaza at the foot of Skygard Aramen in Feidreh.
Plump		Name of one of God's three Sisters.
Prin	Erejhen	Priestly cantors who form the Oregal under the direction of Irion; the backbone of the power exercised by the

Glossary

TERM	LANGUAGE	REFERENCE
		Mage and Irion; their true language is Malei.
Pulleypod	coined word	Cars that ride up and down the carbon cables from Skygard facilities.
Rao	symbiont dialect of Alenke	Name of the Prime who comes to Aramen as an ally of the Dirijhi. He is also referred to as the God Rao.
Russ		Tributary river that flows into the Silas in northern Greenwood. At the place where the two rivers merge, the land between the rivers is called Lower Land of Flowering Silas.
Rui Fal	Alenke	Enforcement commander on Aramen.
scuppling	Anin	Name of a variety of southern tea in Irion.
Senal	Alenke	The Home World of the Hormling, colonized by

TERM	LANGUAGE	REFERENCE
		humans from the starship *Merced* in the year 10,001.
Seris Annoy	Erejhen	Prin member of pononter couple assigned to Cueredon Tower; see *Faltha Menonomy.*
Sherry File	Alenke	Short form legal name of Cherry Ann File, Keely File's sister.
Shoren	Anin	Prin who is aide to Vekant, fifth rank cantor, training to sing pivot in a choir of a hundred.
Shu Shylar	Erejhen	Park adjacent to Citadel on the island Avatrayn in the river Trennt.
Silas Ford	composite	Ford across the Silas River just south of Dirijhi country, where Dembut was founded; the ford was later dredged and replaced by a bridge. Site of the treaty negotiations between the

Glossary

TERM	LANGUAGE	REFERENCE
		Hormling, the Erejhen, and the Dirijhi.
Silas River	Aramenian dialect of Alenke	River that runs through the north continent of Aramen; one of the main rivers into and out of Greenwood.
Skygard		The lift system that serves as primary transport for cargo and passengers from space to the surface of a world; Skygard facilities are owned and operated by the Hormling Ministries. Each Skygard is named for the world it serves. There are two Skygards for Senal.
stipple-ball	coined word	Name of a sport played on Senal and likely on other Hormling worlds; teams of eight, sticks, and an energy ball.
Svyssn	Erejhen	The territory of one of the so-called Uncreated

TERM	LANGUAGE	REFERENCE
		Races, the Svyssn, who maintain a very basic hunter-gatherer society, minimal agriculture, ruled over by the Great Wife; also the name of the people who live there.
Svyssn Husband	Erejhen	The Great Husband of the Svyssn Wife, poisoned by acht and replaced every decade.
Svyssn Wife	Erejhen	The Great Wife of the Svyssn, the immortal female being who rules the Svyssn, one of the so-called Uncreated Races of Iraen.
Thin		Name of one of God's three Sisters.
thuenyn	Erejhen	Leaf used to make a poultice to promote healing in most wounds; also used in certain kinds of Prin medicine.

Glossary

TERM	LANGUAGE	REFERENCE
Tosh Unrotide	Aramenian dialect of Alenke	Spokesman for rebel forces.
Treaty of Silas Ford		Treaty signed at the Silas river ford near the edge of Greenwood along the river; treaty governs the relationship between the Dirijhi and the Mage.
Trennt River	Alenke	River that flows through Feidreh-Avatrayn.
Truss	Alenke	Pack-bird used in Greenwood.
Twelfth Fleet		Fleet based in Red Star system for defense of Aramen and the Anilyn Gate.
Twil Gate	Alenke	The gate that links the country Iraen with the Hormling home world Senal; in Erejhen it is called the Eseveren Gate.
uduvarii	Erejhen	The Great Cantor of a Prin choir of ten thousand.

TERM	LANGUAGE	REFERENCE
Unyur-thrupen	Orloc	City near Chulion in the mountains; also called Middle of the Mountain.
Urtuthenel	Alenke	Minor Orminy family whose exodus from Senal is part of Fineas Figg's daily news cycle.
Vad	Aramenian dialect of Alenke	The ocean between Jharvan and Ajhevan.
Vekant Anevarim ad Kiram	Erejhen	Great Cantor (uduvarii) of the Prin Choir of Ten Thousand on Aramen.
Wider Ocean		The northern ocean in the part of the northern hemisphere not occupied by Ajhevan.
Young		Name of one of God's three Sisters.
Yron	Erejhen	Honorary second name given to Jessex by the Sisters. Yron is the root for the name Irion and the later name Iraen; his

Glossary

TERM	LANGUAGE	REFERENCE
		later name, Great Irion, thus derives from this honorary name.
YY	Erejhen	The name of God.

Author's Note

Many of the characters here have their antecedents in short stories; Kitra first vowed to free Binam in "Into Greenwood," which also involved a journey through Dembut and told the tale of her conference with the Dirijhi; Fineas Figg's three hundredth birthday party is the central event of "The 120 Hours of Sodom," and Figg adopts Keely at the end of that story; some of the tale of Hanson is told in "Perfect Pilgrim"; and other connections are here but not yet ready to be discussed. The stories cited were all published in *Asimov's Science Fiction*. A number of characters have their origin in earlier novels *Kirith Kirin* or *The Ordinary* and I will not list those.

The glossary is not intended to be all-inclusive; I have excluded some minor names and definitions. I have attempted to avoid giving plot-related information. For some names there is considerable history attached. Character names specific to the present book are listed in the glossary though only their opening roles in the story are defined; again, the list is not intended to be complete, since minor characters are not noted. Important locations are cited here,

Author's Note

although at times without reference as to their importance in the story.

Thanks to Paul Stevens, Tom Doherty, Peter Hagan, Sheila Williams, Gardner Dozois, Madeleine St. Romain, Donato, Frances Foster, Despina Crassa, Paula Vitaris, Joseph Skibell, Kevin Yony, Natasha Trethewey, Bruce Covey, and Lynna Williams for various kinds of help during the writing or for helping to publish the stories drawn from this world.